The
MESMERIST

ALSO BY CAROLINE WOODS

The Lunar Housewife

Fräulein M.

The MESMERIST

A Novel

CAROLINE WOODS

DOUBLEDAY
New York

All rights reserved. Published in the United States by Doubleday, a division of Penguin Random House LLC, New York, and distributed in Canada by Penguin Random House Canada Limited, Toronto.

www.doubleday.com

DOUBLEDAY and the portrayal of an anchor with a dolphin are registered trademarks of Penguin Random House LLC.

Jacket image: (circular background) Swillklitch / Getty Images
Jacket design by Oliver Munday

Library of Congress Cataloging-in-Publication Data
Names: Woods, Caroline (Caroline Courtney), author.
Title: The Mesmerist: a novel / Caroline Woods.
Description: First edition. | New York: Doubleday, 2024. |
Identifiers: LCCN 2023048387 (print) | LCCN 2023048388 (ebook) |
ISBN 9780385550161 (hardcover) | ISBN 9780385550178 (ebook)
Subjects: LCGFT: Thrillers (Fiction) | Novels.
Classification: LCC PS3623.06752 M46 2024 (print) | LCC PS3623.06752 (ebook) |
DDC 813/.6—dc23/eng/20231013
LC record available at https://lccn.loc.gov/2023048387
LC ebook record available at https://lccn.loc.gov/2023048388

MANUFACTURED IN THE UNITED STATES OF AMERICA

1 3 5 7 9 10 8 6 4 2

First Edition

For my parents

The splendid city of Minneapolis . . . In no place I have ever seen (and I have been in many) were the winter nights so clear and beautiful, and the stars so many and so bright as there.

—COLONEL JOHN H. BLISS, *REMINISCENCES OF FORT SNELLING*

"Wherever you go, madam, it will matter little what you carry. You will always carry your goodness."

—HENRY JAMES, *THE BOSTONIANS*

"And, ach! what a beautiful skeleton you will make!"

—GEORGE DU MAURIER, *TRILBY*

PART I

Minneapolis, October 1894

1
ABBY

*T*he poor young woman, the one everyone would take to calling the "ghost girl," or worse, in a matter of weeks, found her way to the Bethany Home for Unwed Mothers by walking the railroad tracks. Later, this would be one of the things that made the other girls suspicious. Could someone in her condition—if she really *was* in said condition—traipse at least five miles in the sticky humidity of a growing thunderstorm, in a heavy satin gown, no less?

In Abby's view, the new arrival's trek didn't imply dishonesty. It suggested desperation.

The thunderstorm, with all the crackling friction it gathered in the air and the impressive black anvil cloud over southern Minneapolis, ended up petering out into nearly nothing: just one bright streak of lightning at around three that Sunday afternoon, followed by a powder-keg boom.

Abby Mendenhall, treasurer and board member of the Sisterhood of Bethany, paid a railway switch operator to watch the comings and goings of the First Avenue red-light district and report back to her—which brothel was the current mayor's favorite, which madams were trading girls down the river to St. Paul, who'd been raided by the police. Later, the switch

operator told her he'd seen what he called a banshee picking her
way over the railroad tracks about ten minutes before the crack
of thunder. He had shouted at the girl to watch herself. He was
Catholic, an immigrant from one of the Slavic countries. He'd
crossed himself when she turned, and he saw her face.

"But I didn't see no face," he reported to Abby, his hands
trembling. "She looked at me, and it seemed—there was no face
there. Or, as soon as I saw it, I forgot it. All I remember is she
wore purple."

Abel Stevens, who owned a small dairy barn just around the
corner from the Bethany Home, on East Lake, saw a waif coming toward him at the instant when veins of lightning split the
sky. He'd known immediately something was wrong—she wore
no hat or gloves, and her hair hung ragged and loose. Her skin
glowed as pale as the lightning, as if something had scared the
color from it. Abel had wanted to help her, but his wife stood
beside him on the curb as they emptied buckets of slop. His
eyes had met his wife's. Both knew what that garish purple gown
meant. His wife splashed her bucket violently, drenching the
girl's high-heeled boots as she passed them. Then—boom—the
thunder. Stevens flinched. When he opened his eyes, she was
gone.

As for Abby, she'd been in the Bethany Home's parlor with
Mrs. Van Cleve and the two male callers when the storm made
its one announcement. She'd delayed her tea until three so that
she could accommodate these two fancy gentlemen in their
brightly patterned waistcoats, the gold chains of their pocket
watches gleaming.

Wealth, she thought as she stirred her tea. Something she
saw little of in her early years here, when the streets were no

more than rutted logging routes and the mighty waterfall had
been clogged with timber. There was still very little established
wealth here, not like in the bigger, older cities; any Minneapolis means had traveled from New England. To see very young,
Minnesota-born men wearing boastful watch chains both annoyed and enticed her. She'd been the treasurer of the Bethany
Home since they were in short pants. It irritated her more than
it should to still have to grovel for donations, but this was probably the Lord's way of keeping her humble.

"A hundred dollars apiece would be wonderful," she told the
two young ones, trying to sound grandmotherly. She was sixty-
three: old enough to be their mother, at least.

"A generous sum," Mrs. Van Cleve—Charlotte, Abby's friend
and another board member—said in her vociferous, off-key
voice, her ear horn balanced in her lap. "I assume you'll be making your contributions in . . ."

"Are banknotes acceptable?" the man on the left said, the one
without any facial hair. His smooth cheeks and bright hazel
eyes made him seem as if he might be scarcely out of sailor suits.
He'd been nosing about since he arrived, peering upstairs from
the foyer, stooping to inspect the brass plates on the parlor art-
work. Men tended to snoop when they were allowed entry to the
Bethany Home, especially the youthful, eager ones. "We have
gold to back it up, if you don't trust greenbacks. Mr. Hayward
and I are in fine shape despite the Panic. We didn't invest heavily
in railroads."

"Or in Argentina," the other man added, with a laugh. This
one seemed a bit older, in his early or middle thirties, with a
substantial mustache. His eyes held Abby's for a bit too long,
then shifted away.

"Gold is preferable," Abby replied. The men turned those bland smiles toward her, appraising her appearance: her silver hair, her plain black dress. Ah, she could see them thinking, a Quaker. How dull her paltry life must be.

"But we will accept banknotes," she added in a hurry, hoping they'd still offer gold. They had to know, didn't they, that most banks had become unreliable? It wasn't just railroads and Argentine investments. The price of wheat had collapsed in the past year, as well as silver. The number of men walking around covered in flour dust—mark of the well employed—had plummeted as the mills let laborers go. The change in fortunes had Abby worried. Where did men take out their frustrations in times of trouble?

"We'll take any donation," Charlotte chimed in. "We aren't affiliated with a church, like the Home of the Good Shepherd in St. Paul, so we receive no tithings."

"Which allows us to run this place a bit differently," Abby added. She wanted to say more but knew she shouldn't. She hoped her weighted expression hinted at what was rumored to happen inside the Home of the Good Shepherd and its laundry.

The man with the mustache sneezed, picked up one of their best linen napkins from the sideboard and blew his nose on it, then dropped it on the embroidered settee. Abby's and Charlotte's eyes met. They might not have to answer to any priest or bishop, but they still had to suffer fools.

"What of the fines you collect from the city?" his friend asked. "Shouldn't they—"

"We do, however, collect two-thirds of the fines the city imposes on prostitutes and madams," Charlotte continued, as if she hadn't heard his question. Abby took a sip of Ceylon and hid her smile in her teacup. Impossible to tell, sometimes, whether

Charlotte hadn't heard someone, or if she simply wanted to interrupt.

"Doesn't that compromise your mission?" the man pressed Charlotte, a little smile lifting one side of his mouth. "You want an end to the social evil, yet you're reliant on its continuation for your survival."

"Our mission isn't confined to ending the 'social evil,' " Abby replied. The edges of her ears had grown hot. "It's also to house, feed, and care for any unwed mother, then send her on her way with the means to support herself."

The man grinned. "You're saying there's always going to be gals getting themselves in trouble, whether they're sporting women or not."

Abby looked to Charlotte, who set down her ear horn. "We're saying that if we could persuade the city to impose the fines on *men*—and it's four of every five men, mind you, who have visited a brothel at least once—instead of the girls, we would."

The room went blue-white with lightning. God Himself, putting an exclamation point on Charlotte's sentence. In the instant when their faces were blanched with fire from heaven, the two men exchanged a glance. Thinking, perhaps, what Abby was: that Charlotte could have exaggerated that statistic to make her point. It wouldn't be the first time.

"Anyhow," the younger man said smoothly, "our interest is primarily in you."

BOOM. The belated thunder rattled the house, vibrating the windows.

"In us?" Abby replied.

"All of you, the Sisterhood of Bethany. You built this place from the ground up, isn't that a fact? And you command a surprising level of political influence." He cleared his throat, perhaps waiting for them to thank him for the compliment. "We're here because we're in favor of Mr. Pratt's campaign for mayor. Can we count on your husbands' votes for Pratt in the election, a week from next Tuesday?"

Abby met Charlotte's eyes again. She would have been astonished if she hadn't heard this many times before: a request for the neck of the household to make the head turn.

"I would ask my husband who he plans to vote for," Charlotte said, gruffly, holding up her ear horn, "but, you see, I can't very well hear his reply."

Abby snickered into her handkerchief, then remembered they were supposed to be courting donations. "Sirs, of course our husbands shall vote for Mr. Pratt."

"I serve with him on the school board," added Charlotte. "Good man. Besides, you wouldn't expect us to back a Democrat, would you?"

The men nodded, though they still seemed oddly unsatisfied. They rubbed their palms on their trousers.

At last, here was the matron, Miss Rhoades, with the refreshments. She set a tray of tartlets next to the Chinese teapot: butternut tassies, made with Gold Medal flour milled right in Minneapolis.

Miss Rhoades took a deft step backward toward Abby's chair. Her fingers tapped Abby's arm. Once, twice, with a firm pressure.

Abby reached for her hand. "Does something require my attention?"

Miss Rhoades shrugged, a casual gesture belied by the urgent grip of her fingers. "Cook has a question for you, ma'am, in the kitchen."

"Please excuse me," Abby said, rising with Miss Rhoades's assistance.

The men leapt up. "Is anything the matter?" the younger one asked.

"No, no," Abby said, indicating that he should sit down at once. "I'm wanted in the kitchen, that's all. It shan't take more than a minute."

He sat down, looking disappointed. Abby could hear Charlotte begin squawking as the parlor door shut behind her, "Now, about your donations . . ."

Once she was in the hallway, Abby could hear a muffled commotion coming from the kitchen. Pearl, one of the cook's apprentices, stood waiting for them beside the cellar steps. She was about twenty years old, willowy, with hair the color of wild-flower honey. Overly aware of the admiration she attracted, a trait Abby had tried, gently, to iron out.

"Cook's at her wits' end. Imagine, arriving unannounced—"

"Shh. Hold your peace, Pearl," Abby whispered.

They followed the stairs down to the cellar, where the kitchen, baths, and inmates' dining room were, and went quickly through the chilled, damp hallway. The polished-wood scent of the first floor gave way to basement mustiness. Pearl led the way into the kitchen, eager, as was Pearl's custom, to get to the epicenter of trouble.

Crouched near the back door of the kitchen was a wet lump of a person, tangled dark hair and ruined purple silk, two pale hands with fingers interlocked, cradling the back of its neck, head down. Mary O'Rourke, whom the girls called Cook, had her foot wedged between the figure and a crate of acorn squash, yelling and trying to protect the produce from those filthy skirts. Miss

Rhoades went to crouch in front of the girl, one hand on her shoulder, the other lifting a handkerchief to her own face, presumably to cover a smell. As Abby grew closer, she saw scabbed gashes on the girl's bare hands, then caught the scent in the air: urine.

"Oh," Abby said, more an intake of breath than a word. "Oh my."

"She's soiled herself!" Cook moaned. "Right here on me clean floor."

Pearl stifled a laugh. Miss Rhoades glared up at Cook, then turned back to the stranger. "My dear, please . . ." She tried prying the girl's fingers apart. "We'd like to help you, if you'll only let us clean you up."

Abby knelt as well. An unannounced arrival wasn't completely unheard of; Abby made sure to spread word about the home when she visited taverns, the jail, the court, the workhouse. Her network—the uncorrupt policemen; the madams she'd helped avoid prison, or bury their unfortunate dead; the boxcar operators who saw girls streaming in from the east and out toward the west—knew what to whisper if they sensed a girl was in trouble: *The Bethany Home will take you in.*

"You're safe here," she told the stranger in a firm, clear voice. "There's a bed for you if you need it, friend."

The girl's shoulders stopped trembling at "friend." Amazing how the word, so common and ordinary among those who practiced plain speech, could lift the spirits of people unfamiliar with the custom. Slowly, the girl unlaced her fingers and picked up her head.

Pearl gasped. Cook had gone quiet. Abby refused to react. A face was a face, just like any other, no matter how beautiful or unusual it might be. God had made this face just as He'd made all the rest. She stared calmly into the girl's eyes, the color of a churning sea, and asked her name. The girl didn't answer.

"Choose a name to use while you're here," Abby told her. "Not your own. We can mark your birth name in our register later, if you're willing to share. Come, now. Choose a name to hide behind, if you need."

Evidently, the girl had heard; she pursed her lips, thinking. Her cheekbones shone, pink and wide, despite the pallor of her skin. Light freckles dotted her nose and eyelids.

"Deaf, ma'am?" Miss Rhoades asked.

"I don't think so." Abby put her hand on the girl's shoulder. "What brought you here?" She lowered her voice. "Is a child on the way?"

The girl's injured hands went to her stomach. She gave a small nod.

"Miss Rhoades," Abby said, turning back to the matron, "why don't you suggest a name for her?"

Miss Rhoades had lowered the handkerchief from her nose. "How about Faith? We haven't had a Faith here in a while, ma'am."

Again, Pearl snickered. Faith, in a harlot's dress. Abby threw her a sharp glare, and she stopped.

"Faith, then. Will that do?" Abby asked. "How about Faith Johnson?"

The strange girl nodded.

"Miss Rhoades can explain the rules of the house in detail," Abby continued. "Expectant mothers are contracted to stay one year, regardless of when the baby arrives. During this time, you'll learn a skill—in the kitchen, or with the seamstress or laundress. That'll help you get on your feet when you leave. Some girls stay in the city, some go west to do farmwork and get away from old acquaintances. And some are married right here in the chapel."

Faith stared at the floor and rubbed her arms. Nothing Abby had just said seemed to entice or encourage her; she appeared miserable.

"You may keep the child," Miss Rhoades said gently, "or we can help with an adoption placement when the time comes."

Faith's eyes widened, but, again, she didn't respond.

Abby turned to the rest of the women. "Now that's done, it's time to get our new arrival clean and clothed. Pearl, there's an empty bed in your room, is that correct?"

Pearl wrinkled her pretty nose. "Yes, ma'am."

"Help Miss Rhoades take Faith upstairs. She can be your roommate."

"Yes, ma'am," they both said, Miss Rhoades with greater enthusiasm, and each of them reached for one of Faith's upper arms to lift her from the floor. As she stood, wobbling, something fell from her skirts, a little sachet. It hit the floor with a metal thump, and Faith's eyes met Abby's, full of meaning.

An ocean, hidden there in those curious eyes. Abby felt cold suddenly, overwhelmed with the urge to open the door and send this girl back up the cellar steps. Something about her did not seem right. *Away, away with her.*

But no. The girl had been delivered to her doorstep, and now she was Abby's to keep.

"Mrs. Mendenhall?" Miss Rhoades touched Abby's arm.

"Leave us, please," Abby said. "Leave Faith with me for a moment."

Once they were gone, Abby reached down to the floor, her fingers outstretched toward the little velvet pouch, but Faith got in front of her and crawled on her knees to pick it up. Being alone with Abby had transformed her. She almost looked eager. She took Abby's hand and placed the pouch inside, then curled Abby's fingers around it.

Abby felt ill. She didn't need to open it to know what was inside. Gold bullion coins. The crinkling of paper between her fingers, too: several greenbacks. She didn't want to know where or how Faith had acquired this bounty. Her urge to send Faith away intensified.

"You don't need to pay to stay here, friend," she said softly.

Faith nodded, but she pushed the bag of money back toward Abby's chest, and when Abby tried refusing, she shook it. The gold clinked. *Keep this for me,* she seemed to ask. Somehow, Abby heard a voice in her head, even though the girl's blanched lips did not move. Her face truly was astoundingly lovely, if unsettled and deathly pale.

"Very well, very well." Abby slid the pouch inside her pocket. No one could know about this, not Charlotte, not Euphemia Overlock or anyone else on the board. Abby would figure out what to do with it later.

The girl was shivering now, and yawning; Abby shouted for the matron. Miss Rhoades came back in, followed, unfortunately, by Pearl, who buzzed through the kitchen's swinging door like a mosquito in summer, hungry for blood.

"That'll be all, Pearl," Abby said sharply. When Pearl had gone, sulking, Abby lowered her voice. "Beth, I've changed my mind. Is May Lombard still bunking alone?"

Miss Rhoades chewed her thin lower lip. "Well, yes, but—"

"Take Faith to May's room." Better May than Pearl. May might recoil at Faith's appearance, but she would ask no questions. May talked too much on her own to interrogate a roommate. That, and her year was up; she was due to leave. "Please, help Faith change into a clean chemise and dress. See that there are fresh linens on the bed."

"Yes, Mrs. Mendenhall." Miss Rhoades hesitated, scratching the hair behind her ear. It had grayed since Abby had hired her, fading from rich chestnut to the color of sun-bleached cedar.

"Funny," said Miss Rhoades, "don't you think Faith looks a little like Delia did?"

"No, I do not," Abby replied. "Off to the linens you go, Miss Rhoades."

She felt drained of energy when she reached the foyer to find the clean-shaven man with his hand on the doorknob of the matron's quarters. "Can I help you?" she asked, her tone sharp.

"I thought I might see the library," he replied. "Or the living room—is that in here?"

She took him by the arm and led him back to the reception room. "I'm afraid the library is for the inmates, dear sir. We must respect their privacy."

They found his friend sitting glaze-eyed as Charlotte held forth on temperance. He rose from his seat when Abby came in. The men waited for her to take her chair, but she didn't.

"Thank you both, very kindly, for paying us a visit," Abby told them. "We happen to have donation envelopes right here in the basket on the hearth."

Their smiles faded. "Can't we have a tour?" asked the man with the mustache.

"We're being exceedingly generous," his friend added. "You should at least vouchsafe to us a peek at the innards of this place. Make sure our money's well spent."

Abby did her best to maintain a polite visage. "We are not a museum, sirs."

With a harrumph, the older one went to the mantel and took

two envelopes, then handed one to his friend. Both took out their billfolds and stuffed all the banknotes they had in them into the envelopes, then handed them to Abby. She and Charlotte thanked the men as they went, muttering and fussing, to the door. They turned and bade the women a polite, if hasty, adieu.

Abby and Charlotte watched them stride toward their carriage, talking animatedly. At one point they stopped—the older one gesticulating toward the house, the younger listening with arms crossed. Then they left.

Charlotte shook her head. "I thought you might ask for their addresses, so we could include them in the monthly solicitations."

"They wouldn't have contributed a penny more," Abby replied, watching their driver prod the horse, who'd stalled on the roadway. "All they wanted was a glimpse at the girls." She exhaled, thinking how close they'd been to witnessing a real spectacle.

The maid had already come with Charlotte's wrap. Her coachman would be bringing round the barouche. Mrs. Van Cleve was somewhat famous, despite her age and sex, and was frequently pulled in many different directions: public lectures, philanthropic events, school board meetings. Unlike Abby, who, as treasurer, paid several visits a week to the home and had to keep track of everything from the store of coal in the coffer to the need for new bedsteads.

Charlotte grasped Abby's sleeve. Her milky eyes hovered somewhere around Abby's forehead. "I trust you know what's best, Mrs. Mendenhall."

Abby patted her shoulder. "Thank you, my friend." Faith's pouch felt heavy in Abby's pocket. She waited until Charlotte had gone to finish her reply: "I hope you're right."

2

MAY

$\mathscr{S}$omeone to care for. Someone who needed her. It was all May Lombard had ever wanted, though in her dreams her dependents took the form of a doting husband and an array of children, not a bedraggled, silent wretch who'd crawled here from God knows where.

The afternoon Faith arrived to take over half her room, May had found a spare moment to work on her embroidery, a cheroot cigar case, which she sat busily embellishing with a pair of mallard ducks. She had given careful thought to the design: subtly romantic—a drake and a hen with wings crossed—yet masculine enough so that Hal would be well pleased.

May still found it bewildering that she'd ended up here, at the Bethany Home, among girls with all manner of tragic backgrounds and circumstances. Her own trouble had started in the most honest way possible. Her late father, who made what he proclaimed were the finest leather shoes in the Midwest, had chosen the youngest son of their closest neighbors, the Riccis (of Ricci & Sons' restaurants, known for their risotto and kidneys), for her to marry. May and the boy, Lorenzo, had fallen head over heels for each other. Enzo, she called him. They were good Catholics, chaste, but they'd given in to passion one humid night after a parish festival. Everyone had drunk too much wine, and her chaperone—Aunt Cassandra, with the black nose-hairs—had fallen asleep in the back of a carriage. Lo and behold, it had taken just that one time with Enzo for May to fall pregnant. Just the one time.

The other girls at the Bethany Home had heard the story more than once. If they were growing tired of it, May didn't care. Where she came from, the Near North Side of Chicago, people liked to talk. Too much, in fact; it was why her mother would never let her come home unless she'd found a husband. Enzo, unfortunately, was long since off the market. Hitching one's wagon to an eligible bachelor was not an easy task when one lived in a home with thirty-some other women, but May was resourceful. Though no male visitors were ever allowed upstairs, or in the nursery, she kept her room tidy and cheerful, a bowl of wildflowers on the sill when she could get them, floor swept, and baseboards dusted. She even washed the white curtains that billowed around her window, so they wouldn't turn drab and yellow, or gray and cobwebby.

Sometimes, when she had a spare moment, she'd take the others' curtains down and wash and iron those, too. Incredibly, the other inmates never bothered to thank her for this effort. They seemed annoyed, in fact. Many of the girls here had worked in some of the houses of ill fame that lined the Mississippi. The very thought of it made May shudder, but she tried to remember that not everyone was raised in a home like hers, where her mother taught her to respect her elders and the space in which she lived, to be a good steward to God's Earth. Her father educated her to be kind, gregarious, helpful to her neighbors. May had never once poked fun at a resident of the Bethany Home, no matter how disheveled or feebleminded she seemed, nor had she whispered behind the back of her hand about how ugly so-and-so's baby was, the way Pearl and her nasty lot liked to do. They were all God's children, after all, no matter what they'd done before they got here, and deserved a clean slate. Especially the babies. Nothing any of their mothers had done was the babies' fault.

"How sweet."

May jumped, knocking her embroidery hoop to the floor; the thread unspooled, her needle lost somewhere in her skirts. Pearl—the most beautiful girl here, but as mean as they come—stood at the door to May's room. The pearl of great price.

"Land sakes, Pearl." May began wrapping the loose thread quickly round her embroidery so that Pearl wouldn't comment on it. "You could learn to knock."

"Who's that for? Wait, let me guess."

Sighing, May stood, and the missing needle fell to the floor with a pixie *plink*. She went to her mattress and knelt before it as though she were in confessional, Pearl watching, smug now in her silence. From under her mattress May retrieved her eyelet handkerchief and unwound a snippet of Mail Pouch tobacco. Stolen from Cook, daily, for Pearl, who also worked in the kitchen but had found a way to make May do her dirty work. She handed it to Pearl, who tucked it into her own handkerchief with one finger.

"Thank you, Miss Lombard, how kind of you," Pearl said, patting her pocket.

May took a deep, long breath in through her nose, the way the matron had taught her. She shut her eyes, briefly, and imagined she sat alone in a peaceful maple grove.

"Don't let them get your goat," Miss Rhoades liked to say, but she didn't know what Pearl held over May. Hal, May's beau, had no idea May lived in the Bethany Home, and she needed Pearl to help her keep it that way.

"I came to warn you," Pearl said. "The matron's on her way. She has a present for you."

"A present?"

"A bunkmate."

May's heart sank. She could hear the matron climbing the curved staircase to the second floor. It had been weeks since she'd shared her room with someone, and she looked now at the other narrow bed, which she'd covered in needlepoint pillows and a soft blanket, a makeshift love seat where she could do her sewing or fold her laundry.

If only Pearl would go away, take her prying, perfect nose back to her room across the hall. Trip, for good measure, and land flat on her face. But that was an evil thought; May tried to push it down as she shuffled everything from the other bed to her own, leaving the bare mattress exposed. She gathered her embroidery from the floor—the needle nowhere to be found—and heaped it atop her desk. Terrible, an awful mess: she'd give a slatternly first impression, and that simply wouldn't do.

"Do you mind—" she began to snap at Pearl, but Pearl had vanished, and standing in her place were Miss Rhoades and some sort of horrifying creature.

"Miss Lombard," Miss Rhoades said crisply, "this is Miss Faith Johnson."

Not her real name, of course; the place was crawling with Smiths and Johnsons. Despite her horror at the newcomer's appearance, May curtsied. "How do you do?"

Faith did not answer, only gave May a small nod. Her hair was a wreck, damp and tangled, undone, but that wasn't the worst part: she wore a bright purple gown, a color suited exclusively for a king or a queen. Here in this plain white room, it could only be a strumpet's color, a beacon of shame. When May closed her eyes, she could still see it tattooed on her eyelids, like a mark left by the sun. With it came unspeakable images of what this girl might have done to get herself sent here.

"Oh my, Miss Rhoades," May said, gesturing toward the new girl as if to say, *What do we do with her?*

Miss Rhoades offered a weak smile. "Faith just arrived this afternoon and will be sharing your room. Won't you help her feel welcome?"

May swallowed the lump in her throat and went to her dresser, the one she'd now have to split with Faith. "Let's start with a clean chemise." She smoothed the garment out on the spare bed, then took a step back.

The stranger stared at it. She reached one scabbed hand forward to stroke the plain fabric.

Miss Rhoades coughed lightly. "May, come with me so that Faith can change in peace. Faith, after you put that on you may come down the back staircase to have your bath." She placed the back of her hand on Faith's forehead. "A tepid bath will do."

May could hear Pearl complaining in the hallway: "She gets her own bath?!"

Miss Rhoades sighed. "Yes, she gets a bath," she called. "May, a word in the corridor?"

Out in the hallway, Miss Rhoades took May by the arm. The matron had very thin skin, freckled and spotted; now it gathered between her eyebrows like a drawn curtain. "As you might have noticed, the girl doesn't speak."

"Doesn't speak?" Of course they'd stick May with a roommate like this, right when they were poised to show her the door. They were probably hoping this beast would scare her away. Her hands balled into fists, but she kept her voice calm. "Can she hear?"

"Yes, we think she's a mute. She can hear you, but she seems unable to talk. And, May . . ." The corners of Miss Rhoades's mouth crinkled. "I believe this girl has been treated poorly. It may feel a shock to you to have been given such a roommate, but I ask you to be gentle, and show fortitude, for her sake."

"I'm more worldly than you think, Miss Rhoades."

"Right. Thank you, May. That'll be all."

May bent her knees in a curtsy, and the matron hurried away. The door to May's room was closed. It didn't feel like her own anymore, and she felt sheepish entering, but it was possible Faith needed her help and couldn't ask. She knocked softly, then, not expecting an answer, pushed open the door to the room.

The girl still stood in the center of the knotted rug, as purple as ever. Her neck was twisted toward May, and her elbows bent at odd angles as she struggled with the pearl buttons on the high, boned collar of that awful dress.

"Oh, goodness, here," said May, "let me help you. I used to do this for my cousin. My aunt and uncle lived right next door to us . . ."

Faith turned so that May could undo her buttons, which were slightly too big for their snug little buttonholes. May chattered on as she worked at the buttons, somewhat pleased to find that Faith wouldn't interrupt her. She told Faith about her two siblings and the cousins who would tumble in and out of one another's houses, the bean soup her mother kept at a simmer on the stove every day in winter, so that any child who hungered could help himself to a bowl. It was a cozy picture she conjured, and she felt Faith relax, slowly, into wistful silence.

The final button gave May trouble; her fingernail stabbed the pad of her thumb in her effort. Faith turned to see why she'd yelped and the purple collar fell open, revealing her neck.

May dropped her hand. Now it was she who was speechless, fixated on the stranger's pale throat.

It was circled in bruises, purple ones that matched her gown. The marks were shaped like ropy fingers. The bruises were darkest in the middle, over the voice box, where phantom thumbs had pressed hard into the skin. May's fingers crept to her collarbone. She swallowed hard.

"Oh dear." Perhaps this was why the girl wouldn't, or couldn't, speak. "Why don't you . . ." May cleared her throat. "Turn around, now, let's get you out of this dress."

Faith obeyed. Her shoulders drooped. May worked the last button above the black velvet waistband, afraid of what else she might find underneath the fabric. As she undid Faith's corset, the girl sighed audibly in relief, but still said nothing.

May had never been able to abide a loaded silence. A question burst forth. "Who did this to you?"

Faith hung her head. May wasn't sure why she'd asked, knowing she wouldn't get an answer. She tapped Faith on the shoulder to let her know the gown was fully unbuttoned, and Faith began peeling off the sleeves. As she did, she lifted her chin slightly over one shoulder, toward May.

The voice was tiny, nearly inaudible. Hoarse, from lack of use, or worse.

"Oh," it said. "You know."

"No, I don't," May replied, waiting for Faith to elaborate. Faith had the gown down to her waist now, and May could see the top of her chemise, stained yellow with age, her breasts soft under the fabric. Totally indecent. Completely inappropriate, this entire interaction. The air was too close; May needed out.

"I thought you were a mute," she said, and before she backed out the door she saw Faith flinch at her comment, as though she'd been struck. Whatever had opened behind Faith's eyes closed itself off again.

3

FAITH

*T*he bed was comfortable; the quilts were thin but soft. She wanted to go to sleep so badly. She had to wait while the matron assembled her new belongings: two white aprons, a washbasin and jug with fresh water from the cistern, a hobnail lamp, a calico dress, stockings. After her bath, Miss Rhoades presented it all to her with a flourish, as though she'd never had possessions to call her own.

She had known finer things. She had also known worse.

Miss Rhoades fussed over her. She tucked echinacea into a vase, helped her comb out her hair—this hairbrush would be hers now! All hers!

The girl who was now called Faith nodded and smiled. Yes, she did feel better having shed her corset. Her aching breasts throbbed under her new chemise, but she didn't say this to Miss Rhoades. She'd never been much for speaking. It was difficult to do without her voice shaking, or, sometimes, without tears running down her face. But this was something new. Speaking had become impossible. Why, look what had happened when she'd tried to say just one little thing to her roommate. A disaster. Said roommate was now nowhere to be seen. She wondered where May had gone, and how many other girls there were in this place. By the number of rooms, it seemed there would be thirty or forty. She'd seen girls of varied complexions and nationalities, who seemed to be sorted into bunk rooms by skin color, just as the brothels were segregated. There were girls whose bellies betrayed just a hint of a swell, some who were far gone and out of breath, others flat-stomached, like May.

No one familiar, not yet. Would any of them be girls whom Faith knew, or who recognized her? She wasn't sure if that would be a fortunate turn or not.

When the matron prepared to leave her, she did her best to show gratitude for all Miss Rhoades had done. Because she was, indeed, grateful. For the locks on the door and the window, she felt most grateful. She tugged Miss Rhoades's striped skirt.

The matron met her eyes and smiled. Miss Rhoades wore her goodness plainly on her face. "You know, I'd say you do just fine without talking," she told Faith, brushing a lock of hair out of her eyes. "You just wait and speak when you're ready. Or not at all—makes no difference to me."

A tear slipped down Faith's cheek. Miss Rhoades reached for the hankie on the stool that held the washbasin and pressed it to both of Faith's cheeks. "Mind you, leave the window open, so you don't catch disease."

She left, and Faith pulled the window shut and locked it. She settled in to snatch a wink of sleep before the dreams began.

4

ABBY

When Abby arrived at the Bethany Home a few days later, her husband, Junius, in tow to begin the process of winterizing the gardens, the front door flew open before she'd had time to reach the knob. The matron stood there, panting.

"Mrs. Mendenhall, you'd better come in. There's trouble."

Abby rocked back on her heels. She was holding a bunch of hothouse blooms, the last roses of October, for the foyer vase. "What's the matter? Is anyone hurt?"

Miss Rhoades's mouth twitched impatiently. "Well, no, not exactly."

"May I assist?" Junius asked.

Abby turned to her husband, a slight, narrow-faced man, who waited beside her with his spade in one hand and walking stick in the other. Dressed entirely in plain black, just as she was. "No, thank thee, dear man. Thou can find the rest of the tools in the gardener's shed. He arrives at nine, and he and the custodian can help thee."

She watched the back of her husband's gray head as he walked round the side lawn and toward the shed. It would pain her to see him reduced to such simple domestic tasks—he hadn't worked in banking since the Panic of 1873—if she didn't know what satisfaction he derived from gardening. His health benefited, too, from the fresh air and a turn in the sun.

The matron had the side of her thumbnail in her mouth. An ungodly habit. "You look worried, Miss Rhoades." Abby tugged the woman's hand down, then made sure to offer a reassuring pat on the shoulder, a smile. "There you are."

Abby was used to switching from plain speech to vernacular, depending on whom she was talking to and whether they were Friends. She could be one person with Junius and another with Miss Rhoades. With her husband, who suffered from sciatica, rheumatism, chronic bronchitis, she could move slowly, hushed and humbled by their accumulated decades. She knew the language and rhythms of frailty, having been sickly in childhood.

With everyone affiliated with the Bethany Home, she became someone else. A woman who knew the back entrances to saloons.

She raised her silvery head half an inch taller. "Now show me this trouble you speak of."

The foyer, Abby was surprised to see, bustled with life. Normally, all the inmates would be at breakfast now, and the babies and children would be with their nursemaids, but here a cluster of young women stood whispering, a group who'd arrived together from Ida Dorsey's brothel; one of them was absently rocking her infant. Another pair of inmates looked up guiltily at Abby; they were sharing a piece of cold chicken, a drumstick, between them, eating right there in the open with greasy fingers. A boy stood on the stairs and reached down through the railing for one of the wilted calla lilies on the calling-card table. Abby went to him and stopped his hand.

"Miss Rhoades," she called to the matron, holding firm to

the boy's wrist. Everyone in the room stopped what they were doing. "What is the meaning of all this?"

Miss Rhoades tapped one of the whisperers on the shoulder, signaling them to move on. She snatched the chicken bone and used it to point down toward the cellar. "You'd better come and see."

"There wasn't any breakfast!" the boy screeched when Abby let go of him.

On the way down to the kitchen, Abby could once again hear Cook shouting at someone, but this time, the sun shone brightly through the basement windows. There was no dark figure in a puddle on the floor, but the plump form and flushed face of a girl who'd given herself the name Dolly, her cheeks streaked with tears as she took the brunt of Cook's tirade. May, Pearl, Leigh, and Faith were nowhere to be seen.

"Seventy biscuits," Cook raged at Dolly from under the massive black hood of the cast-iron stove. "How one girl ruins seventy biscuits meant for an entire household, I'll never know."

Dolly trembled visibly. She'd arrived at the home only a few months ago and had yet to deliver her child, though the event had to be imminent. Her face had a bee-stung look to it, lips and cheeks pink and engorged. Under her skirts, her boots were untied, giving her a slovenly appearance. Swollen ankles, most likely; Abby wasn't always clear on these matters, having no children of her own. Still, it troubled her to see someone behaving so harshly to an expectant mother. "Mrs. O'Rourke," she said, silencing Cook, "kindly explain yourself."

"She ate everything! Woke up with me this morning, as usual, helped me bake today's biscuits. No sooner I turn me back than she's eaten the entire lot of them! Breakfast was meant to be biscuits, butter, and jam, Mrs. Mendenhall. What am I to serve now, jam alone?"

Abby noted that it smelled, tantalizingly, of bacon in the kitchen as well, though that was surely meant only for the staff, for any board members who happened upon the home this morning, and for Cook herself. In years past, they'd been able to serve bacon to the inmates, but tightened finances had put an end to that luxury.

"I didn't mean to," Dolly burbled, between tears. "I don't know what came over me."

"Really, Cook, seventy biscuits?" Miss Rhoades said, before Abby could ask any more questions of her own. "How is that possible?"

Cook reached behind her for one of the two baking pans and thrust it before the women's eyes. Thirty-five or so biscuits, all bitten and half eaten, or shredded to crumbs. "See for yourself. The little thief made sure to take a bite of every last one."

Miss Rhoades's face paled. Dolly looked horrified.

"What I can't figure is how she expected to get away with it," Cook said, slamming the pan back onto the range. "I came back in and there she was, stuffing herself."

Something was amiss here, but Abby couldn't quite put her finger on it. "Well, Dolly?" she said. "What do you have to say for yourself?"

Dolly sniffed. Her eyes were huge, red-streaked. "I'm sorry, Mrs. Mendenhall, Cook. I don't know why I did it. You were gone, and—and it was only myself and the new girl here. And the biscuits smelled so good. I can't say what came over me."

"You were gone for how long?" Miss Rhoades interjected, one eyebrow raised at Cook.

Cook's cheeks reddened. "Can't say exactly. Not more than twenty, thirty minutes."

"While you did what?"

Cook's eyes rolled toward her ruffled cap. "All right, whilst I took a short nap, Miss Rhoades. I let the girls do it, too. You try rousing your bones at four in the morning, before the fires are lit, all to make sure everyone gets a warm biscuit for breakfast, only to have a greedy little—"

Abby interrupted her. "The new girl. Was this Faith Johnson?"

Dolly nodded. "Yes, she's been working with us in the kitchen."

A knot formed in Abby's stomach. She'd hoped that, with a bath, some clean clothes, and a fair share of the chores, Faith would be able to blend in with the others, that her dramatic arrival wouldn't be followed by further upheaval. "Mrs. O'Rourke," she asked Cook, "how has Faith been getting along?"

"Quiet one, she is," said Cook. "But, aye, she's been finishing her work as well as any other."

"This morning, though," Dolly said, tapping her fingertips together thoughtfully, "after Cook left, Pearl and Leigh went out to take a walk before the sun came up, and May headed upstairs to rest. There were only Faith and me in here." She pointed to a footed bronze timer on a shelf beside the stove. "We waited till Cook's timer rang; then we took the biscuits from the oven. And then . . ."

She made the other women wait, holding their breath, as she tapped those fingers together. Dolly was concocting a story. Abby watched it happen behind the girl's eyes. A story she already half believed herself. She'd be repeating the story for all who would listen, for days and weeks to come.

This, not the nibbled biscuits. This tale would be the trouble.

"Faith was just gazing at the biscuits, her nose a few inches from them. She started doing something strange with her hands, lifting the scent toward her nose, and when I came closer to see what she was doing, to tell her to stop fooling around, she started waving her hands toward me." Dolly's fingers rippled in front of Abby's eyes, each one a charmed snake undulating to its own rhythm. "Then she *smiled* at me. And before I knew it, I was eating."

Cook thumped her hand to her chest. "Christ in heaven. And today's Hallowe'en."

The other women, save Abby, gasped. Her gaze wandered to the high cellar window. Thick clouds had gathered, blocking the morning's sun, and were moving quickly eastward. Blades of grass, already dormant and blond, scratched at the glass like fingernails.

Abby exhaled forcefully. "Where is Faith now?"

"Upstairs, changing her apron," Dolly said. "Thank goodness." She locked eyes with Cook. The tears on her face had dried. "I am sorry, Cook. But she cast some sort of spell on me. She made me do it. With her mind."

By the time Abby sat down in her office with May Lombard, as the matron closed the rolling doors with a decisive *snick*, Dolly's story had spread. Abby could feel it crackle, as though the girls themselves were dry kindling: those working with the seamstress in the airy sewing room, the girls changing cot sheets in the nursery, those working with the laundress and Cook, who most likely was engaged in a breathless rendition of the tale herself, right now, in the basement.

Miss Rhoades had tried to insist that Abby speak with

Faith herself, but Abby didn't see where a one-sided conversation would get her. "Bring May Lombard to me," she told the matron with an air of finality, and Miss Rhoades had done as she was commanded.

Why shouldn't Abby turn to May? The girl had a good head on her shoulders. As they sat facing each other, Abby had the sense they were the only two in this house who weren't currently aflame with the story. It felt as though they sat together, bewildered, in a kind of smoking crater.

"They're saying she's a Mesmerist," May blurted out. "Some of the girls have met her before. They've watched her do . . . whatever a Mesmerist does."

"Before." Abby let the word linger. May would understand what she meant. "Before" didn't matter here—that was the gift the home bestowed on its inhabitants, the reason for their pseudonyms. Many arrived with sensational or traumatic stories, far more scandalous than Faith Johnson with her bag of gold bullion. Abby could easily have sold the details to gossip columnists or authors of penny dreadfuls, but she wouldn't dream of it. She liked to think of herself trimming these histories from her girls with invisible shears of righteousness.

Faith's "Before," however, felt relevant in a way other girls' hadn't. Abby would have to find out where the money had come from before she could decide what to do with it.

"They say she was called Marguerite the Magnificent," said May in wonder.

"Marguerite the Magnificent." The name sent a cold rush down the back of Abby's neck. She took a pen and a square of paper from her desk and wrote it down, then dropped the pen into its holder. "What do *you* think, May?"

May leaned closer. Her light-brown hair, parted in the middle, shone cleanly. She had the kind of face Abby liked best: even, small features, nothing in excess, beautiful in its plainness. "It's nonsense. Dolly and those biscuits, too. Besides, Faith isn't even a true mute. She spoke to me on the night she arrived."

"Oh?" This Abby hadn't expected to hear, and it troubled her. Maybe Miss Rhoades had been right: she should have brought Faith in here. "What did she say?"

May stared at the scrimshaw tooth Abby kept on the desk, carved with an image of the whaling ship *Morgan*. "I can't remember. But— Oh, there were bruises around her neck. The worst of it here." May gripped herself around the throat with her thumbs in the middle, pressing her own trachea. Abby's stomach dropped.

"Bruises. We've seen those. Part of the abuse inherent in the sale of human bodies. Men purchase a body and believe that entitles them to do what they will with it." Abby had gotten out of breath, a bit passionate; she touched the back of her hand to her forehead.

May, too, had turned bright red. "It's an awful business," she said quietly. "Do you know for certain she was engaged in it?"

"She arrived with more money than I've ever seen in one set of hands. But don't tell anyone that. I wouldn't want any of the girls to be tempted." Abby gestured toward the drawer of the desk, where she'd stowed the money. "I've a task for you. We laundered the dress Faith wore when she arrived. I'd like you to return it to its dressmaker. Find out who originally purchased the garment, then tell me. Only me."

"Yes, ma'am," May replied reluctantly; she looked as though she'd rather keep at least ten feet between herself and that dress.

After Abby sent May away, she sat by herself and thought. Bruises, for heaven's sake.

She rested in silence for a time, holding Faith in the Light.

On her way out of the parlor, she was nearly toppled by a boy and a girl, between the ages of three and five both, a boy with brown skin, the girl with red hair, pale-faced. The boy was running, mouth open wide with glee and mock horror, as the girl chased him with outstretched arms and waggling fingers, shrieking like a ghoul. "Easy, now, children," Abby said as she caught the girl by the arm. The boy tripped on the corner of a rug and went sprawling, and finally a nurse ran in, out of breath, a guilty expression painting her face.

"Winter will arrive too soon," Abby reminded her. "These children should be outside." She handed the girl to the nurse, who murmured a fervent apology. As Abby went round to tell Miss Rhoades she meant to collect Junius and go home, she heard the boy telling the nurse it wasn't his fault they'd been running in the hallways. The girl, he claimed, had mesmerized him.

5

MAY

*M*arguerite *the Magnificent.* The name invoked such grandeur, such power, that May couldn't help feeling a little jealous. Still, it was only gossip, likely untrue, and if Faith had ever merited such a lofty title, she'd sure tumbled far.

Occult practitioner or not, Faith definitely showed no interest in attending church. The girls were encouraged, though not required, to practice religious observance, either at the home's chapel or with their own congregations. As May dressed for worship in silence, she studied her roommate of one week: a tangled, sweaty mess of dark hair and pale skin. Despite the murmurs that Faith didn't bathe or bathed in blood (a particularly vicious and ridiculous rumor), May had come to expect her to keep a clean room, to rise, reliably, in time to bake the morning's bread, and to complete her morning toilette with a cloth and ordinary water, just like everyone else.

May studied the veins at her roommate's temples, the translucent skin of her throat. She crept to her table and pulled her own hand mirror out of the drawer, the glass splotched and cracked with age. Carefully, she applied a sweep of lavender powder over her face and neck. She dipped her fingertips into a pot of (forbidden) rouge and dabbed them lightly on her cheeks.

The trick was to look just a bit consumptive, a bit bluish and haunted—she applied the rouge under her eyes as well—but not too much. Not like a whore.

"Farewell," she murmured to Faith as she left. Faith's mouth twitched at its corner.

If only she would speak. She hadn't even defended herself when Pearl, at lunch, had accused her loudly of having tricked Dolly into ravaging those biscuits. Everyone in the dining room watched in stunned silence, waiting for Faith to protest, but she'd said nothing, and Pearl had helped herself to the browned half-apple and slice of holey cheese on Faith's plate.

This exchange only doubled the rumors: to allow Pearl to take tribute from her like that seemed an admission of guilt.

"She isn't even with child," Pearl said that morning as they flowed with the crowd down the front steps of the Church of the Redeemer. Leigh and Dolly walked behind her, their arms interlocked, forcing May to bring up the rear. It was a spectacular early-November day, sky like a bluebird and a manageable chill to the air, yet May walked with head hanging. Hal hadn't shown at the service this morning, for the third week in a row. Sometimes, she knew, he slept late on Sundays, which she took to mean he cared more about sleep than he did about her. She felt foolish with the finished cigar case in a carpetbag on her shoulder.

"Certainly not," Dolly replied, stepping slowly down the stairs, holding on to Leigh for support. "All skin and bone, that thing. Her mams look like they haven't even grown yet."

The other girls erupted in laughter. "Dolly!" May hissed, as a woman in a feathered hat cut them a stern look.

"If she isn't knocked up," Leigh said, "what would she want with the Bethany Home?"

"What do you think, May?" Dolly prodded her. "What would the new girl want with the Bethany Home?"

Pearl saved May from having to answer. "You kidding? Bed and board."

A strong arm flung itself around May's waist, stopping her momentum and causing her to drop the carpetbag. Her embroidery and a length of purple silk spilled out onto the stone steps. Churchgoers grumbled and stepped around them.

Pearl shaded her eyes with her hand, looking up at the man behind May and, fortunately, not the mess on the ground. "Well, hello, there, Hal," she called, lips pursed.

May felt a rumbling laugh in the chest of the man behind her. He had her pressed up against him, her tailbone to the front of his trousers.

Blood thundered in her cheeks. The rouge hadn't been necessary after all.

"Damn it, Pearl, you gave me away." Hal let May go, and she hurried to retrieve her bag, her thoughts racing. He was here. Had he heard Leigh say, "Bethany Home"? He offered May his arm, and they began strolling down the steps, the other girls in front of them.

"Anything I can carry for you, darling?" Hal asked.

"No, thank you, I'll manage." She wished that she'd fiddled with her dress the way Pearl had, to make it more fashionable. Pearl had gored her skirts so they'd lie smooth along her hips, then used the extra fabric to puff up the sleeves. If it weren't for Pearl's worn leather boots, she'd have been a Gibson model.

"The sheer size of this church makes it awfully hard to find someone," May told Hal. "I assumed you'd stayed in bed." She shut herself up at the word "bed," distracted by the thought of Hal in his sheets. Her sordid mind at work, yet again.

But, Lord, he was handsome. A better match for Pearl, the two of them with their fair hair and their tall, proud carriage. Yet he chose to have May on his arm. One of life's mysteries, and not one May wanted to resolve anytime soon.

"Will Amelia allow you a promenade with me?" he asked May when they reached the street. "Or are you wanted at home?"

The others' faces broke into broad, knowing smiles. May glared at them. Dolly, who'd largely escaped punishment for ruining everyone's breakfast earlier in the week, was especially conspicuous. It would be a miracle if Hal hadn't noticed her girth or the lack of a wedding ring. Scrawny Leigh—who hid tobacco inside her bottom lip and liked to dispose of the evidence in the home's potted plants—had surrendered her own baby for adoption right away, in the spring. And Pearl had bragged with sacrilegious fervor the entire streetcar ride to church about one of her regulars when she'd worked at Jennie Green's parlor house, a man who once made her howl like a coyote. Lumberjacks, she claimed, made the best lovers. Pearl had a three-month-old son, currently in the care of the nurses at the home, whom she was still deciding about.

May hated them all. They were pretty ceramic vases that, if you looked closely, were riddled with cracks.

Pearl locked eyes with May, grinning wickedly. "Ah, yes, Cousin Amelia. How lucky you are to have a cousin to live with, May, while we're stuck in a mere boardinghouse."

"But we're not due back till three at least," Dolly replied. "I think we've time for a pint and a slice of cake, don't you, Leigh?"

"Golly," said Leigh, "but I didn't bring any money. May, what've you got in your change purse? We'll pay you back, of course, next time we see you."

May gave a tight smile and placed six Indian-head pennies

into Pearl's outstretched hand. Her heart ached as she saw them go. The thirty-dollar stash she'd arrived with last year had dwindled nearly to nothing, thanks in large part to this kind of extortion.

"Mighty kind of you, May," said Leigh, turning with Dolly to go.

"You're a true friend, May." Pearl pocketed the change. "Say hello to Amelia for me! Farewell, May! Farewell, Hal!"

May and Hal watched them charge down the block, Pearl's arms thrown around her friends' shoulders, the three of them howling with laughter. A dark fantasy came unbidden into May's mind: herself holding raw eggs, launching them at the girls' backs. How satisfying it would be, the sounds of shells cracking, the drip of yolk down their coats and onto the sidewalk. She wondered how badly the eggshells would hurt the girls as they broke.

She blinked away the thought. "You'll have to forgive them," she said to Hal. Her own voice sounded funny to her. "They weren't raised in nice homes. Not their fault."

"Unlike you." He grinned, his handsome face framed by the mostly bare branches of a ginkgo that was still clinging to a few yellow fan-leaves. His mustache, as always, looked perfectly trimmed and combed, almost fastidiously so. His blue eyes gleamed, the pupils small in the sunlight.

A crisp breeze caressed May's cheek, sensuously lifting the hair on the back of her neck. Her fingers moved to take the cigar case from her carpetbag, before her better sense took hold of her. A drake and his hen, a matched pair—was she daft? How presumptuous, to assume he'd want such a thing from her. This was the extent of their courtship so far. He'd take her arm and walk with her, around the block and to the streetcar.

But he had his hand in his pocket, and he was pulling out a billfold. "How much do you need, darling, to recoup what they took? Five? Ten?"

"Goodness! But that's much more than . . ." *Take it,* a voice in May's head insisted. *Allow him to feel he's taking care of you, so that later you may take care of him.* The bills felt flat and new in her hand. She'd have to break them into coins, somehow.

"That can't seem like much money to you," Hal said. "You were brought up in the lap of luxury, is that right?"

"I don't know about the lap of luxury, but we had a good life." She took his arm and continued walking. "Father invested in leather, once they built the railroads and could bring goods from the ranches out west to Chicago." Her father had been a shoemaker, so this was not technically untrue.

"And how, again, did you find yourself in Minnesota?"

"Chicago had become dangerous, so crowded and dirty. Mother suggested I come stay with my cousin, Mrs. T. S. Winfield, and enjoy the fresh air of Minneapolis."

May had told him before about Amelia and her red brick home in Kenny. She left out the fact that Amelia lived, along with her four children, above the stables of that fine house, where she worked as a maid. During May's brief stay with her cousin, Amelia had risen before dawn and returned in the evening to scream at the children, at May, at the absent husband, whose whereabouts May never ascertained. She'd moved out before the newest baby was born.

Hal laughed. "Minneapolis isn't so fresh anymore." They were passing the bread line that formed beside the church's rectory every Sunday. Shabby, ghostlike figures shuffled forward, waiting their turns for a heel of bread or a cup of soup.

"I do miss Chicago sometimes. It's my younger cousins I miss the most . . ." May could see the streetcar stop ahead. It could be weeks before she saw him again, and all she'd have done was bore him. Who knew what he'd be up to in the meantime? She could tell by the cut and fabric of his clothing that he had money. He'd spend their time apart at fancy salons while May kneaded dough in a basement.

"I liked the sermon today," he said, changing the subject. "The bits about Darwin—now, that's religion I can get behind."

"I must admit I didn't listen to the sermon," she said quietly. She'd been looking for him.

"Oh, May. Why do you even come to church? Not for the entertainment, surely."

What could she say to that? She did view church as entertainment—it was the best part of her week. An excuse to get out in the fresh air, to ride a streetcar and feel like a regular citizen of this city, and, above all else, to see Hal.

To think she lived all week for the chance to talk with this man for only a few minutes. How desperate she was. How pathetic. She took a deep breath. "I attend because, at this church, there's no confession."

Hal stopped walking. For a moment she regretted her surge of honesty—he'd think her a heathen. Then his face broke into a broad smile. "Why, Miss Lombard! What have you done that would turn a priest's collar?"

She felt a bit startled that she had at last gotten his full attention. And said something her mother would've whipped her for. "I shan't tell a soul," she replied, trying to sound coy.

"Not even me?" he murmured, coming close to her. They stood facing each other. A wind off the river rushed down Eighth Street, causing all the trees to say *hush*. He took her left hand. She inhaled as he began plucking at the fingertips of her glove, one by one. Her glove off, he lowered his face slowly, never taking his eyes from hers. When his lips had nearly reached her hand, he paused. He smiled teasingly. He'd never kissed her before.

She felt warm between her legs, dizzy. She wished he would just do it, just kiss her. Her skin itched for it.

"I'd like to court you properly, May," he said, lips an inch from her hand. "Shall I call on you next week?"

She couldn't answer. She felt stunned, watching him. Instead of kissing the top of her hand, he turned it over—her heart shuddered—and touched his lips to the inside of her wrist. She felt the tickle of his mustache, the wet touch of his lips. Her veins pulsed rapidly. When he pulled away, the damp mark he'd left behind turned cold in the wind.

"That sounds lovely," May said when she found her voice. She wanted his lips on her mouth, his bare, flat stomach against hers. But that was a bad thought—*bad*—the kind of impulse that landed her in the Bethany Home to begin with.

Behind them, the church bells rang, lazily, a few notes of a Westminster chime. Quarter past the hour. It brought May back to her senses. If he were to call on her, he'd have to find out where she lived. "My cousin is very strict," she told him quickly. "She wouldn't allow you to see me without a chaperone. And she's a terribly nosy chaperone."

"Oh?" He lifted one fair eyebrow. "You've had other suitors, then?"

"No, I . . ." Her face burned. She was saying, and thinking, all the wrong things. She could hear her mother's voice in her head: *You are ruined.*

Hal pulled his pocket watch from a chain in his pocket. "I

have somewhere to be," he said, taking a few steps back. "Until next time, then, Miss Lombard? Next Sunday?"

Her shoulders drooped. He'd asked to court her, and she'd rejected him. "Next Sunday." But what if he slept late next Sunday? What if he never came to church again?

Before she could think better of it, she added, "If you can rouse yourself."

She'd only meant if he could wake up in time. She caught the double entendre too late. Hal caught it, too. He shot her that grin again as he strolled backward, his gait improbably confident.

"Oh, I can rouse myself," he called to her.

She hurried away, face flushed, blood pounding in her earlobes.

"Miss, I assure you," the dressmaker said twenty minutes later. She pulled a stern face, brows furrowed under her curled black hair, as she tut-tutted over the state of her presumably once-beautiful purple handiwork. "No gown bearing my stamp has ever been sold to a sporting house. Not here, not in New York, not ever."

"I am sure," May murmured, mortified.

"What sort of business do you think I run?" Miss Catherine Ging, the dressmaker and, incredibly, store owner, flung out her hands. "Do I look like the personal clothier of Nettie Conley?"

May was surprised Miss Ging knew the name of one of the madams. "No, miss, of course not. I beg your pardon, please. It's only, this dress . . ."

She stalled, looking around. The front room of the store, on fashionable Nicollet Avenue, was papered in satin, with polished wood floors and a brown-and-white cowhide rug. Dress patterns were tacked to the walls, and a three-sided mirror with an oak pedestal sat in the corner. A neat cabinet held spools of thread, a rainbow of gleaming colors. A shopgirl flipped idly through a stack of fabric swatches, from fine chiffon to weighty velvet. The soft whirr of sewing machines, feet on pedals, drifted from the back room. For the first time, May wondered if she should have taken up work with the seamstress, rather than Cook.

She swallowed and tried a different tack. "You own this store? How extraordinary. How did you do it?" What she'd meant was, how could a woman own anything that wasn't a brothel?

Miss Ging sighed. She wore the latest fashions, of course, a creamy white blouse with full sleeves, tucked into the tiny waist of a delaine-wool skirt. A small fur hugged her collar. "I have loans to repay, many loans, if you must know." She began folding the dress, expertly, crisply, to fit back into the carpetbag, wrinkling her nose again at its sad condition.

"New York, it was? That's where you came from? I grew up in Chicago."

"You don't say." Miss Ging perked up as the bell over the front door rang; it was only the mailman, however, and she nodded at him, crestfallen, as he dropped a few envelopes into the basket by the door.

"Bills?" May asked quietly.

Miss Ging gave an exhausted huff. She thrust the bag at May. "Good day, miss."

"Look," May said, setting the carpetbag back on the counter. "I'm an inmate at the Bethany Home. A girl came in a week ago wearing this dress. We're attempting to find out who she is or where she came from, but the girl's a mute. Can you help?"

Miss Ging blinked a few times. For the first time, it seemed, she really looked at May, taking in her plain gingham dress—her best—with the white collar and cuffs; her shawl, a hand-me-down; her straw bonnet, a bit out of season now that the weather had started to turn.

Miss Ging's eyes cut to the shopgirl, who went back to organizing her fabric swatches. "All right," said the dressmaker. "I do enjoy a good mystery." She produced a pair of square-framed glasses and unfolded the dress. "It's a polonaise, see? Before the hem tore, the overskirt cut away to show off this black satin. A trifle old-fashioned, but some people still favor the style."

She turned the collar inside out to examine the stamp. May leaned forward, so that the tops of their heads were nearly touching. The tag was simple: tan grosgrain with "Made by Catherine Ging" stamped on in faded pink.

"The problem is, this is my old tag," Miss Ging said, removing her glasses. "Now they're embroidered with the customer's name. I don't remember who I sold this to, as it was more than a year or two ago. But she was a lady, I can assure you of that."

May wrinkled her brow. Everyone at the home assumed the purple dress signified brothel work, though it would be rude to say this. But perhaps, on the right lady, paired with a proper hat and gloves, the gown could be acceptable.

Miss Ging seemed to read her thoughts. "I don't sell to whores," she said again. "It would've been a gentlewoman. This heliotrope hue was the height of fashion a few seasons ago."

"Then it must have been stolen. It didn't arrive on a gentlewoman."

Miss Ging shrugged. "Maids can have sticky fingers."

Maids. May hadn't thought of that. Everyone implied Faith had been a sporting woman, but what did they really know about her?

"Or," Miss Ging added, "if we're looking for the least outra-geous explanation, the owner of this dress outgrew it and offered it to a servant. It's rather small. Sometimes ladies order vanity gowns, which never have and never will really fit them, and even-tually they give them away. The wealthy are curious people."

May began folding the dress, poorly, back into its bag. "Thank you for your kindness." She meant it; the dressmaker hadn't recoiled in judgment when she'd admitted where she lived. Rather, it had seemed to cleave her sympathies to May.

The bell rang as May let herself out. A gust of wind yanked up a corner of her shawl, and she pulled it tight, walking with her head down.

"Oof." She ran face-first into someone's broad chest, just as she was hit by the acrid smell of cigar smoke. That someone gasped in surprise.

"May?"

"Hal!" He stood in front of her, Hal in the flesh, smoking a cheroot cigar. Her heart felt as if it might burst. Guilt overtook her, as if he'd caught her in a lie, but then she remembered she hadn't mentioned where she was going. Neither had he. "What are you doing here?" she asked, just as he blurted out a version of the same question.

She replied first. "I had an errand to run for a friend."

"The same," he said. For once, Hal didn't seem entirely in control of his body, his face. He looked distracted, pulling on the cigar, blue eyes darting up the street and then behind him. Someone passed with a stout dog on a chain, and he jumped back a little.

May's fingers curled in her gloves. She'd been much too for-ward with him earlier. Now he couldn't even look at her.

"Listen, May, you got me thinking." He huffed a nervous

laugh, his hand on the back of his neck. "Can you give Amelia the slip, and get out without a chaperone? I've a dinner to attend on Friday, at the house of a friend. A party of about twelve. Er, rather, there are eleven of us. Fancy making it an even dozen?"

She couldn't believe her ears. "Are you asking . . . You would like me to . . ."

He smiled, a brief motion, up and down. "Would you accompany me to dinner?"

"Of course. Oh, Hal, yes, of course I would." Was she still being too forward? "Sounds nice."

"Good, good. Have you a . . ." He clenched the cigar between his teeth and mimed paper and pencil.

"Tell it to me. Address and time. I've a mind like a bear trap: once the teeth set, it holds on to everything."

Hal stared at her for a moment. "All right, then." He told her where to be, at six in the evening the following Friday. He flicked the cigar away, then took her gloved hand and kissed it once, perfunctorily this time, dry lips to cotton. A bit deflating, after what had happened earlier, but still. He'd invited her to dinner. She could scarcely breathe.

"Farewell, Hal, until then!"

"Farewell, May." He reached for her cheek and patted it twice. She stood dumbfounded as he hurried past her. Her hand went to her face.

She heard the bell of Miss Ging's store ring behind her as Hal went inside. What in the world could he be doing in there? Something to wonder about later.

The butt of his thin brown cigar, still rolling, came to rest near the curb. She hesitated, thinking how nice it would be to put her lips to something he'd just held in his. She wrung her hands for a minute, waiting for a break in the crowd strolling on the sidewalk, then decided she didn't care. She bent to pluck the cigar from the ground and puffed at it—once, twice—it was still damp—careful not to inhale lest she start coughing. When she opened her eyes, she caught a man looking at her out the window of a butcher shop. She walked away quickly, head down. He might be thinking her a lunatic, which she figured was fair. That, or sensationally poor.

6

FAITH

*T*here were only a few girls in the home who would talk to her. Her roommate, for one. May had been chilly at first but now seemed to appreciate having an audience who would not interrupt her sermons about the amorality of the other women in this place, and, since Sunday, her monologue about her beau, Hal, and the dinner party she'd been invited to. Should she wear the gingham? The gingham was her best, but he'd seen her in the gingham several times at church. The only other option was a dark-green calico skirt and a blouse. Far too plain for a dinner party. Did Faith have an opinion? May didn't wait for an answer.

"She's wound awfully tight, May is," Tuva said that week, one evening after supper, when she and Faith sat on the steps behind the kitchen, sharing an apple.

Tuva was her real name, she'd told Faith. Everyone else here called her Constance. Faith had met her before, once or twice, when she'd gone to court to pay her fines. Once, Tuva had offered her a smoke, on a bench outside the courthouse. Faith had hated going there to be publicly shamed. She remembered that gesture from Tuva as a warm ray of humanity.

Now that Faith had eaten several meals in the dining room of the Bethany Home, she'd noticed a few other familiar faces as well, none of whom had a smile or a spare word to offer her, save for Tuva. Mostly, Faith listened in on conversations wafting from nearby tables. Talking about one's past was frowned upon here, but once they sat down to supper, the girls opened up like broken faucets. They spoke wistfully of their regulars, throwing a gauzy sheet of nostalgia over their memories, and competed over who'd gotten the most elaborate gifts—a jade comb, a pair of scarab earrings, a fifth of Jamaican rum.

Tuva, too, had spoken at length of her best john, a clergyman by the name of Willard. When she got out of here, she aimed to rendezvous with Willard. She wished he'd have turned out to be the father of her baby, Luke, but, alas, the boy had been born with dark eyes and curly hair.

Tuva had recognized him, though. Right away. She'd recognized the baby. That was all she'd say on the matter.

"Why's May so keen to stay here?" Tuva said now. "We all know there's worse out there, but we also know there's better."

Faith crunched through the green-and-pink skin of the apple. That wasn't quite right. May did seem determined to move on; she was simply hell-bent on leaving with a husband.

"Suppose I can't blame her," Tuva continued. "They like to send the girls here to farms, to be homestead wives. Last place I want to be is back on a farm." She scratched under her arm, and her ample breast jiggled in response. Nobody here wore a corset, Faith had noted, or ribbons, rouge, or lace. There were very few looking glasses about. Their hair went into careless buns; their cheeks shone from a clean scrubbing and nature's pink exertion. They laughed with abandon; they blew their noses loudly and stuffed their hankies into sleeves. It felt as if they were all on a brief holiday from a world that included men. Most of the women appeared to enjoy it, but Tuva seemed to miss the attentions of the masculine sex.

Tuva Larsen, born into rural squalor; she came to the city when she'd heard there was a demand for domestic work. Maltreated and fired by several mistresses, she ended up going for two dollars an hour in the First Avenue red-light district. A familiar story. Her baby had already been adopted, but she'd only arrived here five months ago, right before he was born, so she had seven months to go. Seven months of drudgery, as she put it to Faith.

"Sure, they feed us fine, and they don't beat on us if we make a mistake, like the mistresses do in the big houses. Miss Rhoades, she's a pushover. But I don't like the way they look at us," Tuva told Faith that night, as they watched the branches of the trees turn black against the purpling sky. Faith took "they" to mean the Sisterhood of Bethany. "Like we need to thank them all the time. You can grow a bit sick from it, eh?"

Faith cleared her throat. Her lips parted.

Tuva continued, not anticipating an answer, because why should she? "They make such a great deal of there being no bars on the windows, no lock on the front door. All of us free to go, et cetera. Yet you'd have to leave in the dead of night unless you wanted a hundred eyes on you. That's how girls do it. They go back to the trunk closet and fetch their belongings, if they're still there, then shove off in the middle of the night."

Faith raised her eyebrows. The trunk closet?

"Sure, what do you think they do with all the fine dresses these whores arrive in?" Tuva laughed; she had nibbled the apple down to its pips. "Keep them in the trunk closet, that's what, up in the wing by the seamstress's sunroom. Once every few months or so, they donate them to be cut up for scraps. And make a big fuss of it, so everyone knows how charitable they are."

Again, Faith cleared her throat. A clutch of phlegm gathered at the back of her tongue. She swallowed it down, and when she spoke, her words came out rough.

"You sound as if *you* want to leave."

"Uff da!" Tuva mimed tumbling off the step. "It's got a voice! Can't recall I've heard you speak before." Slowly, she handed the stripped apple core back to Faith, eyes slanted in exaggerated suspicion. "Is it true, Faith, what they say about you?"

Faith nibbled around the stem, finding every bit of apple flesh. The name—"Faith"—she was beginning to feel accustomed to hearing it from other people, but she couldn't yet use it herself, in her thoughts. It felt like wearing the wrong-size shoes.

"What do they say about me?" she whispered.

"That you're Marguerite the Magnificent." Tuva said this as though it were a joke, but then she waited for a reply. Faith detected a bit of curiosity. Tuva wanted to know. "But that isn't right, is it?"

Faith grinned, sadly, and shook her head. That one didn't quite fit, either.

7

ABBY

*M*iss Rhoades called Abby at home on Election Day, Tuesday, November 6, from the telephone in the matron's office. "I know you're working on this month's ledger," Miss Rhoades began.

"Yes, the board meets next week," Abby replied. She'd finished her morning devotions and had been sitting at her little desk in the solarium, writing in her journal, when the telephone in her hallway rang. "Do we have a new entry for the ledger? Don't tell me—did Dolly's baby come?"

"No."

Abby could almost hear Miss Rhoades wringing her hands. She'd hired Miss Rhoades herself, snatched her up, really, when a woman she knew from the Temperance Society mentioned that her children had outgrown their governess. Clean, orderly, sober, and upright: Miss Rhoades had lived up to Abby's friend's description of her, and Abby had been pleased with her service these last eight years, even though sometimes she wondered if the inmates tended to walk all over her. Showing kindness was one thing; laxity, another.

"Speak, friend," she urged Miss Rhoades. "What is it?"

"A runaway. Constance."

Abby removed her glasses and pinched her eyes with her hand. "When did it happen?"

"At night. I'm sorry, Mrs. Mendenhall. I hadn't realized anything was amiss with her. Although she has been spending time with Faith—"

Abby cut her off. She'd hear no more hysteria surrounding their new arrival. The facts were what mattered, and the fact was, Constance had decided to leave. "I'll have to begin a search, which means it's unlikely I'll be at the home for a few days. Will you let me know if we're near running out of anything?"

"Of course," Miss Rhoades breathed. She sounded relieved to have passed the burden of this news to someone else.

Abby returned to the solarium and stared out the window for a while, watching the wind pluck yellow leaves from a black walnut. "Crows flew by today," she wrote in her journal, then shut it until tomorrow.

She had two girls to track down now, although one was in the unusual position of still being an inmate of the home. She began with her web of informers, asking if they'd seen hide or hair of Constance or had any information that would help determine where Faith had come from. A lumberjack who lived in the Bohemian Flats and a maid at an hourly hotel knew nothing, but the railroad worker, whose children received Christmas presents from Abby every year, and Abel Stevens, the dairyman, had at least seen Faith on her route to the Bethany Home. Neither had any idea where she'd been coming from.

"You should really talk to Swede Kate," Stevens murmured under his breath, so that his wife wouldn't hear. He stood on the curb outside his barn. "She knows everything and everybody."

"I know Kate," Abby replied, causing Stevens to frown in disbelief. She thanked him and signaled to her driver to start the horses. Kate Campbell's parlor house was the last place Abby wanted to go, but Stevens was right. She went home and telephoned the local sheriff's office, insisting on speaking to one deputy in particular: Officer Roland Nye. He agreed to meet her on Second Avenue the very next day.

Abby's driver let her out at eleven in the morning, under Kate's porte cochère. Madams and their girls tended to sleep late, working as they did till 4:00 or 5:00 a.m., so Abby knew to visit well after breakfast. When she arrived, she saw that Officer Nye had beaten her there; he reached for her horses' bridles—Polly and Prince, sister and brother bay Hackneys—and held them as Abby disembarked. She paused for a second after stepping over the wet gutter, a bouquet of flowers for Kate tucked under one arm, inhaling the fishy scent of the river.

Officer Nye watched her do it. He had a jolly face, broad and fair, with a good deal of pink in his cheeks. "Manure, ma'am, from the west." He winked. "That's Minneapolis on a warm autumn day for you."

Nye had been with the force for more than three decades. He and Abby had crossed paths in this district many times, and he was the only cop Kate would accept into her parlor. His sideburns were nearly all white now. Abby prayed he wouldn't retire.

She shook her head. "It's the water I'm smelling. Reminds me of home."

"Were you born near St. Anthony Falls?"

"No, nowhere near here. In Cape Cod." She hoped she didn't sound boastful. Folks from the Bay Colony still ran this town, a coterie that once included her husband. Nye raised an eyebrow but said nothing.

They couldn't see the river from here—mills, factories, slum housing for immigrant laborers stood between them and the muddy banks. But its proximity always reminded Abby of her mother, who'd kept Abby's bedroom windows flung open to the sea all year round. As a child, Abby Swift had suffered hemorrhages of the lungs; not a handkerchief in their household was spared from bloodstains. Her father, one of the last of a Quaker whaling dynasty out of New Bedford, had been gone for years at a time, spacing the Swift siblings in increments of three, four, five years; by the time Abby, the last, was born, her mother was well past thirty. After her eldest children left the nest, to captain ships of their own or raise families, Chloe Swift spent hours holding frail, coughing Abby. She read her daughter Bible stories as Abby watched ships limp wearily into the harbor, sails torn and rudders pocked with barnacles.

"The sea gives its greatest gift to those who remain on land," her mother would say. "That salt air will cure anything."

The gift Chloe gave her daughter was one of freedom: freedom to run barefoot through the dune grasses when her lungs had strengthened, to learn how to drive a carriage, how to butcher a whole hog, how to plant and tend her own wildflower garden instead of sitting inside practicing embroidery. Chloe did not believe in shielding her from the ocean's spray, from the elements, which toughened Abby over time. For years, sand clung stubbornly to her fingernail beds and lodged between her toes.

Chloe had died here in Minneapolis, after living with Abby for the last fifteen years of her life. Abby had given her the sunniest, warmest room in the house, in quiet thanks for being well mothered.

"Shall we, ma'am?" Nye asked, extending an elbow.

"We shall," Abby replied, and they started up the walk.

Swede Kate's had once been a brothel owned by the cunning Mollie Ellsworth, who spread the lucrative rumor that Jesse James had been a client. Kate had taken over after Mollie's death and livened the façade by adding window boxes, which now held purple chrysanthemums. Elaborate topiaries curled up from her planters. Even now, with the city mired in economic woes, Kate had money for decoration, which meant some men still had the coin to buy women. Two such men were just now posted outside Kate's front steps, ordinary-looking men who nevertheless gave Abby a feeling of menace.

A servant answered the door, scarcely out of girlhood, her face still dotted with acne. The girl shrank at the sight of Abby and the constable. Abby knew she could appear imposing: a gray-haired lady in black, with a hooked nose better fit for a bird of prey. She wanted to reach out and gently touch the girl's shoulder.

Instead, she said: "Did someone call for a traveling vaudeville act?"

The girl's eyes popped. She took a step backward, hand over her lips; a giggle was waiting to escape, but she was afraid to let it.

Abby leaned forward. "My colleague here is the acrobat." Behind her, Nye snorted, his cheeks flushed. "I'll be playing the part of the thousand-year-old crone."

Now the girl laughed in earnest, a winsome sound, and led them into the dimly lit foyer, expensively decorated in dark damask with Chinese tasseled accents. A fresh arrangement of flowers, deep-purple hothouse tulips and chocolate cosmos, sprayed from a black-and-gold urn. Funereal, Abby thought with a shiver, her smile fading. Why did the décor have to be so grim?

"Mrs. Mendenhall. Officer Nye." Kate had rustled into the room, a cloud of shimmery midnight-blue fabric and voluminous faded-orange hair. She smelled of bergamot cologne, which reminded Abby of tea. The first time she'd met Swede Kate, nearly twenty years before, Kate had had the air of a young mother caring for unruly children, her face still vivacious and apple-cheeked. Now she seemed more a grandmother, or a frazzled aunt.

"Zinnias!" Kate said, taking the paper-wrapped bouquet from Abby. "Such pretty pinks and reds."

"They're from Mr. Mendenhall's greenhouse," said Abby.

One of Kate's cheeks dimpled. "For affection?"

"I was thinking for absent friends."

Kate's mouth went into a pinch. "These should go in water," she said, handing the flowers to the servant girl. She turned back to Abby and rocked forward on her toes. "Can't say I'm surprised to see you here."

Abby felt her blood quicken. "Why is that?"

"You haven't seen the paper?" Kate brushed past her visitors and through the front door, where she called to the two men lounging by the side of the house. "Go away and come back later. We're not open until four."

One of them must have muttered his displeasure, and she threw up her arms in exasperation. "The girls are at rest, gentlemen. Have some decency." She shut the door with a flourish and brushed off her hands. "Come, we'll talk in the parlor. Gilly?" The pubescent servant girl reappeared. "Fetch us bouillon toddies and today's copy of the *Examiner*."

"No liquor in mine, please," Abby told Gilly as she took her seat. The parlor was just as sumptuously decorated as the foyer, the cushions velvety and supple. On the satin-papered wall behind Kate hung an enormous painting of a Greek goddess, naked except for a length of fabric wrapped up one thigh and over her shoulder.

"The *Examiner* is a rag, Kate. Why should I care what they have to say?"

Kate only smiled, taking the love seat opposite Abby. Officer Nye stood beside the window, peering out suspiciously.

Abby wished she couldn't picture the upstairs rooms of this house, with their deep-piled rugs, gleaming oak headboards, silver hairbrushes, and gilt mirrors, all designed to entice girls into staying there, as much as to impress the male clientele. Each brothel had its theme, its standard visitors: There were the rowdy saloons and gaming halls, which catered to a lower class of men, and lavish feasting-houses for wealthy rogues. Gambling halls staffed prostitutes to take the winners' money and comfort the losers. Kate's establishment had an air of exclusivity, with its warren of private sitting rooms, inviting gentlemen to linger in conversation. This parlor had a library ambience, stacked with works by Henry James and Nathaniel Hawthorne. The man who frequented Kate's would consider himself an intellectual— yes, a misunderstood species of genius—and the women who worked here would be trained to flatter and listen and confirm every grandiose notion he had of himself.

The servant girl came with the newspaper and steaming mugs

of broth for Officer Nye and the women; Kate's, presumably, was laced with Angostura.

"Thank you for the toddy," Abby commented, setting her saucer on the table.

Kate scoffed. "I hear the young ones are serving Colombian coffee now. Another fad I can't keep up with."

"You seem stylish to me." Abby knew little of fashion and cared about it even less, but she had to admire Kate's street gown—a walking suit, she believed it was called—and its big sleeves, which billowed out like legs of mutton and did not deflate even when Kate sat back and drank.

"Look at us," Kate said. "What a funny little reunion this is."

"It's too bad we aren't all here," Abby replied evenly.

Kate hesitated, then gave a stiff nod. "To Delia," she said, lifting her cup.

Abby didn't follow suit. Delia deserved better than a half-hearted toast. She deserved to be alive.

By the time Abby had tracked Delia to this brothel, after the girl had fled the Bethany Home not once, but twice, after Abby had even tried taking her into her own house, she'd found Kate sobbing in the upstairs corridor here; Delia had ingested a lethal dose of morphine. It had taken the Sisterhood's involvement to persuade the coroner to complete his inquest here, instead of bringing Delia's body to the city morgue, which would have guaranteed her a pauper's funeral. Instead, the Sisterhood had paid for her burial. Kate resented the interference, Abby knew—the fact that she'd had to rely on women the authorities deemed respectable.

Despite her best efforts, Abby could never clear the images of that dead girl from her mind. In death, she hadn't looked like

Delia at all: her pale eyes open, pupils reduced to pinpricks; the blue-gray cast to her skin. Abby had arrived just in time (yet too late, infinitely too late) to see lice flee from the body.

Abby watched Kate drink her cocktail. A yellow diamond, at least three carats, glistened in a brooch at the center of Kate's neckline. In front of the authorities, Abby and Kate had presented a united front. Women versus men: an unspoken, unbreakable code. Behind closed doors, they'd fought viciously. Abby had accused Kate of profiting off the girl's vulnerability. Kate, in tears, had insisted she cared for Delia just as much as Abby did. She'd only been trying to give the girl a chance at a better life.

An odd choice of words, Abby had thought; she so often used them herself.

"Don't keep an old woman in suspense," she said now, clearing her mind of ancient grievances. "What's this business about the *Examiner*?"

"Ah." Kate flipped open the paper. "Shall I read you the headline? 'Former Inmate at Bethany Home Alleges Chaos, Starvation Exist Within Its Walls.'"

"Starvation!" Abby's nerves jolted. "Let me see that, please."

The story took up a whole page and bore an illustration of a shapely young woman, leaning with her elbows back on what appeared to be an upright piano. The caption: "Tuva Larsen, Runaway from the Bethany Home for Unwed Mothers."

Tuva Larsen. *Constance.* Abby couldn't bring herself to read on. A dollar sign, however, caught her eye: the newspaper had published Tuva's new hourly rate.

"She's working at Agnes Bly's now," Kate said, her voice silky. Of course, Agnes Bly would allow the newspaper to print her name and a flattering sketch of one of her workers. Free advertising. "Well, at least Tuva's made herself easy to find," said Abby, casting the paper aside.

"She claims you've lost control of the home. Some witch girl has taken charge."

"Witches are not real." Abby felt a headache coming on. No one took the *Examiner* seriously, but a story like this could alert other papers. And what would the City Council think?

"Abby? Abby!"

Abby started. "Good grief, do not snap your fingers at me. I am no dog."

"Will you finally tell me why you've come? I'm a busy woman, you know."

Abby took a deep breath and told her. Tuva's story held a kernel of truth; they'd taken in a girl the others called a ghost, or Marguerite the Magnificent—Kate didn't seem to have heard of this character—who was mute and had spooked the others. "You know I generally do not investigate the backgrounds of the girls we accept. In this case, however, I figured a bit more information might be useful." Abby chose not to mention the gold that Faith had come with.

Kate pinched at her chin, stroking some fine blond hairs. "She's joined the pudding club, I presume?"

"She's in a delicate condition, yes." Privately, Abby wasn't sure. The visiting doctor had examined her and said she must be early in pregnancy, for he couldn't find physical evidence. The home had seen ghost pregnancies before—the inmate might feel unwell for a time, her womb might even grow, but then no baby.

It had happened to Abby herself, once, and had ended in a torrent of blood. Her only pregnancy. But that wasn't something she was about to tell Kate, or anyone else.

"Do you know any girls who fit the description?" she asked Kate. "Unable to speak, dark hair, freckles on the nose? A comely girl, but slight, frail."

Kate shrugged. "I shall ask around."

"You shall do nothing of the sort," Abby said with such force that Nye broke his gaze from the window, and Kate blinked in surprise. "I don't want to put her in danger."

"You're afraid." Kate put her teacup down. She fiddled with her clothes, then rubbed her hands together vigorously, as though trying to warm cold fingers.

"Seems I'm not the only one who's afraid, Kate."

"Women in our line of work need always be afraid," Kate replied. "This past year has been very difficult. When men are in a losing position, you can guess where they come to let off steam. Some of the madams have decided to take advantage of this, and allow their customers to—"

"Please, stop," Abby interjected. "I don't want to hear it." But May had mentioned bruises, hadn't she? Dark-purple bruises, wrapped around Faith's throat.

Kate inhaled. "That isn't the kind of business *I* run, Abby. But there's only so much one woman can do to curb some men's violence." She cast a meaningful look at Officer Nye, though Abby knew it would do little good. The police didn't protect prostitutes. They arrested them, sent them to the courthouse to pay their fines, then went back to ignoring them.

Abby drank the last of her toddy, down to the yellow dregs of chicken bouillon at the bottom of the cup. "Have you heard of any girls being killed?"

"We've had no such news in the department, ma'am," Nye interjected.

Kate gave him a withering look. "Unfortunately, yes," she

told Abby. Nye took out his notepad and flipped to a clean page. "Someone did a sporting girl in a couple of weeks ago, and a madam has just gone missing."

"Which madam?"

"Priscilla Black." Kate hitched her shoulders up a few inches, till those mutton-chop sleeves grazed her long earlobes. "Her girls woke up one morning and she was gone."

"That could mean anything. She could have taken off for a new life."

"Without shoes, a cloak, any money or jewelry? I think not. All her shoes were left in her closet, Mrs. Mendenhall. All of them." This seemed to be a detail that particularly bothered Kate: the shoeless madam. "Can't say her lot were sad to see the back of her, though. She worked her girls to the bone."

"And the sporting girl. How was she . . . ?" Abby prayed Kate wouldn't say strangulation.

"I heard she fell from a high window."

Abby squeezed her eyes closed, her lips twitching in prayer.

Death is but a horizon, and a horizon is nothing save the limit of our sight.

But she could see it: the body of a woman in her prime of life, twisted and motionless on the cold ground.

"The man got away before anyone could catch him," Kate said quietly. "A phantom, they're saying. Must have persuaded her, somehow, to jump. He was already out the door and down the street when they heard the—"

The door to Kate's parlor opened, and Gilly came back in to whisper something in Kate's ear. Kate draped her arm gently about the girl's shoulders, and after she'd listened for a moment, she gave Gilly a nod and a smile, stroking the long braid that went down her back. "My luncheon is ready," she told her visitors.

Kate's motherly affection for the girl filled Abby with a sense of unease, though she couldn't say why, exactly; perhaps it was because the scene felt familiar, like one of Abby's own inmates coming to fetch her. Anyhow, she had to get home so that she could contact the other board members before they saw the *Examiner*. She wished she could talk to Mrs. Overlock, her dearest friend, but Euphemia was on a monthlong trip to New Orleans. Abby would call on her as soon as she returned. Euphemia would know what to do.

Abby gestured for Officer Nye to help her from her chair. She bade Kate and the servant girl farewell, eager to leave this place as quickly as possible.

8

MAY

"What do you think of this?" May whispered. She held up a blue plaid shirtwaist, tailored with tucks around the high neck, wondering if it would be to Hal's fancy. Faith turned around, her petticoat brushing May's, and nodded.

Friday evening had finally arrived, and the girls stood close to each other in the trunk closet. They'd shut themselves inside, one candle dripping precariously into its dish on a rattan chair in the corner. The room stank of camphor balls. Faith had led May here ten minutes earlier, when May began fretting once more over what to wear. She'd nearly hugged Faith when she saw the shelves draped in gowns, skirts, hats, blouses, and gloves, all of which would soon be turned over to volunteers at Mrs. Van Cleve's church.

May licked her lips. The air in the closet had grown stuffy. "How about this one?" She'd found a simple skirt in dark gray. "Will it match the plaid? It's hard to tell."

Faith held up a black cape to go with it: waist-length, trimmed in jet beads, with a matching pair of doeskin gloves.

May clutched the garments to her chest. "Perfect." In these clothes, she just might fool everyone into thinking that she belonged with Hal, that she was on his level.

They smuggled their finds down the hall to their room and shut the door, giggling.

"Locked," said Faith, as she turned the key in the knob.

As May and Faith spent more time in each other's society, May had heard her roommate's voice more, little by little. Mostly very brief answers, negatives and affirmatives, "Good night" or "Farewell," in a musical, gentle voice, scarcely more than a murmur. May hadn't told any of the other inmates; the gossips needed no more fuel for their fire.

She turned her back as she dressed, feeling Faith's eyes on her. Since Constance's departure, Faith had been like May's shadow. She was the one remaining girl who'd allow Faith to sit close during dinner, the only one who'd talk to her.

Faith was like a sickness the girls in the home had caught, which was rapidly spreading.

All nonsense, of course, especially this latest business with Leigh, who'd woken two mornings ago to find that her hair had been chopped off with sharp scissors in the night. Her screams, histrionic in May's opinion, roused the entire floor. Miss Rhoades had to do her best to even it out, leaving only a feathery cap.

Leigh had blamed Faith, of course. But the shears had been on her own nightstand.

May tucked the plaid blouse, which in better light revealed itself to be a rich weave of blue, teal, and green, into the skirt, and turned around. "How do I look?"

Faith smiled wistfully, her head tilted to the side. She'd been holding May's black toque, which she presented with a flick of the wrists and placed gently on May's head. As May did the hat pins, Faith wrapped her in the cape. She held up their small mirror so that May could see pieces of her getup and dab her forehead and nose with rice powder.

They sneaked downstairs to avoid anybody who might recognize May's clothes. She could hear music in the parlor, and
muffled laughter coming from one of the closed bedrooms. Friday evenings in the home were both lively and subdued. The
children who lived in the cottage nearby—those who hadn't
been adopted as babies, and whose mothers were long gone—
gathered in the parlor to hear the matrons tell stories. The
babies went to bed early, as usual, and the mothers met in small
groups throughout the building, playing chaste card games or
reading aloud to one another. Normally, May listened to books;
a cadre of women had been taking it in turns to read the serial
installments of George du Maurier's *Trilby*, and a piece of her
was loath to miss tonight's chapter.

They hurried down the staircase. The moon's soft effulgence
shone yellow through the transom above the front door. May's
heartbeat kicked into a gallop. She was almost there.

"May Lombard! Where on earth could you be going?" Pearl's
voice.

May froze, halfway out the door. Chilly air billowed around
her. She turned to see Pearl standing with her arms crossed.
Faith made sort of a fence between the two of them, her arms
spread wide so that her shawl draped between them in a semicircle and Pearl, May hoped, couldn't see what she was wearing.

"Shh," May intoned. "Pearl, please. I'll give you my breakfast
in the morning."

Pearl stood on her toes to peek at May's outfit. "You're all
dressed up. Where do you think you're running off to?"

May felt defeated. All her life, bad luck had followed her. Of
course Pearl would hold her up, interrogating her. May could
never escape. "I was going to a dinner party."

Pearl's eyes widened. Her mouth fell open, making her look young, vulnerable.

"Can I come?" she asked.

It was May's turn to stare. She had never heard Pearl *ask* for anything.

Faith moved first. She wrapped one hand through the air and brought it under her chin. Slowly, theatrically, she blew something invisible in Pearl's direction.

Pearl blinked, as though she'd gotten powder in her eyes. Then she backed away, three clumsy steps, and turned and ran.

May and Faith spilled out onto the front porch and shut the door behind them. "What was that?" May asked, turning on the top step to peer at her roommate. "When you blew on your hand, what were you doing?"

Faith smiled and shrugged, shaking her head.

"Just a bit of nonsense?"

Faith nodded. "But she believed it," she said quietly. She rubbed her upper arms. "You don't have much time. She may be telling Miss Rhoades." The longest sentences May had ever heard her speak.

"She might." May took a long, cool breath. The lawn in front of the home was empty; the children had long since gone inside. The swelling gibbous moon, the lamplighter coming slowly down the street to illuminate the growing darkness, Pearl's unexpected plea—all of it was exhilarating, almost to the point of being too much.

May didn't want to leave, she found. How nice it would be, to stay here grinning with Faith. Perhaps she was nervous to have dinner with Hal. "All right, then. I should go. I shall be home no later than ten o'clock, but please don't wait up for me."

Faith gave her a puzzled look. May took another step down. "What's the matter?"

"He isn't . . . isn't your beau . . . ?"

May's scalp prickled in irritation. She shouldn't get so angry, not when they'd just enjoyed such camaraderie, but she couldn't help herself. Her blood boiled. Who was Faith to imply that Hal should have come to pick her up? He didn't have a carriage of his own, from what she could tell, so why should she expect him to drive her?

Besides—May felt her face grow hot—asking him for a ride would have required her to tell him her address.

"Of course not," she snapped. "I'm not a child, I can take the streetcar by myself. When you get yourself a beau someday, you can insist that he, personally, cart you around the city in a cabriolet, with him as the horse. See where that gets you."

May's voice had grown harsh, and loud, hardly her own voice at all, she thought in shame. She lowered her eyes so that she wouldn't see Faith's expression and hurried off to catch her streetcar.

The home of Mrs. V. L. Beecher, on Mount Curve Avenue in Lowry Hill, turned out to be a veritable mansion, a stone fortresslike structure with a round turret crowned in battlements and a red tiled roof. Party sounds greeted May upon entry, gleeful shrieks, bursts of masculine laughter, music that might have been playing live. The quiet clink of silverware as servants set the table. Reluctantly, she allowed a butler to take her cape—the best part of her outfit—and her hat. On the streetcar, she'd noticed a tear in the sleeve of her shirt, a stain on the thumb of her glove. She stuffed the gloves into the hat.

The butler indicated the tray of calling cards sitting on the rosewood table in the center of the room, before a large, winding staircase. A hothouse orchid mimicked the bend of the stairs, craning its neck down to the tray. May froze. She had no calling card.

This was it. They'd find her out before her boots left the foyer rug.

"And who, may I ask, is this?"

The hostess had burst into the grand hall. At least, May assumed this was Augusta Beecher. Every movement of her body suggested ownership: the broad sweep of her hips, her outstretched arms, the upward tilt of her chin. She was petite, with a tiny waist and minuscule hands, but the puffed sleeves of her gown and her high-piled hairstyle gave her presence. She looked to be in her middle forties, yet somehow youthful. Was this how women of a certain class were permitted to age? With soft skin and shining hair?

"Miss May Lombard. How do you do?" May attempted a curtsy on wobbly knees. "I'm a guest of Hal ..." She still didn't know his surname. What a complete fool she was. "Of Hal."

Mrs. Beecher threw back her head and laughed, veins stretching in her throat. "So *you're* the young lady our Mr. Hayward invited to accompany him! I thought I'd never see the day. Won't the other gentlemen be pleased."

Hayward, May thought. An elegant name. Mr. Hayward.

Mrs. Beecher took May's arm. "Come, dear, we're just sitting down for dinner. You're in for a marvelous evening, full of surprises. The theme of the party is 'Illusion.' You see, I am a Decadent."

"That's grand, Mrs. Beecher," May replied. She had no idea what it meant to be a Decadent, but she could hear the capital letter in the woman's voice.

"Call me Gussie," Mrs. Beecher said into May's ear as they entered the dining room. A crowd had gathered around the table, holding drinks, waiting for the hostess to take her place. The noise lowered to whispers when Gussie stepped in with May on her arm. May gawked. Twelve place settings of gilt, linen, and crystal graced the enormous tabletop. The room was papered in green brocade, with bouquets of camellias and peacock feathers adorning the sideboards. Eighteen-inch lit tapers teetered in many-armed brass candelabras that resembled giant squids.

After the stark Quaker plainness of the Bethany Home, May's eyes felt almost assaulted. At first, she couldn't even pick Hal from the crowd of men, indistinguishable from one another in their white ties and mustaches.

"Please, be seated. Oh, Mr. Hayward!" Gussie trumpeted. "Look who I found." She deposited May on Hal's arm, then hurried to bend the ear of one of the maids. May caught a snatch of their conversation—"The string quartet should be in here now, *not* in the salon."

Hal kissed May's cheek; he smelled of whiskey. "Aren't you a picture," he said, but then he had to let her go to find her seat. She would have been disappointed, to find him and lose him so quickly to the other half of the table, if she hadn't wandered over to an empty chair between two gentlemen to see her name printed, not even by hand, but engraved, on a place card:

MADEMOISELLE LOMBARD

Pleasant heat rose to her cheeks. She belonged here. She'd been invited, expected. Would it be uncouth to save the card? She slipped it into her pocket, looking around rapidly as she did.

It was only too bad that Lombard wasn't her real name.

The rest of the guests chatted idly as two servant girls poured a clear white wine to complement the first course. The soup, May thought. She was going to have a proper dinner, soup to nuts, as her father used to say. She nearly thanked the maid for pouring her wine, but then noticed no one else did.

The man on her left—Mr. Wolfe, according to his place card—greeted her cordially but did not seem happy to be here. He kept sneaking glances at a woman much younger than he was, whom May assumed was his wife, and who seemed quite happy to be seated between Hal and another man at the far end of the table. The chair on the other side of Hal was empty, which May was glad to see. She was staring at Mrs. Wolfe— dressed all in mauve, with her hair in a gorgeous twist—when the man on May's right introduced himself as Johnny.

"Pleased to meet you," she said, taking Johnny's hand. He was the only man present who didn't wear a beard or mustache.

"Prepare to loosen your belt," Johnny told her with a wink. "Gussie goes whole hog."

May smiled uncomfortably. There was something rather informal about all these people, despite their finery. A stink of cigars and alcohol, a looseness to the men's ties and the women's gazes. Maybe this was how the rich behaved. The man at the head of the table, opposite Gussie, didn't even look to have combed his hair or trimmed his beard. The ragged ends of it trailed in his wine.

Johnny caught her looking. "That's the entertainment."

"The entertainment?"

"A magus, or trance medium, something. Gussie loves that sort of thing. She's a widow, so she gets to host these parties and invite whomever she wants to sit at the opposite end."

May looked at Gussie, her hand wrapped around the forearm of the young man beside her, glove unbuttoned and hitched to the elbow. To be a wealthy widow seemed a wonderful thing. The man seated next to Gussie, now that May studied him, seemed vaguely familiar. He looked up and caught her staring, and she turned her head, glad to see the first course being served.

The soup arrived in disguise. A cup of coffee on a saucer was placed in front of them, the milk swirled on top and dusted with what appeared to be cinnamon. "The evening's first illusion," Gussie proclaimed, and she lifted her soup spoon to her lips to signal that her guests could also begin. May tilted the spoon away from her the way her mother had taught her and lifted it to her lips.

Mushroom bisque. Creamy, savory, frothy soup, flecked with herbs and served piping hot. The richness of it made May want to close her eyes as she ate. It killed her to leave a polite puddle in the bottom when she was done, but she knew she must not tilt the mug to slurp it up.

"Where's Kitty?" Gussie called out, indicating the empty chair, the steaming mug, at the place beside Hal. May gazed longingly at the untouched soup.

"Well, let's see," said Hal. "She had to pass Shaw's, and who knows how many more faro tables on her way here, so that'll have delayed her at least an hour . . ." He winked at May, though she had no idea what he was talking about.

"Hayward, there are ladies present," Johnny called.

"Yeah, and what's Kitty?" Hal replied. Their laughter left May feeling uneasy.

The servants hovered, ready to clear the table, but Gussie made a show of stopping them. "Ah-ah-ah!" she tsked. Everyone waited. "You may eat the mugs!"

The dinner guests, save for the medium or magician at the end, burst into delighted applause. The string quartet broke into a waltz. May and Johnny, laughing, picked up their mugs by the handle and clanked them together as if they were in a beer garden. This was, she decided firmly, the best night of her life.

She took a tenuous bite, and the mug crackled in her mouth. It tasted like a candy cane without sugar. A bit of it stuck in her teeth.

"This reminds me of saltwater taffy," she said aloud. When she glanced up, everybody was looking at her.

"What's that, darling?" asked Hal over the rim of his drink.

"Saltwater taffy," she replied. "Candy made with saltwater."

Everyone at the table, landlocked Minnesotans, looked dubious, so she kept talking. "My uncle Vin brought it back for us once. He used to take the New York Central Railroad all the way to the coast, and once he traveled down the shore in New Jersey and brought us back candy. The taffy came in pastel colors and tasted just a trifle like salt." She could feel heat rising in her face with everyone watching her, even the magus. Yet she couldn't stop herself. "Uncle Vin worked in leather goods with my father. He and my father would tan and dye and polish leather, then make it into shoes to sell in the Northeast." She took a sip of her water. "My father's name was George."

No one said anything. They all avoided looking at her, discomfited by her little speech. Gussie looked mildly annoyed that no one was paying attention to her edible mugs. May tried to catch Hal's eye. Why had she added that last part, about her father's name? Just mentioning him had brought embarrassing tears to her eyes. But why had she said any of it at all? She missed her father, she supposed. It had felt good to be heard, to be seen, for just a moment—or it would have, if anyone had acknowledged what she'd shared.

"Aha!" Hal cried, saving her, rubbing his hands together. "The fish."

"*Bon appétit!*" cried Gussie. She and Hal raised their glasses toward each other. Something was passing between them. Not, May hoped, a laugh at her expense.

The fish course seemed to be eel cooked in nutmeg and garlic but turned out to be sole, molded elaborately in a serpentine shape. It melted into butter in May's mouth, helping her to forget how she'd humiliated herself. She glanced up at Hal just in time to notice the tall black-haired woman hurrying into the room.

"What've I missed?" the woman cried as she flopped into the seat beside Hal. She accepted kisses from Hal on both her cheeks, which sent a pang of jealousy into May's chest. Then the woman caught May by the eye.

May swallowed a fish bone, as fine as a piece of hair. The latecomer was Miss Ging, the dressmaker.

Hal presented her from across the table. "Kitty, have you met my companion for the evening? This is Miss May Lombard."

"How do you do," May said, her voice hitching in her throat.

Kitty nodded back at her. "How do you do." She shot May one more look, then turned a cheeky smile on the rest of the party. It seemed she wouldn't let on what she knew about May, at least not now. Why had May thought it a good idea to tell her where she lived? The fish lost its flavor in her mouth. She watched Kitty mingle effortlessly with the crowd at Hal's end of the table, as though they were all old friends, except for the mysterious entertainer at the head, whose threadbare elbows had been creeping steadily closer to the tabletop. He caught May staring at him with his watery gray eyes, and she snapped her head back toward Gussie.

She stabbed a hard black lentil, meant to look like a fish egg. *Companion? For the evening?*

Out of the corner of May's eye she caught Hal whispering into Kitty's ear. Why did Kitty get to sit beside him? It was an oddity of the formal dinner party, how far away they placed you from your suitor. May chewed hard in frustration, the lentil lodging itself inside one of her molars. If only she could have insisted upon sitting with the man who'd brought her here.

They broke apart by sex after the meal, the men to the cigar lounge, women to the solarium, which turned out to be a drafty room, tiled in white marble, with floor-to-ceiling windows and an assembly of tropical plants. May felt chilled. All the wine and brandy had made her feverish at the table, but now she wished for the cape she'd surrendered at the door. She longed, too, for Faith's company as she watched the other women form whispering pairs, warm and familiar with one another.

"The boys'll want to get to a faro hall after this," said one of the women as she ran a fingertip over the grand piano. She inspected her glove for dust. "You know they like a chance to double their money. And I've brought the wrong hat for a carriage ride."

"Let them go," another scoffed. Johnny's wife, May thought, based on the way he'd gone to her for a moment after the dinner. She was pretty, in a sense, with sharply sloped eyebrows that made her appear perpetually suspicious. "Maybe Gussie will let us stay and have a cocoa, like last time."

All the others laughed. Clearly something had transpired over cocoa.

"I have to keep an eye on Thomas," said the first woman. "He can get himself in all kinds of trouble in a gambling hall, and I'd rather go with him than have him delivered to me dead."

"Dead I could handle," replied Johnny's wife. "It's maimed I wouldn't want to deal with. All that maintenance."

"Hear, hear," said Mrs. Wolfe.

May gaped at them as the others tittered. What a terrible thing to say, and about her own husband! Didn't these women realize how fortunate they were?

"How do you know our Mr. Hayward?"

It took May a moment to realize someone was speaking to her. Beautiful, young Mrs. Wolfe, her mouth in a mauve pinch.

"I met him in church."

"What was that? Speak up!"

"She said she knows him from church—go easy." Kitty had come into the room, later than the others. May scarcely had a chance to wonder where she'd been when she took May's arm and led her, with no small force, around to the other side of the piano. They stood together against a tall plant with rubbery leaves. Up close, Kitty's face looked older than it had in the muted light of her dress shop. May could see rouge settled into her skin's pores. "You're the girl who came into my store, aren't you?"

She spoke quietly enough, but May could sense the others straining to listen, standing on tiptoe to see around the open lid of the piano. May nodded.

Kitty glanced over at the women. "You shouldn't be here," she said quietly to May.

"I beg your pardon." May wouldn't allow herself to be intimidated. All throughout dinner, Kitty had been laughing with Hal, whispering with him, cooing at his jokes, and slapping him playfully on the arm. Quite obviously, she wanted him for herself. "I've just as much right to be here as you do. I was invited. Hal invited me."

Kitty closed her eyes as if she had a headache. She stood a few inches taller than May, which unfortunately gave the impression of a moral high ground.

"I know who ordered the dress," Kitty said under her breath.

May's mouth fell open a half inch. "Who?"

"Ladies, ladies!" Gussie strode into the solarium, a petite ball of energy. She'd put on a hat, a satin cap with a diamond brooch and an ostrich feather dyed peach. "Please, join us in the drawing room. The entertainment portion of our evening shall begin presently."

Kitty mimed locking her mouth with a key, then followed the other women into the drawing room.

To May's delight, Hal beckoned to her as she entered. She settled beside him on the velvet love seat. She would not think of the dress right now. The dress was Faith's problem, and Mrs. Mendenhall's. It really had nothing to do with her.

"Have you enjoyed the evening, darling?" Hal asked, handing her another brandy. Some of the others had grown red-eyed and blotchy-complexioned since dinner, but not Hal; he looked as fresh and clean as he did at church.

"Oh, yes, it's been marvelous." The arms of the sofa curved in, heart-shaped, and she scooted closer to Hal. Blood pounded in her temples as he draped an arm, the one not holding his drink, around her. She tried meeting Kitty's gaze. Kitty sat with a few other women on the fainting couch opposite them, staring straight ahead.

"Just you wait," Hal snickered, gesturing toward the strange man, the one from the head of the table, who now stood in front of the fireplace. "This should be good."

The man did not move as Gussie's servants went around dimming the gaslights and putting out candles, and the noise in the room lowered to hushed giggles and whispers. In a swift gesture, he raised his hands, then threw them back behind him, causing the fire to pop and spit and, for a moment, blaze green.

Everyone exclaimed at once, clapping and laughing, just as they had for the edible mugs. Hal took his arm away from May's shoulders to lean over and whisper something to Johnny, who was seated on the floor. Kitty cut her eyes toward May.

"Copper," the man said abruptly. His voice had a ragged quality, a bit slurred, though he did not seem drunk. His dark eyes were sharp below the shaggy eyebrows. "Do not clap, for this was no magic display. I threw copper powder into the fire. Any of you could do it. It is science." May couldn't take her eyes off him and had the sense no one else could, either. Hal had gone quiet beside her.

"Mesmerism..." the man continued. May held her breath, thinking of Faith. "...is also science. All animate and inanimate beings are connected by a web of invisible threads of energy. I tug on one and..."

With a jolt, Mrs. Wolfe sat forward, led by her chest. Her lithe arms flopped backward. Everyone else gasped. She looked around the room, laughing nervously.

The man crooked a finger and she rose to her feet, unsteady, arms out to balance herself, as though these feet now weren't her own. He gestured, and she walked, quickly, to a chair beside the fireplace and fell into it as though dropped there. Muted laughter: everyone seemed to be waiting to see what happened next. May turned to see Gussie perched on the edge of a wing-back chair, her feet propped on a stool, looking absolutely delighted.

The man stuck one hand out flat in front of Mrs. Wolfe, as though he held her there with an invisible force. He turned back to the room. "Have you ever wondered why asylums overflow during a full moon? The moon sends its own energy, which overtakes the mind's good sense. Illness, of the mind or body, can come from anywhere and all directions." He turned back to Mrs. Wolfe and stroked his gnarled beard. "You have an aching head."

"I . . . I do," she said. "A brandy can make me . . ."

"Would you like to know where your headache came from?"

"As I said, the brandy—"

He held up a finger and she quieted. To the rest of the guests, he said, "Shall we see just how far this misbegotten energy has traveled?"

"Indeed!" said Gussie, as a few of the men thumped the cof-fee table.

"We will not know until we hear the language." The man went to Mrs. Wolfe and placed his hands an inch from the top of her head, grazing her chignon. Caressing the air, his hands went around the back of her neck and under her chin. He grasped the air in front of her mouth and began to pull, one hand in front of the other, as though he were a sailor raising an anchor lodged inside Mrs. Wolfe's throat.

For a moment, nothing happened. Instinctively, Mrs. Wolfe had opened her mouth; her eyes looked up at the man in a sort of terror. A log fell in the fire, causing a spray of sparks, faintly greenish. May felt, secretly, a little glad to see Mrs. Wolfe forced into a weak position.

"*Siurrisa!*" A shriek, perhaps a word, though not one May had ever heard before. It had come from Mrs. Wolfe and yet not Mrs. Wolfe. The voice did not sound like her own. A sprinkle of murmurs echoed through the company. Mrs. Wolfe looked as surprised as they did. The man went on tugging.

"*Siurrisa teppanek brimightom vanishet kloor maniperrat!*"

The words poured out of Mrs. Wolfe as the man leaned into pulling that anchor, his knees bent as if holding a great weight, and the fire in the hearth grew. The dinner guests shifted and glanced at one another and covered their mouths, unable to believe this strange language was really coming from Mrs. Wolfe. Her husband appeared truly disturbed. He stood, looking ready to put an end to the display, then sat back down and frowned when Gussie caught his arm.

The Mesmerist lowered his arms, and Mrs. Wolfe's chin dropped to her chest. "That settles it. Mrs. Wolfe caught her ailment on the trade winds. There was a storm in the Sahara just days ago, bringing sands across the Atlantic. Her pains came from Morocco." There were a few gasps. He went to her and picked up her chin in his hand. "Your headache is gone."

Mrs. Wolfe faced the room, beaming. "It is."

Everyone applauded, even May, although she couldn't yet make up her mind about what she'd just seen. When Mrs. Wolfe stood, the color was high in the tops of her cheeks, but she beamed and curtsied, as though she'd just had a hand in this display. She went to take her seat on the divan as the man scanned the room for his next subject.

He held one hand out flat, like a butler with a serving tray. After the applause died down, he blew on his hand. Then he dusted off his fingers, as though Mrs. Wolfe's headache had sat there on his palm just a moment ago, and now he'd officially freed her from it.

The gesture felt so much like what Faith had just done to trick Pearl that it made May squirm in her seat. A coincidence, she hoped.

"And who shall be the next beneficiary of my services?" The Mesmerist peered out at the dinner guests, rubbing his hands together as they looked at one another and chuckled nervously. May assumed he'd choose a man this time, but then his eyes landed on her. He crooked a finger. She didn't move.

"A stubborn case," he said.

Hal looked at her and gestured toward the fireplace. The next time the man summoned her, she rose.

The Mesmerist brought the chair to the center of the hearth, facing the room. May sat down, her heart pounding; eleven pairs of eyes were fastened on her, more if you counted the servants, who leaned with arms crossed in doorways and glared as if they saw right through her. May sat on her hands, her knees and ankles pressed tightly together.

The man walked in slow circles around the chair. "Something heavy weighs you down," he said. He stank, slightly, of clothes left to molder. May knew the odor, that of a poor bachelor. It triggered memories that were better left untouched. She pinched her eyes shut.

"Very heavy, like lead, like iron," the man said. He sounded as if he needed water, but he kept talking. She wished he wouldn't. "I believe it is guilt."

May opened her eyes, panicked, to look at Hal, to gauge his reaction. But his head was turned to the side. He and Kitty were exchanging a glance, full of meaning May couldn't decipher. A mutual smirk.

"But who put the guilt here? Whose sins has this poor young woman swallowed? Whose energy has coiled inside her, waiting to be drawn out?"

May trembled so violently that she felt sure everyone present could see, yet no one moved, no one urged the man to stop. Her underarms felt both cold and wet. Hal looked on in bland amusement. She wished, fervently, that she'd stayed home tonight.

"I could make her levitate, above this chair, and allow the guilt to sink below her . . ."

"Yes, do!" called Gussie. May gripped the cushioned seat.

The man shook his head. "That is not the best remedy for guilt. Guilt stems from secrecy, and the best way to remove a secret is to give it voice."

He began, again, with the invisible rope. One hand in front of the other, his filthy, hairy knuckles grazing the air close to May's lips. She did not open her mouth to him. She wouldn't. She would not let him offend and humiliate her any further. When his penetrating gray eyes became too much for her, she closed hers.

Whose guilt *was* she carrying? Whose secrets? She forced her mind back, further back than the sins of her adulthood, back past Cousin Amelia's house and the secret of Amelia's abandonment, past dear Enzo and their nights of passion. May went all the way back to the day her cousin Anthony had gotten cross with her for refusing to let him look beneath her skirt. He was called Little Anthony to differentiate him from his father, but he was bigger than she was and had forced her down the cellar stairs and locked her in the dark. It wouldn't have been so bad if his mother hadn't sent the dog down there earlier to keep his wet paws out of the house. Lupino, that was the dog's name, a big Irish wolfhound with long, yellow teeth. Now she wasn't sure he'd actually bitten her, but in the pitch darkness, when she was nine years old, she'd been terrified as he pawed and scratched and barked, then knocked her to the cold floor into a puddle of his urine. All because she hadn't given Anthony the simple pleasure of seeing under her clothes.

She opened her eyes. Mesmerism wasn't real, of course, and half the people here knew it. She wanted to be one of them, exchanging knowing smiles. She didn't want to play along, like stupid Mrs. Wolfe. She didn't want to be like Dolly or Leigh or Constance, half hysterical and absolutely convinced that an ordinary girl with no power in any sense of the word could somehow control their every move.

But then May looked at Hal, who had his hands clasped, elbows on knees, concentrating on her. His blue eyes gleamed red in the firelight. If anyone here wielded an invisible influence, it wasn't the bedraggled buffoon tugging the air before her. It was Hal. She wanted, more than anything, to please him.

She turned back to the Mesmerist and opened her mouth. She began to howl, hoarse and ferocious, like an Irish wolfhound.

"Thank you," May said quietly, sometime later, as she accepted the jet bead cape and her hat and gloves from the butler. Her body felt exhausted, her eyes strained, as if she'd spent the last hour attempting to read very small text. She'd left Hal in the cigar lounge, where everyone had gathered after the Mesmerist left, talking intimately with Kitty. The two of them hadn't even noticed May slip out.

She didn't care if it was rude, if she should have thanked Gussie. She was glad no one saw her leave, that no one came after her now as she descended the brick front steps. The more bottles of wine and liquor they'd opened, the less attention anyone paid May, and the more they'd all been engaged in infuriating side conversations. The men, or at least Johnny and Hal, had insisted on paying the Mesmerist for his services, and had whispered and cackled as they assembled his fee between them. The women rolled their eyes and hissed behind their fans. No one shunned Mrs. Wolfe, but everyone had treated May as a kind of pariah after her turn with the Mesmerist. She couldn't understand it. Hadn't she given them what they wanted?

She felt tears well in her eyes as she passed through the gate of Gussie's walled property. Her boots slipped on the cobblestones. Likely, she'd never see any of these people again, not even Hal. She could stop going to church. She could stop letting Pearl gouge her. Perhaps that would be for the best.

The doeskin gloves did little to protect her from the cold. The wind bit at her fingertips. She stuffed her hands into the cape and began walking down the sidewalk. They had sidewalks here. The rich really did have everything.

"May!"

She turned around. Hal, his jacket open and white tie askew, was coming toward her round the curved street. She let him catch up to her. Why must he insist on being so handsome? The effort of running after her had brought color to his face. His eyes looked glassy now; his intoxication must have finally caught up with all the others'.

He offered her his arm. Warmth radiated from his body. "Come, let me at least take you to the next streetlight."

They walked in silence, following the waves of the appropriately named Mount Curve Avenue. Tangle towns, they called these: streets that twisted and interlocked in complicated braids meant to confuse outsiders. The mansions' windows glowed yellow in the night.

She was surprised he hadn't chastised her for leaving without a goodbye or asked why she'd left early. Finally, she said it: "Everyone was laughing at me."

"No, darling, they weren't at all, you were brilliant."

"You were. You, and Kitty, and Johnny, you were all sharing a joke that I wasn't part of." She sounded like a child, but she'd had enough brandy not to care.

Hal ran a hand down his face, all the way to his chin. He'd left his gloves inside. "I'm sorry you thought that. We were laughing at the Mesmerist. We paid him in green goods."

"Green goods?"

"False money. Greenbacks—they're easy to counterfeit." He shrugged.

"Hal, that's . . ." Scandalous. Shocking. She couldn't fathom him doing such a thing. "It's illegal. Isn't it?"

He laughed. "Of course it is. But the man's a quack! I could've put on a better show of Mesmerism than he did. That old coot took advantage of poor Gussie. Rich woman like that, he knows he can charge an arm and a leg—just throw a little copper in her fire and she'll rain gold coins upon him. It's no sin to defraud a fraudster." He guided May around a little pile of dog waste on the sidewalk.

"Poor Gussie? What about poor Mrs. Wolfe?" *What about poor me?* May wanted to add, but then she'd really sound childish.

They were almost to the streetlight, its gas lamp flickering, and the little patch of grass that was Fremont Triangle. "Mrs. Wolfe is her own brand of fraud. As for you, you were a gem. Still, I'm awful sorry for putting you through that. It's a fast crowd, I'll admit. Too fast for you."

"You seem to like them. You seem to like Kitty."

"Kitty! She's the worst of them. Kitty is my neighbor in the Ozark Flats. I love her, but talk about fast."

May processed this. They had reached the streetlight; the road had turned into Fremont Avenue, and her motor stop wasn't far. He loved Kitty—he said this in the way a brother might about a sister. He lived in the Ozark Flats. A block of apartments. This hadn't been what she pictured. Maybe it put them on more even footing.

At the corner, Hal took her elbows in his hands. "Farewell, May. I won't be far behind you. I should be getting to bed." His lower lip came out in exaggerated penance.

"You aren't going out to play faro, then?"

"Faro, me? Darling, I detest gambling."

He came closer to her and tapped his finger on the tip of her nose. Her body responded to his touch, a quickening of the blood. "Is there anyone waiting up for you? There should be."

She thought of Faith, whom she had specifically told not to wait up. Now she hoped Faith hadn't listened. "Yes," she replied.

"Thank heaven for that." He kissed her hand through the glove. "See you in church."

"Church," she said mechanically. A throb of desire, fiendish, unbidden, pulsed through her at the touch of his lips. She wanted him to take off her glove again, to do more than that. She longed for him to ask her if she'd come with him to the Ozark Flats, even as she knew how wrong that was. Her face burned so feverishly she had to look away.

She let go of his hand and watched as he disappeared back into the shadows of Gussie's curvy road. Quickly he was out of sight.

No one was around. The streets were empty, alerting May to

how late it must be. Or how early. Wind whistled off buildings. Would the Bethany Home's front door still be unlocked? She'd never been out this late. The home was still so far away, and she was tired, tired.

She crossed the road, normally a busy one but quiet now, lit sporadically by weak streetlights. The thick black cables of the electric streetcars snaked left and right on Douglas Avenue, but she didn't need to walk far before she reached the tracks heading south on Bryant.

Her boots clicked on the pavement. Halfway there, she stopped and slowed. The streetcars had stopped running. She'd expected to be home by ten, but dinner had gone on for hours and hours. Now she'd have to walk the twenty or thirty blocks home. What a ninny she'd been.

She picked up her pace. One foot in front of the other. Eventually, she would get there.

Fremont Avenue was residential, tree-lined, with overlapping branches that must have been charming in daylight but created a canopy of darkness at night. She looked into the windows of the homes she passed, where all were sleeping peacefully, masters and mistresses nestled in down pillows, maids ready to shake themselves from bed at the first hint of dawn. She wondered if anyone would notice if she stopped to rest under one of their neatly trimmed shrubs.

She was at the middle of a particularly dark block when she heard footsteps behind her. Running. A man in a rush, she thought, and naturally she stepped aside to allow him to pass her on the sidewalk.

Instead, he barreled straight for her. She got a look at him before they collided: a horrible, ugly, pug-faced man with bulging eyes and a large mustache. Hands outstretched, he lunged at her, and she was too surprised to cry out before his thick fingers wrapped around her neck.

He pushed her down by the throat, pressing her spine to a low brick wall and hedge. She tried, in a frenzy, to hit him, but her hands flapped uselessly at the coarse fabric of his coat as he crushed her windpipe. The pain of it shocked her. All she could see were branches, and his wretched red forehead, beaded with sweat. Her vision began to cloud with bursting white stars. The man growled as he strangled her. He grunted, as if it took all his effort to do this.

Mother! Her mother would not know what had happened to her. Her sister. Her brother. Her cousin Amelia. Emmanuel.

She thought of her father, who perhaps could see her now. *Oh, Father! How ashamed of me you must be!*

Her vision nearly blacked out completely, she made one last weak effort to push the man away. Incredibly, he let go of her. She fell over, coughing, onto her hands and knees. Her eyes gushed with tears. She spat blood onto the sidewalk. A sobbing, keening sound came from her, outside her control.

"I'm sorry," the man said in a hurry. He took off, running quickly for someone of his bulk, back up Fremont, the way he'd come.

And she did lie by the hedge, arms and head resting on the corner of the low brick wall belonging to some distinguished family who would not treat her kindly even if she cried out. She waited for she wasn't sure how long, frozen in fear that the man would come back, swallowing saliva in a vain attempt to soothe the burning in her throat.

She closed her eyes and let the darkness overtake her.

PART II

9

ABBY

*T*hank goodness, Abby thought on Saturday morning, for Archibald Yost and his tuba.

He'd grown into a fine young man since his time at the Bethany Home, sturdy as an oak, a living reminder of how many children and mothers the home had served. Archie, they'd called him in his youth, when he had cornsilk-fine curls. Now he stood with his small brass band at the top corner of the front lawn, their varied horns tooting out a Sousa march. Watching them from across the sunlight-streaked yard calmed Abby's nerves. When Dolly waddled over, asking fretfully where to put the tray of pumpkin pies now that the refreshment table was full, Abby managed to respond with measured patience.

"You can squeeze them in beside the pitchers of cider, dear," she said. "The more plentiful the table appears, the better."

This party, a harvest picnic to celebrate Mayor-Elect Pratt, had been pulled together in under forty-eight hours, and, fortunately, the weather had cooperated. A wan sun shone through thin clouds. November 10 was a bit late in the season, but Abby had still been able to produce a few more sunset roses from her greenhouse, which she had tucked into pitchers with sprigs of dried peony leaves, for luck. The baby nurses had brought all the charming infants from the nursery, and now lined up prams and white blankets on the lawn. One of the nurses, dimpled and young, lifted a plump little cherub high in the air, cooing at him, before laying him gently on a blanket to bat at wisps of cloud overhead. The older children had come with their matron from the cottage, and they danced happily and longingly in front of the desserts, dragging hand kites in their mittened fingers, the ribbons caressing their faces.

A hand landed on Abby's shoulder. "What a fine event you've planned."

Abby turned to face her friend. Euphemia Overlock had a wide brow, dark deep-set eyes, and gray hair that turned abruptly to black in a tight little bun. Just the sight of her face quieted the butterflies dancing in Abby's stomach.

Yost's band switched to another march as Abby embraced Euphemia. "I can't tell you how happy I am to see you. I trust you had a refreshing time in New Orleans?"

"We did, although the journey home was a trial. You know I'm a snug fit for a Pullman berth, and we were stuck for hours outside Memphis." Euphemia stifled a yawn, pressing two fingers of her kid glove to her lips. "Now, tell me. Why have you staged this last-minute party? I hear you invited not only our next mayor, but also a reporter from the *Tribune*."

Abby took a deep breath and filled Euphemia in on Tuva Larsen's interview in the *Examiner*, the hubbub surrounding Faith, and Swede Kate's report on the missing madam and murdered girl, as they watched two sewing apprentices hang a row of bunting. The purpose of the event, Abby explained, was twofold: to generate a positive news story to counteract Tuva's, and to sit down with Robert Pratt to figure out if he'd be a friend to the Sisterhood after he took office.

"I'm sure we have nothing to worry about there," Euphemia replied sunnily. "By all accounts, he's a good man."

Abby only nodded. She worried he might be too good, but she kept this to herself. When Pearl and Leigh came down the steps with a bucket of floating apples, Abby pointed out Leigh's unfortunate haircut. "There, you see? She claims Faith Johnson made her do it."

"Preposterous." Euphemia flipped open the fan she always kept hanging from a silk rope at her waist and fluttered it rapidly, her habit when bothered. "It's folly to believe someone could mesmerize you into picking up the scissors."

"Folly or not, it's what the whole household believes." Abby gazed at the home, its wrought-iron porch, central squared turret, and impressive addition. It looked proud and righteous, not at all the site of such chaos. "They won't go within ten feet of her."

"Speaking of those I'd rather give a wide berth, have you met this missing madam, Priscilla Black?" When Abby shook her head, Euphemia tutted, "Dreadful woman. I went to bail her out once, and she just about spat at me in return. I wouldn't be surprised if she has her share of enemies."

"Perhaps her disappearance and the sporting girl's murder are unrelated." Abby caught herself hoping this was true. Otherwise, it meant a more sinister agent of evil was afoot.

Euphemia shut her fan. "I'll see what I can find out about Mesmerism. Horace may have a book on it. You know he likes to divert himself with supernatural twaddle."

Abby smiled. "It is good to have you back."

Carriages had begun to arrive, and people were taking their seats in a semicircle of wooden chairs they'd staged around a podium. Charlotte was to give a lecture, an occasion that sometimes cost four or five dollars a head and had now gathered a crowd of well-heeled guests, mostly women. Euphemia went to sit in the front, right beside the row of seats roped off for Mr. Pratt and his aides. The journalist from the *Minneapolis Tribune*, Herbert Block, was easy to pick out, having arrived on foot in a cheap, rumpled suit. His sketch artist was a pockmarked boy who looked no older than fifteen. They hovered near the buffet table, guiltily sneaking hand pies. As far as Abby was concerned, they could eat as much as they wanted. The *Tribune*, a Republican-leaning paper, tended to treat the Bethany Home fairly, unlike some of its competitors, who over the years had implied that the Sisterhood tended to overstep their bounds, or were nothing more than busybodies, rather than effectual agents of progressive change. Abby could mark the dips in donations they received after a story like that was allowed to run; it could take months to recover.

Here was Charlotte now, descending the steps of her buggy. Her round glasses gleamed white in the muted autumn sunlight, making her appear profoundly blind and helpless; within minutes, however, her voice would boom across this lawn, captivating everyone present and, Abby hoped, convincing the new mayor that the women who ran this home were the very bedrock of this city, deserving of whatever funding they'd already secured, and more.

A flash of movement to her left drew Abby's eye. Cook had run up to the front door, panting, to accept a tray of candied apples from Faith.

The girl looked more relaxed than Abby had seen her before, a gentle smile lifting the corners of her mouth. She seemed oblivious to the steep wave of tension that her appearance caused to ripple through the yard. Movement slowed. Eyes went to her. A few of the society women who'd come to hear Charlotte craned their necks and began to whisper.

Faith offered Cook the gleaming caramel apples, decorated with sugared violets, with an air of pride. She must have prepared them herself. Abby watched, a sick feeling in her stomach. Friend or not, the reporter would be intrigued by the ghost girl, the alleged Mesmerist. What if his artist drew a sketch of her?

Beth Rhoades appeared beside Faith on the front steps and looped her arm through Faith's. Abby hurried toward them, trying to avoid the divots of the lawn, the uneven ground. Fortunately, they were chatting, or at least Miss Rhoades was, and Abby made it to them before they'd had a chance to leave the porch.

"Good morning, my child," she said. "Beautiful work on the violet apples."

Faith's pale cheeks flushed a lovely pink, and she bent her knees in a curtsy. Miss Rhoades was watching Abby with a strange look on her face.

"That'll be all, Faith," Abby said. "Run upstairs and rest. An occasion like this will only prove difficult for someone who cannot speak."

Miss Rhoades's mouth fell open. She turned to Faith as though she wanted to contradict Abby but felt she couldn't break ranks. Archie's band chose this moment to launch into a full rehearsal of "Stars and Stripes Forever," cymbals crashing, and Faith's eyelids fluttered in discomfort. She fumbled another quick curtsy in Abby's direction, then in Miss Rhoades's, then disappeared into the house, closing the door gently behind her.

"Mrs. Mendenhall," Miss Rhoades began, "Faith has every right to enjoy this party."

Abby interrupted her. "It's for her own good, Beth."

"I've a mute sister myself." Miss Rhoades's voice trembled, then grew louder and higher pitched. It seemed she might cry. "I know my sister wouldn't want to be left alone."

Abby took Miss Rhoades's cold hand. She'd forgotten about the matron's eldest sister, who still lived with their parents; she wondered, fleetingly, if this was why Miss Rhoades had never married and had been working since the age of twelve. Sometime she would have to sit with Miss Rhoades and ask. But now was not the time, not the time at all. The guest of honor had just arrived and taken his seat.

"The press will be looking for a witch among us—we have Tuva Larsen to thank for that. We cannot abide any more scandal. Now, please make sure there are plenty of clean napkins on the buffet table."

As Abby left Miss Rhoades, she glanced toward the upstairs windows, then slipped into the last row as Charlotte began her lecture.

"Temperance," Charlotte bellowed, before the crowd settled and quieted, the murmuring drawing to a whisper. On the lawn, the nurses shushed the babies and held the children back from the apples, the buffet table. The top of Charlotte's head came just over the edge of the podium, her white hair curled in ringlets, rhinestones gleaming in her trademark velvet headband.

"When we speak of temperance in whiskey consumption, we

understand our efforts must be two-sided. The publican displays temperance in how much he serves; the patron decides how much to partake, if at all. As long as the patron exists, so will the provider."

Abby gripped the back of the empty seat in front of her. She could suppose where this was going, and a tirade against the men of the city wouldn't be the best entrée into their relationship with soon-to-be Mayor Pratt.

"Why do we, then, approach the 'necessary evil' as if it were a one-sided problem? Placing responsibility squarely on young women without means, and ignoring the men—many of whom are in our own homes, our own churches, our own . . ."

The lawn chairs creaked as everyone shifted uncomfortably. A few of the women were nodding their heads. The men sat still and silent. Abby tried to bend her neck so that she could see Pratt's face. He remained motionless in his seat, gazing at Charlotte, his expression unreadable.

The rest of the speech, thank goodness, avoided blaming men directly. Instead, Charlotte lauded the growth of the great twin cities, ended on the question of what the cities could be if vice were not allowed to flourish, and named Robert Pratt as the best candidate to lead them all into that future. Everyone, including Pratt himself, applauded with enthusiasm.

Herbert Block, the reporter, came to Abby after the speech had ended and everyone had made good work of the buffet. A crumb of piecrust clung to his mustache. "The feature should run on Monday," he told Abby. "I'll write a nice scene, with a few choice lines from Mrs. Van Cleve's speech. My sketch boy got a good picture of the crowd." He indicated the seated cluster of people, including Pratt.

"Thank you, Herbert," said Abby, inching away from him.

Best not to make it look as if she were orchestrating her own press.

Block whistled for the sketch boy, who sat on a hay bale near the children bobbing for apples. "Until next time, Mrs. Mendenhall," said Block.

Abby didn't hear him. She was looking over his head at a girl who'd stumbled up the path in disheveled evening clothes, her hair askew, the whites of her eyes bright red. Abby's breath caught in her throat as she realized it was May Lombard. Block followed her gaze, and she heard him swear under his breath. The sketch artist, who'd joined them, began fishing in a pocket for his charcoal.

Abby reached for the artist's wrist. "Friend, please. Respect this girl's privacy."

"Who is it?" Herbert had his pad out. Of course: he loved a scoop just as much as the rest of them did. "Is that the ghost girl they're talking about?"

"There is no ghost girl." Abby had been about to tell him May's name was none of his business, but then an idea dawned on her. "This person is a stranger to me." A lie. Lies could be necessary, couldn't they, to protect the vulnerable?

Miss Rhoades had reached May and was holding her by the elbow, hurrying toward the house. "Please show our *new arrival* to a room, Beth," Abby said, giving her a pointed look.

For the second time that morning, Miss Rhoades stared suspiciously at Abby, but she didn't argue. She led May past the flower-strewn tables, through the kids with their pinwheels and kites, all of whom stopped, ribbons drooping, to watch May stumble by.

Abby glanced at the reporter and artist, both of whom had

their eyes narrowed at her in skepticism. As they should have. The back of her collar stuck to her neck, drenched in sweat. What good did it do to live and dress simply if she didn't speak the truth?

"Well, it was a very nice party."

Robert Pratt sat in the parlor opposite Abby and Euphemia as the sounds of the picnic continued outside. A pinched-faced man with a shiny head and small glasses, Pratt gave off a studious and almost delicate air. He looked run ragged from months of campaigning. Abby had a hard time imagining him holding a rifle, let alone leading the Vermont infantry to puncture the Confederate line at Appomattox.

"Mr. Pratt," Abby said, worried her voice sounded hoarse. The exchange with May had left her feeling out of breath. "You can expect the full support of the Sisterhood of Bethany in your first term. Whatever you need from us, please, let us know."

"In exchange," Euphemia said, coolly passing Abby a glass of water, "we trust we can count on *your* support once you've taken office."

Pratt inhaled through his nose and held the breath, looking upward, then brought his head down in a slow, deliberate nod. Something about it felt condescending to Abby. It was a gesture she'd seen priests make, on the occasions she'd attended Mass with friends, when the priest was about to launch into a particularly scathing homily.

"As your friend, Mrs. Van Cleve, so aptly noted . . ." His nose twitched slightly, and he sat forward to button his waistcoat. "I look forward to having the opportunity to scour this city. To set it back on its proper, God-fearing path."

Abby set her cut-glass tumbler in her lap. It sweated through her skirt. "Are you proposing anything in particular?"

He smiled at her sadly, preparing her for news that might hurt. "The Bethany Home's reputation is not what it once was, Mrs. Mendenhall. When former inmates are going to the press—"

"We've helped more than five thousand women and children, Mr. Pratt," Euphemia interrupted him. "I hardly think one vocal, dissatisfied girl negates that."

"I don't believe it's only one girl. Inmates coming and going, engaging in immoral activities right under your roof. Occult activities."

"Preposterous," Abby sputtered. Beside her, Euphemia snapped open her fan.

"We have the same objective, Mrs. Mendenhall, Mrs. Over-lock." Pratt opened his palms. "We'd all like to see an end to the social evil in this city. I'll ensure that happens within a year."

"How do you intend to do that?" Abby asked.

He snorted, as though the answer were right in front of them. "Shut down the red-light districts. Seize the madams' proper-ties on First and Second Avenues, and on Main Street."

"Many of them are owners, not tenants," Euphemia coun-tered. "I can't imagine the law allows you to dispossess them at your will."

"They belong in prison, Mrs. Overlock. They've broken the law in those houses, and so the buildings must be seized. The era of tacit approval, of this outrageous system of fines, is soon to be over."

Abby pressed her hands to her skirt to stay their trembling. "The social evil will not disappear if you simply shut down the district. It will disperse and become more dangerous, for all involved. Unless, of course, you find a way to dissuade the clients."

Pratt cocked his head at her. A child shrieked outside, making them all jump. Abby was relieved they hadn't heard a peep from the second floor, from May or Faith.

"As a Christian woman, you're telling me you *don't* want me to close the houses of ill fame, Mrs. Mendenhall?"

Abby bit the inside of her cheek. When she and Junius were younger and argued more, when he was sharper, he liked to tell her she didn't understand how money worked. Perhaps to spite him, to prove him wrong, she'd become the Sisterhood's treasurer. Now she understood a great deal about money. The men of this city spent an awful lot of it on women. It then went into the pockets of the madams, of the girls, and, through the city's vice tax, to the Sisterhood of Bethany. It went into the bellies of women and children in the form of food, it bought warm clothing, it purchased the very chair Abby sat on now. It kept the lights on and the fires burning in the parlor houses, and, yes, despite her disapproval of what those women had to do to earn a living, she was glad they were clothed and fed.

If the brothels no longer existed, would all that uncollected money be spent on the greater good? Or would men simply hoard it to use on something else?

"If you close the vice district, it will be very hard for the city to collect fines," she told Pratt. "Without the fines, there will be no Bethany Home."

He offered her an infuriating, simpering smile. "Without the sporting houses, we will *need* no Bethany Home. Surely, this is what you've prayed for."

She'd prayed for a gradual end to brothel work, of course she had. Shutting them down in one fell swoop wasn't the answer. But if she were to say this out loud, Pratt would retort, *Then what is the answer?* And she wouldn't know what to say. They couldn't very well round up every single poverty-stricken woman in this town and give her food, clean garments, and tutelage in a skilled trade. And then guarantee that her employers would pay her fairly. Abby had been trying to do just that, one person at a time, for the past twenty years, and she knew from experience what a daunting task it was.

Pratt shook his head. "Here I thought you'd be grateful for the news," he said. "To think, two Christian women who'd rather see the madams win. Well, you still have the City Council on your side, though I've heard that more than a few of them have concerns about the Bethany Home." Pratt stood. "Thank you for the invitation. It really was a very nice party."

Abby and Euphemia didn't see him out. They heard his aide close the front door, hard.

"Do you think it's serious this time?" Euphemia murmured. Her fanning had slowed. She pressed the lace to her lower lip, staring off into nothing.

"No," Abby said decisively. "The Bethany Home will stand." It had to. Yet her thoughts drifted once again to money. The previous month, their expenses had been near eight hundred dollars; their revenue, including donations, little more than nine. No one else, save Euphemia, knew what razor-thin margins they maintained here. Abby didn't want to concern her fellow board members. Worse, she worried they'd take it as a sign to appoint someone younger, with a keener mind and fresh ideas, as treasurer.

"We still need to pay the greengrocer," Euphemia said quietly. This afternoon, the man would return to collect his empty crates as well as payment for so many pumpkins and apples. Abby stared with glazed eyes at Charlotte's portrait hanging on the parlor wall.

Something slid into place in her mind. A bolt shunted out of its lock. She stood.

"I'll be back in a moment," she told Euphemia.

The hallway between the parlor and the office was mercifully empty. Abby shut herself into the office and unlocked the desk drawer. Faith's money was just where she'd left it. Without touching the gold, she retrieved four five-dollar bills.

When she handed twenty dollars to Euphemia, back in the parlor, Euphemia stared at the money, mystified.

"That should more than cover the grocer's bill," Abby told her. "Why don't you pick up this month's coal as well, tomorrow morning? I've a few errands to run with Miss Rhoades."

"Is this a donation?" Euphemia asked. "Has it been logged?"

"I'll log it. Thank you for fetching the coal."

Abby's body tingled anxiously. She longed to go home and hide, yet she couldn't stand the idea of sitting down. After she saw Euphemia out, she climbed the stairs as quickly as her tired legs would allow, gripping the banister.

She found May lying back on her bed, eyes closed, huddled under her thin blanket. Faith had pulled a stool beside her and was wringing a cloth over the washbasin. She'd been about to place it over May's forehead, but she jumped when she saw Abby, and May flung her elbows back and sat half upright.

"Mrs. Mendenhall," she said hoarsely. "I apologize. Last night—"

"Enough." It was hard for Abby to see May this way, clearly in the grips of a bad bout of bottle-ache. May, one of her favorites, if she was being honest. She felt no favoritism for the girl right now. May's recklessness, on today of all days, could help cost them everything, if Herbert Block mentioned her ungainly behavior in his *Tribune* piece.

"Miss Lombard, you have three weeks. Miss Rhoades and I will make work and housing arrangements, but I want you to prepare yourself to leave this place."

May cried out. Broken blood vessels clustered around her eyes; the eyes themselves were bloodshot, as if she'd vomited recently. Abby didn't want to know.

"I need more time." May's face crumpled like a child's. Abby tried to steel her heart against it.

"Three weeks *is* more time, Miss Lombard." Abby took an unsteady step backward when she noticed Faith glaring at her, eyes narrowed like a viper's, her lips moving slightly, as though she was whispering an incantation.

Rubbish, Abby reminded herself. It was all rubbish.

"That'll be all," she said, but her stomach was in knots, and she left the room in a hurry.

10

MAY

*T*he door closed, and she and Faith were left alone.

May threw her forearm across her eyes. The encounter with Mrs. Mendenhall had left her trembling. To be censured when she craved comfort! Her attacker's fingers had seemed to close around her neck once again.

From outside came the squawks of sandhill cranes riding the thermals, heading south for the winter. The lawn party, fortunately, was winding down. The children's matron called for the young ones to line up and return to the cottage.

Cold fingers took May's arm, moving it aside to apply the damp cloth to her forehead. May opened her eyes to see Faith hovering, her delicate face crumpled in sympathy. It was strange: When she and Faith were apart, May had trouble picturing her. Her mind would assemble the features—dark hair, violet eyes, creamy complexion—but they would add up to nothing. Yet here Faith was, real and solid. A fair-faced girl with ordinary pale freckles and the tiniest wisp of dark hair on her upper lip.

May cleared her throat. Her voice box felt swollen and bruised. "I simply couldn't tell her what happened."

Faith's lips twitched to the side. She nodded in understanding.

May shifted her quilt, exposing her neck down to the collarbone. She waited for Faith to flinch at the bruises, but the girl regarded her with steely eyes.

"It wasn't . . ." Faith swallowed. ". . . him, was it?"

It took May a moment to realize Faith meant Hal. "Oh, no! Of course not. It was a stranger. A horrible, ugly man." She described her assailant for Faith: his bulky physique, his broad, scraggly mustache, his pug-nosed face. Faith's eyes widened, and she nodded as though she was familiar with this sort of person.

"He's still out there," May rasped. "He ran away. He said, 'I'm sorry.' And then he was gone."

Faith's brow wrinkled. "He apologized?"

Downstairs, the front doors banged open. Women's voices, skittery from sugar and coffee, punctuated the air like the chatter of a dozen birds. Feet pounded up the stairs. May and Faith were due in the kitchen. May began to sit up, wincing, then froze. Her stomach dropped. She had been ordered to leave in three weeks.

"What am I going to do? Where can I go?" She preempted any question about Hal with a sweep of her hand. "He hasn't asked me to marry him yet, and it's not as if I can ask him."

An idea came to her. Hal had just inquired whether she had family looking out for her, and one of her last thoughts, just before stars began to appear in front of her eyes, had been of her mother. Perhaps her mother could spare some help for her, especially if she hinted she was in danger. Then May could rent an apartment for a little while, maybe even one of the Ozark Flats. She handed the rag back to Faith and went to the desk for a scrap of paper.

"You bake well," Faith said in her quiet way, squeezing the cloth over the washbasin. "The layers, in your biscuits . . ."

"Have you ever sent a telegram?" May asked. The inkwell was

nearly dry. She blotted and dabbed the nib. "I can't recall how many words you're allowed before the price goes up."

Faith shook her head no. "You could apply to bake bread somewhere. A hotel, perhaps." Her voice was so soft. "Night work. But you'd rest in daytime."

Night work. It sounded obscene. May paused and looked at what she'd written so far. "Let me concentrate, please."

Faith obeyed, stayed still as a statue while May completed the note to be transcribed. She'd never sent one to her mother before, these few years she'd been in Minnesota. She had been waiting for an occasion to relay some good news.

"There," she said. She read the message aloud, to make sure there were no errors.

Mother, In good health but suffered small injury at work. Seeking new job need money to stop gap. Love to all at home, Your Daughter.

"Twenty-five words," she said, satisfied. When she looked up, Faith was staring at her. "My mother believes I still work at the woolen mill." The very mention of the place brought back a scalded feeling to May's hands and the sharp tang of lye. "Mother also thinks I live with my cousin Amelia, even though I left Amelia's in summer of '92. It's better for everyone, including Amelia, if we let Mother keep believing that."

The wary look on Faith's face didn't change. May crossed her arms. "I couldn't have told her I was attacked while walking alone at night. Then she certainly wouldn't send me any money." She sniffed. "It's not exactly a lie. I *was* injured at the woolen mill. More than once."

Faith looked her up and down, from the bruises at her throat to the worn toes of her stockings. May's palms went cold and sweaty. Why had she mentioned how long it had been since she'd left Amelia's? Sensing a question brewing, May turned away and began stripping off last night's clothes, the tartan blouse and dark skirt, her petticoat, all of which now smelled of smoke and whiskey, and which she'd be happy never to see again.

"If you wouldn't mind," she said over her shoulder, "I'd like some privacy." She heard Faith set down the washcloth before their door opened and shut.

"Oh, my darling May, what horror has befallen you!"

To her delight, Hal had not only shown his face at church the next day, but he'd also searched for her ahead of the service. They sat in a pew together, which meant she'd been able to leave Pearl and the others behind, scowls on their faces. So much had happened to May in the last couple of days, and Hal's solid form beside her, his thigh along hers, felt so distracting that she had trouble keeping still during the sermon. She'd left church wanting to burst.

And now, incredibly, he'd taken her to an upscale ice-cream saloon with a full menu, where she'd told him what happened to her on the way home from Gussie's party.

"If only I'd walked you home," he cried. "Why didn't I remember that the streetcar stopped running at ten? It's completely my fault."

She tried not to smile. Had she wanted to make him feel guilty? Perhaps just a trifle. She'd worn her calico dress with the higher neckline, a shawl draped around her shoulders. She let it fall an inch or so, to give him a glimpse of her black-and-blue skin.

"Well," she said, taking in the walls lined in gilt-framed mirrors, the burgundy tiled floor and tin ceiling, the ornate scrollwork around the cash register. "I am feeling much better now."

"Thank heaven for that, darling."

It was pleasantly warm in here, though May could feel a draft emanating through the fogged glass window beside her. She could just make out the huddled shapes of passersby, heads bent against the falling snow. Any other day, she'd be one of them. Today, she was here with Hal, and he'd ordered them a veritable feast: blue-point oysters; an omelet for her and Salisbury steak for himself; a plate of toast, butter, and chocolate; steaming mugs of coffee with cream and sugar. She lifted the shell of a broiled oyster to her lips and hesitated. Was it polite to slurp, or did one use the tiny fork? Hal slurped his, and she followed suit, savoring the briny flavor peppered with breadcrumbs, sharp cheese, and green onions.

He reached across the table for her fingertips, ducking his head charmingly so that he had to peer under his eyelashes at her. "What did your cousin Amelia say when you came home in such bad shape? I hope she won't forbid you to see me again. That is, if she knows I exist."

"Certainly, I've told her about you," she replied, without thinking it through. He'd caught her off her guard. She hoped he couldn't tell how slick her palm had become.

His eyes brightened. "Then she wouldn't mind me coming to call on you? I love to visit Kenny. I'm sure her home is delightful."

The skin on her collarbone began to itch, as it did whenever she lied. She scratched, trying not to be obvious. Her fingers brushed the wounds on her neck. "I don't know if that's such a good idea."

"Why? Do you think she'd disapprove?"

"No, but . . . her husband is away, and I don't know if it would be proper. He's inspecting livestock in the Dakotas."

Hal squinted. "I thought you said he worked in railroads."

She wet her lips. She had said that. Last she'd heard about Amelia's husband, he'd been a Pillsbury boxcar loader. Now she'd gotten him mixed up with the stories she told about her father and uncle. "He did. He does. He's there with Union Pacific, something to do with"—she waved her hand in the air—"freight."

Hal slipped another oyster down his throat. "That must pay well."

"I'm sure it does," she murmured. Why were they stuck on Amelia's husband? There were still three warm oysters on the copper platter in front of her, and she hesitated before reaching for one of them. She put it on her plate and looked at it.

"I'd like to see where you live," she said, peeking up at him, then back at the oyster. She meant it; she longed to be alone with him, to sit on a soft divan or a mattress, instead of across from each other on these hard wooden benches. It made her squirmy, being so close to Hal and yet unable to touch him. Under the table she dug the heel of one boot into her other toe.

Hal looked through the window and took a sip of coffee. "I'm afraid you'd be sorely disappointed by the Ozark Flats. A dingy place. All manner of crime happening in and around those walls."

Then why did he live there? The shellfish seemed to lodge in her throat, like glue.

"What about your parents?" Hal said abruptly.

"Pardon?" She tried washing the oyster down with water. "What about them?"

"Now that you've been attacked, what will they do to protect you? Why don't they hire you a driver to take you around?"

The idea was so absurd that a hoarse laugh burst out of her. She pressed her fingers to her lips, embarrassed. If only he knew. She'd be grateful if her mother sent her five dollars.

She studied Hal as he ripped apart his bread. He'd always given off an air of aristocracy, and she'd assumed him well heeled, only to find he rented an apartment and dealt in counterfeit money. Everyone knew it was uncouth to comment on how much someone made, too, and here he'd done it about her cousin. Who was Hal, really, besides a handsome face? And who was he to pry about her family, when she'd already endured such scrutiny from Mrs. Mendenhall?

Her father had told her a story once, about a merchant who tried selling him faux-leather bootlaces. The man had taken his time in getting to know May's father, George, flattering him about his craftsmanship, bringing trinkets for the children. He'd sold George real leather cord three times before passing him the imitation. The man was a masterful actor, according to May's father. Nothing in his manner had betrayed anything suspicious about this lot.

"But I knew," her father told her. "I knew from the moment he set foot in my workshop that I'd have to inspect anything he brought in with double the scrutiny I gave anyone else. Because all along he'd been selling me a hell of a lot more than leather."

May slid out of the booth. Hal's blue eyes widened in shock.

"I have to go," she said, pulling her woolens on. "Thank you for lunch."

The waitress nodded at her in approval on the way out, as Hal scrambled for his belongings and called after her to stay. The girl likely assumed May was playing coy for his affection when, in truth, she was tired. Tired of lying, weary of performing for the affection of someone she had begun to understand, deep in her soul, was only *her* best option, not the best of men.

"May!" Hal didn't take long to catch up to her, even after paying the shopgirl. In green goods, or in real greenbacks? May's lip curled at the thought.

He swung her around by the arm. His eyes searched her face. "What's the matter?"

"I haven't been honest with you," she said. What did Miss Rhoades always say? Speak truth even when it's difficult. She hadn't done enough of that lately. "I don't live with my cousin. I live in a boarding house." She still couldn't bring herself to tell him it was the Bethany Home. "I live with Leigh, and Dolly, and Pearl. I'm the same as them."

His mouth fell open, pulling his mustache down at the corners. He let go of her arm and put his silk top hat on, slowly. She could nearly see the gears of realization turning inside his head. "How did you end up there?"

"My father died, and my family couldn't afford to keep me." She drew her shawl tighter, shielding herself from the damp. "I came here to work. I've worked in the woolen mill, and now I'm a cook. I have no fortune to my name. You needn't lead me on if that's what you're after."

Hal was quiet. The snow had turned to sleet, little nettles of ice that stung May's cheeks. They hit Hal's top hat and melted, leaving streaks of water in the silk. A gig clopped by, and he watched the driver swat the horse's haunches.

Finally, he said, in a gravelly voice, "I'm sorry to hear about your father."

"Thank you," she said. Tears sprang to her eyes. Hal noticed her crying and reached into his pocket for a handkerchief. He folded the corner into a triangle and dabbed at her gently. When she'd caught her breath and could look up at him, he was smiling. His face glowed under the brim of his hat. Something had shifted.

"May, darling, I'm so glad we can speak frankly with each other now."

"You are?"

"Yes. You must have thought me a villain for using green goods. A terrible business, not something I'm proud of. But, you see, my family has fallen on hard times as well. Our home, my birthright, recently burned to the ground, and as it turned out, my parents had no insurance."

"Oh," she breathed, "how awful."

He chuckled. "And here I was, worried *you* were after *my* money!" He slipped a bold, searching arm under her cloak and snaked it around her waist. She could feel the heat of his hand through his glove, through her clothes. Her body responded, her heart working to send blood to her groin. He'd never grabbed her like this before he learned she lived on her own. She decided she didn't care. He drew her closer, his face tipped toward hers. The brims of their hats touched. He tilted his head to bring their lips closer. "I should have said something sooner, to make my station clear," he said, his voice husky. "But you should have, too."

She felt the bristles of his mustache first, tickling her upper lip, but then they gave way to his soft, wet mouth. Her lips parted under his. His mouth was warm. Her cold nose pressed against his cheek. The kiss lasted long enough for her to run her hands from his chest, up and around the smooth skin of his neck.

Kissing a man on the street! What would Mrs. Mendenhall

think? May switched her nose to the other side of his and kissed him again, letting herself enjoy the feel of his slick mouth, the length of his body against hers. She wouldn't be under Mrs. Mendenhall's thumb much longer. She let her hands fall so that they rested on his slim hips and pulled him toward her. Wicked thoughts, scandalous, shameful thoughts, ran through her mind, and for the first time, she let them. She could imagine the whorl of hair that would begin at his navel and disappear into his trousers. His face hovering over hers, a drop of sweat falling from his forehead to her nose . . .

Hal was the one to break away first. He lifted a hand to her cheek, caressing her with the backs of his fingers. "I am fond of you, little rogue."

"Don't say that. I'm not a rogue." The lower half of her body had turned to liquid.

"It's all right, we can be a pair of rogues." He tucked her arm into his, and they began to stroll. Perhaps she'd been too critical of him a moment ago. He was, as far as she could tell, a man who accepted her—or at least the parts she'd been willing to show him, which was more than she'd shown anyone else.

"Listen, May. I might come into some real money very soon. Won't that be nice for us?"

They passed a shop that smelled of gingerbread, an enticing aroma. "I might get my hands on a few bucks as well," May said, thinking of her mother.

"Good fortune, May. Forget what I said about hiring your own driver. How about a gun?"

"A gun?" May felt dizzy. The soles of her boots crunched on some thin ice. "What on earth do you mean?"

"Nothing unwieldy, just a lady's pistol, one to tuck into your handbag. Your little secret, for the next time some cretin interferes with you." He placed his gloved hand over hers, to keep it warm. "You'd have a nice surprise waiting for him."

May looked up at the gray sky, its clouds oppressively thick. She imagined herself surprising that horrible man. Whipping a pistol at him, watching his expression turn from menace to abject fear. Just imagining it intoxicated her. Why, she wouldn't even have to squeeze the trigger. She could fend him off just by scaring him.

Or maybe she would pull it. Maybe she'd want to.

"I might fancy that," she told Hal.

He flashed her his brilliant white teeth, and her stomach fluttered in response. "I had a feeling you would."

11
FAITH

The telegram arrived while May was out. Faith was surprised to see it delivered here, to the home. She didn't intend to read it, but Miss Rhoades had already taken it from its envelope, as was policy. And it was so short.

BEST NOT WRITE FOR EMMANUEL'S SAKE
LOVE MOTHER

Faith sat on her bed and stared at the message. She wasn't surprised May's mother didn't seem concerned about May's reported injury. (The choice of the word "love" felt particularly harsh.) No one from Faith's childhood had been capable of safeguarding her honor or well-being, either. But she ached to think how the reply could send May deeper into the dangerous spiral Faith had observed in the weeks they'd lived together. Her roommate appeared to be unraveling at an unnerving pace.

Dust had collected on May's side of the room. She had even forgotten to make her bed this morning. Faith hurried to tuck in the sheet corners and plump the pillow before May returned. Maybe she'd be so distracted she'd believe she'd done it herself.

Someone had once taught Faith to look for unseen forces

behind any sort of dramatic change. People were not only like magnets, they *were* magnets, able to attract and repel one another, changing one another's paths, nudging them toward safety, or toward the abyss. This particular teacher of Faith's had proved himself to be, by Faith's reckoning, an agent of evil, and she wasn't sure how much of his instruction she still believed. But there did seem to be many potent influences acting upon May now: Mrs. Mendenhall; the beau, Hal; the grotesque man who'd attacked her. Too many voices for one person to bear.

Another point that couldn't be ignored: May's woes seemed to coincide with the arrival of Faith herself. What if May's fall from grace was Faith's fault?

She remembered the Pullman conductor who'd tossed her and Madam Irini from the train in Decatur, Indiana, as if they were bags of mail. The old palm reader had seemed unfazed, clearly used to this sort of treatment, but Faith had been shocked by his callousness.

"If I see you on this train again, bringing your bad luck, I'll have you both skinned alive," he sneered at them from the top of the ladder. The engine had hit another deer and was stalled. Passengers dangled from the half-open windows. A band of boys in their teens leaned out to ogle the two women, calling them hags.

"Come on," Madam Irini said, dusting off her skirt. She made no mention of the tickets they'd paid for, which had been meant to take them all the way to Chicago. "Let's walk."

Madam Irini had already been on the train when Faith boarded in Buffalo, and had set up shop in one of the sleeper cars: her tarot cards and silk pillows, the gauzy red scarf she hung over the window, her crystal ball the size of a grapefruit. She'd noticed Faith in a coach car on her way to the toilet.

Faith had been huddled against the window, knees pulled to her chest. Madam Irini leaned over the florid-faced man snoring beside her and asked Faith to come help an old woman count something.

Money, it turned out, and lots of it—that's what she needed Faith to count. As the train rambled west, she showed Faith how to read palms, or, rather, how to read people: to determine what they wanted to hear and give it to them. She let Faith stay in her sleeper car and traced her head, heart, and life lines, teaching her how to manipulate readings of them, how to bend the story.

"Everyone's in love with someone they have no business with," Madam Irini told her as they swayed back and forth with the train, their noses nearly touching. Her lips curved in a thin smile. "That's a good place to start."

Madam Irini rode trains back and forth, north and south. She had no home in the soil, as she put it. Railway travelers were an easy mark for fortune-tellers: they were either bored and captive, restless, or running from something and anxious for reassurance. Madam Irini looked ancient, with creased, soft skin and watery brown eyes. She told Faith late one night, after Faith helped her count her coins and store them safely in the lining of her carpetbag, that she'd been born enslaved in Georgia.

"I say I'm a Gypsy," she said. "Folks don't look too closely at me anyway, only at their own palms."

After the conductor threw them out, they'd walked to the station in Decatur, Madam Irini hobbling with her heavy carpetbag, insistent on carrying it herself. Even after a day and a night in each other's company, Faith still had the sense the woman didn't trust her, or anyone else, to hold all that money.

Yet, at the station, she'd surprised Faith by handing her a ten-dollar bill. "Where are you headed, dearie? Won't you come east with me? I might as well go back to New York, then down to Florida to see my sister."

Back east—Buffalo . . . Faith shivered. She shook her head.

"All right," said Madam Irini, "you go on ahead. I see nothing but good news for you in the West."

The words had comforted Faith at the time, even though she already knew Madam Irini told people only what they wanted to hear. Now Faith wondered if the conductor had been the more accurate soothsayer. If bad luck followed and clung to her like gnats on fruit.

She placed the telegram face-down on May's quilt. Her fingers had scarcely left it when the door opened.

"What's that?" May was breathless, face flushed, back from church with the piquant aroma of griddled bread and coffee clinging to her clothes. She crossed the room in three steps and plucked up the telegram, then sat down with a *whump* on her bed.

"You told your mother your address?"

"No. I asked the telegraph office to forward it here. Oh," May said, after she'd read it, and for a second Faith thought she might cry, but then she crumpled the telegram angrily and tossed it at the wall. She kicked off her shoes and peeled down her stockings, then sat on her bed and began fanning herself with a temperance pamphlet someone had left on their table.

Slowly, Faith lowered herself to her own bed, so that they were facing each other.

"Who is Emmanuel?" she asked.

She waited for May to accuse her of violating her privacy, but May didn't. Her fanning slowed, and she took in a deep breath.

"He's my little boy," she said after a while. "But he thinks my sister-in-law is his mother."

"Why?" Faith asked, even though she could guess the answer.

May sniffed, looking toward the window. The milky light amplified red blotches on her cheeks. "My brother is married. Emmanuel shares their last name and could fit neatly into their household. It was best for everyone. He was born, and I came here to live with Amelia."

Faith knew she would have to be selective in asking questions, and so she filled the gaps in her own mind. In a crowded Italian neighborhood in Chicago, where there could be no secrets, May and this fellow, Enzo, had had a tryst—probably more than the single night of lovemaking May liked to reminisce about—resulting in the boy Emmanuel. Enzo wouldn't marry May, so Emmanuel became her brother's son. And May was cast into the wilderness.

People could be so strange, Faith mused, especially when they thought their neighbors might judge them. The more someone cared about being proper, the odder, and often crueler, their behavior.

Faith had saved May a piece of soda bread, but when she brought it to her, wrapped in a napkin, May waved it away. She continued staring out the window, her expression fluctuating between grief and bitter anger. Faith sat back down and took a bite of it herself, wishing she'd thought to smuggle a pat of butter from the dining room. Hunger gnawed at her these days, following her around like a begging dog. She longed for the courage to ask for more food, or to ask May if she, too, had been consumed with hunger and thirst while pregnant.

What else would she ask May if she knew she'd receive an answer? To start, how old was Emmanuel? Old enough to read a telegram, perhaps, or close to it, which didn't fit with May's version of events. May told the story of her doomed romance with Enzo as though Emmanuel was the baby she'd been carrying when she arrived at the Bethany Home. But Emmanuel had never left Chicago.

"Did you—" Faith blurted out, louder than usual. May startled backward on her bed, as though a hand had shoved her in the chest. *Magnets.*

Faith swallowed the last bite of bread and cleared her throat. She looked down at the napkin. For all Madam Irini's teachings, she still couldn't always get people to spill their secrets. Especially people she cared about.

A train of words burst out of her. "Did you have another baby? Why does Mrs. Mendenhall want you to leave?"

Two questions. Ask two questions, you're unlikely to receive even one reply.

May sat up, and her bare feet smacked the floor. Her mannerisms seemed off, unlike her: more confident, in a sense, but more erratic. She put on her stockings and shoes, fastened the toggles on her woolen shawl, and tossed one side over her shoulder. "I'm off to buy something. I shall see you at dinner."

The white sky outside threatened more snow. Faith hated to think of May out there in the cold, missing that afternoon's fireside reading time, the pleasure of a warm blanket, and the cool trickle of Miss Rhoades's voice reading *Trilby*. She reached for May, longing to atone for her invasive questioning and beg her to stay, but words failed her.

May flinched. "Don't follow me" was all she said, her finger pointed at Faith's nose. She flung herself out the door with such force it felt as though she'd been squeezed out of the room, as though Faith and her questions had swelled to fill all available space.

12

ABBY

*A*gnes Bly was no friend of Abby's, not even in the way she and Swede Kate maintained their tenuous truce. Agnes's parlor house lacked the charm of Kate's, too: the Bly girls occupied a dim brick building on Main Street, in the shadow of Jennie Jones's three stories of bright awnings. Bly's had the feel of a spillover house. If Jennie's was too busy, Agnes could be relied upon to offer second best.

The ride across the river had left Abby feeling shaky-kneed, a little damp. The falls were roiling, fed by the recent snow, and she regretted asking her driver to take them in the open-sided phaeton. A light spray still dusted her face.

At the curb, Miss Rhoades took Abby's hand and helped her from the buggy. The air smelled of river algae mixed with a doughy whiff of wheat waste. Agnes's brick façade was filmed in a greenish moss. Church bells, somewhere nearby, chimed eleven.

Miss Rhoades sighed. Abby knew she hated this sort of business, pouncing on the madams unannounced. This wasn't even their first bordello visit of the day. In the morning, they had ridden to one on First Avenue to fetch a new arrival's trunk.

Under normal circumstances, Abby herself didn't mind con-

THE MESMERIST · 125

frontation. Enjoyed it, even; she'd been known to show up in brothel parlors just to read the Bible aloud. Today, however, her stomach churned like the Mississippi. She watched her driver lead the horse round to the back of the building, where there would be a trough of water.

"Tuva should be awake by now," Miss Rhoades said, taking a step forward. "Should I knock, or will you?"

"Don't knock." Abby caught her sleeve. "I need to say something, Beth."

The corner of Miss Rhoades's mouth crimped as she stared up at the house.

"I worry you think I've been too hard on Faith, and on May Lombard." Abby laid a hand on the matron's shoulder. "Yet I mustn't show any of them special consideration. There are too many lives dependent on us, and we need to be fair: every girl is allowed one year."

She'd expected Miss Rhoades to push back, to bring up the lie Abby had told the reporter about May's being a new arrival. Instead, Miss Rhoades looked at her awhile, face impassive. Her gaze then shifted away, up to the second-floor windows of Agnes Bly's.

"We all protect our hearts somehow," Miss Rhoades murmured.

Abby thought about asking what she meant, then decided against it.

They went in the back door, Abby in the lead. She had long since learned she'd be turned away from most of these places if she attempted to knock; she'd also discovered that in the morning hours, especially on Fridays, cooks and maids tended to leave their back entrances unlocked as they took out garbage and brought in supplies.

She and Miss Rhoades surprised a scullery maid, always the last to be fed, leaning against the kitchen wall, eating cold grits with her eyes closed. The maid took one look at them, at Abby's black frock and white bonnet, and shrieked for the madam.

"You can tell her I'll see her in the reception room," said Abby as she made her way there. Miss Rhoades's mortification wafted, in palpable waves, behind her.

"You have quite a nerve, you know, showing up here like this."

Agnes Bly sat on the divan opposite Abby and Miss Rhoades, a shawl pulled tightly around her, her mouth puckered as if she sucked sour candy. She was known for her high crown of golden hair, her cascade of blond sausage curls, which Abby had always suspected belonged to a wig—something she could now confirm. The hairs clinging to Agnes's scalp were wispy and gray, no longer than Leigh's after the chop. She looked like a perturbed fledgling hawk.

Tuva sat beside her, hands between her knees. She wore a modest day dress, dark blue, costlier than what she would have worn in the Bethany Home, with a draped overskirt and full sleeves. She wouldn't look at either Abby or Miss Rhoades, or at Agnes, but kept her eyes cast toward the metal boot-scraper at the far corner of the reception room, beside the front door.

Abby looked into Agnes's bloodshot eyes. "We'd like a moment alone with Tuva, please. Just to make sure she's getting by."

Agnes scoffed. A speck of spittle landed on her skirt. "She's getting by. She's better fed here than she was with you, isn't she?"

"That could be," Abby conceded. Her heartbeat had quickened, but she kept her voice even and benign. She knew Agnes would find it maddening. "We have many mouths to feed." She tried addressing Tuva directly. "My child, we shan't lecture you or attempt to drag you back with us. We aren't angry about what you said in the *Examiner*. May we talk?"

"You won't believe what Cook's done now," Miss Rhoades added, a hint of conspiratorial humor in her voice.

Tuva's mouth twitched. She looked at Miss Rhoades from the corner of one eye, then at Agnes Bly. With more insolence than Abby would have predicted, Tuva told Agnes, "You can shove off. I don't mind sitting with them."

Agnes muttered something about pulling out the girl's tongue, but her words felt ineffectual, weak. When she had left the room—stiffly, her chin held in an indignant pout—Tuva moved to the center of the love seat and sat back against the bolster, taking up as much room as she could.

"Tell me about Cook," she said to Miss Rhoades with Agnes gone.

Miss Rhoades filled her in on the "night in Venice" supper gone wrong, Cook's attempt to substitute catsup for tomato sauce. Abby studied Tuva as she laughed, fingers interlocked around one knee, bouncing her heel. Tuva looked to be doing fine, thriving, even: her cheeks had good color, her arms were plump, the whites of her eyes, unlike Agnes's, were clear. Youth, Abby worried, could sometimes hide neglect of the body, of the spirit.

When Miss Rhoades handed Tuva the scant belongings she'd left behind—her two dresses, a pair of clean aprons, sturdy work boots—Tuva accepted them with a grim smile.

Something about the clothes seemed to jog a memory in her; she looked up sharply.

"What about Faith?" she said. "How is she getting along?"

"I'm concerned about her, to be frank," Miss Rhoades said

before Abby could answer. "Without you, I'm not sure she has a friend left in the place. With May about to leave..." Miss Rhoades trailed off. She put her hands up and let them fall, limp, to her lap. She looked at Tuva, then, quickly, at Abby, leaving Abby to wonder if she'd intended to guilt them both.

Tuva bit her thumbnail.

"What about you, Constance?" Abby asked, using her Bethany name deliberately. "Are you well? We would gladly have kept you the rest of the—"

But Tuva was still on about Faith. "Is she showing yet?"

Abby and Miss Rhoades glanced at each other. "She will," replied Abby.

"You won't make her leave, will you, if she doesn't show? If it turns out to be a ghost baby?"

Abby felt Miss Rhoades watching her. "No, child, we won't make her leave. She can stay the one year. As I was saying, so could you—"

"There was a man here asking about her," Tuva whispered.

Abby started. She looked down at Miss Rhoades's hand squeezing the couch cushion, bones visible through her thin skin. Somewhere beyond the swinging parlor door, Agnes loudly admonished a servant. They didn't have long.

"Please, tell us about it," Abby said quietly.

Tuva told them, excitedly, that she enjoyed some notoriety now as a recent Bethany Home inmate, especially one who'd been featured in the paper. Customers liked the idea that she'd been out of service for a while, that she was "fresh."

Abby kept a straight face as she took in this information, even as her heart sank.

"I could leave here tomorrow and work in any number of sporting houses," Tuva explained, but she liked the big room

Agnes had given her. "A four-poster bed," Tuva boasted. "All to myself."

Not exactly, Abby thought. "And the man who asked after Faith...?"

"He was a young one, baby-faced. Seemed like a goody, to me. Saw me in the paper and had to wait a few days to get on my dance card." Tuva pursed her lips. "Afterward, he wanted to know if I'd seen a girl in the home with long dark hair and freckles. A mute, he said. He was after a mute."

"What did you tell him?" asked Miss Rhoades.

"Told him I'd never seen the likes of her, of course. What do you take me for?"

Abby's shoulders came down, just an inch. "Did he say what he wanted with Faith?"

"I don't want to make trouble for her, but he said she stole from him."

"You haven't gotten her in trouble, child." They asked Tuva if she'd learned his name, at which she laughed hard, and then they asked if she could describe him: young, in his late twenties or early thirties, light to medium hair, slim build, and, as she'd said, a boyish face.

"Wish I could give you more details than that," Tuva said, twisting the strand of pink pearls around her neck. "But, as I told you, I've seen a lot of gentlemen these last few days."

A voice came from upstairs, hollering that they'd run out of hot water. A maid's feet came scurrying.

"Constance, child," Abby said, launching into her plea even though she knew it would go nowhere, "you *can* come back with us if you want to. We'll keep you the rest of your year without question. In fact, we'd love to have you return. Miss Rhoades and I. Faith."

Tuva winced at Faith's name, but then she slowly shook her head. "I can't go back. That place makes me think of him."

Abby puzzled over this for a moment, wondering who "him" could be at the Bethany Home, but then Miss Rhoades said, softly, "Luke."

The baby Tuva had given away. "Why, Luke is—" Abby started to say that Luke was doing just fine, he had been adopted by a kind, Christian couple, but Miss Rhoades's expression stopped her.

Tuva swiped a tear from under her eye with the back of her pinkie. Her voice turned harsher. "What did you expect me to do, anyway? Go work as a seamstress? They're paid three dollars a week now, Mrs. Mendenhall. A month's bed and board can be as much as twenty. How's a girl to live?"

"We'd help you find better work than that. We'd help you find a—"

Tuva's eyes were red now; her neck was splotched above the collar. "The only good way out is to get married, Mrs. Mendenhall. You don't teach the good trades, like rolling cigars. Instead, you boast how many of us have been married in the chapel. It's catch a husband or back to the sporting house. Everyone at the Bethany Home knows it, except for you."

Abby felt as if she'd been kicked. This wasn't true—surely, it wasn't. But Miss Rhoades wouldn't look at her. "I'm very sorry to hear you feel this way," she said. Her own voice sounded odd to her, far away, as if she were speaking under a bridge. "But I assure you, you're mistaken. Countless girls have left to pursue fulfilling work." There were many of them, but her mind drew a blank at their names.

"The lot of us think this is the better life," Tuva continued, her voice rising in volume, the words coming one after another as though she'd been waiting to say this for years. "You know what it is, to look after a man, and children. Men who beat you. Children who die. At least here we've got someone taking care of us."

Someone shoved open the parlor door: Agnes. Abby had never been happier to see her. "Time's up. No more visitors today, Tuva. Not till four." She jutted her chin at Abby. "You can show yourselves out through the front." They heard her bang through the kitchen. Something metal clanged to the floor. She hollered at the cook to keep the back door locked.

Tuva had composed herself. She gathered her Bethany Home bundle into her lap. "You'll have to excuse her," she said with a roll of her eyes. "She's on edge, now they've found Priscilla Black."

"Priscilla Black?" Abby's heart was still racing, her thoughts moving slowly, like honey poured from a jar. Priscilla Black— that was the name of the madam who'd gone missing without her shoes. "Is she alive?"

Tuva laughed, a jaded, incredulous laugh. "I should say not. They found her over at Wessex Mill. One of the water wheels had jammed, and they sent a boy down with a stick to see what had clogged it."

"Have mercy, Lord," Miss Rhoades muttered.

"It was her," said Tuva. "Her body was swollen with river water. They say the black dye had completely bled from her hair. Solid gray, she'd turned, both hair and flesh."

"How awful." Abby tried to remember the words to the prayer for the dead, but her head felt stuffy.

"Strangest thing, too," Tuva whispered just before Agnes burst back in. "One of her eyebrows. I hear it was gone. Completely gone."

"Priscilla Black's?" Abby managed to ask.

Tuva nodded. "Yes. Just the one eyebrow. Now, how's a river supposed to do that?"

Abby rode home from Agnes's in silence, which seemed to satisfy Miss Rhoades as well. She looked out the window at the frothy gray river and considered what Tuva had said, about marriage being the only alternative.

Everyone at the Bethany Home knows it, except for you.

It was true, Abby reflected, that she'd always considered marriage a good option for the girls who entered the home. The Sisterhood didn't make matches, but it did serve to restore girls' marriageability. It cleansed them, in a sense, scraped their records clean. Now that Abby considered this, it did make her uncomfortable, as if they were in the business of scouring women.

Marriage had come late for Abby herself, after she'd passed the age of twenty-five and her parents had resigned themselves to the idea that their youngest daughter, the sickly child, would live out her days as a spinster. Her mother hadn't seemed bothered by it; they'd settled into a comfortable existence in that cottage by the sea, making raspberry vinegar, thinning the irises in spring, and curing bacon in fall. What would have happened if Junius Mendenhall hadn't come to teach at the Quaker school nearby, if she hadn't noticed in him a kindred oddness, a bookish nature, a shy charm that other young women had overlooked? She'd have continued like that with her mother, with their jelly jars and their storybooks, and she might have been just fine.

What if women could live that way forever, not married to men or serving their needs in other ways, but with one another, in peace, for all their years? What if she and, say, Euphemia . . . ?

Never mind. Abby bade a distracted farewell to Miss Rhoades and headed for the office.

The hallways inside the Bethany Home were dark, and her thoughts were similarly clouded. Did the women here wish to be married, for reasons beside the security it provided? Why, she herself hadn't enjoyed marriage at all, at first. Almost immediately, Junius had been drawn west, to chase his fortune in this frontier town. Though she'd kept a brave face for her new husband, she'd initially been horrified by this place: its flatness, the muddy tracks that passed as roads, the white men's ghastly talk of the violence they'd inflicted upon the native peoples when they staked their claims. Only Junius had been allowed to drive their carriage, which at that time was really a lumber wagon, through the rutted and uneven streets lined with frame houses. She'd been more or less a prisoner in their home, or at least she'd felt that way. She'd undertaken the same chores she did on Cape Cod—she blacked the stove, canned preserves, gutted hogs. She used the ham bones to prepare their mutual favorite dinner, New England pork and beans, a dish that reminded her of home. But here, the air smelled of singed wood, not salt, and she had no sea birds, no thatch of wild irises, no mother to keep her company.

Men who beat you, Tuva had said. *Children who die.* Junius had never laid a hand on Abby, but she had seen her share of babies and children taken before their time, had heard their mothers' screams. Not long after she moved to Minnesota, a neighbor's child nearly succumbed to cholera; she'd brought the family a cauldron of soup and paid the doctor's bill. The son of a family of freedmen died in a wagon accident not long after that, and she'd again gotten involved. Junius had begun making serious money, running a bank of his own; Abby took some of it to cover the costs of the child's funeral. She began visiting the workhouse, bringing blankets and tins of biscuits. Two years in a row, she missed her wedding anniversary with Junius: she was out visiting the burgeoning immigrant neighborhoods, tending to the sick. And then a sort of limb dangled above her, which she grasped on to tightly: Charlotte's invitation to form a branch of the Magdalene Society, which would become the Sisterhood of Bethany.

The first two inmates they helped were a pair of madams, whom the city had been poised to imprison. The Sisterhood argued for their release, paid their fines, and brought them back to Charlotte's house, unsure what to do with them next, but excited to have acted so boldly. It had felt exhilarating, and oddly good, to be in all those women's company, even the madams'.

Abby swung open the door to the office to find Euphemia sitting behind the desk. Her hand flew to her cheek, as though her troubled thoughts were written there.

Euphemia cleared her throat. She had something spread on the desk in front of her, fanned out like a deck of cards. Abby took a step closer to see that it was money: the banknotes that had been in Faith's purse.

"We have a problem," said Euphemia.

13

MAY

Dolly went into labor in the middle of the night on the last Monday in November, just as it began, again, to snow.

May was awoken by a scream. For a moment, in the dark, the man's hands were wrapped around her neck again. She sat up, gasping, keeping her woven blanket around her shoulders.

Faith was up as well, eyes shining, dark hair splayed on her pillow.

"What time is it?" May whispered. Faith reached for the alarm clock and held it up: three. Cook would rouse them to make the morning's dough at four.

The air in their room held the wet scent of winter approaching. Faith had finally agreed to keep the window open at night, and now a film of flurries had collected on the sill. May got up to close it, muffling the howl of the wind. Her feet felt as if they'd freeze to the floor, but she took a moment to peer through ice-bloomed glass at the front lawn, covered in confectioners' sugar.

Another moan reverberated under their door, louder this time. Voices murmured in the hallway: the matron and Leigh, who sounded frantic. Footsteps scurried down the stairs, likely off to use Miss Rhoades's candlestick telephone. They'd call the obstetric nurse at the hospital, who'd send over a student.

The doctor who'd delivered Emmanuel had delivered May, too. He'd seemed tired when he arrived at her house—bothered, in fact, by the inconvenience of her pains starting in the middle of the night. He'd examined her painfully, then yanked off his gloves and tossed them inside out on the floor. He chastened her mother for calling him too soon, as May groaned again, another wave cresting; how, she'd thought, how on earth could this not be the moment of the baby's arrival?

"Are you finished?" the doctor had said over her cries. "Can I speak now?"

"You are trembling," Faith said quietly.

May pulled her blanket to her chin. She'd passed a restless night. Hal hadn't come to church the day before, and she'd lain awake for hours, thinking how many days she had left—only six, including today—to stay safe in this house. "It's cold."

Dolly's voice came at them again, whimpering to Leigh. Their voices pulled Faith's eyes toward the door, widened with fear. She must not have given birth before—May could read it on Faith's face. May herself didn't feel fear, but recognition and sympathy mixed with dread. She knew Dolly had no idea what the hours, perhaps days, in front of her held. But May did.

There would be no going back to sleep, so the girls dressed quickly and headed down toward the kitchen. They met Pearl and Leigh in the hallway, both of whom wore resigned, wary expressions. Leigh's face looked pale. A white bonnet covered her chopped, shaggy hair, which stood out at odd angles against the ruffle. The others had tied their locks into tight kitchen buns, parted in the middle.

"Miss Rhoades is with her now," Leigh told May and Faith.

"The nursing student's on her way; then she'll take Dolly down to the exam room."

May nodded. How nice, to be addressed directly. It was the most anyone other than Faith had spoken to her in days. Word had traveled quickly that her time here would soon come to an end, and she had become, like Faith, a kind of ghost, invisible now to the rest of them. Girls who left the Bethany Home shed the names and friends they'd acquired here; that was by design. They were forgotten so that they could leave this interlude behind them, and the process of forgetting May had already begun.

Through the door, they heard Dolly cry out, and this hurried them down the stairs. The wind howled; the snow had picked up and formed small drifts on the windows' mullions. Miss Rhoades had turned on a few electric lights downstairs—only the first floor was electrified—and they flickered ominously as the four walked in silence through the chilly foyer. Late November seemed to have draped its dark blanket on the house overnight.

Cook met them at the top of the cellar stairs, holding a candle. "And our Dolly?" she asked. When she saw their faces, she said nothing more.

By candlelight, in the dank cellar, the bakers' apprentices worked mostly in silence. Leigh brought in coal from the bin outside the basement steps and shoveled it into the stove while May, Pearl, and Faith carried in a hundred-pound bag of flour from the pantry. They got to work, mixing the flour with water and yeast in the trough, their arms soon whitened to the elbows. Cook got her hands in but had to rest when, as was often the case, she began hacking, the tarry cough of lungs blackened from decades in front of a coal fire.

In no time, May felt perspiration beading on her forehead and dripping down the back of her collar. Every time Leigh opened the back door to get more coal, snowy night air met sweat, a phantom blowing on the back of May's neck.

"We're freezing here," Pearl snapped at Leigh. "Can't you shovel faster with those manly hands of yours?"

May's and Faith's eyes met as they kneaded the dough.

Leigh paused in the doorway, snow swirling behind her. Soot smeared one of her eyebrows and the side of her nose. "What's that supposed to mean?"

"Christ, we'll all catch our death from this folly!" Cook went to the door and closed it, then slid the bolt shut. "Enough from both of ye." She turned Leigh toward the stove. "Start stoking the fire or we'll bloody well be here till morning."

May's muscles burned. The dough was beginning to come together, to stretch and give between her hands. Soon they'd be ready to leave it to proof, and she'd be able to steal perhaps another hour of precious sleep. Yet the idea of being alone with her thoughts depressed her. Mrs. Mendenhall had called her into the matron's office the afternoon before and, in an unusual display of humility, declared herself sorry for having ordered May to leave with such sudden harshness. It wasn't a punishment, she assured May, simply May's time. She'd even arranged for May to work at a new commercial bakery on Lake Street, one of the first of its kind in the city. She'd be making loaves, rolls, and pies, to be sold to restaurants and hotels, or in the storefront on the ground floor; she'd have a room of her own on the third, above the owners' apartment. This would not be a grueling position, this would not be the woolen mill, Mrs. Mendenhall assured her: it would be a decent place to live and work.

May hadn't been able to say much, besides a nod here and there, and she must have said thank you at one point.

"It will be all right, May," Mrs. Mendenhall assured her. "I've made certain they pay you fairly—five and a half dollars per week—and only charge you two for the room. You will be able to save some money."

Mrs. Mendenhall's wrinkled, placid face, her implication that May should feel grateful for this arrangement, filled May with an unexpectedly violent anger. A room of her own on the third floor. Those words, strung together, sounded fine, but May could read between them. Could Mrs. Mendenhall? Had she ever slept in an unheated attic in winter?

And what of the couple who owned the bakery? Would they allow May to come and go as she pleased? Would the husband treat her decently? Would the wife?

May had picked up something heavy from the top of Mrs. Mendenhall's desk: a pewter paperweight, shaped like some kind of sea bird. She had wanted to throw it.

The bakery owners were Quakers, Mrs. Mendenhall, oblivious, had assured her. People she knew from the meeting house. As though this satisfied everything.

Someone had once told May that her problem was she'd been spoiled in her youth. Her contented home had tricked her into believing that everyone deserved a comfortable life. Thus, she was unable to see that a bit of sleep, a bit of food, and work—*any* work—were enough, since so many others lived without one or another of them, or all three.

Slowly, her wrist offering a bit of resistance, May had put the paperweight down.

Now she stood up straight, her backbone cracking. She massaged her wrists. Faith, across the trough from her, had stopped working. She stood still, one hand in the dough, watching Leigh work the bellows. May looked over her shoulder. The bellows wheezed in Leigh's hands, but the fire wouldn't start. Leigh pressed the heel of her hand to her eye. She pulled off her cap, hair standing askew.

"You're worried about her," said Faith.

Pearl snorted. "The witch is talking to you, Leigh."

"Hush, Pearl," Cook said, as her own curiosity brought her round the side of the trough to peer at Faith. She'd never spoken in the kitchen before, as far as May knew. It was a miracle the others had even heard her over the slap of the dough.

Leigh turned around, eyes red and full of tears. "Worried about who?"

Everyone's eyes went to Faith. Even in the dim, sooty kitchen, with her hair parted severely and yanked into her cap, she shone with an otherworldly beauty, her lips a deep pink, her eyelashes fanning onto her cheeks. The girl was downright pearlescent, May thought with some measure of envy. The name Pearl should have been Faith's.

Faith gazed at Leigh with what May had once considered an eerie, unblinking focus, and now thought might simply be kindness in the form of close attention.

May didn't expect her to speak again, but Faith whispered, "Dolly."

Leigh's face went red with rage. "You keep her name out of your mouth," she said, stepping toward the trough. "Don't you dare curse her."

Again, Cook leapt to hold Leigh back and turn her toward the oven. "Blazes, what's gotten into you girls today? No blood spilt before morning coffee, that's the rule."

Faith went back to kneading dough. Her chest rose and fell in a sigh. Her eyes met May's, and then widened in concern. May hadn't realized she'd started crying, but now she felt a drip run past her jaw and down her neck. She dragged the back of her sleeve across her eyes.

Faith had only been trying to look out for Leigh. Who would look out for May if she went to work in the bakery? Who would wait up to ensure she came home safely at night?

Later that afternoon, May lurked a few doors down from Kitty Ging's dress shop. Fine snow had been falling all morning, decorating the black sleeves of her threadbare wool shawl with six-pointed flakes. She leaned against the façade of a tea shop, near a downspout that had leaked a puddle of ice onto the sidewalk. Passerby after passerby slipped in the ice, grasping the sleeves of their companions, but May was too distracted to warn them.

She had to enter the dress shop armed with poise, assurance, and a convincing lie. Sure, she could mend and darn and hem, whatever Kitty needed. Needlework had never been one of her strong suits, but with concentration and effort, she could figure it out. Kitty could tell her where a young woman could live on her own in this city without having to engage in brothel work or the confines of domestic servitude.

Carefully, May stepped over the icy patch of sidewalk. Before she could get to the store, the bell rang and the door opened. Hal strode out, flexing his fingers in his leather gloves, and May froze. He was speaking to someone over his shoulder and laughing. Kitty stood in the door, her arms crossed, propping it open with her shoulder. He said something May couldn't hear, and

Kitty shook her head, grinning. Then he took her bare hand and kissed it.

May waited, heart pounding, until he strode off down the avenue, thanking the Lord he hadn't come her way. Then she walked up to Kitty's door and, with a deep breath, opened it.

It was warm inside, the radiators humming, gas and electric lanterns lit. A gramophone's record wobbled in circles, playing something May had heard the matron turn on: Debussy, she thought. Kitty stood behind the desk, lost in thought, arranging a pile of tan envelopes. Her black curls were lacquered perfectly, and she wore a dress of rich cranberry velvet.

"Miss Lombard!" she exclaimed when she looked up, putting her hand on her chest. "You scared the wits out of me; I thought I'd seen a ghost."

"Not a ghost," May replied. But just as insubstantial. She stood with feet pressed together and fingers interlocked, feeling a fool for having come here. What had she been thinking? If by some miracle Kitty offered her a job, and Hal saw her working here, it would look as if she were trying to insinuate herself between Kitty and him. Her desperation would be plain for all to see.

Kitty snapped her fingers in remembrance, startling May. "You wanted to know about the purple gown. The polonaise. I couldn't tell you when we were at Gussie's, but I can now, if you'll swear to secrecy."

"Oh. Yes." May collected herself. She stepped forward, so that the fringe of her shawl touched the edge of Kitty's desk, as Kitty flipped through a ledger. "Yes, I figured it would be more discreet if I came to ask after the gown in person." In truth, she hadn't thought about Faith's dress in days. To prod into Faith's past, now that she knew her roommate better, felt a kind of intrusion. Still, the dress made the perfect excuse for coming all the way here.

Kitty's manicured fingertip landed on a line of the ledger. "Aubergine silk with charcoal satin underskirt, ordered by Mrs. Jonathan Lundberg on May the eighth, '92." She peered up at May, one thick black eyebrow raised high.

"Is that supposed to mean something?"

"Mrs. Lundberg, from Gussie's dinner!" Kitty scoffed. "Surely you remember her. You sat beside her husband."

"Johnny," said May, and Kitty nodded. May tried to remember their faces, but it was their voices that had imprinted more clearly on her memory: the way he'd kindly told her who everyone else at the table was and whom they belonged to. The way his wife declared she'd rather he return to her dead than wounded. "But . . ."

"But what connection could the Lundbergs have with your friend? Well, this city is smaller than it seems. I'm not one to gossip, but I've heard about him and his maids. It wouldn't surprise me if he got one of them into trouble, and then gave her the dress as a parting gift."

May licked her lips, which felt scaly and dry. She'd never heard Faith say anything about having done domestic work, but, then, she hadn't heard Faith speak about her past at all.

"She'd been badly treated when she arrived at the Bethany Home. Since we're speaking in confidence," May added. "Bruises round her neck. Would Johnny Lundberg have done that?"

Kitty shook her head slowly, and May expected her to say, *He'd never,* but she didn't. "I don't think we can ever know what men do in their other lives," Kitty said, her voice wispy. "As their other selves."

Outside the windows, the snow created a blue, filtered light that contrasted sharply with the warm russets and mustards of Kitty's décor. The gramophone had stopped playing, but the record continued going round and round on the turntable, making a sound like fingers grasping at silk. May took an uneven breath. "Would he have given her money?"

Kitty wrinkled her nose. "Maybe a little. The dress itself was worth a lot, before it was destroyed. Seems unlikely he'd feel the need to send her off with money if he knew she was going into a home for unwed mothers. She wouldn't have needed it. Unless he intended for her to take care of herself another way. But then he would have paid the doctor." She closed the ledger and stood up straight. Her neck was long and white, her bosom pleasantly round; May remembered how jealous she'd felt a few minutes ago, how jealous she still was.

Kitty continued, "I'm sorry this raised more questions than answers about your friend. But, please, remember, this conversation stays between us."

May blurted out, "Do you know where I might find Hal?"

Kitty's nose wrinkled. "Savino's, I believe. But, Miss Lombard, it's a faro hall. You don't want to go there."

"It's within walking distance?"

"Well, yes. On Nicollet, a few blocks west. Miss Lombard—"

May was turning to go when one of Kitty's seamstresses came through the curtains separating the back of the store from the front, holding up an unfinished sleeve for Kitty to inspect. Kitty held up a finger.

"If you insist on entering that wretched place," she advised May, "ask for Harry Hayward. You're the only one I know who calls him Hal."

"It's how he introduced himself to me," May said, her tone regrettably defensive.

Kitty nodded. "I'm sure he did. May, please trust me on this. Whatever you think you'll get from Harry Hayward . . ."

The seamstress looked from Kitty to May and back again over her half-moon glasses, seemingly glad to have come in at such an opportune moment.

". . . you won't," Kitty finished. There was kindness in her expression, along with a galling concern. If Kitty knew better than May did, why had she accepted a kiss from the man mere moments earlier? May had a feeling they both knew what he was, and, still, neither could stay away from him.

"Please, do not threaten me, Miss Ging," May replied. "Especially when you seem fond of him yourself."

"Oh, you were watching us, were you?" Kitty's expression hardened. "Good for you. What you saw may have looked like a girl and her suitor, but would you like to know the truth? You saw a girl and her *lender*."

The seamstress's eyes bulged; this seemed to be news to her as well. May felt unbearably hot, with the funnel of her collar giving off an odor of damp wool; the air in the shop was stifling.

A splotch of red had appeared on Kitty's throat. "He's the one who gave me the money to keep my store running, and now that he's come on hard times himself, he's asking me to repay him at his demand. I must act as though I still like him so he won't send someone to break my fingers."

"I am sorry." May shook her head. "I didn't know." She found herself, quite horribly, relieved. Kitty was not a romantic rival. Kitty was a business partner.

"I thought . . ." Kitty's face contorted into a painful smile, more of a grimace. "I thought it would be my ticket to success, letting him come on as an investor. I thought it would allow me to expand. Maybe even open a second store. Turns out I was a fool."

"How much do you owe him?"

"None of your goddamned business." Kitty shot a glance at her seamstress, who was busying herself with the sleeve. "Go ahead, May. Marry the fellow if you can catch him. My debts can warm your marriage bed."

May hesitated for a moment, unsure what she could say to rectify the situation.

"Go!" Kitty bellowed, and May scurried from the shop, the bell ringing behind her.

Hal sprang up when May appeared at the door of the faro hall, almost as if he'd been warned of her imminent arrival. She had only a glimpse at the saloon, a crowded space no wider than the width of two tables, packed with men sitting on wooden stools. It was much quieter than she'd expected, the gamblers' eyes fixated on the green felt of the tables, as they waited for a few standing men in bow ties and suspenders to turn over the house cards. Tired waitresses bent to deliver neat whiskeys and foamy beers. A haze of blue smoke hovered under the tin ceiling, and the floor near the door was caked in boot slush. May slipped as she came over the threshold and let out a little yelp. A hundred eyes popped in her direction.

"May, darling." In an instant, Hal was at her elbow, turning her away from the room. "This is no place for a girl like you." He reached for his coat and top hat from a coat tree behind her, then turned over his shoulder. "Adry, hold my chips."

Adry stood—a pudding-faced man with an oversized mustache who had been eating crisped potatoes—and wiped his hands on his trousers. "You aren't going to introduce me, Harry?"

Hal sighed impatiently. "Miss Lombard, please meet my brother, Mr. Adry Hayward."

"Oh," May said, accepting the man's hand, her face flushed. Adry looked to be at least five years older than Hal and hadn't received the lion's share of the family's good looks. Still, she felt a thrill at meeting Hal's brother, even though she hadn't been invited. "I'm so pleased to meet you, Mr. Hayward."

Adry offered a brief smile and patted her arm. "Remember, you're down," he warned his brother.

"I'll be back," Hal called, pushing May out the door and into the snow.

"I thought you detested gambling," she said, wincing in the cold. The sky felt simultaneously overcast and too bright for her eyes.

"I do, darling. It's an awful pastime," Hal said, steering her. "Never said I didn't play a hand now and then, though, did I?" To her surprise, he headed for one of the carriages out front, a two-seated gig attached to a single black horse. As she climbed in and Hal untied the reins from the post, the horse shook his mane, tossing off a coating of powder. "I'm borrowing this from a friend," he explained as he took the seat beside her, pulling the reins into his lap. "I'll give you a ride home."

"You can take me to the streetcar, the Hennepin stop." The seat felt cold under her bottom, chilling her through to her hip-bones, but she pulled the wool blanket into her lap and felt snug and secure when Hal's leg touched hers.

"I've just been to see Miss Ging," she said after they'd clopped a little way down the avenue, through tire-worn muck. "You hadn't told me you were in business with her."

His mouth disappeared into his mustache for a moment. "How dare she—" He raised a fist to his mouth, collected himself, and started again. "Everyone's in business with Kitty, darling. I don't know how she keeps track of all the fellows she owes. Really, she's going to find herself in trouble one of these days. It's concerning."

May burrowed her hands farther under the blanket, squeezing her fingers together inside her mittens. "According to her, you've been the one asking her for money."

The corner of Hal's mustache twitched. "I've had some additional expenses lately. Look, don't trouble yourself. It's been this way for a while with me and Kitty. Money going back and forth. Hard to keep track of who owes whom. That's why I'm about to shut it down." He pulled a face and made the sign of the cross, as though protecting himself from a witch. "Cut ties for good."

"For good," May echoed. No more Kitty Ging. May let out a held breath. She peered out under the gig's awning. Incredible how quiet the city could appear in the snow. By January, she'd have tired of it, but for now the whirling flakes felt peaceful.

She remembered Dolly, and her spirits dropped. What was happening to Dolly at this very moment, as May enjoyed the quiet company of a warm carriage in a snowstorm?

"How about you, Miss Lombard? Did you arm yourself, as I suggested?"

"I have." She'd taken the last of her savings and bought herself a LeMat revolver originally owned by a Union soldier, now engraved with roses and vines on its frame. The salesman had talked her up from a muff pistol. He'd shown her how to load the gun with black powder and place six rounds in the chamber, but blood had been pounding so loudly in her ears that she hadn't been able to pay attention. Since then, she'd kept the revolver hidden in her dresser.

"How does it feel to carry it, darling?"

"Well, I haven't been, to be honest. It is rather heavy—"

Hal threw up his hands in exasperation, causing the reins to flap and the gelding to lurch forward. "What good does it do if you're not carrying it? You must defend yourself, next time some ratbag tries to mess with you."

A bit of snow blew into May's face. "I don't know how to load it."

"Then let me show you."

The gig rocked to a sudden stop, flinging May forward at the waist. She hadn't been watching where they were going, and she realized Hal had taken her not to the streetcar stop, but to the edge of Loring Park. The little lake spread out before them, a quiet, lovely picture: falling snow; bare, dark trees; the mostly frozen lake, still a bit dark in the middle. Here and there along the banks, other carriages were parked. Steam billowed from their cabins. Pairs of lovers, she thought, her face flushing.

Alone at last, she realized. She and Hal were all alone.

When she turned to face him, she saw that the tops of his cheeks were bright pink, too. He tugged off his gloves with his teeth, and she watched, breath hitched in her throat.

"You could come to my apartment tomorrow night," he said quietly, his voice husky with suggestion, "and I'll teach you."

"You'll teach me?" she murmured. He'd reached out to caress her jaw. His thumb slid over her lower lip.

"How to load it," he whispered. "Unless you'd rather not come to a bachelor's home alone. I'll understand."

His fingers crept under her hat. His hand wrapped around the back of her neck; his fingers snaking through her hair brought gooseflesh to her arms, sent chills through her earlobes, all the way down her back and between her legs. All the while, his crystal-blue eyes never left hers. He knew what he was doing, that was for sure. The man knew women and exactly how to please them. She let her eyes flutter shut. She wanted to lunge for him but couldn't. It was best to let him believe she did not have an equal amount of experience—or any experience, for that matter.

"I've never been to a bachelor's apartment," she replied.

After she said it, she realized it was true.

He paused for a moment, hand still on the back of her neck. His eyes flickered toward the lake; he was thinking. A ghost of a smile appeared on his lips, and then it was gone. "I have something for you. It may help with your worries about impropriety." He reached into a jacket pocket.

"I told you, I've had some additional expenses," he said, opening a small velvet box to reveal a bejeweled ring.

"Hal! My goodness!" May tugged off her mittens and slipped the ring onto the fourth finger of her left hand: a small ruby flanked by two bright diamonds, set in gold.

Hal smiled, eyes crinkling at the corners. "Aren't you a picture," he said, watching her admire her hand.

"Thank you," she said shyly. What else was she expected to say? Should she have responded, "Yes"? There hadn't been a question, no mention of marriage, but surely that was what this ring implied. How perfect, a proposal in the snow. All her uncertainty could come to an end, and what a telegram she could send her mother!

"It's Thanksgiving this week," she said. "Perhaps we could dine together?"

Hal laughed. "I forgot all about Thanksgiving, but why not?" She wrapped her arms around his neck and pressed her lips to his, kissing him again and again. The tip of her nose and her upper lip felt reddened and raw against the bristle of his mustache, but she didn't mind. After a moment his mouth traveled down toward her bodice. He undid her scarf and kissed her neck and collarbone, warming her chest with his breath.

"It seems funny to do this in front of the horse," she said, panting, and she felt him laugh against her sternum.

"You're a card," he said, his nose pressed to her skin.

His hand found her breast where it spilled over the top of her corset, only the thin layers of her chemise and her dress between his hand and her nipple. It was too much, the press of his fingers too intense, and she cried out, which only made him kiss her harder.

She pushed away from him, hand on his rib cage. Breathlessly, she promised to visit him at the Ozark Flats tomorrow afternoon if he could bring the gig to pick her up at the Hennepin Avenue stop. The man who'd attacked her was still out there, after all. She'd appreciate the escort, even if it was only partway.

Two o'clock, Hal promised. He and the horse would be there.

14

FAITH

*M*ay stayed out all day, leaving Faith to eat dinner in solitude.

The dining room was crowded, as usual, the air steamy, redolent with the scent of a boiled dish: Irish potatoes, sauerkraut, pickled pork backbone. The other girls squeezed together on their benches to ensure that Faith would be left to her own pocket of space. All the inmates had their clusters of friends with whom to chortle and whisper; only Faith had no one.

Witch. Ghost.

Look at her, the banshee.

Without May present, the others were emboldened. Their murmurs whirled around Faith, solid in the air, like strands of a nest. Tendrils of the story Tuva had sold to the papers, painting Faith as a wicked enchantress who'd wrested control of this place.

Wind groaned through the high cellar window. Cold drafts broke through the cracks in the whitewashed foundation walls. Faith shivered, remembering Tuva, who used to sit beside her. Another friend who'd ultimately proved herself to be no friend at all.

Aiiiee! someone shrieked. *It's talking to itself!*

At least Faith had space to spread her legs a bit on the bench, making room for the new heavy feeling in her lower belly. "Today is November the twenty-sixth," she whispered. Last time she'd had the curse it was the height of mosquito season, right around July 20. Add forty weeks, that would be the end of April or beginning of May. A fine time to be born. The season of renewal.

She'd begun working for the Lundbergs in April, she realized, her stomach sinking. April 1, the year before. They'd been her third house, after her previous two mistresses both dismissed her, without notice, within her first few weeks on the job. "Don't take it personal," a more senior maid had whispered to her at the second house, as she'd packed. "No mistress is going to keep someone with a face that pretty."

At first, she'd counted herself lucky that Mrs. Lundberg hadn't seemed to notice her face at all, or to care what she looked like, as long as she stayed out of the way and kept the hearths clean. The Lundbergs were young, still childless, though they lived in a cavernous mansion that required constant cleaning. Her duties, Faith realized her first day at work, would never end. The home boasted six fireplaces. The couple hosted callers every afternoon, nearly every evening, save Sunday, and each piece of china and crystal and silver they dirtied had to be scrubbed to a high shine. They drank copiously; they spilled port on their imported rugs. Faith blanched her fingers white trying, as they slept off the liquor, to lift the stains.

One day, Mrs. Lundberg caught her, on a rare moment of rest, reading the cook's palm.

"What are you doing?" she'd said, snappish, as the women sprang apart. Faith had expected to be punished, that Mrs. Lundberg would box her ears—she wore a pronged ring that stung—but, to Faith's astonishment, the mistress took Cook's place on the stool.

"Read mine," she said.

Faith's heart filled her throat, making it nearly impossible to speak. With shaking hands, she took Mrs. Lundberg's warm fingers, thinking her own must feel icy cold in comparison.

"Well? What do you see?" Mrs. Lundberg prompted her.

Faith knew she must be careful. The wrong reading could get her tossed onto the street again. What did she know about Mrs. Lundberg? The woman slept in a separate room from her husband—because of his snores, she said. She also didn't give a fig about Faith or her beauty.

"I see . . ." Faith said, her voice scratchy from lack of use. "I see . . . a stranger?"

Mrs. Lundberg turned and barked at the cook. "Leave us."

When Cook had gone, having blown out two of the candles beside the stove in her huff, Mrs. Lundberg urged Faith, "Go on."

"Here, on the love line. A dark-haired man."

She'd taken a leap, saying he was dark-haired, but Mrs. Lundberg seemed to like it. Her face came closer to Faith's as she looked more closely at her own palm. "What about him?"

"He wants you to wait for him, a little longer. Then he's going to take you . . ." Just about everything was south of Minnesota, so she went with that. ". . . south."

Mrs. Lundberg's face flushed. She pursed her unusually shaped lips, which always reminded Faith of an osprey's beak. Then Mrs. Lundberg snatched her hand back and lifted it in the air, as though poised to deliver a slap. Faith tried not to flinch.

"Don't you dare speak a word of this to anyone," she said.

Faith nodded repeatedly. No, of course, she wouldn't say a thing.

After that, Mrs. Lundberg began trotting Faith out at parties. She read the palms of half the young society women in the Twin Cities, a more difficult task, knowing little about them ahead of time, but she managed to produce satisfactory results. This one would inherit surprising wealth, halfway down her life line; that one possessed a secret genius that only her most beloved would be able to unlock. It exhausted Faith, all the talking: she'd go to bed at two or three in the morning with puffy eyes and a splitting headache.

As the women had their fortunes read, their men looked on, among them Mr. Lundberg—decidedly *not* dark-haired Mr. Lundberg—who'd asked Faith to call him Johnny. The men found her amusing, a sort of household pet; they offered her sips of brandy and sneaked her desserts. Johnny gazed at her with a faint smile on his lips, his eyes sparkling. He'd always seemed sweet to her, gentler and more attentive than the other men whose homes she'd worked in. She liked that he kept his face clean-shaven. Why in heaven would his wife long to leave him for a raven-haired stranger?

One night after a party, long after the guests had departed and the Lundbergs had gone, so Faith thought, to bed, Johnny came downstairs in his nightshirt and found her in the entryway, scrubbing mud from the marble. He lifted her up by the hand, holding the tips of her fingers delicately, as if she were a lady. She felt shy to see him in the loose garment, his hairy legs exposed below the knees, a button open at his chest. She hadn't known where to look.

"I have a friend who needs her fortune told," he whispered. "You're free Sunday afternoon, is that right?"

She nodded. Sundays, she had three hours to herself. She found she didn't mind having Johnny stand so close to her. Mr. Lundberg was someone she liked. His wife was someone she didn't. She felt compelled to make it up to him, the way his wife had betrayed his trust.

"Good," he said. "Wear a street gown, if you have one, and meet me at the carriage house. My friend and I, we'll pay you in gold." He interlaced his fingers with hers. She looked down at them, stunned to feel him touch her. She wondered what she'd find in Johnny Lundberg's palm if she took a serious look.

"It will be our secret," he told her.

Faith stood, now, to bus her plate. Most of the inmates in the dining room were still eating, conversing. Their chatter dulled as she crossed the room toward the sinks. She had to pass Pearl and Leigh, who sat at the end of a table full of women. Dolly's baby had been born late in the morning, still and blue at first; the obstetric nurse had had to slap him into breathing. Faith had heard Miss Rhoades whispering about it in the hall. No one ever assumed she'd be listening.

Faith stopped in front of Pearl and Leigh. Pearl glared at her, but Leigh seemed distracted. Pain radiated from Leigh, so intense that Faith could feel it. The backs of her ears were an angry shade of scarlet, her exposed scalp white; the food on her plate was barely touched. Leigh wanted to be upstairs with her friend, who was no doubt exhausted, stretched to her limit, frightened for her baby, possibly for herself: the nurse had long since gone home. Only Miss Rhoades waited upstairs with Dolly.

Faith could read the questions ticking through Leigh's head as though she were reading a telegram: Was Dolly still bleeding? How had she felt when the nurse struck her baby? Was she happy, looking at him now, or devastated, knowing the best choice would be to give him away?

Was she examining the baby's face for traces of his father?

Faith wanted to offer Leigh reassurance but couldn't. Instead, she simply put her hand on Leigh's shoulder. She could hear a few people gasp. Leigh stiffened under her grip, but didn't move, except to lower her chin down toward her chest.

The hum of voices surrounding Faith intensified.

Witch. Witch. Witch. Witch.

Pearl's voice broke through the din. "Get those grimy claws off her."

Faith found she was unable to move. Her hand felt as if it were fastened to Leigh's shawl.

After a moment, Leigh reached up and held Faith's hand for a blink, then gently moved it away. She picked up her fork and took a bite of potato. Faith went to rinse her dish. When she looked up, Leigh was eating, the rims of her ears still bright red.

"It's a ruby." May had returned just after dinner, in the quiet hour before lights-out, when most of the inmates, including Faith, had already washed up and changed into nightdresses. May stood with slushy boots on the rug, the chill of the outdoors clinging to her clothes. She already seemed like an outsider, and Faith felt oddly embarrassed, and exposed, to be sitting here in the white cotton nightgown her roommate had seen dozens of times before.

She examined the cluster of stones gleaming subtly on May's finger and nodded. She was happy for May, who against all odds had gotten what she wanted. May seemed unable to catch her breath, or sit down; she paced the room, picking up objects like the hot water bottle or a crocheted doily as though she'd never seen them before.

"I don't know how soon we can marry. Hal doesn't want me living in the Ozark Flats, and it doesn't sound as if he can make a down payment on a house at present."

"Dolly's baby came," Faith said quietly. "A boy."

"Oh." A hint of a shadow passed over May's face, bringing her back to the room. "Oh, that is nice."

"She named him Jude." Faith speculated that this, and Dolly's refusal to allow the baby to leave her side, implied she might want to keep him, and she'd thought to discuss it with May, but May seemed far too distracted. She'd removed the ring and was admiring the stones, held up to the lamp's light. Then she frowned and turned it over so that she could peer into the inner rim of the band.

She looked at Faith, mouth pursed in a sheepish grin. "I was checking for engravings, but there are none."

Faith wondered why May would think to look for engravings. She wished to ask but couldn't find the words. She'd also been meaning to open May's desk drawer and point out the revolver May had been hiding in there, under her spare chemise. She wanted to know why May felt the need to own it: was it the man who'd attacked her on the street, or something else?

Faith had started to open her mouth to speak when their door swung open.

Pearl stood on the threshold, her long, slender figure taking up the frame. She held something Faith had never seen with her before: her four-month-old baby, Francis. The boy was beautiful, pudgy, and bright-eyed. He quietly sucked his thumb, resting his cheek on his mother's chest.

"Let me see that," Pearl said, gesturing for the ring.

Faith expected May to refuse, but she stepped forward and handed it to Pearl. May seemed entranced by the baby, and by the cool, benign way Pearl had asked the question. May reached for the boy's sleeve at the exact same time Pearl's face changed. Her lip curled in disdain.

"It's paste," she declared, and she threw the ring at the wall.

May ran for it with a sob, scrabbling at it to get it off the floor. When she saw it was not broken, she let out a cry of relief and clutched it to her chest. "You're horrible, horrible! How could you do such a thing?"

Pearl shrugged and shifted the baby's head onto her shoulder. "Thought I'd do you a favor. Make sure it's real." Her voice aimed for nonchalance, but Faith could see something rattled behind her expression. The act of cruelty had been a way for her to reclaim the normal order. Still, it was not justified, and she could not be allowed to get away with it.

Faith took a step forward.

"You're just jealous," May muttered.

Pearl was still looking down at May, bouncing her baby ever so slightly. Faith took another step toward her, then another. "Jealous, am I?" Pearl asked May. "Jealous of what?"

"Jealous that I'm soon to be Mrs. Hayward," May said with a sniff. "And you'll still be nobody."

Pearl's mouth fell open. Faith's feet stopped moving; her upper body collapsed forward, as though she'd stepped in glue.

Hayward. It had to be a different man. May's Hal... All the times Faith had heard May talking about him, she'd never thought he could be...

Pearl threw her head back and laughed viciously. "You fool, a ring means nothing. He'll never—" She stopped, realizing how close Faith had come to her.

Faith raised her left hand. Her fingers began swirling the air above Pearl's head, plucking invisible objects out of nowhere and pulling them down, her lips forming nonsense words. Drivel, meant to sound like a curse. Her eyes held Pearl's, which looked terrified. Pearl covered the baby's face with her forearm, but she did not move and did not let go of Faith's gaze.

Good.

Faith's rippling fingers came to tickle the air above Pearl's hairline, then hovered at her right eyebrow. They hesitated. Faith arranged her face into an expression of concern, then of disgust. Her fingers pulsed above Pearl's right eyebrow, and she winced.

It was all a show, of course. The real part would begin later.

Pearl would do it to herself.

"Spiders," Faith whispered, with a sympathetic shake of her head. Pearl's lips came open with a spluttering sound, as if she were a fish trying to breathe air. She looked down, her face stricken with horror, at the front of her dress. Two wet circles had appeared over her breasts and begun fanning out through the fabric.

At once, Faith stopped what she was doing. Had she gone too far? It was so easy to forget that Pearl was a new mother, even with the baby hugged to her chest.

As she reached for Pearl, the gas lamp flickered and went out.

Pearl screamed. She stumbled backward into the half-open door, banging the back of her head. Fortunately, the baby was unharmed; cradling his little body, she flung the door all the way open and fled down the hallway.

"What did you just do?" asked May, her voice shaky but curious. She found a book of matches on the desk and tried to relight the lamp, then frowned, turned the key, and peered into the fount. "Oh, we're out of gas." She laughed nervously and slipped the ring back on her finger.

"Hayward," Faith said, her voice a croak.

"Pardon?" May's features were sharp, in the slanted light coming from the corridor.

Faith shook her head. "Hayward," she repeated, her voice thick with tears. It was all she could say. She was afraid to ask any questions. It couldn't be the same Hayward. It couldn't be.

May's lower jaw jutted forward. "I'm going to fetch some oil," she said, holding the fount. She left Faith alone and closed the door, plunging the room into darkness.

15

ABBY

*T*he simplest explanation," Euphemia said the next morning, "is that Faith was paid to perform demonstrations in Mesmerism, or some other unspeakable tasks, and somebody cheated her."

Abby sat at her desk in the office, her fingers at her temples. Faith's money lay in front of her. The gold bullion, coins adding up to seventy-two dollars, was real—that they'd established. You couldn't counterfeit gold.

The greenbacks were the problem. They were all five-dollar notes, totaling fifty dollars. Or they would have been worth fifty dollars if they weren't phony. When Euphemia had tried to spend them the day of the picnic, the grocer had refused the payment—wouldn't take "green goods," as he put it—and Euphemia had had to pay him from her own pocket. She'd then tried the banknotes at her local branch, where the teller examined them closely, declared them counterfeit.

"The Bank of Mishawaka uses brown ink on their seal, not blue," Euphemia had explained, turning them over so that Abby could see. "Besides that, the serial numbers on all these bills are the same. Someone used a stamp."

Abby had felt a sort of release upon learning she couldn't

spend Faith's money. A chance to atone for her lies and tell
Euphemia the truth: that it hadn't been a donation at all, not
unless they considered this Faith's donation to the home. Faith
hadn't asked for any of it back, after all; she'd seemed glad to be
rid of it.

"Someone out there wants to get his hands on this money,"
Abby told Euphemia now. "That man told Tuva that Faith had
stolen from him." And there'd been the bruises at Faith's throat.

Abby felt like tearing the paper to shreds, although that
wouldn't have helped them find answers. She glared at the clumsily copied serial numbers, the smudged face of James Garfield.
The wrong-color ink! How cavalier, how stupid. It filled her
with rage that hucksters had fooled her, had swindled Faith, and
now, very likely, were trying to track the girl down.

"We'll have to place another grocery order for Thanksgiving.
Donors are coming. Will we have the money for it, Abby?"

"We have enough." Abby began to pace, back and forth across
the simple rug, a braided oval donated by a former inmate.
"Something about that gold, in conjunction with all this useless
paper—it doesn't sit well with me, Euphemia."

Euphemia nudged her bifocals higher on her nose. One of her
husband's textbooks lay open in her lap. "Listen to this. 'Mesmerism, or animal magnetism, presupposes that the movements
of the planets, as well as magnetically charged elements running through bodily humors, exert powerful influences on the
movements of people and objects. A "Mesmerist" may refer to
one attuned with these magnetic forces and instructed in their
manipulation; these individuals wield great power and can present a danger to their fellow man.'"

She removed her glasses and rubbed an eye. "There have
been criminal trials, haven't there, where men used this as their

defense? 'Someone made me do it, I was hypnotized.' I've always considered it a bunch of poppycock, haven't you?"

"Of course," Abby replied. She was still thinking about the money. The gold and the green goods. The prince and the pauper. They'd been exchanged for each other in the story, the prince for the pauper, and vice versa. The word "exchange" was turning in her mind when May Lombard burst through the door.

"You have to come at this instant," May said, out of breath. Her gaze fell to the gold, shining under the light of Abby's lamp. "Pearl's gone after Faith."

"Gone after her?" Abby said. "What do you mean, gone after her?"

May's eyes were still trained on the money. "She's liable to kill her, Mrs. Mendenhall. Please, hurry."

Now, with the office door open, they could hear shrieks coming from upstairs. "Oh dear," Euphemia said, quickly shutting the book.

As the three of them climbed the stairs, they heard more shouting, then a thud as something fell. Beth Rhoades's voice, and what sounded like Cook's, spoke in low tones, as they tried to restore order. The seamstress and her apprentices were spilled into the hallway, peering down at the rooms at the end of the west wing. "Return to your work, please," Abby told them, catching the seamstress by surprise; she blushed and tugged her girls away. As Abby and Euphemia made their way down the hall, the screaming intensified, coming from Faith and May's room.

Cook stood in the hallway, clutching a corner of her apron to her mouth. "Oh, thank goodness, you're here. I've never seen anything like it."

"It'll be all right, Mrs. O'Rourke." Abby turned to tell May to run outside and fetch the gardener, in case they needed a set of male hands, but May had disappeared. Only Euphemia stood behind her, eyes wide with worry.

Inside the room, they found Miss Rhoades holding Pearl tightly, as Pearl covered her face and cried. The white globe of a gas lamp had shattered on the floor, leaving the flame dangerously exposed on the desk, the room lit brightly, the shadows harsh. Faith cowered on the bed, one leg bent up in front of her, one hand raised as if she might be struck. Pearl let out a moan and whirled back toward Faith, poised to slap or tear at her as Miss Rhoades struggled to keep her contained. Euphemia rushed to Faith to place her own body as a shield; incredibly, Pearl still lifted her hand to strike.

"Enough!" Abby bellowed.

Pearl stopped and turned around, her eyes swollen from crying. Abby drew her breath in sharply.

One of Pearl's eyebrows was missing. The skin above her right eye looked puckered and bloodied, plucked nearly bare.

"She put spiders in me," Pearl said through tears. "All night, they bit me and bit me, here . . ." Her shaking fingers went to her missing eyebrow. "I'm deformed now. I was finally going to take the baby to meet Cooper. We had plans to see each other next week."

"Shh, shh. Come on, dear." Miss Rhoades shot Abby a look of alarm, then softened as she rubbed Pearl's back. "It'll grow back."

"Not before I see Cooper!"

"I thought we decided seeing him wouldn't be a good idea," Miss Rhoades replied. "Come on, I'll help you wash your face."

She and Pearl left the room, the threat of violence quelled. "Close the door behind you, please," Abby murmured to Miss

Rhoades, who nodded. She bent to turn down the lamp, softening the light in the room, before going to kneel, her knees complaining on the hard floor, in front of Faith.

Euphemia had her arms around the girl, rocking her slightly, her lips pressed to Faith's forehead. Faith had her eyes closed.

"I'm not sure what you did to her," Abby said quietly. "But you did something."

Faith's expression contracted as she squeezed back tears. Her shadow loomed large on the wall behind her. She nodded.

"You've done it before, haven't you?" Abby didn't care to imagine Priscilla Black's bloated body, hair and skin drained of color, clogging the river mill. Its missing eyebrow, the lurid detail provided by Tuva. What was it Swede Kate had said about Priscilla?

Can't say her lot were sad to see the back of her.

Faith contemplated her own palms. The top of her hair shone in the gaslight, her straight part a strip of white. The skin on her forehead was creamy and clear, not a whisper of a wrinkle. She wasn't much more than a child.

Abby repeated the question, more quietly this time. "It's happened before, has it?"

A tiny movement, the chin bobbing up and down. Euphemia stopped rocking her. She looked at Abby with a mix of curiosity and dread.

"Listen," said Abby, taking Faith's hand, "I could call the police." Sharp intake of breath from Faith. "But I won't put you in their custody. We've long held that any slate, no matter what is written on it, may be wiped clean. Still. Some sins ..." She couldn't bring herself to say the word "murder." "Some sins are unforgivable. Is there anything you'd like to tell Mrs. Overlock and myself, anything in your defense? It will stay in this room."

Faith cut her eyes in the direction of Pearl's room and shook her head.

"I meant as regards Priscilla Black."

Euphemia jolted, like a spooked cat. Her dark eyes searched Abby's face, then Faith's.

Faith's posture changed, almost imperceptibly. Her shoulders crept up an inch, as though to protect her neck. Her fingertips met over the tops of her knees, quivering.

Abby waited. If only the girl would say something, anything, to explain herself. But she didn't. Instead, Faith watched her own hands tremble, curling further and further in on herself.

Abby grasped the footboard to hoist herself up. She indicated Faith's pillow and blanket, her hairbrush. "Gather your belongings, child. Don't worry, you aren't leaving the Bethany Home. Give us a moment; I'd like a word with Mrs. Overlock in the hallway."

"Priscilla Black?" Euphemia hissed as soon as they'd shut Faith in. "Where does she come in?"

In a hushed tone, Abby explained what Tuva had told her and Miss Rhoades, about the body's missing eyebrow. "It can't be a coincidence, can it? The girl just confirmed as much. She as good as confessed to Black's murder." Abby worried her own hands together, to stay their trembling. "She must have worked there."

"The poor girl." Euphemia shook her head slowly, studying Faith's door. She rubbed her upper arms against the hallway's chill, looking very pale, her eyelids translucent and bluish, like seashells. "What do we do?" she asked Abby.

"She can't go on living among the rest of the inmates. Poor girl or not, we simply cannot put the others in danger."

"We don't know for certain she's killed anyone."

"We know she did something wretched to Pearl. Though *how* she did it confounds me." *These individuals wield great power and can present a danger . . .* Suddenly, something seemed to be crawling, on spindly legs, up the back of Abby's neck. She swatted the base of her hair.

A gust of wind hit the building, making its joists strain, its bones creak.

"Glory be," Euphemia muttered. "Can it be real? Mesmerism?"

"You know better than that, Euphemia." Abby stood shorter than her friend, but her voice was louder. "We shall take her to the tower room. She'll be safe there while we decide what to do."

They found Faith with her face set in an expression of resolve, holding her bedding and change of clothes. Quietly, the three of them walked past the nursery; its open doors revealed a nurse bouncing a mewling baby, and, behind her, rows of soft cots with sleeping infants inside. Abby looked over her shoulder to see Faith peering at them.

The stairs to the third floor were narrower than those to the second, turning at an octagonal window inside the tower. Behind her, Abby heard Faith reach the window and pause, looking out over Bryant Avenue with a sigh.

"Same view as before," Abby told her. "Come along."

The tower room felt drafty, with slat flooring and a narrow bed. The floor, walls, and ceiling were all painted the same shade of pale gray. The tall window did offer a pleasant view facing east and would provide warming sunlight in the morning, and there was a lamp and a little table with a Bible inside the drawer.

Euphemia stood in the middle of the floor, still rubbing her arms. Faith set her things on the bed.

"I shall ask Miss Rhoades to bring you water, and an apple or two from the cellar," Abby said. Her voice felt overly noisy. It echoed in the bare space. "And a rag rug. That'll help."

Faith sat on the bed and studied her shoes. Looking at her huddled, narrow shoulders, Abby had to remind herself that this person was likely a murderer and that this room far surpassed the comfort of a prison cell or, heaven forbid, the grip of the hangman's noose.

"I'll tell Cook she'll be down another set of hands in the kitchen for a while. It's for the best," Abby said when Faith appeared alarmed. "Miss Rhoades will bring you supper later."

Faith licked her lips. Then her mouth fell open and she gasped, remembering something. "May," she said.

It was the first Abby had ever heard her speak, her voice soft, unexpected, more than a little infuriating—why hadn't she deigned to say anything in her defense a moment ago, only to use her breath on her roommate's name now? "We'll tell May, don't worry."

But where was May? Abby opened the door and peered down toward the empty staircase. May had been the one to come and get them, and then she'd disappeared. Abby turned to say farewell to Faith and saw the girl holding Euphemia's skirt and crying.

"May," Faith said, shaking her head. "You must find May. Don't let her leave."

"What do you mean?" Euphemia asked, her face stricken.

"It's all right, child," Abby told her, trying to sound soothing. "We'll make sure you have a chance to say goodbye to May before she moves on."

Faith buried her face in her hands.

Abby could still hear her sobbing as she went out with Euphemia and closed the door behind her. For a moment, she hesitated, wondering if she should lock it. She and Euphemia stared at the keyhole. Something told Abby that Faith would not be tempted to escape.

Finally, Euphemia let out a breath. "This is one of the saddest mornings I've spent here. I feel used up. Need to go home and lie down."

"Mrs. Mendenhall? Mrs. Overlock? What have you done with Faith?"

Abby looked up to see Beth Rhoades charging up the stairs, her brows pinched together in concern. Her hand went to her heart when she came closer and could hear Faith moaning: "May, May! May! May . . ."

"She's in the tower room. She'll be safe there." Abby began walking down to the second story, Euphemia in tow. Euphemia had her fan out, wafting air at her face. "Please, bring Faith a pitcher of water and some spare linens."

"The tower room?" Miss Rhoades followed them. "Where we put Ida Leeds when she was hearing voices? Why would you send Faith there? Bad spirits in that tower."

"Beth." Abby stopped, now that they were out of Faith's earshot. "The eyebrow."

Miss Rhoades's eyes shifted. "I know, Mrs. Mendenhall. It's troubling. If we could hear her side of the story . . ."

"But we can't hear her side of the story, that's the problem. That's why I've decided to keep her sheltered in the tower."

Miss Rhoades looked pained, no doubt thinking of her mute sister. But her sister had never committed homicide! How could Abby make Miss Rhoades see this her way? Everyone benefited from Faith's isolation, even Faith herself. Abby felt comforted by the idea of her sequestered—relieved, even. The girl she'd worried over the most these last several weeks was now safely ensconced, like an insect in amber. The tower afforded privacy, and the gift of time.

The matron's lower lip trembled. "It's just—it's gotten so cold. The tower . . ."

"The tower is perfectly comfortable."

"In her condition?"

"Her condition isn't something we've been able to verify. Perhaps there's some truth to the rumors, and this is another ghost pregnancy." Was this actually what Abby believed? She swallowed hard, her own words like a bitter medicine she had to force down.

"Just because you've gotten that wrong in the past," Miss Rhoades said quietly, "doesn't mean you've done so now."

The words were like a slap. Abby felt her knees nearly buckle beneath her.

"Miss Rhoades," said Euphemia curtly, "remember your station."

"My apologies, Mrs. Mendenhall," Miss Rhoades said, her face scarlet.

"Quite all right," Abby said in a hurry. She thought about what Euphemia had said, about wanting to lie down. Another blast of wind hit the house, along with a peppering of freezing rain, the sound like buckshot. "Miss Rhoades, make yourself useful and find May Lombard. Let her know she can stay a little longer. We don't need Room Sixteen sitting completely empty, now, do we?"

The matron nodded, an enthusiastic affirmative. Euphemia looked relieved. They'd be keeping May close, giving Faith what she'd asked for.

"Now, if you'll excuse me," Abby said, the joints in her legs still threatening to give out, "I must retire for the afternoon."

16
MAY

$\mathcal{S}$omeone to care for. Someone who needed her. It was all May had ever wanted, yet now that she'd figured out a way to take care of Hal, she felt racked with guilt.

Miss Rhoades called to her just as she stepped from the front walk onto the curb, and May whirled around in terror, certain she'd been caught. She squeezed her pocketbook tightly under her arm.

"May!" Miss Rhoades ran to her, arms bunched to protect herself from the cold. Bits of ice dusted the shoulders of her plain black dress; she hadn't bothered to put on a shawl or replace her house shoes. "I've been looking everywhere for you, child. Where are you going?"

"I..." May blinked the freezing rain, quickly turning to snow, from her eyelashes. She watched Miss Rhoades look her up and down, taking in the worsted-wool skirt, another item pinched from the charity closet. In the commotion surrounding Pearl and Faith, once Pearl had retreated to her room and Mrs. Mendenhall and Mrs. Overlock had taken Faith away—after May had stolen down to Mrs. Mendenhall's office—May had been able to slip back into her room and change.

"I'm going to see a friend," she said, teeth chattering.

"A friend?" Miss Rhoades looked at her with infuriating concern. "I hope this is a true friend, not someone who'll . . . who will use you badly, May."

Miss Rhoades's tone suggested she might know how it felt to be used. Through the scant snow, May studied the matron: her long, thin hands with careworn knuckles, her knobby arms, the large bun at the base of her neck, yellower than the gray at her crown. No one here, from the board down to the smallest child, really looked at Miss Rhoades as anything beyond a means to an end: the helpmeet who kept schedules and broke up quarrels, who could produce a clean handkerchief or wipe away vomit. There were rumors about her: she'd once been a governess to a wealthy family in the Finger Lakes; she spoke French and Lakota and played the piano masterfully; she'd been raised in Indian territory and ran away from her rough-handed husband, a fur trapper. Not all these tales could be true, of course. May wondered now if the matron's background, in fact, looked a lot more like the inmates' than anyone suspected.

She lifted her chin. "He's my betrothed, Miss Rhoades. You needn't concern yourself."

"Oh." Miss Rhoades's expression changed, though May couldn't read it. "Well, that is grand. I just meant to say you don't need to resort to old ways of sustaining yourself. Mrs. Mendenhall has decided—"

"I'll hear no more of this." Abruptly, May turned and began walking toward the tram stop. She was being rude, yes, but Hal would be waiting for her, and she couldn't very well treat him rudely, could she? Her face burned in the biting cold.

Miss Rhoades called her name a few times, but her voice got lost and distorted in the wind. "You can stay for as long as you'd

like, May! That's all I meant. May! Please don't stay out too late!
We'll need you to help prepare . . ."

May crossed the street, walking in a hurry, chin to her chest.
When she finally turned around to look at the home from a safe
distance, she saw that Miss Rhoades had gone inside.

A dowry. That was what the money she'd stolen would amount
to. A sort of hope chest she'd provide herself, in the absence of a
proper offering from her family. It was Faith's money, she knew,
but Faith didn't seem to want it. May might as well put it to
good use.

She'd had a hope chest once, a modest but respectable collec-
tion of embroidered pillowcases, eyelet napkins with a matching tablecloth, crocheted afghan blankets, and five pairs of knit
socks. One set had been meant for a future, imagined baby:
pale-green booties with a matching bonnet. She and her mother
had prepared it all together, when it had seemed she would
marry Enzo, before she'd fallen pregnant. What had happened
to it? Had Emmanuel ever worn the booties? May would never
know. She'd had to surrender everything when she left the city.

She felt wistful when she remembered Enzo, the way his
smooth arms, tanned from working outdoors, cradled her naked
torso as they kissed. Thanks to Enzo, she knew how tender life
could be. Also, how tragic. She couldn't help looking on her
memories of Enzo with wrath in her heart as well. He'd moved
on to a new girl, a fresh, innocent one with a trousseau of her
own, while May's life had never recovered from the mistake she'd
made: loving him with too much fervor.

She reached the streetcar stop before Hal did and stood beside the post, keeping herself moving to stay warm as she watched carriages cut through the slush. What did passing strangers think of her, a woman alone on the street? What did Hal think of her? He'd called her a rogue, but presumably he still assumed he'd be getting a virgin bride, a young woman of no more than twenty-one or twenty-two who'd just left her home in Chicago to find work in a different city. It was a common story: hordes of girls poured in from farms and small towns, lured by the high demand for domestic labor in booming Minneapolis and St. Paul.

In actuality, May was nearly twenty-five and far from inexperienced. She'd been living here on her own for over three years.

Across the street, another girl came to huddle at the tram stop, waiting to travel in the other direction; her head was uncovered, which likely meant she was very poor. May stared at the girl's plain dishwater-colored hair, the red tip of her downturned nose. She wondered how long the girl had been here and if she'd yet turned bitter. May knew how the story went: girl arrives in the city with high hopes, but quickly realizes that the life of a scullery maid—or a weaver in a textile factory, or a wool scalder, working for ninety cents a day with hands reddened, lye-stained, and swollen—can be a fate worse than death.

How long would it take for this girl, plain and skinny as she was, to decide that brothel work would be preferable? The hours, after all, were superior, the pay and living conditions more comfortable.

How long until this girl's turn in the Bethany Home?

A set of black wheels pulled to the curb, right at her toes, and May realized she'd been watching snowflakes fall on the dark fringe at the edge of her shawl. Perfect, innocent, oblivious snowflakes showing off their lacy points, melting into the wool without a care.

Now here was Hal, handsome, red-cheeked, and merry. How had she ever considered him second best? He rubbed his hands together and blew into them. "Get in, daft girl. I've a warmer on the seat."

She laughed and flung herself in beside him. He slapped the horse's back with the reins, and they took off. May made a point of not looking at the girl as they passed her. She exhaled. She felt so relieved to have a carriage to climb into that she put her hand on Hal's thigh and planted a kiss on his cheek. "I have a surprise for you, darling," she told him, and his mustache twitched. He smacked the horse to go faster.

"You brought the pistol, didn't you?" he asked her, eyes on the road.

"I did. I brought something else as well."

She'd braced herself for his apartment to be a disappointment— that's what the money was for, to purchase them a proper home—so she was surprised to find the Ozark Flats clean and elegant, fixed with electrical lamps in the corridors and up-to-date plumbing in the units. The housemaid had left a basket with two pumpkin muffins and a pot of butter beside Hal's door—yes, the building employed one housemaid, he informed May, and a rather disgusting custodian—along with a note asking if he'd like her to clean his apartment on Wednesday.

"Of course, I'd damn well like her to clean," he muttered. "It's her job, isn't it?"

"How grand, to have a maid," May said.

"None of them last long here. Two, three months at best."

May stood in the center of his large living room, still in her boots, hat, and gloves, feeling out of place. The warmth in the apartment hadn't yet penetrated her cold, stiff clothing. The apartment occupied a big corner of the first floor, with tall windows arched at the tops. Heavy taupe curtains provided privacy. She let her fingers drift over the surface of his small dining table. The furniture was sparse but respectable, though there were few pieces of art on the walls and even a couple of empty hooks.

"This is rather charming," she said, looking through his window at the snow-dusted city. How did someone who claimed to be in perpetual debt afford this? "It all feels very modern."

He shrugged and made a face. "My father owns the building."

"Your father! Do you not pay rent?"

He crouched before the fireplace and began propping up kindling and logs, twisting old newspaper. "What's it to you?" he snapped. Something about this seemed to bother him—his father's ownership of the block of flats—though it made no sense to May. And why would he have described it as a rough place to live?

"Nothing," May replied hastily. "Only, I do feel foolish now."

"Why is that?" He touched a match to the newspaper and stuffed it under the kindling. Shaking the smoke from the match, he stood up and pinned her with those beautiful blue eyes.

He'd stopped moving, leaving the two of them with nothing to do but stand facing each other. May felt the weight of his presence and hers, filling the space like a ringing in her ears. All she had to do was take one step forward and reach out her hand, and then she'd be touching him. The magnitude of what they'd come here to do together hung between them, made them break into nervous laughter.

She had to do something. She fiddled in her carpetbag until she found the money pouch, and she handed it to him.

He weighed it, first, in his big hand, then took out the gold and counted it: a bit more than seventy dollars in specie. She held her breath. He fanned the greenbacks—ten five-dollar bills—studied them closely, said nothing.

"I thought we could use this to set up house," she said shyly. "Unless you're obligated to stay here." She had to sneak a glance at the ruby ring he'd given her to steel herself. He wanted this. He wanted her. Didn't he?

"Where did you get this much money?"

May licked at the dry patches on her bottom lip. Hal came to put his hand on her shoulder.

"You can tell me, May. I won't judge you for it."

"I took it from my roommate," she whispered.

He didn't move, just looked at the money for a while, blinking his golden eyelashes. At last, the hint of a dimple appeared in his right cheek, and then he broke into a full grin and turned those impish, sparkling eyes on her.

"Oh, you've made me very happy, May. Very happy indeed."

"Have I?" She smiled widely, relieved.

He nodded. "Oh, yes." He put the money back into its bag on the table, and then he pulled May into his arms and kissed her. "Come here," he growled, half closing his eyes in something like hunger, and tugged her into the dark cocoon of his bedroom.

Half an hour later, May studied the gray light slipping around the curtains and wondered what time it was. The girls at the home would be busy in preparations for the Thanksgiving feast in two days' time, rolling piecrusts and roasting apples. Afterward, they'd go up to bed, chatting, wiping their floury hands on one another's aprons, and sharing nips of cooking sherry.

By God, she wanted to go home.

As with so many of her life's disappointments, she'd expected intimacy with Hal to be one thing, and found it to be quite another. She had worried he'd be able to tell she was no virgin, and feared what he might think of her body, if he'd notice the faint white scars striping her belly below the navel, where she'd stretched to carry Emmanuel.

But Hal hadn't seemed to look at her much at all. As a lover, he'd been quick, perfunctory, leaving her vastly unsatisfied. He hadn't done any of the things men could do to ensure that women had a good time; instead, he yanked her this way and that, dragging her leg here and turning her torso there in uncomfortable and near-painful ways. It was all she could do not to cry out. Meanwhile, his face had taken on a sort of blank expression, a ferocity; he'd vanished into a fog of his own pleasure and seemed almost not to notice she was still in the room. After they shed their clothing, he hadn't even bothered to kiss her.

At first, she'd tried to shut her eyes and picture the bright young man she'd once supposed him to be, the one she had first encountered at church and longed for so profoundly. She was with that young man now, she reminded herself. She should enjoy this.

When that failed, she'd gone to the maple grove.

It was an old trick she'd learned to use, in moments when she no longer wanted to be with her body. She'd picture the underside of maple leaves, backlit by sunlight, and promise herself: *One day, someday, you'll actually be there.* She wasn't sure where the image of the maples had originally come from: A park near her childhood home? A line from a book, made real by her own imagination? Whatever the source, it worked. In uncomfortable moments, she could easily go there, to rest under the maples in early summer, staring up at the veined backs of fresh green leaves, and feeling the sun on her face. One day she would be there, and all this would be behind her.

Hal turned onto his back now and crossed his naked legs, looking down admiringly at his spent, stubby member. He'd pulled a cheroot cigar from his nightstand, and now the air filled with the tangy odor of cherry wood. Smoking, he wiggled his toes, tufted with blond hair. She pulled the sheet to her chin and inched away from him.

"The pistol," he said, scratching himself. "Where do you have it?"

"It's in my little carpetbag," she said, gesturing toward the living space.

He flung himself out of bed and, after a few long steps, was in the parlor, rummaging through her belongings with the cigar clenched in his teeth. Then he came right back, twirling the revolver alarmingly on one of his index fingers. The barrel gleamed.

"Fantastic, a Grape Shot!" he cried. "You've outdone yourself, May. Look at these charming engravings. No mistaking a lady's handgun, is there?"

She watched him pull open the top drawer of his shiny wooden dresser and place the gun there. She sat up against the pillow, still clinging to the sheet and quilt. "What are you doing? I thought you were going to help me load it."

He flung himself back into bed with enough force to drop ash. She worried he'd set the sheets on fire.

"I'm too tired, can't you see? Pipe down, you'll get it back." He blew a sharp breath toward a lock of hair that had fallen across his forehead. "Why don't you tell me a story about yourself? Tell me something you've never told anyone. Go on, I'm feeling bored."

The fire in the living room made a loud popping sound. He wanted her to make him feel important by trusting him with a secret. She knew from experience that this sort of exchange made certain men feel powerful. What could she say? She could tell him she lived in the Bethany Home. She could tell him about Emmanuel. But she wanted to do neither of these things, and she wondered what that meant. Was she afraid of scaring him away? Or was she afraid of him?

She could tell him she was a liar. Or she could simply lie.

"My name isn't May Lombard," she said after a pause. "May was a neighbor of mine, back in Chicago. A girl a few years older than I was, whom I admired. She seemed to have gotten everything right. I guess I wanted to be her, to give myself a chance to be like her, when I came here. My real name is Susannah Green."

A half-truth.

"Susannah Green," Hal said, in a strange tone. Was he mocking her? "You know, I do like surnames that double as pigments. Susannah Green. Priscilla Black. Do you know who she was?"

May shook her head. The name rang a faint bell of familiarity, but she couldn't place it.

He propped himself onto his elbow, the cigar dangling between his fingers. "She was a madam, one of the worst. A purveyor of flesh. A cheat. Do you know what happened to her?"

His pupils were alarmingly large and black, as though sex

were a drug he'd taken, and now he wasn't himself. May noticed that the light coming around his curtains was beginning to dim.

"No," she said, hoping he wouldn't tell her. She wanted so badly to leave.

"They pulled her body from beneath the paddle wheel of one of the mills. Fish had eaten her eyes." His lips were pulled back in a grimace, eyes alight.

"Oh my, how awful." May tried to make it seem as if she were making light of the situation. She began edging toward the side of the bed, feeling around under the quilt for her drawers. "But why do you care?"

"I don't. Care, that is." He laughed, tossing his head back so that his Adam's apple bobbed in his throat. "I just thought it was interesting."

Her fingers located the plain cotton of her chemise, rougher than his sheets, at the far corner of the bed. She grabbed it and pulled it on. "I really must be going." She made her best attempt at a demure laugh. "Can't let you see me this way much longer, you won't want anything more to do with me."

Why did she want to leave with such urgency? As she finished getting dressed, he watched her from his bed, where he was still lying lazily, drawing on his cigar so that the end glowed orange. He made no move to dress himself, nor did he offer to drive her home in the carriage. Good, she thought. The streetcars were still running. She could get home on her own. Never would she be so glad to see her own bed, to lie on her side and look across the room at Faith's familiar face.

She was fastening the belt on her skirt when Hal said, "You didn't ask me."

"Ask you what?"

He watched her, propped on his elbow. "To tell you something I haven't told anyone."

Slowly, she slipped the end of her belt into the loop. She had to find her shoes. "All right. Go ahead."

Those eyes gleamed black. Not a hint of blue remained around the pupils. He blew out a long stream of smoke, aimed at the ceiling. "Would you believe me if I said I'd killed someone?"

She paused, stocking halfway up her leg. Someone scraped at the snow on the walk outside, a grating, awful sound. She cocked her head at Hal, pretending to go along with a great joke, even though her heart had begun to pound. She yanked the stocking upward.

"Now you're just being funny," she said.

"Am I?" He smirked. "What if I told you I offed a man who cheated me at faro? A foreigner. Someone no one would miss. I put the leg of a chair through his eye and sat on it. You should have seen the blood spurt." He burst out laughing. "His skull cracked like a walnut shell. I guess it is rather funny!"

May tried laughing with him, but the sound that came from her was more of a sob. The way he'd put it—"offed"— as though homicide took no more effort than squishing a fruit fly, or returning a book to the library. She took a step backward, toward the door.

"And once," he continued, "I talked a sporting girl into jumping out her own window." He said it as if he was proud of himself, impressed by his own terrible abilities.

May swallowed hard. She didn't want him to see her cry. "Hal, stop it! You know I don't like horror tales." Why in the world was he trying to scare her? What could he possibly gain? It seemed her fear entertained him, which disturbed her almost as much as what he'd said.

She crossed the threshold into the living room and slipped into her boots without lacing them. Her clumsy fingers found her carpetbag as she kept her eyes on him. "Goodbye, then," she said. "Enjoy your . . ." She swallowed.

Her bag felt so light now. He had her gun, and Faith's money. "Enjoy the afternoon," she said.

His mien shifted, and he tossed back the covers and slid out of bed. "Here, I'll take you home." He found his trousers, in a heap on the floor.

"Oh, no, don't worry yourself." Her hand gripped the doorknob. "I prefer the walk to the streetcar. Fresh air. Look, it's stopped snowing." She looked down to unhitch the lock, then back at him. From the front door she could still see him, sitting on the edge of his bed, trousers hitched to his thighs, watching her with narrowed eyes and a sneer curling his lips. The expression flickered away, as though a hand had flipped a switch. He offered her a benign smile, and his gaze softened.

"Farewell," he called, "my utter darling." He tossed her a kiss as she pushed out into the hallway. She took care to shut the door quietly behind her before running for the exit.

PART III

17

FAITH

For hours now, Faith had been alone in the tower, with little to do but think.

At first, she'd felt relieved to have escaped Pearl's wrath, to have a chance to catch her breath. But it was too quiet in here, or not quiet enough: she could hear infants mewling in the nursery, just beneath her; seamstresses going about their work in the upstairs wing; two girls singing "Daisy Bell" as they swept the stairs. Leigh and Dolly had come up, chattering about the tom turkey Mrs. Overlock had brought for the slaughter, a veteran of the yard whose meat was sure to be tough. Still, they hoped that if they helped kill the old gobbler they'd be entitled to the wishbone.

It was hard to listen to them go about their day as though nothing had changed. Restlessness overtook Faith, then confusion, and finally, after Miss Rhoades came and went with her tray of afternoon tea, anger. She'd assumed the Sisterhood of Bethany were good women, with the inmates' best interests, including Faith's, always at heart.

Yet Mrs. Mendenhall had done exactly what Faith's mother used to when Faith became "disrespectful." What Priscilla Black had done, as well.

To the highest tower with you. To the attic, to your room, for the good of the others.

You're making everyone uncomfortable.

Stay here until I say you can come out.

They'd moved to Faith's uncle's house when she was four, after her father died in a mining explosion in Oliphant Furnace, Pennsylvania. Her mother, Trudy, had initially planned to stay for a while in their little company home, collecting her husband's pension checks until she could afford a house on the seashore in New Jersey. Her dream. But people in town began to whisper: it wasn't appropriate for such a young widow, such a pretty one, to collect her husband's pension, or the life insurance furnished by the company, especially when the boy himself had hardly put three years' worth of work into the mine. Quickly, Faith realized that her mother was seen as dangerous, worse even than the stick of dynamite that had buried her father and two other men in rubble. The other mothers pulled their children away when Faith tried playing. The cashier at the company store refused to let her mother shop. Within a fortnight, her mother had packed their things and hired some cart men and had given a forwarding address to the mining company: her brother Clyde's house, in Buffalo.

The mood those first few days at Clyde's felt celebratory. He and Trudy rejoiced that now they'd be able to share Clyde's post-and-beam home and József's pension checks, which neither of them yet knew would stop coming after three years, the length of József's tenure at the company.

Uncle Clyde commented once, as Faith ran a little wooden truck over the carpet and her chubby baby brother bounced in her mother's lap, that it felt nice to have children in his house. That made Faith pause. Without thinking, she asked: Didn't

Clyde have a wife? What about children of his own? She barely
had a chance to watch her uncle's face darken before her mother
set the baby down and whisked her into the dining room.

"Shut your mouth, Peg," her mother whispered.

Faith had been called "Peg" then, a nickname that didn't
sound anything like "Margaret" but somehow made sense:
a name like a wooden peg, something to hang things on.

Her mother's breath smelled of the corn whiskey she and
Uncle Clyde had been drinking. "Don't mention Nicola again.
Christ, you ask too many questions."

Faith had never heard of Nicola before, and she started to
protest, but her mother gripped her wrist, harder than she ever
had before. "Don't say a word about your father, either. Clyde
never liked him, and you're liable to set him off."

It seemed to Faith that her mother and uncle had actually
been discussing her father a great deal, or at least the money he'd
left all of them in death. But she didn't say this. Over the years,
those long, dreadful years in Buffalo, she learned to speak less
and less. Any subject could set her uncle off, especially when he
was three sheets to the wind. She found herself yanked into that
rarely used dining room more times than she could count.

Don't ask Uncle Clyde what kind of work he does.

*Don't you dare press him to send you to school—do you think he can afford
the books?*

Don't talk so much about Pennsylvania.

Don't talk back.

Don't talk. Don't talk. Don't talk.

When she reached her teenage years and surpassed her mother
in stature, her very presence became intolerable to Clyde, even
in her silence. All she had to do was squint and stare at him a
little too long, and he'd become visibly irritated, scratching at

his neck and hollering for Trudy to check the girl's insolence. And Faith began to realize that this ability to cause such a reaction, even a negative one, was in itself a form of power.

Daylight dwindled in the little empty room. Faith wished she had something to do other than reminisce: some knitting, or a jigsaw puzzle. She fashioned her blanket into a shawl, sat on the hard bed, and watched through the oval window, only the tips of her toes balanced on the frigid wooden floor, waiting for May to return. Miss Rhoades had mentioned that May was out, seeing her beau. The matron had been puzzled when Faith responded with a stifled sob, then bit down on her knuckle to keep from crying out further.

She'd have to find a way to warn May about him. And then maybe she and May could snatch her money from Mrs. Mendenhall's desk and use it to leave this place, together. But where would they go? The police would indeed be looking for Faith, if they cared to investigate Priscilla's death. West, maybe, farther west, into unknown and unclaimed territory.

The snow fell all afternoon, as soft as cottonwood seeds. The tips of the grass, grown golden and dry, grew shorter and shorter and eventually disappeared. On tenterhooks, Faith paced, the floor creaking beneath her; she kept wondering what Hayward could possibly see in May, what good he felt she'd do him. His entanglements, Faith well knew, were exclusively designed to benefit himself. After he got what he wanted from you, he'd throw you out like yesterday's garbage.

Or worse.

The Sunday afternoon when she first sneaked out of the Lundbergs' house with Johnny, Faith had expected to meet the woman he'd mentioned, the one who needed her palm read. Instead, Johnny took her to the West Hotel.

She stood shivering, dripping rainwater on the richly patterned carpet of the lobby, as Johnny handed their coats to the valet. The ceiling soared two floors above her head, buttressed by wide marble columns. Clusters of globe lights gave the room a soft ambience. The hotel rivaled the best in the East, Johnny had told her on the way over, and meant Minneapolis had really come into its own. Behind the front desk, the staff in their brass buttons watched her suspiciously. Trying, she assumed, to know what to make of her in her slate-flannel dress, the only decent one she owned, and the leather boots come all the way from Buffalo and missing a button or two.

She forced herself not to cower, to meet their gazes until they were the ones who looked away. By now, she'd had some practice arranging her face into different expressions to put others off their guard or confuse them. She stared at the bellhop as though she were here to inspect his work, and she watched him clear his throat and tug at the ends of his sleeves.

"Ready?" Johnny said, touching her elbow. She felt a little quiver run through her body. She stood close enough to see a line of hairs he'd missed with the razor, just beneath his bottom lip. "Harry's waiting for us in the lounge."

"Harry?"

Johnny's features softened. "You have an exquisite voice, do you know that? I'm covered in gooseflesh when you speak to me. You should do it more often."

He led the way into the hotel lounge, an extension of the lobby, with two-story-high ceilings and a gallery around the perimeter. The space was quite crowded, with mahogany tables and gray velvet armchairs, and men, dozens and dozens of men.

In the near corner, what looked to be the Park Board were celebrating under a banner and some paper rosettes; a man in a sash gave a toast that Faith couldn't hear over all the laughter, sloshing his glass here and there. The underside of his white mustache and top of his beard were soaked in brown liquor.

As they pushed through the crowd, Faith kept her eyes focused on the back of Johnny's head, his close-cropped hair, his neck. Without turning around, he reached slowly behind him, his fingers seeking hers. She grasped his hand. No one could see them holding hands, his warm fingers held close to her waist. It felt like a secret.

"You said 'Harry,' " she murmured, close to his ear, thinking about what he'd just said about her voice. "I thought your friend was a woman."

Chill bumps rose on the back of his neck. "Harry's the one who needs you to talk to her. Here's the bastard now."

The curse had barely a chance to register when she realized they'd reached the far corner of the room, where an elegantly dressed man sat with his back to the watered-silk wallpaper. Mr. Hayward stood and introduced himself to her, kissed her gloved fingers between the second and third knuckles before they all took a seat, the men facing Faith, she with her back to the room. She could study only her two companions, and her eyes were drawn to Hayward. He possessed a cold kind of beauty, his hair the same shade as the sandy icicles that formed along Lake Erie after a vicious winter storm. His eyes were freshwater ice.

He signaled the waiter and ordered drinks for Johnny and himself. He was the one in charge here, Faith noted, not Johnny. Next to Hayward, Johnny looked like a boy tagging along with his older, more self-assured brother.

"And a Jack Rose for the lady," Hayward told the waiter.

She blinked out of her stupor. She'd been staring at Hayward so intently, she hadn't realized he wanted to order her a mixed drink. She shook her head. "Sarsaparilla," she managed, the first word she'd uttered at the table.

Hayward and Johnny looked vaguely disappointed. Hayward nodded at the waiter, who scurried off. "Johnny tells me you're a medium."

Again, she shook her head.

"A palm reader," Johnny corrected him.

"A palm reader! Even better." Hayward drummed his fingers on the table. "Can you explain to me what a palm reader does?"

She inhaled slowly. The air smelled, quite pleasantly, of cherry tobacco and whiskey barrels. Hayward had his right eye narrowed, the side of his mustache raised in a smirk. She wondered what kind of answer he wanted: the mystical, or the realist.

"I'd like to learn the tricks," he added. Realist, then.

She slid her hand across the table, reaching for his palm. He turned his hand over in hers. "If I were reading your palm . . ." she whispered, and she sensed him react to her voice. His wrist stiffened. He leaned in to hear. ". . . I'd notice that your life line is very short. See—here." With one fingernail she traced a line, scarcely touching his skin. "It's bisected by the line of fate."

Hayward listened keenly. "But would you tell me that if I were a paying customer?"

"No."

"What *would* you tell me?" he asked. Their drinks arrived—a red cocktail garnished with apple and a cherry for each of the men, a bubbly sarsaparilla for her—but nobody touched them. Johnny paid the waiter.

Faith waited, and thought, before responding. What did she know, so far, about Hayward? He wore a white tie and tails, as though he were heading to the opera. He hadn't paid for the drinks; Johnny had. Hayward's hands were softer than Johnny's, the nails manicured.

He needed her to talk to someone, a woman. Presumably, to persuade her to do something that would benefit him.

"I'd say you were about to come into a lot of money." She chose an arbitrary spot in the center of his palm and circled it, gently, with the tip of her index finger. "I can see it right here."

Hayward smiled. He took his hand back and lifted his glass toward Johnny. "She'll do." He clinked cocktails with Johnny, then slid a five-dollar coin across the table. "That's for the palm reading," he told Faith. "Plenty more of that in no time, my dear."

She smiled as she took the coin, and the men beamed back at her.

Shameful, she thought now. It humiliated her, how she'd craved their approval, how good she'd felt just to be with those two handsome young men. The men were beautiful, the hotel was beautiful, *she* had felt beautiful in their presence. More than that, she'd felt needed, appreciated, special—as though she were not at all the same person who'd grown up in that dreadful place near Buffalo, her uncle's house. She felt rewarded, even glorified, in her peculiarity; that which nearly everyone else had tried to snuff out in her, these men wanted to ignite.

When Johnny and Hayward had mentioned they had a room reserved upstairs—for talking, they assured her, to get away

from the noise of the crowd—she'd known what they expected
of her, and she'd gone up with them anyway. She had only herself to blame for that. She'd wanted to forestall her return to
the endless drudgery of domestic work. And curiosity, she supposed, had gotten the better of her; she wanted to see how the
men planned to impress her, for she had a sense that both were
eager to win her admiration. She'd have preferred to be alone
with Johnny, but Hayward intrigued her with his mysterious,
dangerous charm, and after a cocktail—eventually, they'd worn
her down and ordered her that Jack Rose—she found herself
squeezed between them in the elevator, the doors rolling shut,
the reflections of all their faces flushed and expectant in the
polished brass.

It hadn't been her first intimate exposure to men. Once you'd
broken that dam, it was easy to do it again. There'd been her
neighbor, Brooks, in Buffalo, and the young stevedore she'd
sneaked out in the middle of the night to see. But both had been
mere boys, amateurish and nervous in their affections. Hayward
and Johnny knew what they were doing. They'd started by kissing her on the white skin of her long neck, one on each side
of her, making her quiver. Under their touch, she felt like the
queen of Minnesota.

She knew now that they'd been testing her, lulling her. Preparing her for something else. Unfortunately, she'd passed the
test.

Faith's stomach twisted. She sat up, remembering that
Miss Rhoades had left her a few sheets of stationery. She
couldn't write very well, her education having ended in primary
school, but she reached for the paper now. Her belly was becom-
ing heavier; though its charge was invisible on the outside, it felt

like a medicine ball on the inside. She scooted across her mattress and dipped the nib in the inkwell.

Mae, she wrote. *Haward is no good. Trust me don't see hem agin. Your frend, Fathe*

After a moment, she added a postscript:

I have money and can help. Come, please come, to the towr.

18

MAY

A man followed her home from Hal's apartment. Not Hal himself, but an older fellow, one with a slight limp. A heavy-set man with sloping shoulders. While May stopped to wait for a streetcar heading south, he lingered several yards away; when she got on and headed for a seat toward the rear of the car, he boarded as well and sat near the front. She watched, her pulse fluttering in her throat, as the man looked closely at everyone who departed at each station stop. A couple of times, he turned around, his dull eyes surveying the crowd at the back of the car, possibly to make sure she was still there. She couldn't see his features—he had a muffler wrapped around his face, protecting his nose and mouth from the cold, but her imagination tried to convince her this was the man who'd attacked her.

May closed her eyes. Some of Hal was still with her, leaking into her drawers. If only she could wash herself, once she finally returned home, scrub him from her skin, but she wasn't due for a bath for a couple of days.

A terrifying thought soured her stomach. What if Hal truly had left a piece of himself inside her, one you couldn't rinse away, a cretinous little copy of its father? She felt as if she'd gone to bed with a human man, only to have him peel back his skin afterward and reveal the monster that had been lurking underneath all along. She squirmed, rubbing the backs of her thighs against the seat, desperate to rid herself of any trace of him. Perhaps another of the inmates kept a ladies' syringe, in secret—but how could she ask?

Just in time, she remembered to pull the cord for her stop. The car had emptied, with only a quarter of its passengers remaining this far down Bryant; when she stood, she saw that the rotund man still sat near the front. The streetcar lurched to a stop, and she stumbled forward, slipping on the wet floor. She was too afraid to get a good look at him as she hurried for the door. A million pins pricked the back of her neck—she was sure he had followed her—as she stumbled clumsily down the steps and onto the sidewalk, toward the looming peaks of the Bethany Home, perched on its little hill. She heard the bell clang and the streetcar pull away. When she'd reached the home's front gate, she allowed herself to glance behind her, one hand gripping the safety of the cold wrought iron.

No one else had disembarked. She felt a bit better—until she realized that anyone watching would have seen her climbing the steps to the gate. He'd know where she lived. She took a moment to catch her breath, snowflakes landing in her eyelashes. Night had nearly overtaken the street. The lamplighters had already been through.

Her boots heavy on her feet, she climbed the porch steps and hauled open the door. The lights in the parlor were dimmed. Most of the inmates had retreated to their rooms after supper, but the lamps blazed in the parlor. Tiptoeing, she took the stairs two at a time and reached her room unnoticed.

Or so she thought. She'd just walked in to find her room

strangely empty, Faith's bed stripped and belongings gone, when she felt a tap on her shoulder. With a gasp she spun to meet a gaunt face, framed by the dim light in the corridor.

"Leigh?" She put her hand to her heart. "You scared me out of my wits. Where's Faith?"

Leigh peeled open May's fingers and placed a folded square of paper inside. "That's what I came to talk to you about. Miss Rhoades just had me bring her dinner, and she gave me this note for you. They put her up in the tower room for a spell. Remember Ida?"

May felt queasy thinking of Ida, who'd been known to shout curses uncontrollably, as though possessed by a wandering spirit. "Of course I do," she snapped. "Why'd they send Faith there? Because of Pearl?"

"I reckon so." Leigh gave herself a little hug, peering at Faith's empty bed. "Seems harsh, doesn't it? Pearl'll survive."

May pressed her knuckles to her breastbone, trying to quell her beating heart. "Yes, I suppose she will."

"Some of us can't help but feel Pearl got what was coming to her." There was something else in Leigh's words, something she wasn't saying outright. It almost felt like an apology.

Still, May wished Leigh would leave, but she seemed to be waiting for May to read the note. May turned her back and scanned it quickly. Her throat tightened. Faith had offered her the very money May had just given to Hal.

Haward, as she called him, was *no good*.

How did she know? What had she to do with Hal? What had he done to her?

May would have to think before she went to see Faith. Perhaps it was good they'd put her in the tower; she'd be safe there, and May could avoid her questions.

She crumpled the note into the tightest ball it could form. "You didn't read it, did you?"

"I'm no sneak. Why, what'd it say?"

"Nothing." May went to the wastebasket and stuffed the paper to the bottom, as Leigh watched. "She said to tell Pearl she's sorry."

For the next two days, May busied herself in preparation for Thanksgiving dinner, grateful for the distraction from her murky thoughts about Hal and Faith. Nobody seemed to notice that the money had gone missing, and no one mentioned May's impending departure, not even Mrs. Mendenhall, who fretted about, looking grayish and wearier than usual.

The dinner, Cook told the kitchen crew, would be simpler than in previous years, what with the financial panic and the need to tighten their belts. The board members would not skimp on the turkey, because it was a nod to the pilgrims. Besides that, they'd serve oyster fritters with cranberry sauce, chestnut stuffing, celery salad dressed in mayonnaise, and mince pies with brandy butter, the children's favorite. Only the donors and board would get mock-turtle soup, specially prepared by Cook, and the girls would have pumpkin pudding. The guests would be served in the first-floor drawing room, the inmates and children down in the cellar, as usual. Both were to be decorated with boughs of grass and red leaves, potted chrysanthemums from the Mendenhalls' greenhouses, and garlands of dried apples and cranberries.

Wednesday afternoon, May sat in the parlor with some kitchen girls, Dolly and a few new arrivals, stringing dried cranberries with a needle and thread. The newer ones were all visibly pregnant, their stomachs bloated, their bosoms pressed high to their necklines. May tried not to stare at them, or at Dolly, who gave off a sweet, milky smell.

May sat apart from the rest, who whispered and snickered together. She felt her face turn the color of the cranberries she worked onto the string. How did a crop of new arrivals already consider her untouchable? She wiped the corner of her eye with the back of her hand and then caught a strange sound, a sort of moaning, coming from upstairs.

She stiffened. One of the new inmates, a girl called Carmen, looked up.

"That's a strong wind," she commented, as the house creaked and shifted.

"It isn't the wind," Dolly muttered. "It's her."

"Who?" Carmen replied. "The one in the tower?"

Their needles all stopped working for a moment as they looked to May, the ghost girl's roommate. She could hear tendrils of wind whipping at the western side of the building, but beneath that, there was something else: a woman keening, the instrument of her grief plucking out a single note, over and over again: "May, May, May."

"It's nothing," May said quickly and loudly. "Just the wind." They blinked at her. "She doesn't speak, remember?"

"That's a lie," Dolly said. "I've seen her speak to you."

May gathered up her half-finished garland and trounced to the cellar steps, making as much noise as she could. "Cook said she needed more hands shucking oysters," she called, by way of explanation. The others just stared at her.

The stairs groaned and creaked as she made her way to the kitchen. By the time she reached the bottom, she'd convinced herself she hadn't heard Faith at all. "You're a sight for sore eyes," Cook said when she came in. Her stout forearms were

204 · CAROLINE WOODS

coated in flour. "I've a can of eggshells and apple peels that need to go out before they set to stinking—would you mind?"

"Not at all," May said, glad for a reason to step outside. She slipped her feet into a pair of loose, well-worn boots beside the back door and hauled the galvanized metal can up the back steps. She remembered with a lurch that Faith and Tuva used to sit out here, not so long ago.

The ground was icy, the walk to the larger trash bins coated with slush, and she had an eye on her boots, her tongue poking from the side of her mouth in her concentration, when she heard someone call her name.

"Well, there you are, Miss Lombard."

Her eyes shot up. Standing beside the back fence, near the garbage bins, were Hal and Johnny Lundberg.

She set down the can and stared at them. The wind whipped through her thin calico sleeves, pressing the fabric to the skin of her arms.

"What in . . ." She swallowed. "How'd you know where to find me?"

Both men offered her a smile in response. Johnny's appeared sincere, Hal's more simpering. They looked infinitely warmer than she felt, both in top hats and thick wool overcoats, Johnny's with a shearling collar. Snow crunching under their winter boots, they took a few steps forward. When she flinched, Hal held up both hands, the fingers of his white kid gloves spread wide to show he meant no harm, as though he were approaching a deer.

"Don't murder me, but I had you followed," he said. "I know, I could have just asked where you live, but I wasn't sure I'd get the answer. You've nothing to be ashamed of, my darling; plenty of fine girls come through here. We've known some."

"You . . ." May began breathing very quickly, her lungs a set of bellows. "You had me followed." She hadn't been imagining it, on the streetcar. She didn't belong in the loony bin. She wanted to grasp the cold metal lid of the garbage can and use it to smash his face.

Hal stood right in front of her now, close enough for her to see his pale eyes reflect the flat white clouds overhead. "I'd grown impatient, you see, having to wait to see you at church. May, darling, you look well!"

Her hand went to her cheek, surely ruddy from the cold, and smoothed her hair in its plain knot. She could have kicked herself for caring what she looked like to Hal.

"Also, I wanted to give you this." He reached into his jacket, inside the overcoat, and pulled out a long, thin ticket, which he laid in her bare hand. He grinned, his eyes twinkling. "An early Christmas present, darling. We're going to the theater next week."

"Pence Opera House," May murmured, reading the scrolly words aloud. "A special evening performance of *A Trip to Chinatown.*"

"You can tell your friends it's no cheap seat," Hal said. "Go ahead and boast: your man Hayward's taking you out to a fine evening. You see, May? I'm not ashamed of you, no matter where you live."

May thought of the girls inside who wouldn't speak to her or even glance at her, of the look that would pass over Pearl's face when May sauntered out to the opera. Then she peered up at Hal, his handsome face framed by the silk brim of his hat. He was beaming, absolutely elated with himself, believing, as he did, that he could tell her he'd beaten a man to death and had her followed and that she'd still drop everything for the chance to take his arm.

"No," she replied.

Hal's mustache dropped an inch. "Excuse me?"

"No, thank you." She handed him back the ticket, then gently nudged him aside so that she could haul the trash to the bins. If her father could see her now, she hoped he'd be proud. "Why don't you take Kitty Ging instead?"

Hal seemed enraged to hear Kitty's name. He thundered after May, the snow crunching under his boots, while her blood pounded so mercilessly in her temples that she almost couldn't see. "What an ungrateful bitch you turned out to be, May Lombard, or Susannah Green, or whatever the hell your name is. I take you out to eat, I give you a *ruby ring*, I book you prime seats at the opera, and how do you repay me?"

May's teeth were set on edge. She tried to do her job and dump the contents of the can into the bin, but only succeeded in dropping slimy eggshells into the snow as Hal yelled in her face, spraying her with spittle. Johnny threw an arm in front of Hal, whispering for his friend to back down, go easy.

Hal shrugged Johnny off and straightened his sleeves, his collar. "You're making a grave mistake, May. Who are you without Harry T. Hayward?"

May's neck went hot. He was right, she was nothing without him, she had nowhere to go after this, and no friends. But maybe she'd be less than nothing with him. She'd taken a big gulp of air, trying to steady her heart before she replied, when Johnny cleared his throat.

"Forget the opera," he said in a low voice. "What I need is to see Margie. I know she's hiding out here."

"Margie?" May searched the corners of her mind. She wanted them to leave so vehemently, she might have told Johnny anything he wanted. "There are no Margies here."

"I think you know her. Dark hair, freckled, doesn't say much?"

A lead weight dropped in May's stomach. She hesitated a beat too long, shook her head.

"So you do know her," Hal said, smiling, his pale eyes locked on hers.

"Please, May," said Johnny, who reached for her wrist and clamped down with more force than she'd expected. "Margie's in serious trouble. I only want to help."

"I told you," May said, trying to shake his grip. "I don't know a Margie."

"I see what's happened here." Hal took a step forward. "She's got you under one of her spells, doesn't she?"

May shook her head, hard. Johnny tightened his fingers on her arm, twisting the skin the way her cousin used to. "Indian burn," he'd shout when she cried out in pain.

"May." Hal had come close enough to touch her cheek again. "I'll let you in on a little secret." He bent down so that his lips touched her ear, his mustache tickling the lobe. "I taught her everything she knows."

May's eyes fluttered shut for a moment. Faith really had known him. Before her eyes, May could see Faith's childlike handwriting: *No good, no good, no good.*

He pulled back, but he was still holding her right arm, and Johnny had a grip on her left. Hal wore a satisfied expression on his face, smiling down smugly at her. He brushed a stray hair out of her face. "Now I know you'll bring her to me. You're a good girl, May, and you'll bring her to me. She's in danger, Margie. She's done something very bad. Only we can help her."

Hal's eyes were the exact same color as the sky. May had never noticed that before. It was as if he had two holes bored into his face, and she was looking straight through to the clouds beyond. She wanted to look away, but she couldn't. She was so tired.

A warning bell sounded somewhere far away, deep in the recesses of her soul, but she couldn't heed it.

"You'll bring the girl to me, May. I know you will. You know you will."

The back of her scalp tingled at the sound of his voice, followed by a rush of gooseflesh trickling down her spine and the backs of her arms. She found that she was nodding.

The back door of the home banged open, and rapidly both men let go of her. May staggered backward. Through her blurred vision, she watched a sturdy figure dressed in black step outside.

"Mr. Lundberg." Mrs. Mendenhall, her voice like a cool glass of water. "Mr. Hayward?"

The men transformed, brushed off their coats. May's jaw dropped an inch upon hearing their names in Mrs. Mendenhall's mouth. Her presence, nevertheless, would be May's salvation. Johnny turned to tip his hat. Hal tugged at his collar, gave May a final sinister glare, then swung his wide shoulders toward the house, smiling.

"Mrs. Mendenhall," he cooed. "Season's greetings to you."

"It's not Christmas yet," Mrs. Mendenhall retorted, eyeing them warily. Heart pounding, skin still flecked with gooseflesh, May snatched up the metal trash bin lying on its side, and its lid, then ran down the cellar steps to stand behind Mrs. Mendenhall.

"What can I do for you?" Mrs. Mendenhall called. "I hope you aren't still after that tour."

Tour? May trembled uncontrollably. Now that she stood closer to Mrs. Mendenhall, she could hear a slight tremor in the older woman's voice; she, too, was nervous. Her bony hand shook a little as it gripped the iron stair rail.

"Oh, no," Hal replied smoothly. "We were simply in the neighborhood and thought we'd see if our money's been put to good use." He pointed up. "You've swifts nesting in the eaves. Wouldn't want them to cause any damage."

"Thank you. I'll have my husband, or the gardener, take a look. They're here all the time. Good day, gentlemen." Mrs. Mendenhall turned abruptly, shooing May inside, and both hurried into the kitchen. Cook and Leigh had gone silent as they watched Mrs. Mendenhall lock the door, their work momentarily forgotten.

"What did those men say to you?" Mrs. Mendenhall asked May. Wires of her white hair spewed from her cap, and a web of pink capillaries stood out in her wan cheeks. "I don't like them nosing about."

"They said . . ." May's head spun. She wanted to tell Mrs. Mendenhall that Faith might be in trouble, but something stopped her.

It wasn't real—Mesmerism—it couldn't be. Yet she felt as if Hal had tied strings to her limbs, to her tongue. A stream of lies snaked from her mouth as though they'd been charmed by a flute.

"They said they left something here, last time they visited." May's mouth felt dry. Now Mrs. Mendenhall might tell her why she'd encountered Hal and Lundberg before.

Mrs. Mendenhall's rheumy eyes narrowed. "Their donations. Perhaps they meant to retrieve them, now Pratt's been elected. Those serpents." She blinked at May, as though she'd forgotten May was here. "That'll be all, Miss Lombard; hurry along."

May turned and bolted back up the cellar steps, her face on fire.

19

ABBY

*A*bby spent the night before Thanksgiving in a restless sleep, her legs tangled in her damp sheets.

She fell, hard, from what felt like a great height: in her dream she'd been perched on a high table, splayed on a platter like roasted fowl, Mrs. Van Cleve and Miss Rhoades hovering about her with knives, prepared to carve her up. She sat up gasping, still in her bed, and glad she and Junius had long been sleeping in separate chambers. She reached for the little German clock on her nightstand: just past four in the morning.

She went to her dressing table to pour a glass of water and lit the lamp. In the amber light, her gray hair hanging loose past her shoulders, she studied her reflection in the looking glass. Her scant brows formed a troubled peak above the bridge of her nose. All her life she'd longed to resemble her dear mother, but it was her father's face that stared back at her in the mirror, weathered and wrinkled; while his visage had been battered by the sea, Abby's was mottled from years of worry.

She closed her eyes, listening for the still, small voice. When at last she heard it, she nodded.

Faith should attend the holiday supper with the other girls. Little harm could come from that. The next morning, however, Abby would have to turn the girl over to the police. When she'd undertaken this work, she'd promised herself to be firm but kind. To be firm *was* to be kind. The two were inextricable.

The frown in her forehead had slackened. Perhaps the police would determine that Faith had had nothing to do with Priscilla Black's death, and the girl could come home.

In any case, it wasn't up to Abby to decide.

After she made her resolution, she felt better. She even enjoyed hosting the tea reception in advance of Thanksgiving dinner, which usually drained her; she preferred not to spend so much time on her feet. With their guests—four couples, all longtime benefactors, plus Officer Nye and his wife—she admired the needlepoint and embroidered linens the seamstress had put on display in the parlor, the sleeping babies lined up in their snowy cots. One of their guests was a judge, someone Abby had petitioned on many occasions to sign adoption papers for a child born at the Bethany Home. He made a light joke that one day he might see one of these infants in court, and she let herself titter with him and his wife, even as the comment broke a corner of her heart.

Longing for a different conversation, she caught Euphemia's eye from across the room and smiled. Abby was starting to make her way over to her friend, itching to tell her what she'd decided, to remove the burden of Faith's presence from Euphemia's shoulders as well, when Cook rang the dinner bell.

"Please, join us for a feast of gratitude in the drawing room," Abby said, gesturing toward the doors that were now being swung open by two of the inmates.

As hostess, Abby stood back, allowing the guests to find their seats at the long table. The inmates stood in a circle around the edges of the room, waiting for the blessing, after which they'd enjoy their own meal in the dining room downstairs. Junius gave her a light kiss on the cheek and a nod of approval as he went in to sit down; Abby was ready to follow him when she felt a hand tap her shoulder.

It was Charlotte, her round glasses still fogged from the cold. She'd arrived late, which was uncharacteristic. "Abby, a word." Her thin mouth formed a single agitated line.

"Dinner's about to begin. Can it wait?"

Charlotte shook her head. She crooked her finger, drawing Abby into the foyer, the heels of her boots leaving wet horseshoe prints on the tasseled rug. Abby nodded for the inmates to let the drawing room doors close behind them.

Charlotte skipped the formalities. "I've just been on the telephone with a reporter at the *Representative*, about a story they're running tomorrow. An exposé about the Bethany Home."

"Oh, no," said Abby. A wave of pain shot through her chest.

"They're claiming we've imprisoned at least one woman here, that we're keeping her against her will." She lifted her ear horn, plugged it into her left, the better one, and turned it to Abby. "Tell me it isn't true, Abby. Tell me you haven't locked away one of the inmates."

Any good feeling she'd been enjoying these last few hours drained from Abby. The *Representative* was a respectable newspaper. People took it seriously.

"It certainly isn't true," she said into Charlotte's ear horn. "We've moved Faith Johnson to the tower room, after a disturbance with one of the other inmates. She's as free to leave as any other." She couldn't tell Charlotte the true reason she'd moved Faith to the tower—how could she confess to allowing a suspected murderer to remain here? Even worse, to inviting said murderer to join everyone for tonight's meal?

"The source is said to be anonymous," said Charlotte. "Someone with close ties to the home. Someone with access to a telephone."

Abby tsked. "Anonymous? Could be any liar."

"Our reputations are on the line, Mrs. Mendenhall. Not only that of the Bethany Home, at which I'm told the new mayor will take a hard look. But yours, even mine. If word gets around that I'm party to imprisonment..."

Abby pressed her lips together so tightly it made her chin hurt. Charlotte had always fretted more about her personal reputation than did Abby or Euphemia. She had to. Her modest fortune had been earned through speeches and personal celebrity, whereas the Mendenhalls and Overlocks could rely on familial wealth. Charlotte had pointed out on more than one occasion that Abby and Euphemia had the luxury of caring about individual inmates more than Charlotte could. She had to consider, primarily, the well-being of the institution as a whole. A blot on the Bethany Home's reputation would damage Charlotte's livelihood in a way Abby could scarcely comprehend. The Sisterhood thus existed in fragile symbiosis: the home needed both Charlotte's renown and fund-raising prowess and Abby's and Euphemia's day-to-day work with the inmates in order to survive.

Abby hurried to take Charlotte's arm. "Enough catastrophizing. We're needed at dinner."

Charlotte hesitated, fixing Abby with one small brown eye, magnified behind its round lens. "Are you sure there isn't something you're not telling me?"

"Quite. Come, now. We mustn't keep our guests waiting."

As she entered the drawing room, Abby's eyes took a quick dart around the walls, searching for Faith. She was there, Abby noted with some relief, looking presentable, her dark hair plaited in a crown from ear to ear. She leaned around the girl beside her, craning her neck at someone: May, Abby realized, following Faith's line of sight. Faith bobbed and ducked her head, trying to catch May's attention without saying a word. Yet May didn't notice, or pretended not to; she stared down at the table, a glazed, fixed look in her eyes.

Abby pulled her chair in at the head of the table. The guests, and the inmates, looked to her expectantly; as hostess, she'd be the first to eat, although she'd lost her appetite. She tried to forget what Charlotte had just told her, instead taking in the picture as an outsider would: the lovely young women of the Bethany Home, their faces scrubbed pink and calico dresses brushed clean. The inmates had decorated the drawing room with boughs of autumnal grasses tied in russet ribbons, with gourds and white pumpkins strewn over the creamy tablecloth. In the flickering candlelight, warm against the pewter clouds gathering beyond the tall windows, the girls' faces looked serene—ethereal even—as if they were a choir of angels surrounding the table.

Charlotte's husband, Lieutenant Van Cleve, stood to deliver the blessing, and the inmates and guests bowed their heads. Words trumpeted from Horatio's mouth—he, like Charlotte, was a gifted orator—though Abby heard none of them. She'd never been much for Presbyterian table-graces, their rote nature, the way your mind wandered as you listened to someone recite familiar and thus meaningless words. She preferred the Quaker moment of silence before a meal, which allowed for reflection.

She took a deep breath in through her nose, eyes closed.

Today was Thanksgiving. A line came to her, from Thessalo-nians: *In every thing give thanks.* What did that mean? Deep down, she still felt like a bad child; she'd never understood why she must always be grateful. What was there to thank God for, when her life's work might soon collapse around her? If the new mayor shut down the Bethany Home, would she be expected to bow in appreciation if she had to send all thirty-seven of these women, some of them far gone in pregnancy, to the nuns in St. Paul or, much worse, the workhouse?

"Mrs. Mendenhall."

Euphemia, seated two places to Abby's left, squeezed Abby's arm, and she opened her eyes. She'd kept them closed far too long; the blessing had ended, and everyone, it seemed, was look-ing at her. A bowl of mock-turtle soup had materialized on her plate. The inmates were already filing from the room, excited murmurs traveling through them like a current, their bellies no doubt growling for the meal. Faith, Abby was glad to see, had already gone downstairs.

"Is everything all right?" Euphemia whispered.

"Yes, I'm fine," Abby said in a low voice, and she smiled benignly at their company and picked up her spoon, tilted it into the broth, and lifted it to her lips to sip. A relieved ripple traveled down the table as everyone followed suit, silver flashing, conversation picking up. Junius stared at Abby a little longer, frowning, before turning to his bowl.

The soup was good, a testament to Cook's talent: the dark broth rich and complex, the meat tenderly cooked. As Abby's belly filled, she felt brought back to her senses. She set her spoon down and took a sip of tea. Euphemia was engaged in a lively conversation with the man sitting between them, something about banking.

She caught Abby's eye. "I was just telling Mr. Edwards about the money one of our girls came in with, the counterfeit bills. He says he's come across some as well."

Abby studied Mr. Edwards, who'd once worked for her husband's bank and had since started his own. A stout man with very little neck, he'd never been someone Abby particularly enjoyed talking to, though he gave generously to the Bethany Home. He pointed a thick finger in her direction. "You know, you should hand over that money to the police." A sprig of the soup's tarragon stuck out between two of his teeth.

Abby was about to reply when a snippet of another conversation pricked her ears. She'd heard the name Priscilla Black. In the middle of the table, Officer Nye was seated beside Charlotte, who'd set down her fork to hold up her ear horn.

"...likely one of her own girls who committed the crime," he was saying. "But they scattered, after her disappearance, and they haven't been easy to track down."

He lowered his voice. Abby couldn't hear what he said next, especially when Mr. Edwards launched into a lecture on free silver and the gold standard, peppered with Euphemia's polite replies. But she could see Charlotte nodding thoughtfully, listening to whatever Nye had to say, staring, all the while, straight at Abby.

20

FAITH

*I*t had taken all Faith's willpower not to race over to May while Mr. Van Cleve said grace. She'd tried giving a little wave, but May wouldn't look in her direction. At dinner, Faith hurried to sit beside her, but she realized after she sat down that she needn't have rushed: no one wanted to be within three feet of either of them.

They were served all the courses at once: turkey and stuffing, salad, cranberry relish, fritters. Faith's stomach whined in anticipation as Miss Rhoades gave another, briefer, blessing. She looked around at the flushed faces of so many women, half of them currently pregnant; in their shining eyes, their bosoms straining against their blouses, their spindly, anemic wrists, she recognized her own hunger, the feeling of being simultaneously full and empty that had plagued her ever since her last monthly curse.

When Faith took a break from eating to stretch her aching ankles under the table, she felt May's eyes flit toward her lower abdomen, looking, as everyone always was, for a swell.

"Did Leigh give you a note?" Faith murmured to May.

The other girls whispered and poked one another—watching

her, even on Thanksgiving. She wished they wouldn't react so when she deigned to speak.

May tilted her chin up toward the ceiling as she chewed. The folds of her eyes were puffed and red. "You needn't have worried. I'm not going to see him anymore."

Faith bit into a cranberry, letting its acrid juice numb her tongue. She watched a clear stream of wax drip down the side of a candle, turn white when it hit the tablecloth. She hadn't expected May to agree so quickly about Hayward, but her demeanor felt awry. The shift of her eyes, the tears brimming, pointed to something more complex than a simple change of heart.

May took a sip of water, swallowed hard. "He came by just yesterday with a man called Johnny Lundberg, asking if I'd accompany him to the opera. And I declined."

Faith put down her fork and laid her hands on the table to steady herself. "Here?" The word came out choked. It was all she could manage. *"Here."*

May still wouldn't look directly at her, just kept tossing glances from the corners of her eyes. "Just leave it alone; I told you, I won't be seeing him again."

But that wasn't up to May—didn't she realize? That would be up to him.

Miss Rhoades came by with bowls of pumpkin pudding, and Faith reluctantly picked up her spoon, took a few slow, custardy bites without tasting any sweetness. The *opera*. The word swelled inside Faith's mouth, the round egg of it. He'd offered to take May to the opera, knowing, as he now must, that May was a nobody. Why would he do it? What would Hayward have to gain from being seen with a girl like May out in public?

As she ate, the truth settled in around Faith. Hayward and

Johnny knew where to find May, which might mean they knew where to find Faith. At this very moment, they could be waiting for her outside. Today was a holiday; that, and only that, might be her salvation. She could get away in time.

She turned to May, who was stirring her pudding absent-mindedly, staring straight ahead. She hadn't taken a bite. Faith tapped the table, trying to get her attention; somehow, she'd have to let May know she'd be leaving soon, and wouldn't come back.

Without looking at her, May slid back her chair, picked up her tray, and carried it to the sink. No one else in the dining room seemed to notice or care as Faith watched her onetime bunkmate, her one remaining friend on this Earth, slip away forever.

Faith went, first, to Mrs. Mendenhall's office, where she sifted through every drawer of the desk, searching for her money. It was nowhere to be found. Anger overtook her, then panic: where would she go with no money? She took a few deep breaths to settle herself. She couldn't dwell on it. There was little time to spare. She waited to be sure none of the guests had congregated in the foyer, then crept up the stairs, back to her dreadful room. Briefly, she considered knocking on May's door, but decided against it.

The tower reeked of mildew. She hadn't noticed it before but did now that she'd spent some time away, and the smell filled her with rage. She yanked her white cap from her head and flung it at the bedclothes. Hairpins clattered to the floor.

Slowly, her breathing returned to normal. She had to think clearly.

The thing to do was leave Minnesota, start over someplace

where no one could find her. But she had no money to catch a train, had not even her old crystal ball, or her divining salts, and what could she do, set up a fortune-telling booth in the middle of the Union Depot? Word would reach her pursuers immediately. They were wily ones, with friends everywhere, it seemed. No wonder they'd been able to use May so thoroughly. Not her fault she hadn't seen it coming—neither had Faith.

Incredibly, she'd been nervous when Hayward took her to read that first girl's fortune. She'd wanted to do right by him, to impress him. He'd showered her with so many compliments ahead of time, on her beauty, on her supposed gifts as a clairvoyant; she'd been anxious to live up to his expectations, and to Johnny's.

By then she had spent several nights in Johnny's bed with him, right in his wife's house. By way of explanation, he'd told his wife he couldn't sleep without Faith's use of mesmeric hypnosis, and it was true that after their lovemaking—quiet, though Mrs. Lundberg slept in a different wing of the house—he'd ask her to whisper him to sleep. His eyes would close the minute she laid her cool hands to his shoulder and knee. She brought her lips close to his ear and recited whatever she could remember: psalms, poems, a little rhyme her schoolteacher in Pennsylvania had taught them to remind them of the days of the week. When she ran out of words to recite, she simply hissed and clicked and blew in his ears. Gooseflesh would fleck his skin and then subside when he finally fell asleep. Then she'd flee to the attic, where the other maids would turn over and huff into their pillows, no longer speaking to her.

But Hayward seemed harder to please than Johnny, more exacting, more technical: her next afternoon off, following their meeting at the hotel, he'd taught her what he knew about animal magnetism, about the metallic humors coursing through every organic body and the way you could manipulate them with your mind. Faith listened, skeptical, until he lifted an eyebrow and said with a devilish smile: "It worked on you, didn't it? When Johnny and I took you upstairs."

She scoffed. She didn't want to think of it that way, as something they'd persuaded her to do against her will. It had been her choice. They stared hard at each other, an invisible force shimmering between them. She felt a small burst of triumph when he looked away first.

"Don't get bent out of shape," Hayward said with a wave of his hand. "Now it's your chance to do it to someone else. I need you to tell this dressmaker to accept a loan from me. Work your magic: you're the one who knows how to tease out what someone really wants. Figure out what Kitty Ging wants, then promise she'll get it if she goes into business with me."

The problem was, she'd liked Kitty Ging. Hayward brought Faith into Kitty's shop dressed absurdly, a silk scarf wrapped around her head, heavy earrings clipped painfully to her lobes. She carried the crystal ball, something Johnny had found in a pawn store.

"This," Hayward declared, "is the famous Marguerite the Magnificent."

Faith blinked. Famous? She'd never been called by that name before. He must have made it up on the spot.

Kitty took one look at her and rolled her eyes. "Funny costume," she said to Hayward, gesturing at Faith with her thumb. Faith was impressed with her height, her lacquered black hair, her fearlessness in dealing with him. "Listen, this is the most unusual birthday present I've ever been offered, but I still think this stuff is hogwash."

Faith bit her lip. Kitty was right, it was mostly hogwash.

"Oh, for certain. You're a churchgoing gal," Hayward replied solemnly, leaning with one elbow on Kitty's desk, one long leg crossed in front of the other. In his gray suit, he cut a fine figure. Everything he wore hung well on him.

"I didn't say that." Kitty laughed and punched him lightly on the arm. It wasn't hard to see what Kitty wanted. Kitty wanted Hayward. She shone in the spotlight of his attention. Faith couldn't be sure if Kitty was sleeping with him already, or only hoping to, though, clearly, the two were formally unattached.

Faith asked him to leave while she read Miss Ging's fortune, and he shot them a wink. Kitty led her to the back room, among bolts of fabric and several iron Singer machines, their bobbins and pedals at rest. They sat at a little table, face-to-face. There were no windows, but Faith could hear low rumbles of summer thunder and the pitter of rain against the back wall. The air in the workroom felt thick.

With a smirk, Kitty held out her hands; her fingers were long, smooth, and white, the nails trimmed neatly. "Oh—face-up?" she said, turning her palms to the ceiling.

One glance at the lines on the woman's palms was enough. Her life lines were short, too. Maybe it didn't mean anything, but Faith didn't want to look closer. She pulled off the earrings and rubbed her swollen lobes, and Kitty's eyes widened.

"You think it's rubbish," Faith said quietly, "so don't let's waste our time."

Kitty removed her hands to her lap and tilted her head to the side, studying Faith. "Then what shall we do? He's paying you, isn't he?"

He was, and he would be expecting results. He'd want Kitty to emerge from this meeting ready to accept a loan from him, and more: he'd asked Faith to urge her to take out a life-insurance policy on herself, naming him as the benefactor. "Tell Kitty the other girls will be after her," he'd instructed Faith. "All my admirers. Tell her one of them's likely to bump her off, and then I'll need a way to collect on my loan." His logic seemed clumsy to Faith, the threats ineffective. She found it hard to believe someone would agree to such a thing when he wasn't even a family member. But maybe Kitty wanted him to be.

"Let him help you." Faith gestured to the ridiculous getup. "Look at the lengths he'll go to, to get you to trust him. He wanted me to tell you the spirits are on your side."

The two of them laughed, like old friends. It felt good; Faith couldn't remember the last time another girl had laughed with her. Kitty looked flattered, her cheeks pink under her eyes.

"I don't know," she said. "My pa used to say, 'Neither a borrower nor a lender be.' Do you know that one?"

Faith shook her head.

"It's from Shakespeare. I forget the play. But, good Lord, I could use the money. It's hard to be a woman alone, running a business. You must know that, Marguerite."

The comment flustered Faith. She didn't know anything about running a business. Her station in life felt far removed from Kitty's. But Kitty didn't know that, of course. She might even have assumed Marguerite the Magnificent had a storefront of her own.

"Maybe he doesn't want you to feel so alone," Faith tried, gently. "If you let him help you, you tie him to you. He'll have a stake here. In the business. And in you."

Kitty nodded slowly, rubbing her arms so that her stiff sleeves rustled. A little smile crept onto her face. An enchanting person, Faith decided. She hoped she wasn't leading Kitty into a dangerous situation. Her next words, however, came so easily—they slipped off her tongue.

"You could make it even more intimate if you asked him to be your next of kin on your life-insurance policy. You have one, don't you? As a business owner?" When Kitty shook her head, she feigned shock. "Every sensible woman who owns a business has one." Implying she had one herself, though she wasn't even sure what it entailed.

Kitty should have been smart enough to see through Hayward, Faith thought later, as she and Hayward celebrated, toasting her success with a new bottle of Tennessee whiskey. Her victory felt hollow, even when he paid her in gold coins. Kitty had appeared addled with love for him, distracted from good sense by the shining reflection of his beautiful face in her eyes. But Hayward seemed blinded by something else.

How could she have done it? Faith stood at the tower window, watching snow coat the road, thicken the tree branches. She'd led an unsuspecting woman into Hayward's clutches. Her own culpability gnawed at her. If she could go and warn Kitty Ging right now not to trust a word the man said, not to have anything to do with him, especially regarding money, she would. But it was too late for that.

Besides, Faith wasn't going anywhere at the moment. She'd tied her belongings into one of her pillowcases, but she couldn't leave in this storm. She'd have to hope for better weather in the morning, perhaps get on the road at first light.

Downstairs, dinner continued. The guests had become louder as dessert was served, although not as loud as they'd have been if there were any liquor involved. Girls were beginning to trickle upstairs in pairs and threes, their voices carrying the cadence of holiday merriment. Faith lay back on her pillow, thinking of May heading to bed alone.

Pieces of their conversation, and her memories, flitted through her mind, like pieces of a puzzle that hadn't been cut to match. Hayward and the opera. Kitty's reluctance to borrow from him. May's secret revolver. Faith should have felt relieved that she'd at least warned May to stay away from him, but she didn't. A bigger plot was afoot, she could sense that, but she couldn't make out the edges of the trap.

What if Hayward were standing before her right now, asking her to read his fortune? What would she tell him?

She heard nothing but the same answer she'd given him many months ago, that first meeting at the hotel: *I'd say you were about to come into a lot of money.* That was the evening when she'd gone upstairs with him, in the hotel. The one time she'd slept with the devil. The memory brought a burning sensation to her throat.

Heartburn, she realized. The life growing in her belly still seemed so insubstantial, but she'd heard the other girls complaining of acid creep, of their babies pushing up into their ribs. She stood and chugged cold tea, then began to pace, quelling the fire in her chest.

I'd say you were about to come into a lot of money. What if Hal *were* about to come into a lot of money? The man seemed determined not to work in the traditional sense, so how would he attain it? She walked back and forth, the thin boards of the tower room complaining under her bare feet, until, at last, she stopped, the answer looking her plain in the face.

21

MAY

Miss Rhoades found her the next morning, fully dressed but lying curled up on her bed, staring at the wall. "May, you'll have to come downstairs," she said as she drew the curtains. The light in the room had scarcely changed, but the temperature had dropped. December announcing its imminent arrival through the open window.

Miss Rhoades's hand shook her shoulder. "Sit up. The police are here."

"The police?" May sat up with a gasp. In fact, she'd been awake for hours, hadn't slept much at all last night; Faith's empty mattress haunted her. She couldn't close her eyes without seeing Johnny grasping her arm, the terror on Faith's face when she mentioned his name.

"Mrs. Van Cleve and some detectives arrived first thing in the morning." Miss Rhoades looked weary, her teeth clenched, skin pallid. She held a fist to her stomach. "They're asking to talk to all the former sporting girls."

"I'm not a sporting girl," May said, making her voice small.

Miss Rhoades flinched and looked over her shoulder, and now May could hear the buzz of voices downstairs, as though the sudden arrival of these men had disturbed a nervous hive. "I'm not asking," she said without looking at May. "We told them all thirty-seven of you would answer their questions, whether you worked for a madam or not. Mrs. Van Cleve says it's imperative that all of you cooperate. Now, come along."

"What do they want from us?"

"They're after whatever happened to Priscilla Black." Miss Rhoades rubbed one of her shins. "Ever meet her?"

May's breakfast, some crackers she'd kept hidden in a drawer, threatened to come up her throat. She shook her head so hard she saw spots.

"Then you're lucky," said Miss Rhoades.

May stood, her knees like butter. She had never met Priscilla Black. That was no lie. Hal had only mentioned the sad condition of the woman's corpse, which the policemen must have already known. She wouldn't have to tell them.

Miss Rhoades followed her out. At the door, she caught May's hand. "You be strong, May."

But May felt the opposite of strong: she felt as limp as a strand of yarn. She sensed Hal's presence surrounding her, as though he haunted her now. Since she'd known him, she'd been powerless to resist his commands, and she had a horrible premonition that she'd end up doing exactly what he wanted her to, with Faith.

The reception room, which just the previous night had been warm and inviting and decorated for the harvest, was now permeated with the scents of sweat and wool. An array of police officers with varied facial hair patterns milled about the room in their long blue coats, each with a star on the lapel and a tasseled nightstick in his pocket. The garlands and gourds had been hauled away, as had the dining table, so that two chairs could face each other in the center of the room.

She'd passed Mrs. Van Cleve in the foyer, locked into an intense conversation with Mrs. Mendenhall. Mrs. Mendenhall held her mouth so tensely that her lips had all but disappeared, and Mrs. Van Cleve held forth, her voice, as always, too loud:

". . . isn't your personal home to run as you please," she admonished Mrs. Mendenhall. "If there's really nothing to hide . . ."

Miss Rhoades hurried May past the two older ladies, into the reception room, and gestured to the empty chair. The only officer who'd removed his hat sat in the other. He seemed a bit older than the other men, and had an air of command about him.

Quietly, Miss Rhoades shut the doors, muffling the sound of Mrs. Van Cleve's voice.

"Good morning," he said cheerfully, scratching the thick fur of a mutton-chop beard connecting his nose to his ears. "Miss Verdoni, is it?"

May looked at Miss Rhoades, who nodded encouragement. She noticed a younger man in the corner, also in uniform, seated at the scroll-top desk with a fountain pen and paper.

"That's your given name?" the man asked again. "Assuntina Verdoni?"

She hadn't heard it spoken in so long. He didn't quite pronounce it correctly. "Yes, sir."

The detective grunted, made a note. Behind him, one of his colleagues paced back and forth. One stood watchful at the window, observing the falling snow, the steady dusting turning to fat, swollen flakes.

"You worked in a brothel, miss?"

Subtly, the movement in the room changed. The policeman who'd been pacing slowed; the officer beside the window glanced casually over his shoulder.

May couldn't look at any of them. She felt as if she'd swallowed burrs. Her hand went to her forehead, her middle finger rubbing between her eyes. Through her fingers, she could still see a bit of Miss Rhoades, enough to catch the woman's nod.

"It's all right," Miss Rhoades prodded her. "You can be honest."

"Nothing to be ashamed of," said the officer, though she could hear the sneer in his voice.

May spoke through her hand. "Just a few times," she said, very quietly. She felt flayed open.

The police officer launched into another question, but she wasn't listening. She stared at the seeds of some dried wheatgrass that had fallen to the floor. The one with the pen was writing something down. She'd spoken it aloud, which she'd sworn to herself she'd never do. And now this man would write it down, scratching her greatest shame into the record. Her hands roamed her florid face. What did it matter now, what she'd done after she left the woolen mill? Her dream of returning home, triumphant, to her mother, arm in arm with her new husband, was dead.

Miss Rhoades coughed, calling her back to the room. "They asked who you worked for."

"It's not Priscilla Black, so why should you care?" she said behind her hand, her voice thick with tears.

The one with the mutton chops adjusted his hips so that he sat taller in his seat. "We care, young lady, because we're trying to solve a murder. Answer the question."

"Agnes Bly," she said toward the wheatgrass seeds on the carpet.

Agnes hadn't abused her, not exactly, but hers wasn't a name May wanted to invoke again. The words brought back the other girls' teasing, not so different from here.

"The fat ones have a liking for you," they'd gibed. "The old ones. That one with a missing leg, see him? It's your turn to take him upstairs." She'd occupied the lowest rung there, too. With fury in her heart, she'd watched the others take the handsome ones to bed, the young men with elegant figures, the fun ones who brought chocolates and biscuits. May had been left with the ones whose bellies drooped.

Agnes Bly's was where May had first learned to go to the maple grove. She could go there now, she realized. With a loud, wet sniff, she ran her hand through the front of her hair and over the back, to smooth her bun. She looked the officers in the eyes and smiled, her lips tight.

"There you are," said the detective, showing his tobacco-stained teeth. "You came here when? How long ago?"

"Just over a year." She sensed Miss Rhoades shifting uncomfortably, no doubt thinking about May's time being up.

"And your baby was born . . . ?"

"It wasn't," said May.

The men looked anywhere but at her. The pacing one put his hand to the back of his curly blond neck, head turned toward the floor. May stared straight ahead, through the window. The snow was beginning to form peaked drifts like little mountain ranges.

"Come again?" said the detective.

"It wasn't born." May swallowed, the burr feeling having returned. This part she could tell them clear-eyed, knowing in her heart that she'd done nothing wrong. Forget what Pearl or anyone else claimed.

She *had* been pregnant, or at least she'd been convinced she was. It had been just like when Emmanuel was first growing in her belly: her breasts had grown swollen and hard, the nipples darkening to brown. Her curse of Eve, normally as reliable as a post-office clock, stopped abruptly. Despite the horror of not knowing which of the sad sacks the other girls had saddled her with had fathered this bastard child, she'd felt relieved. Now she could go with that gentle old lady in black who came to read her Bible in the parlor of a Sunday, the one who ran the Bethany Home and was only too happy to invite May to stay.

But then her waist had stopped expanding. She squeezed her eyes shut, thinking of it, and had to tuck her trembling hands beneath her skirt. Several weeks into her tenure at the Bethany Home, her monthly curse had returned. One ordinary morning, she'd woken early to knead dough and seen the stains on her sheets. She'd been terrified they'd throw her out, so she told no one. She brought her bedsheets down to the laundry and washed them herself, in the middle of the night. Of course, she couldn't ask for a sanitary belt, and so she stole dishrags from the kitchen to stuff into her drawers—washed them, too, in the night. The bleeding had just begun to lighten when Pearl found her early one morning, exhausted and half asleep, elbows deep in pink water. Pearl had immediately sounded the alarm to the matron. And after a humiliating examination, the visiting doctor diagnosed May with a false pregnancy.

"Physical symptoms can even occur," the doctor told Mrs. Mendenhall in her office, talking as though May weren't sitting right there, red in the face and mortified, as he wiped his glasses. "If the girl believes in it hard enough."

"We'll trust May acted in good faith," Mrs. Mendenhall had declared, "and let her stay the full year." She'd patted May on the arm reassuringly and sent her right back to her room as though nothing had changed. But May had to watch as the girls who'd arrived the same time as she had grew plump and flushed and had their babies in the spring, while she lingered around the edges as they called her a burden, a liar.

She began to think of herself as a mother of ghosts. Someone who was unfit to raise the first child she'd brought into this world, and who had been so desperate to change her circumstances that she'd conjured the second from thin air.

A year should have been long enough to get herself on her feet, find a husband. But look at the mess she'd made, putting all her eggs into Hal's basket. Now she'd have to take the job living above the bakery, if that was even still available, and commit herself to a life of hardworking, solitary spinsterhood.

When she dared look up at Miss Rhoades, the matron's eyes were shining, her mouth pursed in a sad, kindly little frown.

"Let's move along," said the detective, tugging at the knee of his blue pant leg. A sliver of hairy ankle emerged at the top of his boot. May glared at the shiny red skin of his nose. She hated him, for making her say all of that out loud before she'd ever had the opportunity to whisper it to a friend.

"Have you ever met, or heard of, Miss Priscilla Black?" he asked her.

"I've heard of her now," May replied. If she answered their questions quickly, maybe they'd let her go. "I hadn't before."

He had a couple of drawings on his lap, she saw now, and he passed them to her. The first was a portrait of a proud-looking, snub-nosed woman with streaks of white hair over her ears, the rest black. The edges of the picture were darker than the middle, as though this likeness had been removed from its frame.

The second sketch, on onionskin, made May gasp. The paper crackled in her trembling hands. Someone had crudely drawn a body, naked and swollen, stretched over a table. May's eyes lingered on the plump thighs, the little bulbous knees, the tongue half hanging from the mouth.

When she handed the sketches back to the detective, he smirked at her, and she wondered what his game was, what effect he hoped shocking her with the drawing would have.

He shuffled the papers. "We've an inkling one of Black's strumpets killed her."

May considered this. From the moment she'd heard the woman's name, and Hal's gruesome description of her corpse, there'd been little doubt in her mind that a man had killed Priscilla. Possibly, now that Hal had revealed himself to be capable of violence, the killer was Hal himself. She'd never imagined one of Black's girls could have carried out the job.

"Could a parlor girl haul that body?" she asked.

The man didn't answer. "Apparently, she had a troublemaker in her midst. A dark-haired gal who read people's futures in a crystal ball. Among other services." A look passed between the others, a collective grin. "One night in October, the dark-haired girl had some trouble with a customer. Miss Black went up to intervene, and the other girls heard shouting. The next morning, Black was gone. And so was the fortune-teller."

May felt sick with fear. Faith had appeared here in late October. She could also sense terror emanating from Miss Rhoades, who'd gone stiff. How many girls had this detective interviewed so far, how many were left to go? All one of them had to say was

Oh, you must mean Faith Johnson, and these lawmen would march up to the tower and haul her away.

May wet her lips. She was afraid to open her mouth. What if Hal's attempt to mesmerize her into handing Faith over—what if that led *her* to turn Faith in? No, his exact words had been "You'll bring the girl to me..." Not to the police. She could keep Faith safe from these men.

"A woman like Black, I'd guess she was killed by a man," May said, slowly and clearly, watching the detective's mouth quirk in doubt. "But if you believe it was one of the girls over at Black's, why don't you check the court records? All their names will be there."

"First thing we did, dearie. Unfortunately, there's no way of knowing whether the girls use their real names in court," he said, calling her bluff. "You lot move to another bordello, choose a different name yet again, and vanish. Like a fart in a skillet."

May put her hand to her cheek, pretending to be embarrassed by his choice of words. Miss Rhoades pushed away from the wall. "May's been a good girl, Officer. I think you can move on to the next." She wrapped her fingers around May's biceps, drawing her upward.

"Thank you, Miss Verdoni. That'll be all." The men watched her leave, their gazes accusatory, penetrative. The air in the foyer felt cool. Mrs. Mendenhall and Mrs. Van Cleve were both gone. Miss Rhoades marched May through the empty corridor toward the cellar steps.

"They know about Faith," May whispered to Miss Rhoades when she felt certain they were out of earshot. "What'll happen when it's her turn?"

Miss Rhoades said nothing. The back of her thin, pale neck appeared frail, but when she whirled around at the top of the steps, her eyes were steely. They softened as she considered May's face.

"Oh, child," she said softly, the back of her hand landing on May's cheek. "It's kind of you to think of her after what you've just gone through."

"Someone's going to tell them about her," May said, feeling tears brimming on the edge of her lashes.

Miss Rhoades's lip trembled for a second, then stopped. "But you didn't, and I'm proud of you for it, May. Now, go down and get your work done, best you can. We'll still need supper on the table tonight. God knows we'll all be looking for some comfort."

For the rest of the afternoon, May sought any excuse to come back upstairs to the foyer, to pass the reception room and try for a glimpse at what was going on, but Mrs. Mendenhall hovered by the doors and fixed her with a stern expression each time she wandered by. As the other kitchen girls were called up to take their turns with the detective—Leigh, and then Dolly, the new-comers, Pearl—May tried to read their expressions when they returned to rolling dough and slicing carrots for what would be the evening's leftover-turkey pie. Had it ever been so quiet, had the silence ever been so thick and portentous, in the kitchen? The girls went upstairs clear-eyed, but came back looking pale, their features drawn, their brows furrowed. They took to their chopping and kneading with agitated fervor. At one point, Dolly's knife slipped and bit into the pad of her thumb. Even Pearl—her one eyebrow bare, still puckered and red—returned heaving tired sighs. May had feared she'd come back looking smug, victorious at last over Faith, but she didn't. Perhaps

236 · CAROLINE WOODS

she felt as weary as anyone else to be poked and prodded by the detective, to be forced to relive the past.

Hope crept in, slowly, cautiously. Would the girls of the home have decided, all of them together, to protect Faith, just as May had? It seemed preposterous, given how they'd shunned and belittled her these past weeks. But no one was laughing now. In the face of the officers who used to haul them to court, who looked at them like they were breeding sows, maybe the inmates had chosen Faith.

After what felt like an age, the kitchen clock struck four, when Cook's apprentices traditionally enjoyed a half-hour rest before dinner. "All right, girls," Cook said. "Go and put your feet up for a tick; Lord knows you've earned it."

They trudged up the stairs in silence, May sandwiched between Pearl and Leigh. Pearl stopped abruptly in the foyer. In front of her, May could see a wall of blue: all the policemen gathered around the front door, Mrs. Mendenhall standing amid their semicircle, Mrs. Overlock's taller, narrower frame just behind her. Mrs. Van Cleve stood with the police.

The front door was propped open, exposing the lavender evening sky. The giant snowflakes had petered to nothing.

"We've spoken to thirty-six of 'em," the detective was saying to Mrs. Mendenhall. "You said there were thirty-seven. Where's the last?"

"Don't make the man go upstairs, Abby," said Mrs. Van Cleve. "If there's a girl you're hiding in the tower, you should tell us now."

Mrs. Overlock turned to Mrs. Mendenhall, her mouth fluttering open and closed, as if she thought she should say something. May couldn't see Mrs. Mendenhall's face, but she felt certain of what Mrs. Mendenhall would do. Upright, honest,

Quaker Mrs. Mendenhall: she'd hand Faith right over to the men. May waited, her stomach clenched, with the other kitchen girls; she had a sense they were all holding their breath.

A sound came from above—someone clearing her throat—and May saw now that Miss Rhoades was coming down the stairs. Mrs. Mendenhall turned to say something, but Miss Rhoades's expression stopped her.

An invisible conversation seemed to pass between the women, a sort of telepathy. Watching them, her pulse quickening, May understood.

Faith was gone.

May stared through the open door at the frigid landscape; the city had shrugged itself under a blanket of hard snow. She felt something touch her hand, then grab on to it: she was astonished to see that Leigh had reached for her. They held hands tightly, the skin of their palms glued together with hot sweat, as they waited to see what would happen next.

Miss Rhoades had reached the bottom step. She offered a wan smile to the detective.

"I'm afraid I'm the thirty-seventh, sir," she said. "It's been a long time since I worked in a sporting house, so I may not be much use. But I'll do my best to answer your questions."

Mrs. Van Cleve's eyes popped open. Mrs. Overlock covered her mouth with her hand. It was hard to read Mrs. Mendenhall's expression, though her eyes widened, too.

May did her best not to gasp, as Leigh's fingers tightened even further around hers. She could feel the other inmates struggling not to look at one another, not to make a sound.

The detective shrugged. "Come with me," he said.

May and the other girls watched Miss Rhoades, her shoulders squared, follow the detective back into the reception room.

Mrs. Van Cleve, Mrs. Mendenhall, and Mrs. Overlock were left staring at one another. "Did you know?" May heard Mrs. Overlock murmur to Mrs. Mendenhall, who shook her head.

"You should have," said Mrs. Van Cleve. "You hired her."

May would have liked to hear what else they had to say, but the girls were scattering in a swarm now, most to their rooms, and their chatter drowned out the sharp whispers of the three board members. May trudged upstairs, thinking she'd fetch her water pitcher and fill it down at the cistern. With each step, her relief increased. She no longer held Faith's fate in her hands. She couldn't lead Faith to Hayward if Faith had disappeared.

The door to her room stood slightly ajar. She must have forgotten to close it. When she stepped inside, it was dark. Someone had drawn the heavier curtain. She went to open it, to let in more light. Behind her she heard the hinges of her door whine shut. Footsteps came toward her, quickly, and she barely had time to yelp before someone clapped a hand over her mouth.

She whimpered against the person's soft hand as her eyes adjusted to the dark. Blue eyes, as dark as indigo dye, wisps of black hair hanging over the forehead: Faith. She held a finger over her lips. Breathing hard, May nodded, and, slowly, Faith let her go.

"What are you doing here?" May whispered. Faith pointed behind her, to her empty bed. The purple dress lay there, sleeves spread wide. Faith pointed to Kitty Ging's label.

There were dark circles under Faith's eyes, as though she hadn't slept at all the night before. "The dressmaker," she said, almost inaudibly. May had difficulty hearing her over the sound of her own rapid breath. "We must warn her. I think Hayward's planning to . . ."

She made a slashing motion at her throat.

May winced, then stared at the label's faded pink embroidery: *Made by Catherine Ging.* In her mind, she watched the stitching unravel, weave through the air, and travel to the center of town, where Hal sat in his living room in the Ozark Flats, the ends of the thread tied to his long, elegant fingers.

He'd been right. She'd bring Faith to him, after all. She was no different from Dolly with her biscuits, or Leigh with the pinking shears. She felt his fingers give a tug, and her stomach dropped.

"I know where Kitty Ging lives," she whispered to Faith, who nodded keenly. May's voice sounded strange in her own ears. "I can take you there."

22

FAITH

*T*hey waited for over an hour, until the rest of the inmates had gone down for dinner, to sneak out the front door. May fetched them woolen capes from the charity closet. In silence, they let the wind whisk them down the walk, and they turned left to catch a streetcar. Mercifully, the snow had completely stopped, the edges of it already browned along the road, the sidewalks tamped by footprints.

They did not speak as they waited for the trolley. May stared straight ahead, her expression glassy.

Faith stamped her feet, trying to keep her toes warm. Ever since she'd pieced it all together—the revolver, the life insurance, the alleged admirers he'd boasted of—*one of them's likely to bump her off*—she'd felt as if she were losing a footrace. She couldn't warn Miss Ging quickly enough. But today was the day Hayward had tickets to the opera. He wouldn't be going after Kitty today. They'd get to her in time.

Faith had expected May to argue, to defend Hayward, even after she'd vowed never to see him again. Mere days ago, May had boasted she was about to become Mrs. Harry Hayward; now she appeared to accept he was capable of murder. Faith hadn't mentioned any of the ways in which she suspected he'd exploited May in his plotting, but she had to guess she'd been used.

"What did you tell the detective?" Faith knew they'd come to solve Priscilla's murder, and that they suspected her. She'd listened, closely, all morning, as girls came and went from the reception room.

May kept her eyes trained on a locust tree across the street, its seed pods shivering in the wind. "I told him I'd never heard of the girl they were after; it sounded an awful lot like you. They think you killed Black, but I know you didn't. It was Hayward himself."

Faith put her hands inside the flap of her cloak, said nothing. How could she possibly summon words for Hayward's defense? The man left a trail of destruction behind him a mile wide. But he hadn't been the one to kill Priscilla Black. May had mistakenly added an extra body to his ledger.

May fidgeted for a while, tucking her hair into her cap, staring up the road in front of the streetcar stop, waiting, it seemed, for Faith to respond. Eventually, May sighed and laced her fingers in her lap. She wouldn't even glance in Faith's direction as the trolley came up the hill, its electric cable sparking against the purple-dark sky. When they boarded, May paid both their fares without comment. Over her shoulder, Faith watched May fish in her pocket for coins, then pull out an old quarter-dollar, Lady Liberty's face worn flat, marred with little scratches. May dropped it into the fare box and turned the crank, collected the dime and nickel it spat back at her. Her change.

Marguerite the Magnificent had started with a purse full of change when she set up her card table and crystal ball in one of

242 · CAROLINE WOODS

Priscilla Black's parlor rooms. All green goods, of course, false money: it had been furnished by Hayward and Johnny. They'd dolled her up in one of Johnny's wife's gowns, a midnight-purple silk, and trotted her over to the red-light district one morning last summer. Not to become a whore, they assured Faith, but to read fortunes and have the opportunity to earn her own.

Priscilla had taken it upon herself to inspect the bills, one by one.

"This one don't look right to me," Priscilla said, laying one of the false banknotes on the table in front of Johnny. "The stamp's off." She tapped it with a long, yellowed fingernail. Her face had a hard look, as though any capacity for kindness had long since been wrung from her, if it ever existed to begin with. "What happens if a customer figures it out, pulls a knife? A number of the fellows we service lost their shirts in Argentina. They're wary of a con." She sneered at Faith when she spoke the word "con."

"Perhaps you could dim your lighting," Hayward suggested with a grin, gesturing to her lanterns. "That way no one looks too closely at his change."

"I'll take fifty percent of the cut and that's final," Priscilla concluded. "I'm the one putting my neck out here."

She made no mention of the safety of Faith, who hadn't said a word since the meeting began.

Hayward and Johnny had presented their plot to her as if it were an exciting, once-in-a-lifetime opportunity. They'd been looking for ways to launder their counterfeit banknotes, and they'd long thought a brothel would be the perfect place to do it. The problem was, you couldn't trust brothel workers: they were likely to run away, or turn up dead. Their little fortune-teller, on the other hand: she possessed the cunning and sophistication to form a partnership with them. All she'd have to do was set up shop in one of the more respectable bordellos, where men with full pockets—"easy marks," Hayward called them—swarmed like dragonflies. She'd read their fortunes and take their gold, giving them change in green goods.

"The Kitty Ging special," Johnny had said, laughing, until Hayward shot him a look that shut him up. Faith wasn't sure what he meant, not yet, but she tucked that phrase into her memory. *The Kitty Ging special.*

Coincidentally or not, Mrs. Lundberg had fired her just that morning. She hadn't given a reason, or even delivered the news in person: she'd had the cook do it for her. "I guess she's tired of listening to you two carry on," Cook sneered, after she mentioned there'd be no back pay. Faith had no choice, then, but to go along with the scheme. It hadn't sounded too disagreeable to her, not at first. She wouldn't mind working alongside bagnio girls; she had an instinct they'd be warmer to her than the servants and cooks she'd encountered. The part she didn't tell Hayward and Johnny was that she didn't plan on staying for long. Once she'd assembled a goodly nest egg for herself, she'd board a train heading west and set up a fortune-telling booth in a mining or cattle-ranching town, somewhere new and raw and ripe with possibilities, where no one had a past, only a future.

In Black's parlor, Hayward tapped his cigar in the ashtray and smiled at the madam. "I'd say our fortune-teller's neck is closest to the chopping block, my dear Miss Black. It's fifteen percent for her, twenty-five for you—for providing the venue—and thirty each for my partner and me." He winked at Faith, showing he'd look after her.

She'd thought he cared about her, at least as an interesting friend, at that point. She hadn't fully understood that the only thing he cared about was money.

"Or we'll take our business elsewhere," he said casually.

Priscilla frowned, stroking her crepey neck; she seemed reluctant to admit they'd called her bluff, but they had. "She's comely, I'll give you that," she said, gesturing toward Faith.

"The most beautiful girl in Minneapolis," Johnny crowed. "None of your customers will be looking at his money."

In the end, they shook hands, and when Faith got up to leave with the men, Johnny turned around and stopped her.

"You'll stay here," he said quietly, looking past her at Priscilla. Hayward was already out the door. Faith's eyes must have jumped in alarm; Johnny's softened in response. "Well, you don't work for me anymore, do you? What did you expect?" He kissed her on the forehead. "I'll be back to visit you as soon as tomorrow. Do good."

This should have been her first sign that something was not right, when Priscilla led her, a smug half-smile, half-frown on her face, to a room in the bordello with a single window that looked out onto a brown brick wall.

"One of our best bedrooms," Priscilla had said in a huff, "so thank your lucky stars."

Faith opened her mouth to thank the madam but stopped. Though she was trying to discern what lurked behind the woman's eyes, Priscilla read like a wall of onyx. Opaque. Guarded. Faith could detect something there, something dark and shrewd. Priscilla's nervous eyes twitched toward a corner of the room, and she wore an odd little smile on her lips. Clearly, the madam didn't want to be thanked. She slammed the door shut without another word and thundered down the stairs.

Faith waited in that room for hours the first night, unsure whether to go down for dinner. Nobody came and got her. No one brought her a nightdress, not yet; she slept in the purple silk, not realizing how dirty and ragged the gown would soon become. She lay awake, listening to her neighbors' doors open and close. Their beds creaked. Their mattresses groaned and sighed.

As their streetcar chugged downtown, the buildings grew taller and more solid, the boulevard got wider, and Faith mused how little she knew of this city where she'd been living almost two years. She'd memorized the attic rooms and back staircases of some of its grander homes, and she knew all too well the warren of parlors and reception rooms, bedrooms and toilets of Priscilla Black's brothel. But she didn't recognize this section of Hennepin Avenue, its theaters with their faux-Greek façades, its bakeries and banks, closed and shuttered this hour of night. The few pedestrians strolling the sidewalks walked with their heads bent into the wind, coats and mufflers pulled over their faces so that only their eyes were visible.

"We're here," May said quietly. She stood up and held on to the metal pole, waiting for the trolley to stop, her body swaying with the motions of the streetcar. Her face looked pale, even greenish.

Faith followed her out onto the street; the air bit at their faces before they'd even descended the last step. The streetcar's bell clanged. As it lumbered forward, Faith got a glance at the building across the street.

"That's where she lives," May said, her voice getting carried away in the wind. "The Ozark Flats."

The Ozark Flats. Faith mouthed the words. The name was faintly familiar. A handsome red brick building with arched windows on the third and fourth floors, covered balconies at some of the apartments. They hurried across the street, the chill from the river whipping at their coats as they emerged from the shelter of the buildings, then into the vestibule of the Ozark Flats. Through the shining glass door, they could see the carpeted interior of the lobby, lit by electric chandeliers. Faith tried the door, but found it locked.

She turned to see May waiting at the bottom of the concrete steps, breathing rapidly. Puffs of her breath, visible in the cold, swirled from her mouth like steam from an engine.

"There's a bell," Faith said quietly. "We could ring Miss Ging's apartment."

"No!" May shrieked. "Don't ring it."

Faith paused, her fingers hovering over the buzzer. May came up and tugged at her elbow. "I've made a mistake. We must go home now. Before anyone sees us."

May had begun hyperventilating, her cold breath making wheezing sounds. Faith led her around the side of the building and into a service alley where the sides of the Ozark Flats and its neighbor pressed together, the brickwork plain and pale. A single weak light illuminated a door cut into the wall, leading, presumably, to the basement. May huddled against the bricks beside the door, her face turned skyward and eyes closed, her chest heaving up and down.

"I'm so sorry," she whispered when she could speak. "I'm sorry I brought you here."

Faith tried to keep her voice even, her mind clear. "Doesn't Kitty Ging live here?"

May nodded and swallowed. "She does. But so does Hayward."

Faith felt as though she'd been kicked by a horse. Her body

went rigid with shock. She leaned against the wall and slid down it, her spine to the bricks, until her bottom came to rest on the wet ground. May followed suit.

"I'm sorry," May said again. "I didn't want to bring you here. I've enjoyed your company, always. He's got such sway over me. He told me to bring you to him and I . . . I simply couldn't resist. I . . ."

Faith shook her head, quieting May. "It's hogwash," she said grimly. "There is no Mesmerism. There is only convincing people it's all right to do what they already wish."

Quietly, May began to cry. Faith might have been too harsh with her, but she couldn't worry about that now. She could only think of Hayward and what he'd done to her.

Whatever shame May felt at having worked in a sporting house—Faith had intuited almost from the beginning that this was the case, even though May had buried the memories so deeply it seemed she had almost convinced herself they didn't happen—it must have paled in comparison with the helplessness, the sheer terror that had consumed Faith when she discovered the true purpose for which Hayward and Lundberg had brought her to work for Priscilla Black. Faith had been so stupid to believe any of them thought men would pay to have their fortunes read at a house of ill fame. The clients were there for something else, something very particular, something she hoped May's johns had never demanded.

A special sort of evil had gone into Priscilla's design for Faith. She'd spread the word through back alleys and channels that she'd gotten her hands on a real Argentine—not only a bona fide Argentine courtesan, but a debutante! A daughter of industry, offspring of the very barons and tycoons the men of Minneapolis had invested money with before they lost it so badly. Priscilla had let her clients do anything they wanted to Faith—encouraged it, even. She must have recognized that she'd gotten hold of a true prize: a girl who wouldn't talk back, who had no friends she could count on. Worse, whose friends had sold her up the river. Faith could never be certain how much Hayward and Lundberg knew about what was happening to her at Priscilla's. But they kept supplying Priscilla with green goods, and continued, Faith presumed, to collect their share of the fat profits, none of which went to her.

Her rage toward them grew over her months at Priscilla's, became a hot, pulsating thing behind her eyes. How could she have misinterpreted their intentions so badly, how could she have thought they truly saw her as an equal, a partner? She'd always been a bit suspicious of Hayward, but Johnny had found a way to slip past her best defenses. She'd enjoyed sleeping with him; she'd persuaded herself he was a decent man.

Faith pressed her fingers to her eyes. She longed to tell May all of this, but May would ask why Faith hadn't simply run away from Priscilla's. How could she explain? There had been ample opportunities, now that Faith looked back: when all of Priscilla's girls would traipse to the courthouse once a month, Faith could have shouted to the bailiff or one of the police officers that she was being held against her will. But who would have believed her? Priscilla had been such a slick talker, and Faith barely able to string two words together without choking on them. Frequently, Priscilla reminded all her girls that they were deeply in her debt, for the bed, board, heat, and clothing she supposedly provided. She could have any one of them brought in for theft if she wanted. To demonstrate, Priscilla invited the sheriff's men to visit the brothel regularly, plied them with the best liquor, or at least cheap liquor in good bottles. Some of them she sent upstairs with Faith.

That last john had meant to murder her, to choke her to death. Priscilla would have let him if Faith hadn't managed to scream, if the few friends she'd made in the brothel—good girls, they were, and not much better off under Priscilla's watch than Faith was—hadn't burst in to pry him off. They'd badgered him into paying her in gold, after he collected himself and pretended the whole thing had been a joke.

Faith had gripped the coins in her fist, as well as the rest of the gold she'd collected earlier that day, and resolved to escape that very night, even if it spelled death. For herself, or someone else.

"Faith, please. We have to go home." May waved her hand in front of Faith's face. "I can't let Hal see you."

Slowly, Faith shook her head. "We're here now. We will find Miss Ging."

As May's mouth opened, they heard a sound coming from the far end of the alley. A man was walking toward them. The two of them scrambled to their feet, May clutching at Faith's sleeve. She tried to focus on the stranger in the dark, his hunched figure.

"It's not him," Faith murmured. This man was shorter, bulkier than Hayward. He was crying, she realized as he came closer. He hung his head, making a keening sound, his eyes squeezing shut as he stumbled forward. His hands were covered in some sort of dirt. He wore simple clothing, a drab brown coat in a rough material, a misshapen hat, gray trousers with muddied hems. A custodian, she thought, which explained why he'd be using the alley door and not the front one.

Faith cleared her throat. She'd hoped May would ask him if he'd let them in to see Miss Ging, but May had turned into a statue.

"Excuse me, sir," Faith said, hoping he'd be able to hear her.

The man looked up and stopped short, staring at them as if he'd seen a pair of ghosts. Then he crept closer—one step, another. His eyes were rimmed with red, his nose running, his burly mustache glistening. He looked to have been out in the cold for some time, his lips purplish, his bare hands chapped. As he came under the glow of the single lightbulb, Faith could see that his hands were red, too, that what she'd assumed was mud was, in fact, somebody's blood. He was covered in it.

A sob lodged in her throat.

"Who . . ." the man said, looking from her to May. "Who are you? Why are you here?" Faith detected a hint of an accent, something Scandinavian. The man sniffed loudly, wiping his nose with the back of his hand.

Neither of them could answer him. May had gone stiff with fear. Faith's veins ran cold as she came to grips with the fact that Hayward had already done it.

Kitty Ging was dead. He'd had this man kill her.

The man sniffed audibly, flaring his nostrils above his bushy mustache. It seemed he might be regretting what he'd just done: look at how he wept. Faith took a timid step forward, her boot crunching the iced-over snow. He flinched, squinting at her with his bulbous eyes. As though *she* might hurt *him*. The realization flooded her with a sense of command, and she found her voice.

"We're here to help," she said soothingly. She had always found it easier to speak to people who seemed desperate or frightened, who she could tell needed her. Somehow, she found it possible to look past the blood on his hands and into his eyes, stricken with an animal terror. "Look at you. You've been through a trial."

May gasped and tightened her hold on Faith's sleeve. She hoped May would understand what she was doing.

The man's eyes darted between the two of them. "Did *he* send you?"

"No," said Faith quickly. "No, we're here in spite of him."

After a moment's hesitation, the man sighed, lowering his rounded shoulders an inch. "All right. All right, come in. Come in, you can help me with the . . ." He trailed off. He used his key to open the alley door, whimpering a little and muttering about his stained coat, the trousers, how he'd have to burn them. He went inside, letting the door yawn open behind him. Through the doorway, Faith could see a set of industrial wrought-iron stairs, leading down into a darkened cellar. She took a deep breath and made to follow him, but May held her back.

Faith turned to peel May's fingers from her arm. "We have to," she whispered.

"No. Please!" May's chest heaved in her terror, her eyes darting from the cellar door back to Faith. "We can still get away from him. This is our chance."

Faith shook her head. She felt her chin tremble. "He'll have killed Kitty with your gun. You must take it back or you'll hang with him."

May's jaw fell open. The pieces, it seemed, were sliding into place for her.

Faith extricated herself and hurried inside, her eyes working to adjust to the dark. She could see the hulking figure of the custodian at the base of the staircase, traveling down a damp, scantly lit hallway, its ceiling a web of dripping pipes. She swallowed and took a step down, then another. The iron stairs felt sharp through the thin soles of her boots.

23
ABBY

"The inmates of this home are not your playthings," Charlotte said forcefully. "They are not your daughters."

They sat in the office, Abby behind the desk, Charlotte and Euphemia opposite her in the two visitors' chairs, which somehow made her feel more vulnerable. Three cups of tea had turned cold before them, untouched. Worse, even, than Charlotte's harsh words was Euphemia's silence, the fact that she hadn't looked Abby in the eye since Miss Rhoades revealed her secret.

"I have never considered them dolls, or daughters," Abby retorted, her face flushed despite the chill air coming from the window. "I didn't send Faith Johnson out into the cold today. She made the decision to leave, without telling anyone."

May hadn't turned up for dinner, either, Miss Rhoades had reported, but Abby wasn't ready to tell Charlotte that. The whole scenario felt dizzying. Abby needed some time alone to make sense of it all.

Charlotte set her ear horn in her lap. "But you took it upon yourself to hide Miss Johnson in the tower. And yet you say, in your view, she had nothing to do with the murdered madam?"

Euphemia shifted her square-framed glasses higher on her nose as she studied the floor. Abby opened her mouth, but no sound came out. She'd been prepared to turn Faith in to the police herself—hadn't she?—just a day before. Perhaps it was her own stubbornness getting in the way now, preventing her from cooperating with Charlotte. The way Charlotte had contacted the detective behind her back, the way they'd stormed in here like torch-bearing villagers hunting a witch—none of it sat well with Abby.

Maybe she did see the girls in here as her daughters, but did she protect them to a fault? It must have been easy for Charlotte to see Abby's devotion in a negative light—Charlotte, who'd been blessed with so many children of her own.

Charlotte stood up, favoring her bad knee, her ear horn dangling in her hand. "This had better not be a repeat of what happened with Delia. You don't need another girl's death on your conscience, Abby."

At last, Euphemia picked her head up, her expression shot through with sympathy.

"That was unnecessary, Mrs. Van Cleve," Abby said. She struggled to keep her voice steady. "Delia, too, acted of her own accord."

Charlotte turned at the door. Abby couldn't be sure she'd heard her. "For your sake and hers, I hope the girl, Faith, has found safety far away from here. And I hope you will dismiss Miss Rhoades with all dispatch." She set her lips grimly and nodded at the two other women, then left.

The air in the room felt notably flattened in Charlotte's wake. Abby and Euphemia were left to sit in uncomfortable silence. Abby could sense her friend's embarrassment on her behalf, or, worse, her pity. Other than Abby, only Euphemia knew the significance of the madam's missing eyebrow, not to mention the fact that Abby had hired Miss Rhoades by herself, had gone to St. Paul to meet her, that she alone had failed to examine the woman's background properly. Abby had instantly taken a personal liking to Miss Rhoades; she'd wanted Miss Rhoades to be the right fit.

"I can be the one to speak with Miss Rhoades, if you'd prefer that," Euphemia said. "I'll offer her two weeks' pay."

"No. No, it's my duty, I hired her." Abby pressed her fingers to her temples, feeling the ridges of bone under her thin skin.

"Thank you," Euphemia said, sounding relieved. "You must remember what Charlotte said," she added, a hint of reproach in her tone. "We simply cannot offer to serve as a reference. Our reputation . . ."

"*We* cannot serve as a reference?" Abby's voice rose, higher than she intended, and she watched her friend flinch. "What's become of us, Euphemia? Our entire mission demands we accept girls as they are, without asking questions, then return them to the world on the premise that they're worthy of a second chance. If we don't believe it's true of Miss Rhoades, can we claim we believe it of any of them?"

A vein pulsed at Euphemia's temple. She wasn't one for confrontation, as Abby well knew. She could count on one hand the number of times they'd spoken sharply to each other in twenty-five years. "I share your concerns," Euphemia said quietly. "But hiring a former sporting woman . . . You know how it looks, Abby. Besides, Miss Rhoades was not honest with us. Would you have hired her if she had been?"

Abby wanted to say yes, but when she stared into the depths of her conscience, she wasn't sure. "You'd best go home, Euphe-

THE MESMERIST · 255

mia," she said gruffly. "The weather's not likely to improve. I
won't be far behind you."

Euphemia stood, a bit shakily. "Are you sure you don't want
me to take you home? My man brought the Concord coach."

Abby shook her head. "I should take my time in talking with
Miss Rhoades. You go home and have a restful sleep."

Euphemia nodded. She reached out and grasped Abby's hand,
her fingernails digging into Abby's palm. Abby swallowed the
lump in her throat and squeezed back.

When Euphemia had gone, Abby locked the door to the
office. She kept a nightgown and a thick quilted dressing gown
in the wardrobe, along with a white silk nightcap. There was a
bed in the infirmary that would be comfortable enough for the
night. It had been years since she'd slept here, when another of
her favorites had gone missing. Her heart beat at a clip as she
changed into her nightclothes and stashed her black dress and
underthings into a drawer. She took the lantern from the desk
and made her way into the darkened hallway.

Miss Rhoades was coming down the stairs, holding a flickering candle in a brass carrier. Abby could scarcely look at her.
Her conversation with Euphemia hammered at the inside of her
skull.

"Are you staying the night, Mrs. Mendenhall? My, it's been a
while, hasn't it?"

"I'll stay in case the girls return," Abby said. "Any sign of
May?"

"No, ma'am. Nor Faith. I'm beside myself." Miss Rhoades
came close and lowered her voice as a group of inmates, also
in their nightclothes, went past. "The mercury's well below
freezing. I checked the closet, and they took two coats, but still.
Those poor girls."

Abby agreed, yet still felt an automatic urge to project authority, to be the voice of law and reason. "They may not be so innocent, especially Faith. Take care to remember that."

A strange look passed over Miss Rhoades's face. "Surely,
whatever she's done, you don't think she deserves to freeze to
death, Mrs. Mendenhall."

She absolutely did not. The very thought made her want to
collapse. "Of course not." Her fingers found the simple silver
cross she wore around her neck and worked the smooth metal.
"Miss Rhoades, we need to speak this evening. After the inmates
have gone to bed."

Miss Rhoades's face fell. "I figured we would." She opened
her mouth to say something else, but then Pearl came up and
squeezed her arm.

"A group of us are heading to the parlor," she told Miss
Rhoades companionably, with a quick glance at Abby. "Won't
you come tell us a ghost story?" She seemed at ease with Miss
Rhoades, as if the two were peers, leaving Abby to wonder how
many of the inmates guessed at Miss Rhoades's history, or knew
by instinct.

Abby laughed lightly. "Why, we're almost a month from
Christmas Eve."

Miss Rhoades patted Pearl's hand. "Certainly, Pearl. I can
tell a ghost story." They turned to walk toward the parlor,
Miss Rhoades at the last second beckoning to Abby over her
shoulder, as if she were an afterthought.

Through the big front-facing windows of the parlor, Abby
could see that the wind outside had grown teeth, snipping and
snatching at the bent-over trees. The glass of each window was
caked in snow, the whole building creaking and settling with
each gust. Nearly all the inmates, thirty of them at least, poured

into the room, bearing blankets and bed warmers, and took their seats in twos and threes on the carpet, huddled around the fire. Abby remained standing by the door, hip bones tired, knees aching. The girls glanced at her and muttered to one another, and she found herself pulling her dressing gown more tightly around her neck. Despite its thickness, she felt strangely exposed, naked. She wondered if they felt that her presence spoiled the occasion, if they acted differently when she wasn't around. They remained quiet as they watched the matron settle into a big chair beside the hearth, listening to the wind whine like a wraith as it whipped around the tower.

"It sounds like *her*," someone sitting near the fire muttered. Leigh, one of the kitchen apprentices. She crossed herself. Dolly appeared beside her and rubbed her shoulder, both staring at the floor. No one else said a word, but the girls cast wary looks at one another. Kindling crackled in the fire.

Miss Rhoades brought a lamp close to her and turned the key so the flame lit her face from beneath in shades of gold, casting the sharp angles of her features into shadow.

"Will you tell 'The Signal-Man'?" Pearl cried, from her place on the settee.

The matron shook her head. "Thought I'd tell a new one today, girls."

The wind gave a shriek of approval, and the inmates huddled closer under their blankets. Miss Rhoades waited a moment, eyes closed, catching her breath. At last, her shoulders relaxed, and just before she began to speak, she caught Abby's eye.

"There once was an old woman," Miss Rhoades said, still holding Abby's gaze, "who lived with her two daughters beside a lake of ice."

Abby's limbs froze. As Miss Rhoades dove into her story,

Abby had the sensation that her soul had abandoned her body, left it stiff and lifeless. Her spirit seemed to hover near the ceiling of the room, over the enraptured figures of all the girls, until she burst out through the roof and could see the scene for herself: the battered wooden cottage; the ragged coast of the lake, crusted in frozen tides; and, finally, the woman and her two daughters, their hair long and as black as magpie feathers.

Miss Rhoades had told her once that her mother came from Donegal, and Abby could hear just a hint of it now in her storytelling, a lilt to Miss Rhoades's voice, hypnotic and foreboding.

"The mother and her daughters were poor, but happy. They sustained themselves on the fish that lived in the lake, and as soon as the girls were old enough, the woman taught them to bait a line, to drill holes in the ice," Miss Rhoades intoned, her features licked by the flames. "She warned her daughters that in early winter, the thin surface ice would only hold if they remained close to shore. The younger girl, called Roisin, was obedient and quiet, and stayed close to her mother. She preferred to read by the fire or sit in a chair by the window and watch birds swoop over the lake. But the elder daughter, Eimear, the old woman's favorite, didn't believe the laws of nature applied to her. She ventured farther and farther, onto thinner and thinner ice, until one winter solstice, the ice cracked under her feet, and she plunged through."

A few gasps rippled through the room, a muffled giggle.

"The woman made Roisin hunt with her for Eimear's body, deep into the year's longest night, even as Roisin begged to return to the cottage. When the mother found Eimear, dead, floating beneath the sheet of ice, she threw her head back and wailed. After her tears dried, she realized her mistake. She'd drawn Roisin too far onto the thin ice and had also lost her to the lake. And now the old woman found herself alone."

The wind raised its voice, and Abby was startled back into her body. An electric lamp in the corridor flickered. A few of the girls squealed. Abby could remember her eldest brother telling Christmas ghost stories, when she was a young girl, and feeling as the inmates must: wrapped in pleasant fear, huddled under a warm blanket while winter raged outside. She didn't share that sentiment now. She felt conspicuous, out of place, as though she'd intruded on a moment that should be experienced by the inmates alone.

"On the other side of the lake," Miss Rhoades continued, "there lived a witch. The old woman and her daughters had always avoided her, but when she came the first evening of the new year—first in the form of a squall, banging at the old woman's door, which in time became a fist, an arm, a body draped in rags—the mother let the witch inside. She demanded to be served hot tea and biscuits, the last of the old woman's food, for she'd been too deep in her grief to do any fishing at all.

"'You may have your daughters back,' the witch promised the old woman, 'on one condition.' The witch could refashion them into being, using the clay of the earth and the water from the lake. But their mother must forbid them to leave the cottage. If they did, they'd melt back into the landscape, and she'd lose them all over again. The old woman hastily agreed, and in the morning, when she woke, her girls were there.

"They looked the same, save for their eyes, which had turned a solid, pale blue. The woman was relieved when Eimear laughed and teased her for eating all their stored food, and Roisin curled up by the window, picking up her book where she'd left off. But when their mother went close to her daughters, she could see how they'd changed. Eimear's skin was cold to the touch and would begin to melt if the old woman laid her hand there too long: she'd been remade out of solid ice. Roisin's complexion glittered like thousands of tiny diamonds, and when she spoke, her whispered voice came out gritty and rough, for the witch had built her out of sand."

No one said anything now. It was only a story, but Abby felt her heart pounding in the fragile cage of her chest, thinking less of Eimear and Roisin than she was of May Lombard and Faith Johnson.

"Because the girls had been fashioned of magic, they remained unchanged even as spring arrived. Eimear didn't melt when the old woman flung the windows open to let in the south wind, but the girl quickly grew restless. She begged her mother to let her go outside, and of course the old woman said no. Eimear wept, her hot tears working tracks into the ice of her cheeks, and she flung her body at the door in an attempt to knock it from its hinges. The old woman devised more and more desperate bindings, to keep her daughter in: a metal cage meant for a hound long since dead, a rope attaching her wrist to her bedstead. But nothing could keep Eimear contained for long.

"At last, in her desperation, the old woman built a fire just outside the cottage's only door, thinking that would hold Eimear back. Eimear stood in the threshold, watching the fire burn. By now her tears had worn grooves so deep in her cheeks, you could see through to her bones. The old woman stood on the other side of the flames, praying she could keep her daughter with her, forever. She was puzzled when Eimear waved, a sad wave of goodbye, and stepped right into the fire. The old woman screamed, but she was too late: in a puff of steam, her elder daughter was gone."

Miss Rhoades paused in her story to take a long sip of tea. The girls were quiet. Abby touched her own face and realized she'd been crying, like a child. She wiped her eyes with the back of her sleeve.

"As her daughter evaporated, the old woman heard what sounded like a sigh of relief on the wind, and a tinkling like Eimear's laughter. She looked back to the door of the cottage and saw Roisin standing there, smiling up into the clouds. As Roisin hovered on the threshold, the breeze picked up wisps of sand from her arms and her face, lifting them into the wind. The old woman cried her name, begging her to stay inside, and a frown crossed Roisin's face. She stared across the fire at her mother, and with a sad little smile, she followed in her older sister's footsteps and walked into the flames."

At Abby's feet, the girl called Leigh had her thin arms wrapped around Dolly's shoulders, their heads touching. Miss Rhoades took another drink, holding the cup and saucer in her hand. Her eyes sparkled in the light of the fire. "Well, the old woman went into the cottage, once again alone and devastated. She understood why Eimear had run away, but Roisin! Her little one, her dependable child—the old woman had never imagined Roisin would leave her. She realized she'd largely ignored Roisin, all these years, so distracted she'd been, worrying after Eimear. And then she heard a knock at the door.

"She went to answer it, and there stood Roisin, a look of calm on her face. Heat wafted from her as she cooled. The old woman stood by, dumbfounded, as Roisin came inside to sit at her bookshelf as though nothing had happened. The mother ran to her daughter's feet and wept, her head in Roisin's lap. Roisin's legs felt firm and solid. The old woman realized then what had happened: the fire had turned her staid little daughter of sand into the strongest tempered glass.

" 'The witch was wrong,' Roisin told her mother. 'I can come and go as I please now. But I'll stay in the cottage with you if you'd like my company. There's just one thing I must do first.'

"Of course, the old woman was terrified to let her daughter back outside. What if Roisin was mistaken, and she'd blow away, grain by grain of sand, if she left the cottage? But the woman remembered what had happened when she tried to force Eimear to stay, and she let Roisin go. And Roisin, now made of glass, did not blow away. She climbed the highest bluff overlooking the lake and built a cairn of stones, which the old woman presumed was for Eimear. Roisin stood for a while, overlooking the lake, smiling out at the blue water. Then she climbed down and came up the path to the cottage, her skin sunbrowned and gleaming, and she folded herself into her mother's embrace.

"They went on to live there for many happy years. And sometimes, when a spring storm blew in from the lake, they thought they could still hear Eimear's laughter."

Miss Rhoades looked at Abby as she spoke the last lines of the story, and Abby was glad she'd wiped the tears from her face. She gave Miss Rhoades a little nod.

"That was a lovely story," Abby said, her voice hoarse. "What's its title?"

Miss Rhoades gave a little laugh. "I don't know. I made it up myself."

"It wasn't really a ghost story," Pearl commented, her voice piercing the room's trance.

The matron shot her a look of amusement. "Well, I'll have to do better next—"

Everyone jumped as the front door of the home blew open and hit the jamb with a bang. Abby was the first to get to the foyer, Miss Rhoades close behind her, the girls screaming and clutching at one another, slipping in their stocking feet as they clamored to see.

"It's Eimear," someone muttered, setting off a ripple of nervous giggles.

"It's nobody," Miss Rhoades said, holding the knob, wisps of snow whirling past her. "There's no one there."

"The wind must have forced it open," said Abby. The electric light on the front porch swung back and forth, blinding her. Before they shut the door firmly, she squinted toward the far side of the street, a sea of blackness, the trees and sidewalks obscured from her view. Anyone could be standing there, and she wouldn't be able to see him. But he would be able to see not only her, but also the matron, and the cluster of inmates behind her. Not playthings, but people, all of them women, with graver concerns than sand, ice, or snow.

It took until nearly midnight for the house to fall quiet. The inmates, riled by Miss Rhoades's story and Faith's and May's disappearances, filled the air with edgy laughter and muffled shrieks for hours until, finally, the last of them had gone to bed and put out her lamp. Miss Rhoades came downstairs, yawning audibly, to find Abby at the sidelight window beside the front door, still staring out at the street.

"You intended that story for me." She spoke to Miss Rhoades without taking her eyes from the road. When Miss Rhoades sputtered a denial, Abby shook her head. "You believe I've . . . I've interfered too much in the lives of my favorites."

"No, I don't, ma'am." Miss Rhoades sighed. "What's happening now, May and Faith going missing—it isn't the same as with Delia."

Abby bit back a quick response. Her throat made a guttural sound, close to a sob. No, it wasn't the same as with Delia; Delia had committed no crime. But Abby had tried to cage her, in a sense, and, just like tonight, it had ended badly. Twice, Delia had run away from the Bethany Home, which would tolerate no laudanum use within its walls. The second time, when Abby had found her in an opium den, asleep, so sickly-pale she appeared to have been pickled in brine, Abby had taken her back to her own house. She'd placed Delia in her mother's old room, the sunniest in the house, given her their best goose-down pillows and comforter, and attempted to fatten her up with meat pies and ice cream. Junius had been wary at first, but he'd warmed to her, in those three months she lived with them. He'd seen her potential, too: the way her eyes lit up when they engaged her in philosophical debates; her clear, steady voice as she read the Bible; her gifted watercolors, the brush strokes as dainty as a mouse's footprints.

Abby had lied to the Sisterhood of Bethany then, too. She'd told herself she'd forgotten to change the ledger, in which she'd listed Delia as a runaway. When Swede Kate called on them to help her with Delia's death inquiry—after Delia left Abby's in the middle of the night, in search of the easy flow of morphine in a place like Kate's—Charlotte had been flabbergasted to learn Abby had been keeping Delia at her home.

"I put Delia in harm's way," Abby told Miss Rhoades now.

"She'd have been safer here, with you, rather than kept and coddled in my home."

Miss Rhoades shook her head. "Delia wasn't a child, and neither are Faith and May. They must be allowed their free will."

Abby narrowed her lips, watching the street. If she'd been consistent in her enforcement of the rules, she'd have sent May back out into the world when her year was up. The girl wouldn't have had time to get to know Faith Johnson, and perhaps she'd have been better off for it.

"I have a confession as well, Mrs. Mendenhall."

Abby turned toward the matron, whose eyes gleamed. "Miss Rhoades, please." Abby took her hand. "You've bared your soul enough for one day, you needn't say more."

Miss Rhoades shook her head. A tear slipped down her cheek. "I was the one who called the *Representative* about Faith being held in the tower."

Abby stiffened. She was still holding Miss Rhoades's hand. The urge to drop it was strong.

Miss Rhoades sniffed. "I thought it might be the way to get your attention, to convince you to free her. I never anticipated Mrs. Van Cleve bringing the police, or what would follow. I didn't..." She wiped her eye with the lace edge of her sleeve. "I didn't mean to cause everyone such trouble."

Abby held her breath. She'd been given strict instructions to give Miss Rhoades the sack, and now she could do so without reluctance. She stood quietly for a moment as the matron dabbed her nose, listening to the grandfather clock tick in the parlor. Miss Rhoades kept it wound, polished, and dusted. She had given many worthy years to this institution, all with an energetic commitment to its mission, always in good cheer.

Had it been so bad, what Miss Rhoades had done in alerting the press? Had Abby in fact needed someone to sound the alarm, to offer a check against the imperious way she sometimes ran this place?

"What's done is done, child," Abby said, softly. There was more she wanted to say, with her defensiveness riled, but she let it go. What was done was done.

Miss Rhoades could only reply with a nod, and an attempt at a smile, and Abby realized, after a beat, that she'd just spoken to the matron as though she were one of the inmates. She wondered if Miss Rhoades could hear a hidden message there, a sign that she couldn't be allowed to stay in her position of authority much longer.

In any case, Abby was tired. She longed to retreat for the evening. Her muscles, held tense since early this morning, felt rubbery. Still, she went on standing there with Miss Rhoades, side by side, the two of them peering out at the road, hoping they might see two little figures returning in the snow, holding on to each other for support.

24

MAY

*T*he man hadn't recognized her. May repeated this to herself, her boots frozen to the ground, as she tried to will herself to follow Faith into the basement of the Ozark Flats. He hadn't remembered.

She could bolt, save herself; she could run and try to find help, but that would mean leaving Faith alone with the man who'd strangled May on her way home from Gussie's house, and besides, *besides*—she pressed her hands to her eyes, her breaths coming so heavily they rocked her back and forth—he hadn't seemed to recognize her. The night of Gussie's party, she'd been dressed like a woman of much higher social standing. He must have assumed this girl before him in a drab woolen cloak and stout boots couldn't possibly be the same person.

She inhaled, the air so cold it seemed to pierce her sinuses, and took a timid step forward. Knees wobbling, she gripped the metal railing and stepped down, down, into the basement.

The man lived in an apartment at the end of a dark hallway, past a hissing black boiler and a maze of dripping pipes. She could hear him whimpering, and Faith speaking in soothing tones—astonishingly, Faith had found the ability to speak at full volume and clearly—before she reached the soft lamplight of his little room. May hovered at the doorway, taking it all in: the slab floor; his unmade, rumpled bed, the sheets stained; a stack of yellowed newspapers that served as a nightstand; a plate heaped with poultry bones, discarded in the corner. The only saving grace was that the room radiated with heat from the nearby boiler. Still, May had never felt a stronger urge to leave a place than she did right now.

"Oh, good," Faith said, her voice flush with relief. "You're here." She cleared her throat and gestured to the man, who'd sat down on the edge of his bed, one arm propped between his brow and his knee. "This is Mr. Blixt."

May nodded rapidly, making her eyes wide, hoping Faith understood, but Faith appeared distracted, pacing the room in anxious little steps, cataloguing her surroundings, like a detective. Finally, she stopped and rested her hand—May had to wince—on Blixt's shoulder.

Faith knelt before him. "Why don't you tell us what happened?" she asked gently.

The question escaped May's lips before she could think twice about it. "Did you strangle her?" Her voice sounded hoarse.

Both the man and Faith looked up sharply at May, and, finally, May saw a glint of recognition in Faith's eyes: this was the walrus-like man May had described. She gave May a nearly imperceptible nod.

"*No,*" the man spat, his expression savage, his eyes still rimmed with red. "I done her quick, so she wouldn't suffer. She didn't even make a sound. That's how he said to do it, make it quick and then bring the gig home."

"But he made you do it, didn't he?" Faith said, kneeling before the murderer. May wasn't sure whether to feel admiration or disgust at her ability to speak gently to this person, to appear sympathetic. "It was all Hayward's idea."

Blixt gave a wet sniff and nodded, looking at his bloodstained hands. "It was like he could get his voice inside my head, messing me up. He'd see me looking at her, and he'd say, 'She deserves to be six feet under.' And I started thinking it, too. I'd see her and I'd think, *That girl should be put in the ground. Someone ought to put her there.*"

There was a little chair beside the door, a wooden chair that looked to have been made for a child. May sank down into it.

"He took advantage of you," Faith said. "He's asked you to do so many terrible, terrible things." Her gaze shifted slightly to the left, in May's direction. A sickening thought came to May as she realized what Faith was implying: that Hal had told this man to come after her. It had been Hal's fingers, on her neck, even if Blixt had been the one to carry out the deed.

"That must weigh heavily on you," Faith said, and even though her gaze still fell on Blixt, May couldn't be sure whom she was talking to.

The man looked up toward heaven, turning his ruddy cheeks to the light. "It does, oh, it does. I put her in the lake, but she was afloat. They'll find her, and, oh, they'll hang me for it. Claus Blixt's gonna swing."

Faith shook her head. "They won't if you tell them how he mesmerized you. How he got into your mind. How he . . ." She paused, and her eyes took another lap around the room. They seemed to land on the makeshift table, the stack of newspapers, where an oval-shaped frame held something May hadn't noticed before, something that seemed improbable: a daguerreotype from a wedding. She could make out a pale triangle, the bride's gown, beside the looming sepia shape of the groom.

". . . how he threatened to kill your wife if you didn't do it," Faith finished.

Blixt perked up and began nodding. "He did, didn't he? He told me he'd kill Frances if I didn't do this broad."

May watched, amazed, as a little smile appeared on Faith's face. How could she have known Hal had threatened the man's wife? Or had she planted the idea in this simple man's head, to turn him against Hayward, when the police inevitably came? May found herself beginning to relax, warmed by the close air inside the apartment and the extraordinary power her bunkmate seemed to possess. This was beginning to feel like David versus Goliath, with Faith in the role of the giant.

Faith shook her head. "He bought insurance on Miss Ging, did you know that? He's about to collect a lot of money, and were you to see a dime?"

"A little of the money's mine, yes," the man grunted, wiping his wet mustache on his sleeve. "And he said I could keep the revolver."

"Oh, Claus, no," Faith said. "You need to get rid of it. That's part of his plan to pin the whole mess on you, don't you see? You need to get rid of the gun and those bloody clothes. Here, why don't you give the weapon to me? I'll make sure it sees the bottom of a lake."

At the phrase "bottom of a lake," Blixt winced, but he got up and went to the bedpost where he'd hung his jacket. He reached into one of the pockets and pulled out May's revolver. The engraved metal gleamed in the lamplight.

May's breath caught in her throat on seeing it. The end was blackened with gunpowder. Faith stared at it, too, as Blixt made to hand it to her, then hesitated.

"It's a lady's gun," he said, some contempt in his voice. He brought it to his sleeve and wiped it off, his movements clumsy. At any moment, it seemed the thing could accidentally fire. May fought the urge to run into the hallway. They had to wrest the gun from him, somehow. Then they'd get home as quickly as they could.

"You'll be all right now," Faith cooed. She stood, getting just a bit closer to the man. Her belly protruded, just a bit, through the gap in her cloak, yet she didn't seem afraid. "Get rid of those clothes and there's nothing tying you to the crime. Why, I'll bet you have a big sink somewhere down here. But you already thought of that, of course."

Blixt was still holding on to the revolver. "I was going to do that after I met him."

"Met him?" said Faith.

"When he gets home, I'm meant to meet him upstairs." The custodian's beady eyes narrowed at the brass clock beside his bed. "After the opera. Shouldn't be long now."

They watched Blixt polish the gun, his movements jerky and harsh, as though he meant to strip off a layer of metal. Faith's eyes met May's over the weapon. She looked as if she was holding in a scream. Slowly, she held out a smooth, white hand and offered it to him gingerly, palm up, the way one might approach a skittish dog. "You don't need to do that," she said, her voice soft and breathy. "I can get rid of it for you."

Blixt stopped wiping the gun, but he hesitated before putting it in Faith's hand. "It's a lady's weapon," he said again. "Hayward said he was going to pin the whole thing on some girl who was jealous. Not on me."

Blood thudded behind May's ears, so intense it was almost painful.

"But that'll never work," Faith replied quickly. "Hand it to me. Easy, now. Before he comes home."

Nobody moved for a long moment. The brass clock ticked. Blixt peered at the two women as they held their breath. Finally, he handed the pistol to Faith, stretching out his grubby fingers, knuckles caked in blood and dirt. When she took the gun, her body visibly slackened, and May felt the air rush from her own lungs.

Without thinking, it seemed, Faith turned and offered it to May, a reluctant sort of smile on her face. May accepted the revolver, feeling sheepish, wanting to fling herself at Faith's feet and explain: she'd let herself believe Hal wielded such an influence over her, just as he appeared to control this awful man.

"There you go," Faith said, and May whispered, "Thank you."

When she stood to go, anxious to put miles between herself and this place, she realized Claus Blixt was now staring at her. The vacant, weepy expression had left his face, replaced with a suspicious glare. It was as if he'd completely forgotten she was here at all, and now he'd decided she shouldn't be.

"What'd you say your name was?" he asked.

A feverish terror ran its course through May's body, making it difficult for her to think of anything more than the last time she'd encountered this man, the way his fingers had gripped the back of her neck as he'd pressed her down to the pavement. He recognized her now, but he was still trying to place her. Another few minutes in this room and he'd figure it out.

He was waiting for her answer. Faith had gone quiet. "Why?" May asked.

"I said, *What's your name?*" Blixt put a sharp edge on the last three words. He lumbered forward, seeming suddenly larger, taller, menacing.

Faith took a step toward the door and pinched May's elbow lightly, urging her to follow. "Claus, remember. If anyone questions you, tell them everything about the way Hayward threatened you, how he mesmerized you. Tell them how he threatened your wife."

He didn't answer. He followed them out of his little apartment, said nothing when they bade him goodbye. May hurried down the dark corridor, willing herself not to look back at him. All she could hear were Faith's ragged breaths as they climbed the iron stairs. At the door, she couldn't help glancing downward. Blixt stood motionless at the bottom of the staircase, peering up at them with narrowed eyes, his thick hands balled into fists.

Outside, the air nipped at their faces as they walked as quickly as they could toward the sidewalk. It was well past nightfall, but the sky, draped in a thick blanket of snow clouds, glowed an eerie yellow, reflecting the city's electric lights. May could see the streetcar stop right up ahead of them, the sign half coated in snow. She'd completely lost track of the hour, of how long it had been since they left the Bethany Home or how long they'd been inside Blixt's apartment. She prayed that the streetcar was still running. They had to get away from here, to put as much distance between the Ozark Flats and themselves as was possible, and never return.

She tensed as she heard footsteps behind them, relaxed when she realized it was the clopping of horse's hooves rather than

274 · CAROLINE WOODS

a man's boots. The horse made a grunt of protest as someone pulled back on the reins, so close to May that she could almost feel the beast's hot breath on her shoulder. She heard shoes hit the pavement, and then a voice, so clear and confident that it was impossible to mistake who'd just stepped down from the carriage behind them:

"Why, May! What a good little girl you are. You've done just as I asked."

It was as if Hal's voice had tentacles, reaching out to grip her forehead, her throat, her arm, urging her to turn and face him. Faith took her hand and yanked her forward, giving her the strength to resist, but then she stumbled, as though he'd grabbed her by the ankle. She let go of Faith, and in the second it took May to regain her footing, Hal caught up with her and whirled her around.

"Where do you think you're going?" he sneered, his white-gloved fingers holding tight to her upper arm. They were a study in opposites, Hal and Claus Blixt: Hal's skin glowed with good health, his eyes were clear, his shoulders broad. May felt a sinking in her stomach. No one would ever believe he, between the two of them, was the real monster.

Another man stood behind him, slightly older, with wiry sideburns but the same piercing eyes. May recognized Hal's brother, Adry Hayward. He frowned in her direction. Both men wore white ties, elegant coats, and heavy cologne. They had just come from the opera, of course; if May had accepted Hal's invitation, she'd have been with them.

"Adry," Hal snapped at his brother, who moved to grab Faith. May could do little to stop him; now Adry had Faith in his clutches.

May looked around, panicked, but the street was deserted, the theater marquees had darkened, the neighborhood was hushed under its blanket of snow. In the distance, she could hear something coming, the muffled ring of a bell. The streetcar approached.

"What do we do with them?" Adry asked Hal. Faith thrashed in his grip like an animal caught in a snare, her boots skidding in the snow.

Hal held May close enough for his mustache to brush her cheek, her arm pinned to his chest, wrist bent backward. He grinned. "We'll take them inside. Give 'em a dressing down."

The streetcar's bell rang again, closer this time. May felt the LeMat weighing down her pocket. She stopped struggling and went limp. "It's not me you want," she said into Hal's collar. "I brought her here, just as you asked. Now let me go."

She felt him hesitate for a moment, his body tensed in surprise. Then, amazingly, he dropped her arm.

"You're more vicious than I give you credit for, Miss Lombard," he said.

Faith seemed to have lost the ability to speak, but a wounded sound escaped from her throat. Her eyes, panicked, seemed to plead as May took a step backward, then another, and another. Too far away for Hal to grab her easily. She hoped Faith could read her expression. She hoped Faith knew that, of all the people she'd met since she left Chicago, Faith was the only one who'd treated her like a true friend.

She hoped Faith knew she was not cruel, but weak.

Hal moved toward Faith, making as if to grab her, but at the same time May pulled the gun from her pocket. Adry shouted, and Hal turned.

"Where the hell did you get that?" he said, his lip curled in a sneer.

May pointed the barrel at him. The handle felt cold in her shaking hands. She prayed it still held some rounds. "Don't move."

The streetcar was coming closer. She could see its light building, as it prepared to round the curve. With her thumb, she pulled back on the hammer and cocked the revolver. Hal gave a wince that was more of a sneer.

"I said, where did you get that?"

She licked her cracked lips, thinking quickly. "It was on the ground outside your building. You must've dropped it there." She narrowed her eyes. "Clumsy."

Hal cursed, his breath visible in the cold. She hoped that he was cursing Claus Blixt, that he wouldn't figure out they'd been to see the man. Hal held his hands up in mock surrender, but he took half a step toward her. She stepped backward, darting the revolver between Adry and him.

"Drop her," she told Adry.

"May," Hal said, softly, "we both know you aren't going to shoot anyone. I haven't shown you how to use it yet." He chuckled. "It probably isn't even loaded."

Behind him, she could see Faith's lips moving. Something like flames danced in Faith's dark-blue eyes. She was saying something, an incantation, over and over again, her gaze trained on May. *Fire. Fire. Fire.*

May pointed the gun above Adry's head and fired.

The noise took her by surprise, the unexpected kickback of such a small gun nearly enough to knock her off her feet. Even Hal ducked, hands flung over his head; behind him, the other man had dropped Faith to cower on the ground.

"This is your mess," Adry spat at Hal. "I'm not ready to die for you, brother."

The two men began shouting at each other. Only Faith appeared unmoved, serene. When May had recovered, she saw that Faith might even be smiling at her.

The streetcar had rounded the corner, its bell clanging frantically; the driver must have heard the boom. The wheels were beginning to screech as it approached the stop.

"Run!" May shouted to Faith, who obeyed. She managed to slip past Hal's blundering attempt to grab her and began racing the streetcar to its stop as May held him off, the gun, its metal now hot in her hands, still pointed at his chest. She began taking steps backward, trying to catch up with Faith, but she felt like weeping. Hal would catch her. She knew he would. It would be impossible to fend him off and board the streetcar at the same time. She hoped that Faith, at least, would make it home safely.

"I'm going to tell them you did it," Hal said, coming closer to her. He stepped into a pool of lamplight, his face turning to a frightful mask of light and shadow.

"Did what?" May asked, still walking backward, hoping not to crash into anything.

"Killed another girl, because you were jealous. I left that gun outside on purpose, May, so you'd pick it up and take it home. They'll come looking for it. They'll come looking for you."

She laughed, a harsh, wet sound from deep inside her throat. His lies were so obvious now; how could she ever have considered him clever? Behind her, she could hear that the streetcar had stopped, but it hadn't started moving again. Not yet.

There was one thing she could do, she realized, that would ensure he'd leave her be, that might allow her an escape. She could kill him. She could prove to herself, for good, that she was stronger than her desire for this man's approval. She could make her father proud.

She laughed again. "Nobody knows who I am. Not even you. They won't come after me. You can't send them. You don't even know my real name."

For the first time, she saw a flicker of doubt pass over Hal's face.

Another shaky step backward. Her arms were beginning to ache. "What was it you said about the man you killed—that he was 'someone no one would miss'? Well, who would miss me? I could disappear tomorrow, and nobody would come looking for me. I'm no one." She lifted the revolver a little bit higher, praying desperately that it still had a bullet in the chamber. "I'm no one," she said louder, to hide the fact that she now had a lump in her throat. Her lips curved into a hint of a smile. "Who am I without Harry T. Hayward?"

She fired just as he lunged for her. She had the weapon trained straight at his head, realizing too late that she should have aimed lower, for a bigger target. Her shot exploded into the darkness, causing Adry to duck once more and Hal to spring forward like a fox snapping at a rabbit.

May yelped and leaped backward, her legs nimble. Her boots planted solidly on the ice. *Not today,* she thought. Hal's fingertips grazed her skirts, missing her by a centimeter and giving her a crucial second to turn and run for the trolley. The driver, having heard another gunshot, rang the bell—a frightened, bleating sound—and began to pull away from the station.

"No!" May cried through heaving breaths. "Wait!"

Faith stood in one of the open berths behind the driver, holding on to the pole with one arm, the other outstretched for

May. Slipping in the snow, May scrambled behind the moving streetcar, her hand a few feet away from Faith's, then more. The streetcar was gaining speed, taking its light with it. Soon May would be left in the dark with these two men. And with Claus Blixt. Perhaps it was what she deserved.

She watched Faith's expression become more rattled as she glanced behind May, who couldn't resist the urge to look back. Hal had gone sprawling in the snow, the front of his coat and tie ruined, but he was getting up.

Run, May, Faith's voice urged her. She could hear Faith's voice, echoing inside her skull, as clear as day. *Run and you'll make it.*

Even though she could hear Hal grunting, gaining on her, she made one last push, sprinting as she never had in her life, and somehow her boots found traction, she caught up to the streetcar just as it prepared to hit full speed, and she grabbed hold of Faith's slim hand. With surprising strength, Faith yanked her into the trolley.

They collapsed onto one of the wooden benches. "You saved me," May said, breathless, but now that the danger had passed, Faith's expression was inscrutable.

The driver turned around to face them, concern wrinkling his brow. "Were those gunshots I heard? I don't want any trouble."

May shook her head. Her hand slid to her pocket, patting the gun. Through the fabric of her skirt and her glove, she could still feel its heat.

"Those men were harassing us" was all she said. When she turned to peer out the back window of the streetcar, she saw that Hal had given up his chase. She and Faith stared at him, a motionless, menacing figure silhouetted against the snow, watching their car vanish into the night.

. . .

No one was awake when they crept into the foyer, not even the matron, but the front doors had been left unlocked. May made sure to bolt them before she and Faith went upstairs.

Faith hesitated for a moment at the threshold of their old room. Her bed, of course, had been stripped.

"It's all right," May whispered. She didn't even feel like changing out of her clothes. She took Faith by the hand and led her to her own narrow bed. "We can share."

They lay spine to spine, which felt comforting to May, protective. She wasn't sure how long Faith lay there with eyes open, as she did, her breaths shallow, her heart quickening at every sound. Slowly, their frigid skin warmed, their pulses quieted.

"I'm sorry," May whispered. She didn't expect a response.

So much lay unspoken between them, but they were too raw, after all that had just happened. May would explain, she would apologize in the morning for not telling Faith that Hayward lived in the Ozark Flats. She would explain who she was: someone who'd never had the luxury of true friendship, though now that she'd found it in Faith, she'd pledge never to let it go.

May tried closing her eyes, but when she did, she could still see Kitty turning the pages of her ledger, Kitty inspecting a dress hem, amused and sure of herself, still in her salad days. What a waste, and for what? A bit of money? May couldn't help wishing that it would turn out to be untrue, that they'd learn in the morning that Kitty Ging's heart still beat.

At last, May's eyelids grew too heavy to stay open. Sleep tugged at her exhausted body, though she realized Faith's breathing remained shallow. Faith seemed to be listening, alert, biding her time, until May dozed off.

She reached for Faith's hand, held tight to it. Faith squeezed back, once.

May struggled against sleep, until it finally got the better of her. As she drifted off, she knew that when she woke in the morning she'd be alone again—Faith gone for good.

25

ABBY

*O*ver the next few days, the news hit the city like a blizzard. First, the horrific discovery of Catherine "Kitty" Ging's body, shot behind the ear and abandoned on the shore of Lake Calhoun in the middle of the night. The story overtook anything else that had run in the papers of late, including any mention of a girl imprisoned at the Bethany Home. Instead, the journalists obsessed over Miss Ging, who'd newly earned a macabre brand of celebrity, chronicling her relative youth and her beauty, her apparent, unusual success as a female entrepreneur. They sensationalized the manhunt that led, quickly, to a poor Swedish immigrant, a furnace engineer who worked in the woman's apartment building. The police had been aided in their search by a young man named Harry T. Hayward, who had an alibi; he'd been at the opera the evening of the murder but, according to the gossip columnists' wagging tongues, had been courting Kitty Ging.

Abby had scarcely been able to discuss any of this with Junius. She'd barely seen her husband as she flitted between their estate, the Quaker meeting house, and the Bethany Home, as she would for several weeks following the murder and Faith Johnson's disappearance. At the home, she did her best to discourage the inmates from gossiping, from dwelling too intensely on the gruesome details of the murder, even though Abby herself was following the news with rapt attention.

Then, one early-December morning—not a week since Miss Ging had been found dead—the *Tribune* broke the news that Hayward himself had been arrested. Abby read the story over her breakfast of coffee, bacon, and toasted brown bread, food that she could at last taste after several days of holding her breath. She read quickly, skipping to the important parts:

Claus Blixt, the custodian, had confessed to pulling the trigger but claimed Hayward had strong-armed him, using only the force of his willpower. The *Tribune* had learned, through an anonymous police source, that Hayward owned ten thousand dollars' worth of insurance on the girl's life.

Abby set the paper down. "Well done," she said, exhaling all the pent-up air in her nose. Junius looked at her curiously. "They've caught the fellows who killed that poor girl, the dressmaker."

Junius nodded in his somber way, then reached his knobby fingers, the joints swollen and shiny, across the table to grasp hers. She took them gratefully and closed her eyes with him.

We give back to you, O God, those whom you gave to us.

The telephone rang. Abby squeezed her husband's hand and excused herself. She walked through the gallery; through its tall windows, she saw the landscape outside, grayed and quiet, in hibernation, reminding her to be grateful for her warm house, her sanctuary, with its many fireplaces and humming furnaces and cozy bedrooms. She felt radiant with relief. Hayward had been arrested.

She caught the telephone on its third ring. The operator asked to put through Officer Nye. Abby straightened her spine. She placed the flat of her hand on the wall.

"Good work, Roland," she said quietly.

Nye grunted into the phone. "Don't thank me yet." He kept his voice low; she had to plug her other ear to hear him. "Hayward's talking. Says he's innocent, that another woman must have hired Blixt to kill the dressmaker out of envy. Claimed he was with a girl at the opera earlier that evening, a rich man's daughter, and he also named some inmates at the Bethany Home. Said they might have been involved."

Abby rubbed her forehead. "Have they found the murder weapon?" She knew very well they hadn't. Miss Rhoades had taken May to the Hennepin Avenue Bridge, in the middle of the night, to toss the revolver into the river. Abby didn't like imagining the two of them engaged in such corrupt business, but she couldn't stop picturing their faces, grim and determined, as they stood on the bridge and watched a bit of silver disappear beneath the current. Abby had to admit it gave her a small measure of pride.

"Not yet," said Nye. "Likely, Blixt threw it into the lake. But, Mrs. Mendenhall, you'll want to be prepared. The deputy and the mayor may pay a call."

She let out her breath and nodded, then remembered Nye couldn't see her. "Thank you, Roland. You've been a good friend, all these years. Don't plan on retiring anytime soon."

He laughed weakly. "I'll have to. My ticker can't take much more."

She hung up and called Euphemia, asking to meet with her at the Bethany Home as soon as was possible. Junius didn't even feign surprise when she told him she'd be leaving, though he did hesitate when she asked if she could take the morning paper.

"I'll return it to thee," she promised, kissing him lightly on the top of his head. "I shall leave the business section untouched."

She was glad to find the inmates still at breakfast when she reached the home, and she went straight down to the dining room, her creaking ankles moving as quickly as she could make them. A few of the girls looked up when she came in, offering her polite nods, but most ignored her. They'd become accustomed to seeing her here nearly every day.

She spotted May Lombard, sitting—she was glad—not apart from the others, but at the end of a long table with Pearl, Leigh, some of the other kitchen workers. May looked up when Abby came in, her expression both anxious and hopeful.

Abby made a little gesture, a lift of the newspaper, a nod. She watched May's eyes close, then the corners of her mouth turn upward. The hint of a smile.

The mayor-elect arrived that very day, tailed by the detective who'd sat across from the women of the Bethany Home, including the matron, and made them all feel small. Miss Rhoades let them in, and it was to her credit that she kept her face neutral, that she didn't spit on the man's muddy shoes.

"Mr. Pratt," Abby said, keeping her chin aloft and very still. She sat at one end of the davenport, Euphemia at the other. Beside Abby, a young man stood at an easel, a pencil in his fingers. He looked from her face to the easel, which he kept turned away from everyone else in the room.

"Have I caught you indisposed?" Pratt asked, even as he and

the detective settled into the two wingback chairs, their elbows comfortably splayed, making it very clear they weren't going anywhere. From the corner of her eye, Abby watched a clump of snow fall from Pratt's boot to the carpet.

"We'll take a cup of tea, thank you," said the detective, gesturing toward the cup and saucer in Euphemia's hands. Miss Rhoades gave him a curt nod and went out.

"To what do we owe such a pleasure, gentlemen?" Abby took care not to move her chin, to keep her head tilted at exactly the same angle, toward the easel. The young man's pencil scratched.

Pratt's knee bounced impatiently. "We've discussed it already, Mrs. Mendenhall. I trust you've brought your ledger?"

Euphemia sat forward, presenting the men with a leather-bound notebook, gilt lettering on its cover. The detective snatched it eagerly. Abby couldn't help watching as his careless hands bent the pages, as he licked his fingers to turn them faster, to get through the months of births and deaths, arrivals and departures, all recorded by her own careful, even hand. The sketch artist had paused, watching the policeman read; she clicked her tongue at him to keep his pencil moving.

"Here's a list of inmates who were here in the last month," he told Pratt, excited, and the two men bowed their heads over the page. Abby had pored over the ledger so many times that she could practically recite the list, the names of the girls in alphabetical order, by surname:

Johnson, Faith
Pollard, Joan
Spence, Natalie
Verdoni, Assuntina

Abby held her breath, even though she knew he'd find nothing of use in the ledger. May had made scores of mistakes, but revealing her true name to Hayward hadn't been one of them. Abby strained her eyes to watch the men pore over the list, feeling a swell of satisfaction in her chest. Despite May's foolishness, the girl did not deserve to hang for Hayward's crimes. Abby would see to it these men didn't lay a finger on May, or on Faith.

"She's not in here," the detective sneered. "Where's Susannah Green? Or May Lombard?" He slapped the ledger. "There's no Margie or Marguerite, either."

Abby shrugged, just slightly. "There could be a Marguerite. We wouldn't know. Some never tell us their given names. Do either of you remember Lillie Hill?"

Pratt shook his head, frowning, as did the detective.

"Before your time, I suppose. She died of consumption while staying here, God rest her soul. Never would tell us her given name. I trust she had good reason not to involve her people, who were rumored to be a good family out of Boston. Her headstone bears her pseudonym."

"I don't believe you," said the detective. "I think you know exactly who we're looking for. You doctored the list, didn't you?"

"My good man," Euphemia crowed, affecting shock. "How could you accuse us of such a thing? You'll notice it's all there in black ink, nary a page missing. We've only ever cooperated, in full, with law enforcement."

Pratt sat back and adjusted his tie. "The deputy's pursuing Ging's murder as a conspiracy. The brother's involved, and the custodian, of course. Both are prepared to testify against Hayward. If one of your girls is involved, she could testify as well."

How benign he made it sound, as though May would receive nothing more than a slap on the wrist. As though Hayward wouldn't try to pin the murder on her. "What evidence do you have connecting one of our inmates to this crime?" Abby asked.

The mayor looked to the detective, who said, somewhat begrudgingly, "Hayward's word."

"Ah. Your murderer." Carefully, so as not to disturb her pose, Abby slipped a hand into her pocket and pulled out a few banknotes. She held them out to Euphemia, who smoothed them in her lap. "It doesn't surprise me to hear that Hayward won't let up about our inmates. He's rather obsessed with them, I believe."

"We've caught him nosing around here twice, in fact," Euphemia added. "Once, when he was campaigning for you."

Pratt gave a start. The curled ends of his mustache twitched. The only sounds were the tick of the gold clock on the mantel and the scratch of the artist's pencil. At last, the mayor-elect sputtered, "I've never laid eyes on the man in my life."

"How curious. He seemed quite passionately invested in your campaign," said Abby. "He made a donation to the Sisterhood that day, but, unfortunately, we couldn't use it."

"Why not?" Pratt said, growing visibly impatient, his foot bouncing.

"He paid us with some of these." Euphemia set her cup and saucer down, brought the greenbacks over to Pratt and the detective, and laid one on the pantleg of each of them. She returned to her seat and flipped open her fan. Through Abby's peripheral vision, she could see her friend smile. "False money. You may want to add that to your investigation; seems Hayward was swimming in the stuff."

"We've been hearing from our girls—the ones who worked in sporting houses—that the city itself is flooded with counterfeit banknotes." Abby locked eyes with the artist and lifted her chin a bit higher, stretching her neck. "It's hard to know what to trust these days."

"I sure hope they aren't going around blabbing about it," Pratt sputtered. He leaned forward and gripped the wooden handles of his chair, which were shaped like gryphon's talons. "If word gets out there's counterfeit money in circulation, it could cause a run on the banks. Or a localized panic."

Abby nodded sympathetically. "Not at all what you'd want to happen on the eve of your first term."

Pratt laughed harshly. "I should say not."

Finally, Abby broke her pose, turned her neck to the side with a satisfying crack. She stretched her fingers in her lap as she turned to face her two visitors. "I think that's enough, Jed," she said to the artist. "Did you get that last line?"

The boy at the easel unclipped the page he'd been writing on. "Shall I read it to you?"

"Yes, please."

The mayor-elect and detective had gone very still, the detective's mouth hanging open an inch, Pratt's eyes cut toward the artist and narrowed in suspicion.

Jed coughed to clear his throat. " 'If word gets out there's counterfeit money in circulation, it could cause a run on the banks. Or a localized panic.' "

"What's going on here?" Pratt demanded.

Euphemia's fan beat so rapidly, Abby could feel the breeze. "I do apologize. I failed to make introductions," Abby said. "This is Jedediah Marsh, a sketch artist for the *Tribune*. He works with Herbert Block. You might remember the pair; they were at that lovely fall picnic we invited you to last month."

"How do you do," said Jed. He turned his sketch paper

around to show his neatly copied notes, their entire conversation recorded nearly word for word.

Pratt shook his head at the women, a sneer curling his lip. "You think you're so clever. I never agreed to be on the record. Besides, the *Tribune* wouldn't dream of printing such a story about me."

"Oh, I wasn't thinking the *Tribune*," Jed said, tapping his chin and leaving a smudge of pencil lead. "Was thinking I'd take this to the *Examiner,* more like. They don't care about no record." He grinned, displaying his crowded yellow teeth.

"You see, we each have something the other needs," Abby told the mayor. "We need you to maintain our city funding. You need us to keep quiet about your connection to Harry T. Hayward. We know quite a few people in this town." A phrase came into her head, one she'd heard someone say, once, though she couldn't quite remember who. "We enjoy a surprising amount of influence."

Pratt paled. "There's no connection between that monster and me."

The detective jabbed his finger at Abby. "If there's a girl here who helped Hayward kill Ging, or who killed that madam, we're going to find her. None of your maneuvers can change that."

"You're welcome to interrogate them again, one by one," Euphemia said calmly. "If you'd care to go to the trouble. But you won't find a Susannah Green, or a May Lombard, or a Marguerite whatnot among them. They don't exist."

"Perhaps you're barking up the wrong tree, gentlemen," said Abby. "Perhaps it's Hayward you should be asking about the dead madam, rather than our girls about Ging."

"I hardly need the advice of a couple of nosy old crones," the detective said, standing to button his waistcoat. The mayor-elect followed suit. They stood there in silence for a moment, each waiting, it seemed, for the other to say something to help them save face.

"We will be back," Pratt said, and then they showed themselves out. Miss Rhoades had never brought the tea; Abby had specifically told her, in advance of the meeting, not to serve the men anything.

"It's not over," Euphemia said after they heard the front door slam. She worked the paper of her fan back and forth in her fist, smoothing its creases, caressing the silk tassel. Abby reached across their skirts to hold her hand, to still its trembling.

"No. It is not over," Abby agreed. She smiled at Jed, who was packing up his easel, and thanked him. She'd pay him double what the *Examiner* would have offered, to keep his notes carefully guarded and to sit on the story, for now.

She had other chess pieces to move: her girls, the matron—people who were not her playthings or pawns but who had entered her orbit nonetheless, and whom she had an obligation to help. She sat still awhile, watching birds out the parlor windows with Euphemia. Miss Rhoades had filled the seed feeder this morning, drawing crowds of hardy winter birds, built to stay: plump chickadees, a pileated woodpecker, a white-breasted nuthatch, the kind most likely to crash into the windows' glass. The more delicate birds, the Eastern bluebird and red-breasted robin—her favorite—had left not long after the first frost, heading south. It would be a long journey, but it was necessary to their survival.

Abby held Euphemia's hand long after Jed had gone. The birds continued to dash back and forth, their wings in a tizzy. Abby imagined she could hear the flutter of their tiny hearts. She could have watched them all afternoon. She wasn't ready to move her bones, which were beginning to complain, her joints as crotchety as she was. She knew her time here would one day come to an end. It would happen sooner rather than later; she might as well stay sitting with her friend and watching the birds. She couldn't care for all of them, couldn't even come close to that. No one had the power to hold the winter back, to keep the robin near. All one could do was offer kindness, day by day and case by case: a handful of birdseed, a warm bath, a place to rest.

26

MAY

$\mathscr{L}$eigh came to see her the night before they were supposed to leave. May sat on her bed, packing, arranging her things with deliberate care by the gold light of her lamp, to quell her nerves. She folded her handkerchiefs into fourths, tucked them in around the tins of hardtack, preserved beef, and dried apricots Cook had given each of them, for the journey.

"What do you think?"

May studied the person standing in her doorway. A stranger, she thought at first, her instinct to shrink from him. A teenage boy, in shirtsleeves, a buttoned vest, and trousers that didn't match: the trousers dark gray, the vest striped. One hand tucked confidently into a pocket, a wool fedora at a jaunty angle over short, ragged hair.

"Leigh." May's heart was pounding. "You can't—please tell me you aren't planning to wear this on the train. You'll get us thrown out, or worse. Arrested."

"Naw, of course not." Leigh stretched her arms out, examining them as though she couldn't quite believe they were hers. "I'll wait until we're in Wyoming. There I can wear whatever I want."

May didn't respond. Leigh seemed to believe the new state of Wyoming would be a sort of promised land, a place where they could do or be whoever they pleased, without consequence. May wondered how she'd never seen it clearly before, who Leigh was, or—May blushed to think of it—who she and Dolly were to each other. The haircut, too, made sense now. May smiled to herself, thinking of what Faith had said about unleashing hidden desires.

"You should go change," May warned her, "before Pearl or any of the others see you." This was one of Mrs. Mendenhall's conditions for providing train and stagecoach fare for May, Leigh, Dolly, baby Jude, and Miss Rhoades—whom May still had trouble referring to as Beth—to head west together. Mrs. Mendenhall didn't want the rest of the inmates to catch wind of the plan; otherwise, she'd have to explain the special circumstances that required May to get as far away from the city as possible, as quickly as possible. Nobody wanted to entwine anyone else in Hayward's tangled web.

Still, it meant leaving without saying goodbye. As Faith had done. May still couldn't quite forgive her for it.

Leigh hesitated, then came over to rest her hand on May's shoulder. She stared down at what May held in her hands: in her left, a cheroot cigar holder embroidered with a pair of ducks, a drake and hen, their outstretched wings crossed. In her right, a ruby ring.

"It'll be good for all of us," Leigh said quietly. "A fresh start."

May nodded.

Leigh pointed to the ring. "What're you going to do with that?"

May held it up to the light. The gas lantern shone dully

through the back of the ruby and brought colorful sparkles to the tiny diamonds. It hadn't broken after Pearl flung it at the wall, which meant it could possibly be of real value. As with everything regarding Hal, the ring's provenance brought up more questions than answers. Had he bought her a valuable ring, and if so, what did that imply about his feelings for her? Or had it been intended for someone else? Why hadn't he demanded she return it? Was it stolen?

In any case, the best gift Hal had given her was the one he'd managed *not* to deliver; the day after news broke that he'd been arrested, her monthly curse—much more of a blessing, in this case—had arrived.

"I'll sell the ring when we get to Wyoming," she told Leigh, slipping it into her pocket. "Can't risk someone connecting me to Hayward while we're here. Who knows, maybe it'll help us buy a horse."

"Whatever price it fetches, it'll be yours to decide what to do with. Get yourself some good leather gloves."

May grinned. "A mink stole."

"Silk drawers."

After Leigh left, May stared at the cigar holder for a while, running the pad of her thumb over her even stitches. She'd worked so hard on the embroidery, had spent a pretty penny on the colored threads. The vivid green of the drake's shining head—she liked that the most.

She dug into her bag for a piece of stationery and a pencil. Tapping the lead against her lips, she thought for a moment about what she should write. It had to sound genuine, but not overly friendly; that wouldn't be natural. A simple farewell would do, a bequest of luck.

Pearl,

If you decide to make a go of it with Cooper, I thought you might offer him this as a present. It's not secondhand. I never gave it to you-know-who. He didn't deserve it, but maybe Cooper does.

Good-bye and best wishes.

She was careful not to sign her name. Mrs. Mendenhall had warned her that the detectives could come back at any time, perhaps with a warrant to search the premises, and that she should destroy anything in her possession with the name "May Lombard" attached. Fortunately, there wasn't much. She'd never owned a passbook, of course, or kept a journal. The one identifying mark tying her to the name had been the initials she'd stitched into her gingham dress and her aprons, "M.L." in red cotton thread. Mrs. Mendenhall had suggested she remove these, in the unlikely case the police hauled her off for questioning or examined her clothes. May had cut them out with the sharp end of a seam ripper, carefully slicing the threads from the fabric, one by one.

The morning after May took her shot at Hal and missed, she'd been overwhelmed with relief to see Mrs. Mendenhall at breakfast, especially after Faith had vanished. Over coffee and chunks of brown bread in the study, May had allowed the entire story to spill out to Mrs. Mendenhall and the matron, leaving nothing out. She'd begun with the purple gown, explaining how it connected Faith not only to Kitty Ging, but also to Harry T. Hayward.

Mrs. Mendenhall had pinched her eyes shut. "I wish you'd told me what you learned about the dress sooner," she lamented. "Please, go on."

May continued, explaining her own shameful entanglement with Hayward. Several times, as May spoke, her voice breaking at points, Mrs. Mendenhall had looked over her head at Miss Rhoades. They both grimaced when she told them how gleefully Hayward had described Priscilla Black's body; he must have been behind her killing as well.

"Very well, May," Mrs. Mendenhall had said when she finished outlining the harrowing events of the night before: the custodian covered in blood, the revolver May had fired and brought home, Faith's midnight disappearance. Mrs. Mendenhall came around the desk and offered May a handkerchief. "Miss Rhoades, I'll need my coach, and quickly. Could you telephone Junius and ask him to send it round?"

As soon as Miss Rhoades hurried off, Mrs. Mendenhall turned back to May. She came close enough for May to see the flecks in her pale-green irises. "You'll need to go about your day as if nothing has happened. If the other girls ask where you were last night, tell them you went looking for Faith but couldn't find her. An uneventful evening. Do you understand?"

May nodded. Her voice was caught in her throat as she did her best to hold in her tears.

"You've acted unwisely at times, May, but this crime is not your doing, and you have suffered enough. Take a moment to gather yourself. I will call for you when the time is right."

Her words were a balm, soothing May enough to get her to her feet and down to the kitchen, where Cook handed her a pound of cold butter to cut into cubes. But her calm quickly wore off, and when a day passed, then another, with nary a word from Mrs. Mendenhall, not even an acknowledgment, May was twisted into a ball of nerves. Even the news that the custodian had confessed and Hal had been arrested didn't bring the relief she'd have expected, especially when she heard the whispers that the detective had returned with the mayor. At last, one unseasonably warm day in the second week of December, when the ground outside the kitchen had turned slick and muddy and the sun was making grayish attempts to penetrate the clouds, Miss Rhoades tapped May on the arm at lunch.

"Come downstairs after lights-out." Miss Rhoades seemed curiously eager. May had been wondering what might happen to her, too, now that she'd made her confession in front of all the inmates and half the Sisterhood. "Meet me in Mrs. Mendenhall's office."

The hours after that had ticked by slowly, seeming unbearably long; dinnertime and washing up were a trial in patience. After lying on her bed for what felt like hours, her feet and knees twitching and knocking together under her thin nightgown, May crept down the stairs and through the quiet hallway. Soft light seeped under the closed door of the office, and the hush of voices. When the door swung open, hinges creaking, to let May in, she was stunned to see a circle of faces wreathed in candlelight: the matron and Mrs. Mendenhall, Leigh and Dolly, who she was aghast to see had also been invited. They all glanced up at her with the same meaningful, animated air Miss Rhoades had exhibited in the dining room, a circle of women radiating a secret knowledge, looking like some sort of coven.

May's legs wobbled. "What's all this?" She lowered herself into a visitor's chair.

"You're going west," Mrs. Mendenhall pronounced. "The day after tomorrow."

"West." She knew what that meant. She would be a farm wife. Men wrote to the Sisterhood all the time, petitioning for mail-order brides. Better than the gallows, much better, no matter who the husband turned out to be. She'd have to remember that. She nodded dutifully.

"We're all going," Leigh said, interrupting something Mrs. Mendenhall had been about to add, as though she'd burst if she didn't share the news. "Dolly and I, and Jude, of course—and you and Miss Rhoades. We're going to homestead in Wyoming."

May listened in incredulous silence as Leigh prattled on about Wyoming, where she'd always wanted to live. Mrs. Mendenhall was giving them the opportunity to take full advantage of all the state had to offer: women's right to vote (since 1869!) and own property. In Wyoming, they'd have the power to claim a homestead in their own names, which they'd do on a few rocky acres adjacent to Leigh's aunt and uncle's ranch.

"What's ours will be ours," Leigh said. "We'll pool our money and start a homestead. No one'll be able to take it from us."

It all sounded fantastical, too radical to be true; May looked to Mrs. Mendenhall for validation. Mrs. Mendenhall gave a slight nod, betraying a modicum of reluctance. "You'll take the Great Northern Railway as far as Bozeman, in Montana, and then the stagecoach to La Barge, Wyoming."

The Great Northern Railway. May had heard of it; it was brand-new. She imagined wooden bridges suspended hundreds of feet above mountain river valleys, rippling fields under the broadest skies she'd ever seen. Without a stranger beside her for a husband, but with these three women as company.

"I have some stipulations to add," Mrs. Mendenhall said, quieting everyone. They could tell none of the others where they were going, nor leave any hint behind. If anyone from the Sisterhood asked, Mrs. Mendenhall would feign ignorance, saying only that they must each have needed a clean break.

"That clean break is paramount," Mrs. Mendenhall said pointedly, looking straight at May. "You are to tell no one, inside or outside these walls, where you are going. Am I clear?"

"Yes, Mrs. Mendenhall," May mumbled. She felt as if she'd been tossed in the air to float for a moment, only to come crashing back to the hard ground. No doubt Mrs. Mendenhall worried that Hal still held her in his command, that she'd try to contact him at the jail, to let him know where to write her. Instead, her thoughts drifted to her family in Chicago. All these years, she'd dreamed of returning to her family on the arm of a suitable man, to be met, at last, with her mother's approval. Emmanuel could know her—not as a mother, she'd conceded, but at least as a respectable and doting aunt.

She stopped listening to the others and hugged herself, her own arms replacing Emmanuel's. Her dream had never had a chance of coming true, with or without Hal. She'd been, for all practical purposes, dead to her family for years. She would vanish into the West and little would change, in her family's eyes. Gone and forgotten would remain gone and forgotten. But perhaps prospects could change, in time, for her.

They left early in the morning, two days later. May dressed quietly, her belly achy and empty from nerves and too little sleep. When she came downstairs, she found Leigh pacing the foyer, restless, her light baggage on the floor beside her. Leigh looked as if she'd been awake for hours. "Dolly's upstairs, feeding the baby," she told May. She chewed at a toothpick, working the wood to splinters.

May nodded and set her bag down, held her stomach. All night, she'd lain awake, thinking that she wouldn't go, that she'd tell the others in the morning she'd changed her mind. She'd stay here and risk the consequences. She'd ask Mrs. Mendenhall if that position in the bakery was still open.

"This time on Thursday," Leigh said, grinning around her toothpick, "we'll be waking to a breakfast of ranch eggs."

May tried to smile. The plan was for all four of them, plus the baby, to stay with Leigh's aunt and uncle while they built their own cabin. It seemed ludicrous, not to mention risky. What did they know about maintaining a homestead? She couldn't shake the feeling that the land they were prepared to claim had once belonged to other people, who might want it back. Nor was she so sure they'd be able to maintain a savory style of life, four women alone, given their histories. Folks might assume they were setting up a sporting house. What would they have to do to survive?

Miss Rhoades came out of her office, holding a velveteen carpetbag, wearing a little burgundy hat and traveling cloak. She looked as nervous as May felt. "All ready?" Miss Rhoades said. She let her gaze wander up the striped wallpaper, to the staircase and back down, at last falling on the drawing room, where she'd told who knew how many stories. May had never truly felt she belonged within these walls; she'd always been eager to find her escape route back to her past. How long had Miss Rhoades called this place home? A decade, at least.

Dolly came down then, with Jude wrapped in her shawl. He was still so little that he slept most of the day and would be quiet—Dolly promised—on the train. This was another reason Leigh claimed it made sense to leave now, before the boy grew a bit and woke to the world. When Dolly came closer, May could see his soft, flushed cheeks, the shine of his eyelids, his mouth open against his mother's chest as he dreamed.

302 · CAROLINE WOODS

Cook came up, sniffling, from the kitchen, and put a flaky, buttery biscuit, wrapped in a clean towel, into each of their pockets. "My dear girls." She embraced each of them, Miss Rhoades the longest. She kissed May on the top of her head.

"Let's go outside," Miss Rhoades said. Her voice cracked a bit. "The carriage is waiting."

They went out to find the street dusted lightly in new snow. A pair of birds trilled in the black limbs of a tree overhead, flitting from branch to branch. Mrs. Mendenhall and Mrs. Overlock, each in her signature pure black or muted florals, stood beside Mrs. Overlock's big Concord coach. May had never ridden in one, with its shining windows and heavy door that would block out the elements. A footman held open the door, and she could see comfortable benches and lap blankets inside. It felt like too much.

"We shan't dally," Mrs. Mendenhall said as they approached. "May God bless all of you on your journey. Take care of one another, friends."

Dolly and Leigh curtsied to the women and thanked them a final time. Leigh shook the coachman's hand. Miss Rhoades lingered. Mrs. Mendenhall smiled at her kindly, her face sad. "You've snow on your jacket, friend," she said, brushing off Miss Rhoades's shoulder, and at last, Miss Rhoades managed to say, "Thank you."

May was the last to board. She felt dizzy with the weight of such a goodbye. She curtsied to Mrs. Overlock, then stood eye to eye with Mrs. Mendenhall. Mrs. Mendenhall lifted one gray eyebrow, as though she knew May had something important to say.

"If she ever returns . . ." No need to elucidate who "she" was; Mrs. Mendenhall would know. ". . . please tell her I wish she could have come with us. I long to have been a better friend to her. Please tell her that."

Mrs. Mendenhall brought her thin lips into a slight smile and nodded once. "I have something for you." She pressed a card, no larger than a calling card, into May's gloved hand. "You may read it on your journey. I hope it will bring you peace, May."

May slipped the card into her pocket, put her carpetbag into the boot of the carriage, and climbed inside. The air felt stuffy already, warmed by the breath of her fellow travelers. No one said anything as the coachman hopped up and flicked the reins. They stared at one another, wide-eyed, rocking back and forth with the motion of the carriage, their collective breath caught in anticipation of all that would happen next.

Just before they reached the train station in St. Paul, May remembered to read Mrs. Mendenhall's card.

Unsurprisingly, she found a prayer set in plain type:

> *Mind that which is eternal,*
> *Which gathers your hearts together, up to the Lord,*
> *And lets you see that ye are written*
> *In one another's heart.*

May hadn't given the Lord much attention in a long while. She'd had more worldly matters on her mind, even when she'd attended church. Still, it gave her comfort to imagine that she'd be remembered, recorded, not in a family Bible, but impressed upon another person's soul. The prayer felt like a reminder that life could be sweet. Her future in Wyoming could turn out to be misery, but it could also be a lifetime of bright, sunny days, in the shadow of the jagged teeth of distant blue mountains; of Dolly's son learning to walk, his soft leather baby shoes on dry yellow grass; of suppers shared with friends by candlelight, treasuring the peaceful exhaustion of growing and preparing their own wholesome food. May had always assumed that bliss wasn't meant for someone like her, that she didn't deserve it. Perhaps she didn't. But she'd come to see good fortune not as a matter of what you earned through virtuous behavior, but of whom you loved and were loved by in return.

As they prepared to disembark, her fingers went to the card in her pocket, to make sure it was still there. She wondered if Mrs. Mendenhall had meant to imply it was Faith who kept May written on her heart, or if Mrs. Mendenhall wanted to indicate that she did, herself.

May decided she'd take it as both.

Epilogue

ONE YEAR LATER

They hanged Harry T. Hayward on December 11, 1895, in the brick-walled courtyard of the Hennepin County Jail. Quite a crowd gathered to catch a glimpse of the man who had, for a brief time, become one of the most infamous in America. By now, he'd confessed to having masterminded Kitty Ging's demise and committed five other murders, including at least one sporting girl and a Chinese immigrant whom he'd impaled, brutally, with the leg of a chair. For nearly a year, newspapers nationwide had splashed his handsome face across their front pages, racing to print the latest lurid scoop. Allegedly, he'd burned down his own family home, hoping to collect insurance money. He'd mesmerized Claus Blixt to kill, Kitty Ging to sink into financial ruin, his own brother Adry—who'd turned on him immediately—to aid his insurance ploys. No one was safe from his hypnotic charms, it seemed, as long as the man lived.

The sheriff led Hayward up the steps of the gallows, dressed in a black shift, his fair hair hidden in a cap. The mob pressed forward, men and women and at least one little boy, perched on his father's shoulders. Hayward appeared to be muttering, chuckling, sharing private jokes with his executioners, and the people strained to hear. What had he just said? Would he repent, would he profess his faith, as the condemned often did?

There had been rumors that he'd escape with the help of the Freemasons, or that he'd charm the guards into unlocking his cell. No one doubted the man was a true Mesmerist, not even the jury hearing Claus Blixt's murder trial. Blixt had successfully convinced them that Hayward had hypnotized him to commit murder, sparing his own life but dooming Hayward's.

Folks even claimed the "Minneapolis Svengali"—the nickname the press had given Hayward, after George du Maurier's character in *Trilby*, of all things—could persuade the sheriff to untie the ropes binding his hands or cut the noose. An almost disappointed sigh rippled through the gathered masses when the sheriff led Hayward to the center of the scaffold and slipped the noose around his neck. A dramatic escape seemed less and less possible. Hayward gazed out at the throng of people, grinning ghoulishly, a star before his audience. He gibed with his executioners, telling them not to muck it up. "Pull 'er tight," he said casually, as though he, too, believed he possessed the improbable power to transform into a wisp of smoke and slip away.

Just before they yanked the hood down over his head, he squinted out once more at the crowd. Johnny Lundberg must have been there, hidden among the throngs; he'd have a lump in his throat, glad no one had connected him to Hayward's crimes, yet fearful, as he would be for the rest of his life, that someday someone would.

At the last second, Hayward locked eyes with a woman in the back. The new children's matron at the Bethany Home for Unwed Mothers.

His pale eyes widened a bit, in recognition. Then, whoosh, the hood.

The children's matron didn't flinch when the trapdoor fell. She didn't look away as his body twitched for eleven full minutes, as the cries of the crowd grew more and more hysterical. The sheriff had miscalculated the length of the rope.

She waited until she could be sure he was dead. Then she left, keeping the brim of her hat low, her eyes on her skirts. She didn't want anyone to recognize her, save Hayward himself.

Faith had stayed at Mrs. Mendenhall's house, in the cozily upholstered bedroom where Mrs. Mendenhall's mother, Chloe, once lived, until Faith's daughter arrived. She'd named the girl April, after the month of her birth. April had just turned four months old when the two of them moved into the children's cottage, which sat half a block from the Bethany Home on its own little green knoll, surrounded by sugar maples. They'd waited until there were no longer any inmates left at the Bethany Home who would recognize her except Cook and Mrs. Overlock, both of whom were sworn to secrecy. They seemed to enjoy being in on a conspiracy. A confederacy of women, which fortunately didn't include Mrs. Van Cleve. Charlotte had never met Faith during her time as an inmate. As far as she knew, Abby had hired a stranger when she reassigned the current children's matron to the main house and turned over the care of the cottage to Faith.

No one called her that anymore, of course. She went by her birth name, Margaret Bartos. She dressed comfortably, in warm flannel dresses with lace collars, her dark hair wrapped into elaborate knots. The children called her Mrs. Bartos, which always made her think of her mother.

Mrs. Mendenhall exclusively used that name for her, too.

Ever since Faith and April settled at the cottage, Mrs. Mendenhall hadn't once mentioned anything about her past or how she'd come here, even when they were alone. There seemed a tacit understanding between the two of them. Mrs. Mendenhall was the one person on earth who had figured out exactly what happened between Faith and Priscilla Black. If Mrs. Mendenhall had pressed for details, Faith would have supplied them: How she'd put spiders in Priscilla, as she did, in smaller measure, to Pearl. How the spiders had consumed Priscilla, imaginary though they were, following her wherever she went, until, desperate, she leapt into the river in a doomed attempt to shake them from her skin.

But Mrs. Mendenhall never asked. Instead, she read Faith the letters Leigh and May sent from Wyoming. Faith would lift her chin, close her eyes, and smile, as though their news carried a bit of Western sun to shine upon her own face.

Faith knew Mrs. Mendenhall had taken an enormous personal risk in hiring her, especially after what had recently happened with Miss Rhoades. Mrs. Mendenhall had made it clear that Mrs. Van Cleve could never learn the details of Faith's history, or the board would have no choice but to cut her loose. Yet Faith did not believe she'd been hired out of pity or charity, as she felt quite confident in the quality of her work. She had never been afraid to speak to children; she did so in a soft, gentle voice. She felt no need to use Mesmerism, or whatever it was, not with them. It was easy for her to intuit their needs, their fears, their relative strengths, especially as compared with the previous children's matron, who everyone agreed was better suited to the care of adult women. Faith now had sixteen girls and twelve boys in her care, with the aid of two nurses; the children ranged from three to fourteen. She attempted to see herself at that age in each one, and to give them all the encouragement she had lacked.

Beatrix, for instance. The oldest girl at the cottage. She'd come to Faith—Mrs. Bartos—sobbing, convinced she'd soon die. Blood, she'd whispered. There was blood soaked through her underclothes, staining her bed. Faith had been sure to embrace her first, because that was what she herself had sorely needed when her own first blood had arrived. She'd explained it meant that Beatrix's body could now carry a baby, even though her mind was certainly nowhere near ready.

She told Mrs. Mendenhall about the incident the next morning, over hot cocoa in the main house's office. It was mid-November, winter and the holidays approaching. Harry Hayward's upcoming execution had her on edge, plagued with a feeling of unfinished business. What if he somehow escaped punishment, as everyone said he would? The cocoa did little to quell her nerves.

Mrs. Mendenhall didn't seem embarrassed by the mention of menses, but she sighed over Beatrix. "That poor girl. She'll be out in the world soon, and what will become of her?" Then she muttered, almost to herself: "I can't make them all a matron. Can't put them all on a train to Timbuktu." The rate at which Mrs. Mendenhall was declining into old age seemed to have accelerated. The events of the past year had taken their toll. Perhaps because she could see the end of life on the horizon, she seemed, also, to have lost faith in her own ability to make a difference. "Every day, this city grows more and more wicked. And I can do nothing about it."

Faith offered a sympathetic smile, though she disagreed. One person could wield a great deal of influence on the lives of others, often with little effort. A few calculated moves, some watchful waiting, and you could convince an evil woman she was going mad, so mad she was driven to yank out her own eyebrow hairs and fling herself into the river.

You could place a gun in May's hands, knowing beyond a doubt that she would take her shot, even if it turned out she missed.

Faith reached the children's cottage before breakfast ended; the execution had begun near dawn. The sweet smell of griddle cakes greeted her at the door of the dining room, as did April, sitting in a baby stool, smiling with her two tiny teeth as a nurse spooned her oat porridge. The children's matron went around touching her charges' shiny heads, blessing them, silently, as she always did:

You will prosper. You are loved. And you, you are a good little soul.

"How was the hanging?" the baby nurse, Ingrid, asked her. "I don't know if I'd be able to stand close to that man without screaming."

Faith took April from the chair and wiped her face with her bib. The baby's little neck was a stack of folds, plump and milk-scented. They were fortunate to be here, together. Lucky, but not entirely safe. No one ever was. She thought of Johnny Lundberg, the last remaining of the trio who'd forced her into working in that brothel. Occasionally, she asked the Bethany Home's coachman to drive her past the Lundbergs' house. Risky, but she had to study his habits, and those of his wife, who appeared not to have left him for her mysterious dark-haired lover. Quietly she kept track of them, their routines, their schemes.

"Next time," she told Ingrid, "I shall take you with me."

Ingrid gave a shudder. With that, Faith banished the black

cloud coloring her recollections. They had Yuletide decorations to assemble. The older girls were learning embroidery at the main house; today, the four- and five-year-olds would bake gingerbread. First, however, there was time for a story. She hardly had to say a word to get them to follow her into the sitting room. Only gestures were needed, a gentle touch at the base of a spine, a tap on the shoulder of a boy who'd been poking his neighbor. The children waited quietly, a sea of flushed cheeks and runny noses, for their sweet new matron to spin a tale. A scary one, though not too dark: just enough to remind them of the cold outside, the warmth within.

Author's Note

While *The Mesmerist* is a work of fiction, the story is based on a real place—the Bethany Home—as well as a true crime that happened in Minneapolis in 1894. Many of this novel's characters were inspired by real people. I'll use this brief note to honor the dead, separate fact from speculation, and point curious readers to some great works of nonfiction for further reading.

The Bethany Home for Unwed Mothers, run by Charlotte Van Cleve, Abby Mendenhall, Euphemia Overlock, and a handful of other churchgoing society women, is what drew me to 1894 Minneapolis in the first place. The home was, in my opinion, surprisingly progressive for its time, respectful and relatively compassionate toward not only unwed mothers, but also madams and "sporting women," for whom the Sisterhood of Bethany occasionally went to bat in court. For source material, I read the complete correspondence and journals of the fascinating Abby Mendenhall, which is where I learned she used plain speech to correspond with her Quaker Friends, and vernacular with everyone else. Some of her better lines in this book—"Crows flew by today," or the description of the Thanksgiving turkey as "an old gobbler"—I took from Abby's journal and owe her the credit. Despite a sickly disposition, Abby roamed Minneapolis freely, searching for women who she felt needed her help. She really did burst into the back doors of saloons, unannounced, spend the night at the Bethany Home when an inmate was sick or missing, and take at least one girl into her own house to care for her.

"Delia" is an amalgam of two inmates of the home, one who lived with Abby for a while, and one who died of an overdose after running away to Kate Campbell's brothel. The Kate Campbell in this novel is a bit of a composite as well. "Swede Kate" was the moniker given to another contemporaneous madam named Kate Johnson, but I liked the nickname so much I applied it here to Kate Campbell, who ran Mollie Ellsworth's old sporting house on Second Avenue North. Agnes Bly and Priscilla Black are products of my imagination.

Every story needs a villain (or two or three) and I fear I've made too much a villain of Charlotte Van Cleve in this book. As a popular public speaker, she did not shy away from calling out male privilege and pointing out the role men played in creating unwanted pregnancies. I don't have evidence that she would have brought the police to the home to hunt down a potential murderess; to the contrary, she once helped hire a lawyer for a "ruined," poverty-stricken young woman who killed the society man who sexually assaulted her—and succeeded in getting the girl acquitted. Charlotte was, however, of a different social standing than Abby and Euphemia, more reliant on her speaking fees and public persona to survive, which I riffed on to create her character.

Now for the real baddie: Harry T. Hayward, who just might have been this country's first confirmed serial killer. (Hayward's crime spree happened a few years earlier than that of Dr. Henry Howard Holmes of *The Devil in the White City* fame.) While awaiting execution for conspiring to kill the dressmaker Catherine Ging, Hayward boasted of having "offed" at least five other people, including a sporting woman in California and a man who'd beat him at faro. Historians, however, have no way of verifying these murders. Identity was slippery in the 1890s, pre–Social Security numbers and standard government IDs, something my fictional May Lombard and Faith Johnson use to their advantage.

Claus Blixt, custodian at the Ozark Flats, was the triggerman who sealed Kitty Ging's fate, but he avoided the gallows by claiming to have been mesmerized by Hayward to commit the crime. Spiritualism, the belief in invisible means of communication with both the living and the dead—séances, telepathy, hypnosis—enjoyed great fervor in late Victorian America, as a nation of mourners endeavored to contact their Civil War dead. For a brief time, not only the Twin Cities but also the entire country was enthralled by salacious news reports detailing Hayward's alleged hypnotic powers. Not coincidentally, George du Maurier's *Trilby*, in which a teenage girl is hypnotized to death by the Mesmerist Svengali, was the most popular novel of 1894. The public was thus primed to believe Blixt's claim he'd been mesmerized to kill, and he managed to save his own life, though not his freedom. He died at Stillwater Prison in 1925.

Catherine Ging was murdered on December 3, 1894; Claus Blixt shot her behind the ear with a .38 revolver and left her on the road beside Bde Maka Ska (then called Lake Calhoun). Initially, Harry Hayward pretended to aid police in the search for her killer, but within a week, law enforcement learned of the $10,000 insurance policy Hayward had persuaded her to take out, naming him as a beneficiary. For the sake of this novel, I moved up the date of Kitty's murder so that it would happen closer to Thanksgiving (which fell on November 29 in 1894) and simplified the borrower-lender relationship between Hayward and Ging. Allegedly, the two were borrowing and lending from each other so much that it becomes hard to figure out who owed whom. It's safe to say Ging was likely giving Hayward real money, while he paid her back in green goods. After Ging's death, muckraking journalists engaged in some victim blaming, suggesting she was morally loose or potentially a criminal herself. I decided to portray Kitty Ging as a good-humored, clever businesswoman who made the mistake of borrowing money from a handsome man with a black heart. The scene of her murder at Bde Maka Ska has now been named Kitty Ging Green, a picturesque park that honors her memory.

The matron at the Bethany Home in 1894 really was named Miss Rhoades. I found little record of her besides what's in Abby's diary, and I have no way of knowing whether she ever worked in a brothel. I did, however, come across something uncanny as I made my way through Abby's journal. In December 1894, Abby wrote, "Miss Rhoades; called—much to do, my girl not pleasant—many trials and crosses to bear." When I read this line, I had already outlined Miss Rhoades's and Abby's tense conversation while waiting for May and Faith to return in the snow. I felt like I was on the right track.

May Lombard and Faith Johnson are fictional characters. I knew I wanted to write from the point of view of two Bethany Home inmates, who were largely impoverished young women, many former domestic, factory, and brothel workers, whose real names were rarely recorded. After reading how bleak conditions could be in all these professions, I think it's safe to assume that many of them experienced PTSD, disassociation, or selective mutism due to trauma, which I attempted to show in period-accurate detail. At first, I wasn't sure how these characters would connect to Harry Hayward, until I came across the fact that Hayward hired a trance medium to help him convince Kitty Ging to accept his loan. I wondered about that woman, too: what might have led her to become a medium, or what sort of danger she risked in doing such a favor for Hayward. I wanted her to find a way out of that danger; I knew *The Mesmerist* should give the fortune-teller a future.

For further reading on Harry T. Hayward, the Bethany Home, and the sex trade in 1890s Minneapolis, I highly suggest *The Infamous Harry Hayward* by Shawn Francis Peters and *Minneapolis Madams* by Penny A. Petersen. These texts provided a backbone to my research for *The Mesmerist* and offer fascinating portraits of the Twin Cities at the turn of the twentieth century.

Acknowledgments

As always, I owe a thousand thank-yous to my sensational agent, Shannon Hassan, and my brilliant editor, Carolyn Williams, who prompted me to investigate Gilded Age stories and served as a beacon throughout the creation of this novel. Thank you to the rest of my wonderful team at Doubleday, including Laura Baratto, Jess Deitcher, Kathleen Fridella, Sara Hayet, Anna B. Knighton, Felecia O'Connell, Denise Stambaugh, and Johanna Zwirner. Thank you, and kudos, to Oliver Munday for designing this book's gorgeous cover.

Three women in Minneapolis helped tremendously to make this book as accurate as it could be. Thank you to Penny Petersen and Tamatha Perlman for your insights on the Bethany Home and the lives of women in turn-of-the-century Minnesota; and thank you to Michele Pollard at the Hennepin History Museum for allowing me access to the archive and sharing everything from Hayward trial transcripts to the architect's blueprints of the Bethany Home.

Thank you to my friends and beta readers, Kathleen Carr Foster and Madeline Kotowicz, for reading early drafts of this novel and making the perfect suggestions.

Thank you to my dear parents: Susan and Barry, Jim and Jane, and Jim and Julie, all such devoted champions of my writing; and my beloved siblings, Stephanie, Michael, Kyle, and Cory.

Thank you, as Abby might say, to my favorites: Camille, Clare, and Colin. I love you.

This book is for survivors of human trafficking and exploitation everywhere; may we listen to them as they tell their stories. May we say their names.

About the Author

CAROLINE WOODS holds an MFA in fiction from Boston University. She has taught creative writing at Boston University, the Boston Conservatory, and Loyola University Chicago. She is the author of the novels *The Lunar Housewife* and *Fräulein M*. Raised in Delaware, she now lives near Chicago with her husband and two daughters.

A NOTE ON THE TYPE

The text of this book was set in Centaur, the only typeface designed by Bruce Rogers (1870–1957), the well-known American book designer. A celebrated penman, Rogers based his design on the roman face cut by Nicolas Jenson in 1470 for his Eusebius. Jenson's roman surpassed all of its forerunners and even today, in modern recuttings, remains one of the most popular and attractive of all typefaces.

Composed by North Market Street Graphics, Lancaster, Pennsylvania

Printed and bound by Berryville Graphics, Berryville, Virginia

Designed by Anna B. Knighton